T0278751

THE BLONDE DIES FIRST

ALSO BY JOELLE WELLINGTON

Their Vicious Games

Joelle Wellington

SIMON & SCHUSTER BFYR

NEW YORK   LONDON   TORONTO   SYDNEY   NEW DELHI

SIMON & SCHUSTER BFYR

An imprint of Simon & Schuster Children's Publishing Division
1230 Avenue of the Americas, New York, New York 10020

This book is a work of fiction. Any references to historical events, real people, or real places are used fictitiously. Other names, characters, places, and events are products of the author's imagination, and any resemblance to actual events or places or persons, living or dead, is entirely coincidental.

SIMON & SCHUSTER BOOKS FOR YOUNG READERS
and related marks are trademarks of Simon & Schuster, LLC.
Simon & Schuster: Celebrating 100 Years of Publishing in 2024
For information about special discounts for bulk purchases, please contact
Simon & Schuster Special Sales at 1-866-506-1949 or business@simonandschuster.com.
The Simon & Schuster Speakers Bureau can bring authors to your live event.
For more information or to book an event, contact the Simon & Schuster Speakers
Bureau at 1-866-248-3049 or visit our website at www.simonspeakers.com.
Interior design by Hilary Zarycky
The text for this book was set in Garamond.
Manufactured in the United States of America
First Edition
2 4 6 8 10 9 7 5 3 1
Library of Congress Cataloging-in-Publication Data
Names: Wellington, Joelle, author.
Title: The Blonde Dies First / Joelle Wellington.
Description: First edition. | New York : Simon & Schuster, 2024.
Identifiers: LCCN 2024003359 (print) | LCCN 2024003360 (ebook) | ISBN
9781665922456 (hardcover) | ISBN 9781665922470 (ebook)
Subjects: CYAC: Survival—Fiction. | Demonology—Fiction. | Twins—Fiction. |
Sisters—Fiction | Friends—Fiction. | African Americans—Fiction | BISAC: YOUNG
ADULT FICTION / Thrillers & Suspense / General | YOUNG ADULT FICTION /
Romance / LGBTQ+ | LCGFT: Novels.
Classification: LCC PZ7.1.W435516 Bl 2024 (print) | LCC PZ7.1.W435516 (ebook) |
DDC [Fic]—dc23
LC record available at https://lccn.loc.gov/2024003359
LC ebook record available at https://lccn.loc.gov/2024003360

For the Brooklyn kids—have some respect, this place made you

The developer burns, I think, my stomach knotting up. *Did I do it wrong?*

It's a creeping kind of burn, that chases from my eyebrows up my temples and races along my tightly greased edges. Sweat beads on my forehead, and I can feel the baby hairs starting to lift. The Vaseline surrounding my eyebrows feels dangerously close to sliding down my face and into my eyes.

I probably shouldn't have decided to bleach my eyebrows so soon after getting my hair braided. With hair so fresh, the tension combined with the burn of bleach is a recipe for pain. But the way my yellowing brows plus the darkness at the roots contrasted with the white blonde of my hair? No cohesion. And I want to be put together for the party.

I'm going to show up and show out to all of Drew's little friends.

"It kinda burns," I admit finally, rubbing at my edges, but Leila swats my hand away. "Yo!"

"Don't touch your edges. You have developer on your gloves," Leila reprimands.

I wince. "*Ow.* Ma did the braids really tight."

"There's nothing wrong with the developer, though. Turn, Devon," Leila commands. "You missed the edge. Right here." Her tongue peeks out from the corner of her mouth. There's a dark curl hanging between her eyebrows, chasing the slope of her nose. She leans in with her brush, smearing 30-volume developer over the few loose hairs that aren't part of the proper arch. I could just thread them, but Leila is an *artist*. "There. All good."

She sits back on the toilet, pulling her socked feet up on the edge, and she leans back. "And now we wait."

"Now, we wait," I agree.

I sit on the side of the claw-foot bathtub, gripping the edge between my legs. We're silent, but that's not an issue. We exist well in silence, and it brings a kind of peace that soothes my mind. Leila hums to herself, drumming a beat on the bowl of the toilet. She always has to be doing something with her hands. I listen to her beat and revel in the feeling of coming home.

I like to bleach my hair and eyebrows. The very first time I did it, at thirteen, it was just because of my sister's dare. My eyebrows came out the same neon yellow as a highlighter. When I looked at myself in the mirror, I knew it was off, but there was something so alien about it, I fell in love with my own reflection for the first time and resolved to try again. But the time after, I'd hated them so much, I'd just decided to shave them off. Luckily, they grew back normal instead of the patchy mess that my mom would constantly remind me was possible. When I tried a third time, though, I still couldn't get it right.

That's where my best friend, Leila Benady, came in. She took one look at me after the fourth attempt, the summer after our freshman year, and vowed that she'd never let me bleach my eyebrows by myself again, no matter how much my parents and twin sister insisted that I looked fine.

"No, Devon, girl, you *don't* look fine. You look terrible. *Hadras i baranas*," Leila had said, with so much conviction that I hadn't been able to do anything but laugh.

Two years later I still don't have it down to a science exactly, but I usually manage to fix it up fine on my own. Leila's just around for the nostalgia. Or to check my work, she'd claim—not that she's any better at math.

"You're serious about going to this party?" Leila asks, interrupting our silence. She takes down her sagging bun, sending big dark curls spilling over her shoulders and down her back.

"Yeah," I say. "I'm sure." I have to be sure. Because if I'm not, that means I'm doubting my genius plan, and there's no way I'm doing that, because, like, my plan *is* genius. "The beginning of the 'Best Summer Ever™.'"

Leila sighs, the sound laden with meaning.

"Nah, don't do that," I say flatly.

Leila resecures all that hair, pinning it in a more secure position at the nape of her neck. I purse my lips, staring at her, and when she looks back, she does that thing where she makes her eyes round and wide, shiny like two cue balls. "Do what?"

"You know," I say, leaning in.

"I just don't know why you're pushing this so hard, Devon," Leila says. "And also why you haven't even . . . like, told her? Some of this stuff, man . . . it's kid stuff. Like the carousel? Last time we went to the carousel, we were, like, eight and I'm pretty sure you threw up."

"Drew threw up. We laughed about it three weeks ago," I say sharply.

Leila snorts. "Devon—"

Stubbornly, I stare forward. "You know why. It's her last summer. Our last summer together. We have to make it perfect. And fun."

Leila hums. "Sometimes . . . you sound more like Drew than you think, you know," she retorts. "Perfection is overrated."

"Not in this case."

And that's enough to silence Leila. She knows that in a battle between her will and mine, she'll always lose when it comes to Drew.

There's no resentment between Drew and me, not really. I had the complete luck and fortune of being born first and blessed with the skill of crochet, while Drew is just a genius.

It had manifested itself early. Drew was the first to walk and talk and eat on her own. She was the first to learn to read, too, which our parents realized when they found her reading *Brown Bear, Brown Bear, What Do You See?* to me, after we'd been put to bed, sometime around two years old. That's not when they'd put her in her fancy little private school, though. That had come later, around middle school, when they decided that we both had the social skills to function without each other. Or, as I later came to suspect, that *Drew* had developed the social skills to function without me and our friends.

The transition had been seamless for Drew, but that was certainly not the case for me. No, there was no smoothness to the sudden jagged absence of Drew by my side. I felt it deep, but I learned not to question it, because *Drew needed a challenge, and she certainly wasn't going to get it in the New York City public school system*, according to my parents. Drew needed her fancy private school and all the bells and whistles it offered more than she needed me, because she was a genius, and she was going to *do something* for the world. This was the truth that held me together every time she was off doing something I didn't know, until finally the raw edges began to dull into something resembling a new normal.

"You ever even met these people?" Leila asks.

"Nope," I say. I'd never felt the need to, never understood Drew's need to have them either. Not when we had all of this, right here, right near home. "But they're probably on her Insta."

"You know she doesn't post," Leila says, even as she thumbs off one of her gloves and pulls her phone out of her back pocket to check. She flicks it unlocked, searching through Drew's followers, presumably. "Ugh, they're all private. What's the point of being rich if you're not going to show off all your cool stuff to poor people?"

"Wealth whispers or whatever," I say with a shrug.

Leila guffaws violently. "Our wallets must be screaming then. They live in Brooklyn? Not around here, right?"

"God, I hope not," I say without shame. We're lucky enough as it is to not have been priced out of Crown Heights yet without the added influx of *more* rich people.

The timer on my phone goes off, having reached the fifteen-minute mark. Leila leans in to inspect my eyebrows before I can even turn to look in the mirror myself.

"Oh, I think this is the winning combo. No extra coat for you," Leila says.

She's right. My eyebrows have come out wispy and white like dandelions against the brown of my skin. I smile at my own reflection, beaming. We abandon the bleach mixture on the sink and rush out into the creaky hallway, down the steps, and through the pocket doors into the living room, which smells like aloe vera and freshly pressed hair.

"Auntie Carole, that's *tight*," Malachi whines. He's not sitting in her hairdresser chair; instead, he's on the floor between her legs, perched atop a pillow.

Mom smacks his hand away from his scalp. "It's supposed to be tight but not too tight, and I know it's not too tight. You're just tender headed," she insists. "Always have been."

"I'm not tender headed, you're just rough," Malachi retorts.

Mom snorts but doesn't say anything else. She brushes her hands over the slightly raised sides of his head and mutters, "I'll shave the sides too. Clean it up. You wanna look sharp, right?"

"No one's said 'look sharp' in like three decades, Ms. Harris," Gael says, and she gives him a warning look. Out of the six of us, Gael is the only one who's still required to call Mom by "Ms. Harris," the aftermath of a particularly bad episode in our sophomore year when I was caught with his weed by my homeroom teacher after Gael had begged to slip it into *my* bag because our homeroom teacher liked him enough to keep it a secret once, but a second time was not gonna fly.

We don't have a name, the six of us, but it has always *been* the six of us, since we all went to Miss Carter's day care three blocks over from the house. I remember it less clearly than Drew does—she remembers down to the color of the bo-bos Ma put in our hair—but with more swathes of feeling. Like how it felt to talk to Leila for the first time when she was assigned to sit next to me by our teacher. The excitement of finding out that my cousin-not-cousin-godbrother Malachi was *also* going to be in our same class. My fury when Gael shoved Drew out of the way to be the first to recess, and the satisfaction of tripping him into the sandbox, his knees getting scraped raw. Then how he'd laughed like he knew he deserved it.

Most of all, though, I remember Yaya.

"Your eyebrows look good," Mom compliments.

I can't help but preen, touching a finger to each perfectly white-blonde brow, until I'm interrupted by a familiar voice floating in from the kitchen: "Are you going to draw freckles on tonight?" After a beat full of rattling in the cupboards, Drew emerges with a bag of chips tucked under her arm.

"Would that be a problem?" I ask.

The thing is that while Drew and I are twins, we don't strictly look the same. At least, not anymore. For the first few years of our lives, our resemblance was strong in the inherited slope of our noses, the fullness of our cheeks, even the curves of our necks. But as we've grown older, our aesthetics have settled firmly at the opposite ends of the spectrum. I am all neon colors and bleach-blonde hair. Dark freckles drawn across my cheeks and the bridge of my nose, to go with graphic liner. Drew, on the other hand, is clean and classic, with long black hair kept in perfect health by our mother's careful hand. While she wears it straight, she prides herself on the fact that her scalp has never known the chemical burn of a relaxer, only the touch of salon-grade heat protectant and Mom's hyperexpensive ceramic blow-dryer. Drew looks the part of a private-school girl, a preprofessional Black. Almost immediately, the familiar thought that Drew might not want her friends to see me—*know* me—rises like a churning panic before I remind myself that Drew's first loyalty is to us. Me. And our friends. She's always loved us best.

"No, just wondering," Drew confirms. She's already dressed, but she's always the first to be ready to go anywhere. Her long hair is pulled up into a ponytail, glossy with oil and stray touches of gel to press the flyaways down. She only needs to slide into her carefully cleaned Converses. "I'm excited for my friends to finally meet you."

But she doesn't sound excited at all. She sounds as skeptical about the idea as she was when I'd overexcitedly floated it to her in the midst of her asking my parents if it was okay for her to go. I can still so clearly see her raise of an eyebrow, can hear her hesitant "You wanna go to a *party*? With *my* friends?" Oddly enough, her skepticism had faded only when I'd mentioned bringing the others, too.

I deserved Drew's skepticism. Especially after how I'd reacted when she'd told me that she was graduating a year early. The memory is hazy at the edges, in contrast to the sharp despair that had lanced through my gut as Drew had sat me and our parents down, and just laid it plain with a strident, "My graduation will be at the beginning of June." It had been even worse when I realized that our parents had already long known about it all, and that really this was just her revealing it to me. I had been out of the loop on this, and for far longer than I had realized.

Soon, there would be no more dinners with my sister. No more passing each other by on the way to the bathroom or bumping into each other with an awkward laugh on our way to do laundry. No more bickering over whose night it was to do the dishes. None of the innocuous, reassuring ways that I was used to seeing her. Drew wouldn't just be gone a weekend or two a month, out with friends or at some extracurricular. Drew would be gone forever, and I wouldn't know her at all.

"Well, you shouldn't be excited for your friends to meet her. She looks like an alien," Gael says. Like Drew, he's ready. His hair looks freshly washed, curls hanging in his eyes and stuck to the nape of his neck, dampening the collar of his white T-shirt, which reads, SPLATTERFEST '23. He wants some girl to ask him about it probably, so he can revel in her horny sighs when he reveals that he's a short-film-maker. A *horror auteur* or whatever.

"You think so?" I ask, pleased.

"Not a compliment," Gael promises.

I'm careful that Mom doesn't see when I give Gael the finger. He's not nearly as careful as he mimes sucking dick right back at me.

"Funny, because she doesn't do that," Mom says, without an ounce of humor in her voice. "If you're going to be vulgar, you can wait on the stoop." She sounds exhausted with him, and I smirk because it really is everyone's default setting with Gael.

"No, I'm sorry, I'll stop. It's too hot to sit out there, and I forgot my fan," Gael says. "And that lady at the end of the block complained about the ice-cream truck again last week so he's *still* skipping us."

Mom sucks her teeth but doesn't say anything else, thankfully. I've heard *more* than enough about Kendra Thompson-Bryant, dead Mr. Thompson's daughter, who finally moved back to the neighborhood just to gut his brownstone and turn it into over-priced apartments.

"You *could* go back six blocks to your house and then maybe you could catch him," Leila suggests innocently.

"*Clever*, Leila, but nah, I'm good," Gael says with the attitude of someone who doesn't find Leila clever at all. He throws himself onto the couch next to Mom, watching her fingers, slick with loc butter, twist at the roots of Malachi's locs. She's nearly done.

"When y'all are walking to the subway, I need you to do me a favor," Mom says idly.

I narrow my eyes at her, suspicious. "What kind of favor?"

"I need you to take the stack of flyers just there and give them out to the neighbors. And hang them on the streetlights," Mom says, nodding over to the short pile of pale-blue paper. "Leila, go on and take that roll of tape from the mess drawer."

Malachi groans. "Why?"

"I'm twisting your hair for free, little boy," Mom says snarkily, and Malachi sighs because there's really not much he can say to that.

I stand over the coffee table, peering at the words upside down, but it's easy enough for me to glean the information—an invitation to this year's block party, in just about two weeks. The bubbly letters are all printed out evenly in dark ink. Mom probably went to the UPS Store on Bergen and Nostrand to get it printed, all professional and stuff. She may be just announcing it, but like every year, I know she's been planning this for months and I can't help but smile. The block party always feels like the official-*official* start of the summer. In my head, I amend my list for the Best Summer Ever, tacking on "Make it the best Block Party ever" at the end.

"Everyone on the block?" I ask apprehensively.

The implication of Kendra and all the nonsense that entails is heavy in my tone. It would be hard to make it the best one ever if Kendra shuts the block party down like she did the ice-cream truck.

"*Everyone* on the block. And the next until you run out. Just put them in the mailboxes," Mom says. She pats Malachi's shoulder and adds, "You're done, baby. Go on."

I'm still not. Rifling through my canvas bag, I find my freckle pen and lean over the console to stare into the mirror as I haphazardly spatter them across my cheeks. Messier than I like, but we're already cutting it close, especially now that we have to disseminate the flyers. Leila scoops up the roll of tape, Malachi grabs the stack of pale-blue papers, and then we finally spill out onto the block.

Drew takes charge: "Let's divvy up the pile between the five of us. Devon, Malachi, you get this block. Hit all the mailboxes. Gael and I will do the other side of the block. Leila, you can hit the streetlights."

So not the pair of us. That's cool. Fine, I guess. We've never been the Wonder Twins.

Leila folds her arms, pursing her lips. "Mhmm, got it, *Captain*," she sings. She gives me a roll of her eyes that isn't particularly subtle before taking her section of flyers and rushing down the block to fulfill her duty.

I pass over half to Gael and Drew, then turn to Malachi. He takes his portion and we take the block slowly, sliding flyers neatly into each rusting mailbox that sits on the little gate out front.

"So Drew's finally letting us meet her friends, huh?" Malachi asks with a hum, raising his eyebrows. "That's . . . *super*."

"I'd *love* if you could be a little more enthusiastic, Malachi," I say.

Malachi pastes a fake smile onto his face, shaking his head at me tauntingly. I do it right back, and he giggles.

11

"Nah, I'm just saying, I'm glad that we're finally up to standards," Malachi says with a sniff.

"Oh, don't pretend that you've *wanted* to meet them," I retort.

Malachi raises his eyebrows as he runs up the next stoop to deposit a flyer under the door. From the top, he says, "Oh, I'm not. It's a privilege for them to meet *me*. Just a shame they've been denied this long." He runs back down, two steps at a time, and nearly crashes into me, but slings an arm around my shoulders like nothing happened.

I lean into him, laughing as we walk down the block. Between the five of us, it's quick work, and before I know it, we're nearly at the brownstone I know that we're all dreading.

That *I'm* particularly dreading.

Sure enough, *he's* sitting on the stoop when we finally get to the end of the block.

Keith Thompson-Bryant calls out, "Yaya is waiting at the subway." He's staring out at the street, a book open halfway in his lap. He's always got a different paperback, but I'm not even sure he can read any of them.

Keith Thompson-Bryant is not a huge part of my life in any way, shape, or form, but he is a constant. When we were younger and Mr. Thompson was alive, Keith would visit every summer, but as we grew up, his visits to his grandpa would become an every other Christmas or Thanksgiving kind of thing. His family lives mostly in California, somewhere expensive like San Francisco, because his dad is a tech guy, and his mom, Kendra, does *something* film related. Something about being a production designer, which apparently makes her qualified to be a wannabe HGTV star.

Keith always manages to show up when no one wants to talk to him and ask after Yaya, who he has had a noticeable crush on for years now. When he used to come every summer to stay with his grandfather, he would stare at her from inside and stutter when she invited him to hang out with us. He hadn't had the courage then, not to talk to Yaya properly or put up with Gael and Malachi's taunting. That had suited me fine. I liked Keith best when he fawned from afar.

It hadn't been weird back then, because we were all so young. But then Keith got older. Keith got braces, then got them off. Keith finally found a Black barber to give him a decent line-up. Keith *graduated*. He started feeling himself because suddenly he's got good teeth and a sharp hairline, and he's smart and goes to USC and he's a boy, which means, of course, a girl like Yaya has to like him.

Yaya still never even notices, but she humors his attempts at conversation with pleasantries. She doesn't like when we complain about how annoying he is, insisting that it's probably lonely to be shipped off to New York every summer where you don't have friends. Yaya is more than nice, she's *good*, so it makes sense that she would make it a point to be kind to Keith.

It's, unfortunately, had the side effect of Keith thinking that he has a chance with her.

To me, though, it's always felt like Keith still wants Yaya just because she's the last remaining item on a checklist. Something he's always wanted and never been brave enough to ask for.

"And why the fuck do you know that, weirdo?" Gael asks, folding his arms. He doesn't even bother looking at Keith, but Drew shoots him a glare. She purses her lips, folding her arms over her chest as she eyes Keith up and down, using her powers of disdain for good. Keith shifts, self-consciously, and a strange little laugh rattles from his mouth.

"What?" he asks. "I was just letting you know Yaya is waiting for you at the station."

"You think we don't know that?" Leila sniffs.

Drew clears her throat and offers a flyer from between her fingers. "Here," she says. She makes no move to get closer, and Keith slowly stands, approaching us like we're a pack of wild, roving dogs. He snatches the flyer from Drew's hand and glances over it.

"A block party? Really?" Keith asks. "*This* block?"

"Yeah, what other block would it be?" Malachi retorts.

Keith shakes his head. "That won't work. We'll still be doing construction," he mutters to himself. He looks over his shoulder and shouts, "Mom—"

"Shut *up*, dude," Gael groans, crumpling a flyer in his fist and lobbing it at the back of Keith's head.

"Hey—" Keith retorts, head swinging around.

He's nailed with another crumpled flyer to the face, and I have to smother a laugh in my arm. Leila looks extremely proud of her aim.

But our amusement is a short-lived thing as the door swings open and Kendra Thompson-Bryant's hellish presence emerges.

"Are you disturbing the peace *again*?" she asks coldly.

The "again" could be referring to so many normal things that she considers "disturbing the peace." Hanging out on the stoop is disturbing the peace. Walking to the corner store is disturbing the peace. We once were a little too loud coming home from school while she was showing an unfinished apartment, and she considered *that* disturbing the peace. That was the one that resulted in the ice-cream truck being taken away the first time.

We wait patiently for her latest accusation.

Sure enough, she continues, "Littering on my land?"

Kendra Thompson-Bryant looks nothing like her father, with her razor-fine features, all long-limbed and smooth, with the kind of silk press that would fall off the bone. It's the first thing I noticed when I met her at his wake. Mr. Thompson was short and curled up, like his spine had cracked and fallen to pieces with age. He'd had a large head and wide features, and had exclusively worn flannel tucked into khaki pants with a thick, weathered black belt. Mr. Thompson had been well loved, a neighborhood cultural touchstone since the seventies. He was a curmudgeonly old Black man who would complain about how much noise we were making late into the summer nights but would still offer us Italian ice from his downstairs freezer when the sun beamed down too hot. He always had a soft spot for Drew, but that wasn't surprising. Most adults have a soft spot for Drew. They love a Black kid who proves all the white people wrong—identity politics strike again. But at least he hadn't hated the rest of us, who screamed and ran around. Not like his daughter does.

The day of his funeral, a somber late May afternoon, it was uncharacteristically hot, just like the days he would call us in to cool off. We'd known the second we met her, though, that with Kendra Thompson-Bryant now owning that home, we'd never get a free Italian ice again.

The next week the construction started.

"There is no *land*, Mrs. Thompson-Bryant. This is the sidewalk, you see, and no one can own the sidewalk," Gael says, voice *too* bright, *too* pleasant.

Kendra's eyes narrow immediately at his smart-assery. She snaps at Keith and he scoops up the two balls of paper quickly, stuffing them in his pockets with a nasty look back at us.

"We're just passing out flyers, ma'am. Sorry," Drew says. "We'll go now." She takes a step back and gives all of us a steely-eyed gaze, jerking her head. I remember now—Mom was clear that everyone was invited. No need to taunt the beast of the block and ruin Mom's party.

"You can keep your . . . flyer," Kendra says, voice dripping with her disdain. It's a coveted dismissal, one we take.

"Tell Yaya I said *hi*." I turn and see Keith looking shockingly smug for someone who needed his mommy to save him.

I'm not nearly so restrained.

"Why doesn't your grown ass get a job instead of watching what we're doing?" I bark.

Keith bares a smile that he probably thinks is charming, the smile of a boy whose mama and daddy have good dental insurance, which is sick because *nobody* has good dental insurance. He shouts after us, "I'm on my summer break. From USC! It's practically an Ivy—"

"Fuck off," Gael finishes for me, and then he breaks into a run, dragging me after him. My blonde braids whip behind me as I cling to him to keep up, giggles overcoming me, and I let go of the idea of sending the rest of the flyers off in a civilized matter.

Whooping loudly, I toss a flyer onto each stoop without stopping, feeling the intoxication of summer wash over me. I'm free to do as I please, to throw flyers to the best block party of the summer, to call out Keith for being the worst, to party with Drew's friends. I can't let Keith and Kendra ruin this, because this isn't just any summer now. It's my last summer with Drew. My last summer with *all* of us before everything changes.

By the time we make it to the subway, there's only one more flyer left, and Leila expertly sticks it to the streetlight on the corner.

"Train in, like, two minutes. Let's hustle," Malachi says, squinting at the LED sign right beneath the Nostrand Avenue sign.

Even from street level, I can hear the rattling of the tracks.

As we thunder down the steps, Drew casts me a look and says, "You could stand to be less rude to our neighbors. Especially Mrs. Thompson-Bryant. Mom is having a hard enough time with her because of the ice-cream truck and the construction and everything. Let's try to make life easier for her."

I bite back my irritation. Drew's not wrong, but I hate when she lectures me like this, like we're not the exact same age. I can't push back, though, because it'll start another fight and ruin *everything*, and I'm trying. I'm trying so hard. I have to try harder.

I force a smile onto my face and salute.

Another amendment to the list: "Don't fight with Drew."

The Best Summer Ever™

1. Go to one of Drew's friends' parties. Bring the crew. Remind Gael to not be a piece of shit. Remind friends to be _friendly_.

2. Go to the Prospect Park Zoo. (We've never been, it'd be funny.) Drew likes animals—maybe interested in zoology? [NOTE: What DOES Drew want to do in college? Ask, maybe?]

3. Ride the carousel at Brooklyn Bridge Park like we used to.

4. Make nice with Alexis so that Mr. Ahmed doesn't have to tell me off for making her cry again → parents won't be mad at me for Alexis's snitching to her mom → shows Drew I can just ignore Alexis like she's always telling me to.

5. Girls' night at Movies-in-the-Park biweekly. (Checked the schedule and there's a summer series of rom-coms. W!)

6. Vet each and every one of Malachi's dates—no repeats of what happened last summer. Be on Malachi shift with Drew?

7. Make the Block Party the best Block Party ever. It's Drew's last one (maybe).

8. Don't. Fight. With. Drew.

CHAPTER TWO

The thing is, I don't strictly want to go to this party. I'm going to go and I'm going to drink these rich people's alcohol and smoke their weed and take up space in their fancy-ass house. But I don't want to. It's never been my idea of a good time.

That's what I said to Drew during our first year of high school, when we'd revisited the idea of maybe meeting up with some of her friends at brunches in Midtown or going to house parties in Cobble Hill. My idea of a good time is hanging out in the back of Leila's parents' brownstone and disguising the smell of our weed with burning incense and Gael's disgusting aftershave. Or even getting my hair rebraided while watching *Living Single* reruns with Mom. And so Drew had assured me that that was fine. After all, she still made time for us when she could; her presence was sparing during the school year, but it's not like she disappeared off the face of the Earth.

But. *But.* Now that has to change.

This is Drew's Best Summer Ever.

It has to be.

With graduating a whole year early, come fall Drew is going to college to be brilliant in whatever she does. Of course she's going to be brilliant. But she's going to be far away, and even when she comes back, she's going to have to be an adult, which means internships and summer jobs that aren't bullshit like working as the temp secretary at Yaya's mom's ballet studio. So, I'd begun to plan the Best Summer Ever for her.

But also for me and for our friends. To remind Drew that she loves us and that we love her, and maybe a little bit of a "this is what you'll be missing." I've even written it out in my journal in a numbered list because Drew is so *organized*, and if it works for her, it'll probably work for me, okay? And it starts with this party tonight, whether I want to go or not, because this party will be a reminder that even when she's gone, I've tried. I've *tried* with her friends and with all the things she likes, and so she has to try with me.

I'm rattled out of my thoughts by the sound of a Euclid Avenue–bound train coming from across the platform, and I'm the first to see her, because I always am. She's lingering by the MetroCard machines, wiggling because she can't quite stand still.

"Does anyone have five dollars? I need to reload my Metro-Card," Yaya asks.

"Please just use Apple Pay like a normal person," Leila says, waving her phone in front of the turnstile. Yaya turns up her nose.

"Or be a *real* New Yorker and just"—Gael punctuates his snobbery with a well-executed hop over the turnstile while Malachi hustles through in the same swipe as Drew, pressed up against her back.

"I have five dollars," I say, reaching for the ratty bill tucked into the back pocket of my shorts. I offer it to her between two fingers, and Yaya beams.

"Thank you," she says, moving to fill her MetroCard.

I rock back and forth on my heels as I keep one eye on the

monitor for the train times and the other on the way Yaya's hair sits against the swanlike length of her neck. Her curls are bound in two braids, with teal ribbons woven through like flags. They trail down her back, touching the waistband of her low-rise jeans. I notice the skin between the bottom of Yaya's camisole and her jeans and fidget, my fingers itching. I used to find so many reasons to touch Yaya, to hug her or to hold her hand. Until the first time I kissed a girl and realized I wanted to do that and so much *more* with Yaya.

Now I try not to touch her at all.

I manage to look at her like a normal person again just in time for her to finish up and beam at me with the brightest, whitest smile in the world.

"Ready," she says, and then she grabs my wrist and tugs me along.

I never said Yaya made the no-touching rule easy.

When we get through to the platform, I very pointedly ignore the knowing stare that Leila is giving me. Leila loves looking at me that way, like she knows all about my horny Yaya-occupied thoughts. Which she does. But still.

"They don't live that far," Drew says, staring down at her phone. She's texting so hard that I can hear the rhythm of her words. "We transfer to the G at Hoyt and take that to Bergen, and then we walk."

So it's in Carroll Gardens. I've never found a reason to be in Carroll Gardens in my entire life. I want to say so, but Drew looks up from her phone suddenly and stares owlishly right at me. It's a reflex, the way I beam back at her, and Drew's surprised smile makes it all better; my plan is working. I'm *not* complaining about how her friends don't know anything about Brooklyn besides Jay-Z and Smorgasburg and their little expensive slice of the borough. She's not snippily calling me judgy while she skips out on one of our group hangouts to go to the Hamptons for the third time that month. Everything is A-okay. Nothing wrong with a little bit of Carroll Gardens.

The A Train rattles into the station with the loud screeching of brakes. It's a familiar sound that settles where my molars used to be. Only three people exit the train where we stand—two white guys in head-to-toe Supreme and an Asian girl with one of those expensive beaded bags looped over her shoulder.

Very loudly and obnoxiously Gael calls, "There goes the neighborhood." One of the guys looks over his shoulder, nose wrinkling, and Gael stares back balefully. He only gets on the train before the doors close because Leila pulls him through. She lays into him immediately. "Do you have to do so much *always*?"

"Yes," he says, unbothered.

I tune them out, wishing that I'd remembered to bring my headphones. The train isn't *full*, but it's certainly not empty, I note as we spread out in search of a seat. Gael and Leila are already paired off, still arguing. Malachi and Yaya are next to them, whispering. Finally, I spy Drew sitting by the window. There's someone eyeing the seat next to her, a girl with box-dyed red hair, but Drew doesn't even flicker a glance the girl's way, just sets her flimsy little purse right on the chair to claim it. The other girl stops in her tracks, affronted, and then takes another step, ready to say that snide "Excuse me" that we know so well. But I don't let her. I slide right in next to Drew quickly and then meet the girl's eyes.

She does a double take and then slinks back as I smile. Victory.

Drew doesn't even notice, though. She's still looking at her phone when she says, "My friend Avery is excited to meet you."

I rack my brain for anything she might have said about Avery. All I know, though, is that he's the party host. Drew talks about her school friends as if they're cartoonishly unreal characters in a beloved television show, one where I should know every single member of the cast despite never having seen an episode. Which makes anything she does tell me hard to follow.

Drew can tell I'm coming up empty, and she sighs in a long-suffering way. I fight the urge to roll my eyes.

"Avery is Lydia's ex-boyfriend. Christophe and I sided with Avery in the breakup," Drew says. More names that I don't recognize, but I nod anyway, and Drew seems pleased by my feigned interest. "I think you'll like them. They'll definitely like you."

"'Definitely' is such a strong word."

"Do you not *want* them to like you?" Drew questions.

"Couldn't be further from the truth." *I can be proper too,* I think. *I can say things like "furthermore" and "regards" or whatever shit you sign off with when you text your friends that aren't us.*

Spite is so sour, it turns the stomach, and I can't afford that. Not tonight. We're leaving the passive aggression at the *door*.

The train pulls into the next stop, allowing us to reshuffle. Malachi grabs a now-vacant seat near us, and Yaya perches on his knee, curled forward, chin resting on her fist as she doesn't make an effort to hide that she's now listening to our conversation.

"Have they graduated like you? Or . . ." I trail off.

"No, they'll be going into their senior year as planned," Drew says, still looking at her phone.

"Oh. Oh, wow. Bet that bums them out," I try. "You leaving and all."

"It does."

We fall into a silence far less comfortable than the ones I share with Leila, but then Drew sits up and sets her phone face down in her lap, looking me in the eye intently. It's either *too much* eye contact or none with her. "This is kind of like my graduation party."

A beat.

"Oh, shit, are you serious?" Malachi interjects before I can figure out what to say.

"Of course I am," Drew says, raising a waxed eyebrow. She is so rarely unserious that it makes Malachi's question a little ridiculous. "Avery wanted to throw it since he's especially 'bummed' about it all. I told him I just didn't think it was a productive use of my time to continue there."

Yaya nods sagely. "Yes, that makes sense."

"Only you would resent a year of coasting, Drew," Gael sighs, shuffling nearer. "I wish I had an extra year. I'd spend it all doing what I actually want to do."

"And what's that? Making low-budget splattercore monstrosities?" Leila asks derisively.

Gael grins. "Exactly."

The ride really isn't so long, but when we get off, we have to wait a whopping fourteen minutes for the G Train. It's a train I take so little that once we do finally get on, I have to look at the overhead map three times to remind myself where we need to get off. It's strange to have lived somewhere your entire life, to have that place in your veins, and to not know parts of it at all.

"The G is so weird. You know——" I start, but the end of my sentence is drowned by the screech of the brakes.

"Here," Drew proclaims, and she exits the air-conditioned comfort of the train car without looking back. She never looks back, never afraid that she's forgotten something. I envy Drew's self-assuredness.

I choke on the sweaty heat of the train station as I follow her, only seeing and breathing normally again when we get up to ground level.

"Okay?" Yaya asks kindly.

"Yeah. Just no stamina," I admit. A humiliating thing to confess to someone like Yaya, who I've seen do six-minute ballet routines without breaking a sweat. But she is kind enough to rub my back as I heave. Of course that means my heart never stops racing, though. The two of us walk slower than the rest, and like with Drew, my silences with Yaya are never comfortable.

I reach for something to fill it. "I . . . Keith was talking about you today," I say quickly. Yaya tilts her head, squinting into the air, trying to place the name, until I add, "Kendra's son."

"Keith Bryant?"

"Thompson-Bryant," I correct, because the hyphenated last names are a point of pride for Kendra and her son, and I can't help but mock it.

"Isn't he, like, twenty?" Yaya asks slowly. Like she's finally cottoning on to how Keith is weird for that. The being obsessed with a teenager of it all.

"Nineteen."

"Sure." Yaya snorts out a laugh. She doesn't explain the joke, but she shakes her head. She's always been like this—dismissive of all interest in her, even the noncreepy kind. She's never dated, never has the time, she claims. But sometimes it seems like, really, she's just *waiting* for something, like the doll in a music box, anticipating being wound up.

"Do you know the guy who's throwing this party?" she asks, changing the subject.

"His name is Avery."

Yaya's eyes go wide. "Oh, he's the one who was dating Lydia until Lydia tried to have sex with Christophe, right?"

It fills in the blanks from Drew's story on the train, but I don't remember hearing any of this. It just makes me feel shittier, like I should've studied before throwing myself headfirst into this party and my plan.

"Drew's been going to that school for like a million years and I've never met any of her friends," I say, even though of course she knows. "Does that make me a bad sister?"

"No," Yaya says immediately, like she anticipated what I was going to say before even I did. And she says it with such conviction, I should just believe it.

Still, I question her. "Are you sure?"

"I'm sure," Yaya says, and then she loops her arm through mine, tugging me close, without taking her gaze off Gael's back. "You made an entire list of how to make this her best summer ever. That doesn't really make me think of you as a bad sister."

Maybe a selfish one, though.

"Okay," I say feebly as we turn into the more residential area.

As we follow Drew, I notice the streets over here are calmer, quiet even though it's only just past eight, and the sun is still cresting the horizon, bathing the world in a stringent orange. These brownstones are so different from the ones that Leila, Drew, and I live in. This one is clean on the outside. There are no jutting rounded parts or sloping steps up to the parlor floor. It's all so . . . strange.

"Are you sure this is the right house?" Gael asks.

Drew sends him her most withering look before she rings the doorbell.

We wait for only ten seconds. And then when the door swings open, a wall of sound slams into us, so loud that I feel like I've gone deaf for a second. A light-skinned boy with a shock of red hair and freckles across his dusty brown cheeks says something that I can't make out. Then he gathers Drew into a tight hug and looks over at us, grinning widely.

"Welcome to my humble abode," Avery-I-presume says, sweeping into a low bow but not quite letting Drew away from him. "So . . . let me see if I get this right." He looks at each of us, pointing in order. "Yaya, Leila, Gael, Malachi . . . and you've *got* to be Devon. Holy shit, you both really do look alike."

Drew snorts. "We don't, but okay, you got it right."

"You're right, she looks way cooler than you, you square," Avery says, and then he presses his face into her hair and inhales. Drew doesn't even seem to notice.

We certainly do, for how weird it is. Malachi elbows Gael hard in the gut as he takes a deep breath, probably preparing to say something stupid. Gael grunts but takes the hint, then extends a hand, shaking Avery's free one. "Nice to meet you, man. Can we come in?"

"Yeah, yeah, of course," Avery says, shuffling inside like a crab with Drew still attached to him. Their closeness feels alien. "Drinks are on the bar. Drugs in the bathroom. If you want food,

27

raid the fridge, or Andrea has my Uber Eats account on her phone; get anything you want. We're here to celebrate her after all."

The sound of her full name is a jump scare, and I have to physically stop myself from flinching. Drew hasn't gone by her full name in a literal decade. Except, clearly, she has, if Avery feels so comfortable using it.

"Fuck off," Drew says, but she allows the tiniest of smiles to creep across her face. Then Avery tugs her off into the crowd, and the room seems to swell with even more noise, everyone's voices booming their congratulations over the droning of Sheck Wes.

For a moment we stand in the middle of the foyer like a bunch of assholes. Malachi leans over, staring at the pile of shoes that sits underneath the empty coatrack. "Look at those ugly Balenciaga sock sneakers."

"How much do you think they would go for on GOAT?" Leila asks.

"Without the box? Not much," Gael sighs.

"Damn."

I roll my eyes and turn to look at them. "Stop trying to steal these kids' sneakers and let's have fun," I insist sternly, like someone who has never experienced fun in her entire life.

Gael salutes and says, "He said drugs in the bathroom." And then he's off, ingratiating himself with a comical ease. There are already at least three girls eyeing him and the way he smiles so easily and shakes out his loose glossy curls as he passes.

"Come get a drink with me," Leila demands of Malachi, but Yaya grabs her wrist with an "I'll go." Leila winces and gives a half shrug, leaving me with Malachi, the only one who still looks as uninterested in being here as I feel.

"So that Avery guy. He's into your sister," Malachi says as we ease our way into the party. It's all open concept, a stark difference from our own brownstone full of dark wood and pocket doors. All of that's been blown away for a sleek, soulless modern kitchen and a bright, open living room with a back wall made of glass.

I snort. "Yeah, I suspect so."

"How much do you want to bet that she doesn't know?"

"I'm not going to take that bet. There's a one thousand percent sure chance that she doesn't know at all," I say, lingering in the kitchen, tracing my fingers along the edges of the speckled marble counters. I've never thought of Drew as particularly primed for romance.

I search the crowd and it's like I have a tracker on her; that's how easy it is to find Drew, even amongst the crush of people. She's sitting on the arm of the most central couch, surrounded by a swell of people that I don't know, but she looks . . . *comfortable*. She holds herself differently, keeps her shoulders a little looser than back at home. Her usual slight aloofness just makes Avery sway closer into her space, his hand sitting on her thigh like both a reassurance and a claim, but she doesn't seem to mind.

I don't get a chance to process this further because my vision is suddenly obscured by a bouncy redheaded girl, tall with lean muscles. Volleyball muscles.

"You must be Devon. You look just like Andrea," she says, without introducing herself.

There it is again—*Andrea*.

"I mean, of course you're blonde and edgy and alt, but yeah, you've got to be Andrea's sister, right? I'm totally right," the girl continues, not waiting for confirmation. She leans one hip against the edge of a kitchen counter and unsubtly leans in, assessing. She likes what she sees—that's easy enough to notice, particularly with the smirk Malachi sends my way—so she continues. "When Andrea talks about you, it's like she expects us all to know you and she always seems so confused that we don't. It's kinda funny, especially, because . . . you know Andrea." She wiggles her eyebrows.

"Totally," Malachi drawls, in a way that's very much making fun of her, but she doesn't catch the insincerity.

"Yeah, *Andrea* is literally never confused," I confirm, trying to be nice.

"Right? Half the time she's correcting all the teachers," the girl says. She continues to chatter about Drew and I let her, because I'm curious about this *Andrea Harris*. The one that everyone else here seems to know.

Apparently, Andrea Harris is composed and confident, which is no surprise. But when I learn that her role as president of the student council, a position of ridicule at my school, is a coveted one that she got because of her six-part campaign strategy but most of all because she's popular, that *does* surprise me. Andrea Harris is *popular*.

Malachi checks out of our conversation and does his Instagram sleuthing as one drink turns into two. I pick up more bits and pieces from Volleyball Girl, interspersed with Malachi whispering to me about how the boy two seats down from Drew is a newly graduated senior who's going to Princeton for lacrosse, or how that girl against the wall who's pretending not to stare at me is the girl who owns the house in the Hamptons that Drew always ends up at. Each bite of information is a new porthole into the shape of Drew's life—no, *Andrea Harris's* life. Each contextualizes her a little more, and I can see that just like she's a cut above the rest back in Crown Heights, she's smarter than everyone else at her school too.

"Your hair . . . ," the girl says, suddenly shifting gears.

"What about it?" I ask. I still don't know her name, and it feels too late to ask it.

She leans in, flicking her gaze up and down again in a way I think is supposed to be flirtatious.

Jesus. The girl's not particularly good at it.

"I know that's, like . . . not your *natural* color. But Andrea has long hair—is that all *yours*?" the girl asks.

Malachi snorts violently and he says, "Chile, we should go."

I blink once, twice at the girl, and then I turn on a heel and walk away. There's really nothing else to say after that. Besides, she doesn't seem that close with Drew. It doesn't technically count as me breaking the *friendliness subrule* of the Best Summer Ever if she's not an actual friend.

"That wasn't . . . that wasn't, like, out of line, right?" I ask.

"The girl's question or you walking away?" Malachi retorts as we shoulder through a conversation to get to the bar. He makes an appreciative sound in the back of his throat as he looks at the assortment of treasures. This is top-shelf liquor—Casamigos, Goose, and Johnnie Walker Gold, amongst others. Either they're sparing no expense, or Avery genuinely doesn't know the meaning of the word.

"No, no, like she was definitely out of line," I say, as he mixes both of us a Jack and Coke. "I meant me walking away. I just don't want to make trouble for Drew."

"Drew is a big girl and that other girl embarrassed herself. Though I guess she doesn't know you're not hooking up with anyone here unless it's Yaya," Malachi says.

I flinch but don't protest. I've learned to get over the teasing about Yaya. I've never been able to be subtle. Everyone knows.

Everyone but Yaya, that is.

Malachi and Leila clown me often about my refusal to do anything about that, but even the idea that I might throw off the friend chemistry is a big enough threat to keep them silent around Yaya. An exercise in caution . . . and maybe a little fear.

"And what about you?" I ask, looking at all the boys there. All stubbly faced and pocked, with that boy smell. Not something I've ever found particularly attractive, but Malachi probably picked his target the moment we stepped into the building.

"There's potential. That one is the son of a famous photographer. And that one is the rumored ex-boyfriend of that guy who got caught trying to sleep in the Met overnight. You know the one?" Malachi asks. I'm not sure who he's pointing at, the boy in the Arsenal jersey or the one wearing sweatpants. The white boy in a button-down or the Asian kid with perfectly fluffed hair. The longer I look at this crowd of rich people, the more they blur together.

I scoff. "No, I don't. Because I don't live on IG, Malachi."

Malachi sniffs. "You just don't know culture, Grandma."

"Crocheting doesn't make me—"

"Whatever," Malachi drawls, tugging his phone out of the back pocket of his extremely tight cutoffs. "Anyway, I don't have my eye on anyone just yet. I feel like I *know* who's gay, but I can confirm."

Malachi is a creature of habit. I don't even need to look at his phone to know that he's on Grindr.

"How do you even know they're on there? Don't you need to be eighteen to be on that app?" I ask for the millionth time, nose wrinkling.

"Don't you need to be less of a prude?" Malachi retorts. He bites his bottom lip. "I'm just looking, all right?"

All in all, it's not a particularly bad party. It's not *fun*—the kids are too curious about public school, as if it's an alien world they're unfamiliar with, and they're a little too fascinated by the fact that Andrea Harris has a "secret" twin—but it's bearable.

Once or twice Drew looks up from her conversation to find me and tilts her head, assessing. I make sure to smile and lift a full drink when I see her watching from the corner of her eye. Then I turn back and pretend that I'm super into this conversation with some rising sophomore who wants to know the cool restaurants in Bed-Stuy, even though we live in Crown Heights. I wait a few seconds, then glance back and smile at her, and Drew tentatively grins back.

Everything is going to plan. Everything feels perfect. Whoever owns the aux is good, the drinks are strong and smooth, and most of all, Drew is happy. And even though it feels like I don't know her here, I'm trying to. I won't make the same mistake again. I'm trying and she's trying and all of our friends are talking to her friends, and it's going *good*. As it should be.

Because this is the Best Summer Ever. And that is how it'll stay.

CHAPTER THREE

I do away with any of the last remaining preconceived notions I have about Drew when she doesn't seem ready to leave the party within two hours. If anything, *Andrea Harris* catches a second wind after the first batch of people leaves to go to whatever other engagement they have.

She's sitting on the couch now, legs tossed over Avery's thighs. I'm not sure whether to approach or not, but Drew catches my eye and beckons me forward, so I drag Malachi with me to meet her.

"You seen the others?" she asks, her once-formal tongue loosening from liquor.

Avery looks thrilled by it.

"Last I saw Gael, he was chatting up some girl. Haven't seen Yaya or Leila since we got here," I say honestly. Almost to be contradictory, I see Yaya and Leila slip back from the depths of the townhouse, giggling to each other. Yaya looks up, like she feels my gaze on her, and grins, waving happily. I helplessly smile back at her before dragging my stare back to my sister.

Drew nods slowly and she smiles up at me, extra toothy. It's a cautiously good sign for the effectiveness of phase one of my plan.

"And you. You having fun?" she asks.

I nod because it's not like I'm *not* having fun. So yeah, that must mean I'm having fun.

"Are you?" I return.

Drew's smile widens. "Yes." She leans around Avery, searching for someone, and then crooks a finger. "This is Christophe. You know."

"I know," I say, even though I don't. "Hi, Christophe."

"Oh, wow, you really are Andrea's twin sister," Christophe says, blinking in surprise.

"It's like they've never met twins before," I say, smiling at Malachi. The laugh I let out is a little more cutting than I'd like it to be.

"It really is," he affirms.

Christophe notices Malachi instead of my comment, and I know he's lost. Having attractive friends is so funny. You just get used to conversations dropping off, and they always get the double take. I get the double take too, but that's usually due to my white-blonde eyebrows or the makeup I've scrawled on like a child taking crayons to a coloring book, ignorant of the lines, just the way I like it. The sheer messy creativity to Drew's carefully curated elegance. Christophe looks down at Drew, who is being very Andrea and nodding encouragingly, like she doesn't know exactly what Malachi likes.

I'm picky about my secondhand wares and personal style, but I have nothing on Malachi and dating. Malachi wants an epic kind of love with someone who checks off all the right romantic boxes on his list—he's organized like Drew that way—and, excruciatingly, who is about three to five years too old for him. I can already see Malachi's disinterest take root, just as quickly as Christophe's fascination grows.

"Hi, I'm Christophe," he says.

"I'm sure," Malachi says.

Christophe has the put-off look of a boy who's used to being fawned over, or at least let down easy. Malachi's not a coddler, though.

"Well, *I'm* bored," Avery declares before things can get any more awkward. He turns to Drew and says, "Let me read tarot for you."

I can't manage to smother my snort of disbelief, looking over at Drew to commiserate. The glare Drew shoots me in response is absolutely poisonous. Arsenic-smothered.

My fingers twitch at my sides and I dig them into my thighs, exhaling noisily through my nose. That's an unknown factor. That's *new*.

"Yeah, sure. Not a huge spread, though," Drew says, indulgent. *Patient.*

Avery grins at her and rushes off, probably to fetch his tarot cards. Drew drags me down to fill the warm spot that he's left, and she lets her head fall on my shoulder in a way that she hasn't done since middle school. When she looks up at me, she hums.

"Tarot, huh?" I ask.

Drew scoffs. "He's . . . into it. I don't want to hurt his feelings," she mumbles. She leans up closer, and I can feel her breath against my cheek as she asks, "Are you really having fun?"

"Yeah, I am. I like your friends," I lie.

"I do too," Drew murmurs. She sounds sleepy, her lids lowering just the slightest bit. She is unbound and vulnerable with alcohol in her. It's why the words "I think they're easier than *our* friends. Easier than you" slip from between her teeth so easily.

I'm too stunned to demand to know what she means.

Then there's no time, since Avery returns just as fast with a box tucked under his arm and we swap places once again. He clears the coffee table of the red Solo Cups and the empty top-shelf bottles, making just enough room for a small spread. Drew frowns and reaches out for him since he's returned to sitting a regular distance apart.

"Come back; you were warm," she sighs.

Avery beams at her. "I know I said I was gonna do a reading, but . . . I found something cooler." He spreads something on the table, and it becomes clear his idea of cooler is an old Ouija board. Everyone oohs and aahs at it. Well, almost everyone.

"Oh, hell no," Malachi murmurs, gently redirecting me away, putting just a little more space between us and the table.

I've never seen a Ouija board in person. I've heard of them. But even I know that they are not to be messed with. Drew knows that too. I hear the suspicions of our mother and father so clearly in my head—"Don't bring no Ouija board into this house," my mother spat every time we saw one on television and expressed even a little bit of interest. "Don't invite them in."

"This is a bit much, hm?" Drew says.

Avery frowns, looking up at Drew in confusion. "No, come on, it'll be fun," he says gently. Drew doesn't even fight back. She simply collapses into his side with a slow nod.

Drew's tolerance is all the more confusing, though, not just because of Mom and Dad but because she's her. She always finds the illogical so insufferable. She's quick to dismantle the mysticism in any of Gael's horror films, but now she's forcing herself to be patient with Avery as he commands everyone where to put the candles?

"Shh," Avery calls finally. He's kneeling in front of the Ouija board, something balanced across his palms. I rear back when I make out the shape of a jagged knife with a blade made of black glass. The hilt is heavy and wooden, runes marked across it.

"What kind of demonic white shit does Drew have us at?" Malachi mutters from the corner of his mouth. His eyes are narrowed into slits, and I can feel him drumming his fingers against his thigh, his knuckles brushing with mine. "Devon, what the hell—"

"Gather round. Closer, closer," Avery calls, and he's smiling at us directly, beckoning us specifically. Malachi scoffs, refusing to make any moves, but I latch on to his wrist and drag him closer too. "Good, we want to keep the circle closed. Nothing to come in . . . nothing to get *out*." Avery waggles his eyebrows for good measure, inciting a swell of nervous, muffled laughter.

I am *not* laughing.

"I swear this reminds me of something," Gael says, slightly too loudly, as he reenters the room, slipping out from under the attention of two girls, both pretty and blushing. He earns a glare from Avery, but Gael has never been embarrassed in his entire life, so he just shrugs. Yaya smiles, strained, from her perch on the arm of the sofa, next to him.

"He just watches a lot of horror movies. I'm sure at least some of the screenwriters do their research. Go on, Avery," Drew says encouragingly.

Avery nods but doesn't quite shed his pout. "Well, this isn't a movie," he says.

"Of course not," Drew says indulgently, and she preens when Avery finally relaxes and releases his petulance.

This time Gael makes a loud sound of disgust in the back of his throat. It's followed swiftly by the sound of a hand smacking against a chest, and I don't need to look to know that Leila has moved to stand beside him, as per usual. I look anyway and see his hair is mussed, her collar rumpled. Those are the only things out of place, but I know there'll be a story to get out of her. Later. After this charade.

"When I was growing up," Avery begins with more gravitas than he's earned, "my mother used to tell me scary stories. About the known, the unknown, and everything in between. These were not stories she told for entertainment. No, these were warnings, for she had seen much, and sees much even now. My mother is a collector of stories. Warnings, such as this one." And he presents the knife to us, showing it off. Pressed to the pale flesh of his palm, the glass edges seem sharper than before.

"Tell us," Christophe prompts. His interest becomes everyone's interest, and they lean in closer, giggling and shoving, taken with this manufactured idea of the forbidden.

"Yeah, tell us about the knife," Gael drawls. To everyone else it sounds mocking, but I know him well enough to tell when he's on edge. I look over at Yaya, and she seems to have noticed it too. There's even more uneasiness in her smile now.

"This is no ordinary knife. My mother calls it an athame," Avery says. "It is a knife with *purpose*. It cleaves. Of course, 'cleave' has two very distinct meanings. To bring together. And to split apart."

I don't like how he's conducting this circle. It *is* a bit much. Too much. The words sit heavy in the air, and I can see the smiles of even Avery and Drew's friends beginning to dim. He speaks like he actually believes this instead of just being someone who is having fun messing around at a party. It's all too serious for a game. But even still, I can see Drew's expression, enraptured.

"What does it bring together?" I ask. I flourish under the grateful look that Drew sends me. Sorry, *Andrea* sends me.

"Us," Avery answers. "And the other."

The beat of silence that echoes from even Avery's friends is interrupted as Gael lets out a bark of laughter. "Oh, fuck, I recognize that speech. I *knew* it sounded familiar. That's *Read Your Rites*."

As soon as he says it, I know he's right. Gael had managed to drag all of us, even Leila, notoriously terrified of all things horror, to see it. She hadn't even needed to cover her face; that's how dull it was. The rest of the room seems to recognize the name too, and the tension drains out like a wheezing old balloon, crackling with smothered laughter.

Avery flushes angrily. "Okay, and? My mother consulted on that. This really is an athame."

"Yeah, and that movie really did *suck*," Gael retorts. He leans in, a familiar arrogance coming over him. This is how he gets when he talks about film. "It had *all* the clichés. Gratuitously bloody first kill of a blonde woman, killed the gay kid to prove that you *can* still kill the gay kid in 'these times,' and a shitty romance plot that barely romanced. No cast chemistry, and holy shit, they pulled the camera when the Final Girl finally got rid of the demon. You don't even know what she really did. Like, come on."

"Maybe the writers just aren't very creative," Drew says. "I bet the real legends are fascinating."

"The Bible begs to differ," Malachi says.

Drew scoffs. "Don't tell me you suddenly believe in the *Bible*."

"My grandma certainly does," Malachi says firmly. "I'm not messing with no demons, Drew."

"Andrea, your friends . . . are being . . . a *bore*," Avery says, dragging out each and every word, his eyes hardening.

The rest are fine with that. But I can see the annoyance in Drew's eyes. Her grip on Avery's arm tightens, and she looks straight at me, her bottom lip jutting out in the slightest plea.

"No, we're not. We're not being bores," I say immediately, ignoring the hiss from Malachi and my own annoyance that she doesn't even think of sticking up for us. "Come on, show us how you do it. I've only seen Ouija boards in . . . probably *Read Your Rites*."

"Yeah, because we may not be geniuses, but *we* are too smart to mess with that stuff," Malachi mumbles in my ear. But Drew smiles broadly up at me, so I shake him off to focus on the coffee table.

The Ouija board is still glossy and new. Like it has been purchased for this very moment, not just found upstairs like Avery said. There's a big YES in the left corner. A big NO in the right. The alphabet falls in two distinct arcs. Numbers beneath. And most hauntingly, at the very bottom—GOODBYE.

"This will be fun. Usually, you use a planchette," Avery says, dispensing with the dramatic lines and waggling his eyebrows. He nods at the heart-shaped piece of wood. "But we have something cooler. The athame."

I pretend to display interest, leaning forward and smiling. I can feel Drew's approval, and it's just even more encouragement to humor her friend. Every moment of her approval means I'm proving her wrong—I *am* interested in knowing her friends. I *can* get along with them. I can do it again when she goes off to college.

"Okay, cool. Are we talking to someone?" I ask.

"Is there someone you want to talk to?" Avery asks, almost like a challenge. Then he leans back and repeats the question to the group at large. "Who do you want to talk to?"

"Madame Curie."

"Mahatma Gandhi."

"Bela Lugosi." Gael, of course.

But Avery doesn't heed any of them; none of the names called out seems to be what he's looking for. He's looking only at Drew now, waiting for her input, because she's Drew and Drew always knows all the answers. Very quietly, she says, "The other."

It makes Avery smile at last and he nods. Another gold star for Drew. "The other."

"How charmingly vague," Malachi mutters. "Not threatening at all."

I hush him again, as Drew leans over Avery's shoulder. He nods at the athame he grips with two hands, and Drew wraps her own hands around his, guiding it toward the Ouija board. Avery sends her a goofy smile over his shoulder, and Drew's softening gaze confirms that I've made the right choice. Drew is pleased, despite the oddness of it all, and it's not like any of this is real. I hold my breath as everyone falls into a silence like it is, though, staring hard at the pair of them as they touch the tip to the board.

The candles flicker dangerously. A well-timed coincidence that definitely adds to the ambiance.

"How do we contact the other?" I ask.

"Call to them," Avery says, all his focus on the board before us, but I know he's speaking to me. "They will answer. They can't help it. Loneliness is a terrible thing."

Malachi's hand tightens on my shoulder as Avery and Drew draw the knife steadily up the center of the Ouija board, right where it folds, tapping over the logo. Drew looks over the board, right at me, quirking an eyebrow. Daring me to commit.

I don't back down. I lean forward, staring hard at the board, and even though it feels stupid, I whisper, "Come to me."

Nothing changes. Of course.

Except Avery sits up straight, a jolting move that startles even Drew. She turns to look at him, but he's staring curiously at the board.

"Again," he commands, without looking at me.

"Come to me," I repeat, a little more uneasy this time around.

Again, nothing changes.

Or almost nothing.

One of the candles flickers out, but it's easily explained away by someone exhaling or shifting nervously by it. No one notices but me. Still, it sets my teeth on edge. I lean into Malachi's side to ground myself.

"What do you want to know from the other?" Avery asks. "What does everyone want to know?"

"Do you know us?" Christophe asks.

The athame drifts—no, Avery and Drew move it, obviously— toward the word NO.

"Cool—" Christophe begins, and then stops, because the athame is drifting again.

Avery frowns, looking over at Drew. "Are you moving it?" he asks.

Drew just gives him a look that says it all. I look back down at the Ouija board, following the knifepoint—I W-A-N-T T-O.

"Fuck no," Gael murmurs.

Drew asks the next question: "Who? There are a lot of us."

Y-O-U.

Malachi jumps hard, hand slapping the back of his neck, and he looks around. I frown, looking over at him.

"What's wrong?" I ask.

"I thought . . . I thought something touched me," Malachi murmurs.

But there's nothing there. Just space once occupied by some kids who left, bored by Avery's fake summoning.

"Nothing touched you," I sigh, turning back to the board just as it finishes spelling out D-R-E-A.

It doesn't take a genius.

"Me?" Drew murmurs, laughing to herself.

No one else is laughing.

I'm not laughing.

"Why me?" Drew asks.

The athame drifts again: C-O-N-G-R . . . Drew giggles with her delight as Avery tries to keep a stern face, to pretend that this isn't him, but it is, and the other partygoers catch on quickly, all bursting into quick laughter.

I look over at Yaya, expecting her to be laughing too. But she's not; she's cradling something in her palms, her brow furrowed.

"What is it?" I ask.

"My rosary snapped. I'm trying to make sure I don't drop the beads," she says.

I lean forward, cupping my hands together under hers to make sure that I catch any that spill over. Drew and Avery continue their fit of laughter as we work, dropping the athame on the Ouija board in favor of whispering to each other.

"Got them?" I ask.

"Yeah," Yaya says, pushing the beads into her pockets, smiling over at me gratefully.

I'm grateful we can move on, but then Gael calls out, "You didn't dismiss it. The other."

Avery stops in his whispers of sweet nothings to my sister. "What?"

"You have to tell it goodbye. Or it's going to stay," Gael says firmly.

For a moment I think Avery, too, will finally declare that it's all not real. He does look annoyed with being interrupted. But whether because he actually believes or he's committed to the bit, he picks up the athame and imperiously says, "Go back, other. I'll call you again."

And then the knifepoint drags toward the word GOODBYE, before Avery abandons it again.

"That was cool," I say generously, and Avery flashes me a smile. I mean to ask more about his spiritualism or maybe his mom's influence on it, to humor his "journey" or whatever, but someone taps on my shoulder, and I look up into Leila's stern expression. "What's wrong?"

"We need to chat," she says coolly.

With trepidation, I walk with her back toward the entrance, near the pile of shoes. Malachi trails behind me, and Yaya and Gael round us out. Suspicious, I pull my phone out of my pocket and see that the group chat has been *very* active in the past thirty seconds alone.

"What's going on?" I ask, trying to read the texts.

"Don't bother. I'll just say it," Malachi says. "I hated that shit. And I hated that you went along with it."

I stare at the group of them, incredulous, and they all stare back, pursed lips, waiting for my excuse. "It wasn't real," I blurt out.

"Yeah, but we hated it," Gael says. "*You* hated it. I saw your face. Why didn't you tell her that? She probably would've told him to stop."

I look away. I'm not so sure how true that is.

"We know . . . you want to make this a good day for Drew, but . . ." Yaya trails off, shaking her head, hands reaching for the rosary that is no longer there around her neck.

"Yeah, that was . . . ," I start to agree.

"That was what?" Drew seems to have finally peeled herself off the couch. She doesn't look perturbed by the fact that we're having a little group meeting without her. If anything, she's arrived like she's been invited. She smiles lazily, a beer in her grasp.

"We're never doing that shit again, you hear me?" Gael says as a warning.

Drew shakes her head, waving away his concerns. "It wasn't real, Gael," she echoes me unknowingly. "You know how often Avery does this kind of show? It's his regular party trick. That and predicting someone's future from the soles of their feet or whatever."

"It doesn't matter. It made me uncomfortable. *Us* uncomfortable," Malachi says with a sincerity that actually grabs her attention.

Drew struggles under it, the stares and annoyance, but then

she puts herself back together, rather masterfully for someone under the influence. "Fine," she says with a smile, loose and excited. "But there's still a party going on. A party that's being thrown for me. I make the rules, and the rules are that you are my friends and you have to have fun. So have fun."

Drew's brusqueness isn't outside of the ordinary. But it's early in the summer still, and the awkwardness of distance has yet to be shrugged off. It's never been more obvious than this moment, the way they all look at Drew like she's an alien entity, and then look at me, like I've introduced a foreign species.

And I can't let us fall apart. I can't let them decide that she's not worth the detox.

I won't.

I step between the opposing forces and smile too. "You know how Drew likes rules," I say with a teasing lilt to my voice. "At least we can follow this one. Let's have fun."

The quartet look at one another, having a silent conversation. The only problem is that we're just as much a part of their group, and we can follow every unsaid word. Malachi's side-eye is enough to tell me they're already tired of my Best Summer Ever if Drew's gonna be like *this*. I widen my eyes, bottom lip jutting out just so, making my plea evident.

Finally, Yaya announces their decision.

"Let's have fun," she says.

So we forget the Ouija board and we do.

CHAPTER FOUR

I t's never smart to agree to midmorning plans the night after a party. It's even less smart to be the architect of those plans. Still, my lateness to our meetup in Prospect Park isn't the intentional blunder you would think it was from the withering look that Drew sends me when I arrive at our meetup spot, sticky and sweaty with exertion.

"It's not hot enough to be fee-fi-fo'ing like that, Devon," Malachi says.

"Hey, I just *sprinted*," I say, collapsing like my puppet strings have been cut. I lie in the grass, despite the fact that there's space next to Malachi on his blanket, and inhale its freshly cut scent. The sharp blades dig into my skin, but it grounds me in a way that I've been craving since the night before. "Where were you this morning?" I ask Drew.

"Waking up at a reasonable hour to get here at the agreed-upon time," Drew says with a wry smile.

"You couldn't have woken me up?" I demand, frustrated, as I search through my bag for my spoils. I sigh in relief, pulling out my wrapped bacon, egg, and cheese (complete with salt, pepper, and a tiny bit of ketchup).

"I tried," Drew insists. "You were late and still stopped for breakfast?"

"I'm *starving*," I whine. "But Mr. Ahmed definitely knew I was hungover."

"What'd he say?" Leila asks.

"Nothing. Just was giving me *judgy* looks and rattling the bottles at the register while I waited on my food. Then he took a little too much pleasure in saying I'd be working with *Alexis* for tomorrow night's shift," I say. They all offer long looks of sympathy. Even Yaya.

"Godspeed," she says. She looks cute today as always, dressed in her frilly white bloomers and a pink sweatshirt, but it's the red heart-shaped sunglasses sloping down her nose and the pearl glasses chain keeping them around her neck I notice most. Her birthday gift from me last August.

"Cute glasses," I say.

Yaya smiles knowingly. "Yeah? My friend got them for me."

Leila feigns a gag behind Yaya's back.

"Where's Gael? He's taking forever," Malachi sighs.

Yaya checks her phone, no doubt searching for him on Find My. "He's not far. He's by the museum," she says.

"Who does a drug deal on the steps of the Brooklyn Museum?" Malachi groans loudly.

"Why don't you just announce to the park that we're waiting on weed?" Leila says, her face twisting sour. Malachi looks at her with mock offense, sputtering and scoffing away his slight embarrassment.

Drew looks at her with a dry twist to her smile. "No one cares." The ingratiating process is in motion as she lounges on the grass. There's no lingering tension from last night's events. Once she'd told us to have fun, I'd thrown myself into the command and wrangled my friends into following suit, which wasn't hard.

Good music, good snacks, and good alcohol will do that for you.

And now we're reaching our normal state in the summer, and for once there's not an empty space where Drew should be, and no one is questioning her presence or lack thereof. It feels *right*.

Yaya perks up. "Oh, he's on the move."

I lie back on my elbows and look over at her, quirking an eyebrow. "Are you smoking today, or do you have rehearsal later?"

"I'm smoking *and* I'm going to rehearsal. I just won't smoke *too* much. I'm on the second passage and I'm refusing Mami's help. I want to be able to say that I choreographed it too in my audition," she says.

"Your mom was a literal ballerina. Isn't it kind of impressive to say that she choreographed it?" Malachi asks.

Yaya shakes her head. "It's different. Like . . . I want to be able to show that I have a versatile skill set. There are plenty of daughters of ballerinas," Yaya says.

Drew purses her lips. "I mean, there's only one daughter of Karina Betancourt, but sure."

Yaya is the only daughter of a former principal ballerina of the American Ballet Theatre, and she has always felt responsible for her mother's early retirement from ballet, but I've always said that that's on Ms. Betancourt and Mr. Powell for forgetting that contraceptives exist. It's not as if Ms. Betancourt resents her either. She still teaches at her own ballet studio, Bet-On-It. It's prestigious. Entrance is never guaranteed. There are tests and everything, and Yaya earns her spot at the top of the list, having inherited her mother's talent and her father's tenacity.

"But all the admissions officials won't know that's who I am. I'm not a nepo baby," Yaya says, and it's the chilliest she's ever sounded about the matter, the end of the conversation. But then she melts just as quickly, eyes scanning the park entrance until she points. "There he is."

Gael skates over on his stupid skateboard, his camera bouncing against his chest. He's such a cliché, but he revels in it. He even finds the time to wink at three girls leaving the park as he skates by. When he gets to us, he skids off the skateboard, letting it roll to a stop in the grass, but he keeps going until he crashes onto the ground, long knobby legs folding up. Then he leans forward, elbows perched on his scabby knees.

"Okay, Steez gave me a quarter for the price of an eighth, because he's the homie, so next time you see Steez, say thank you," Gael says by way of greeting. He roots through his fanny pack and presents his treasures with a shit-eating smile. "Also, Leila, you owe me ten."

"Why are you buying your weed from Steez? You know there are dispensaries now," Drew says, unimpressed.

"Some of us support small businesses, *Andrea*," Gael bites out. "Feel free to go to the dispensary by yourself. Oh, *wait*, you're not twenty-one, *nor* do you have a fake. So—"

"All right, all right, that's enough," I interject, before he can antagonize her further. "Can you just roll? I'm exhausted and I have a headache."

Gael glowers at me but does as I command. He always rolls the best and he knows it. The sun is intense and the air is lazy, and no one looks twice at a bunch of kids lounging and picnicking in the grass.

"Don't call me Andrea," Drew finally says.

Gael does a double take when he realizes how long she's been sitting on that one. He rolls his eyes. "*Avery* calls you 'Andrea,'" he sings. "And so does everyone else from your school."

"Okay, but I introduced myself as 'Andrea' to them. *You* don't have permission to call me that," Drew says firmly.

Gael guffaws. "*Permission?* I didn't know I needed permission to use your name." He lifts the joint to his eye, presenting it for admiration, before he tucks it between his lips and holds out his hand for Malachi's lighter. He lights it, inhales for a long time, then passes it over to me before he even exhales. "Oh, and by the way, your friends are weird."

"They aren't," Drew says defensively.

"Be so fucking for real, Drew," Gael sighs. He looks over at Malachi. "They pulled out a *Ouija board* to summon a demon."

Malachi purses his lips. "I less than enjoyed that."

Drew shakes her head. "Avery is eccentric. It was just a party trick."

"You don't mess with demons, Drew. Not even as a party trick," Gael warns. "My abuela taught me that."

Drew looks at all of us, clearer-eyed now. To her, last night's events hadn't been a big deal. To the others, it very much had been, and they'd made their thoughts perfectly clear after the strange mess. I sigh, leaning forward, looking at each of them.

"Look . . . demons aren't real—"

"Not you too," Gael interrupts dramatically.

"Demons aren't real." I start again. "They were trying to include us in the game, and it just didn't jive for us. That doesn't make Drew's friends weird. They're not weird. They're . . ." I drift off, mouth already cotton sticky from the weed, my mind drifting to nebulous stupid details.

Like how Leila still has the pigment from her pastels smudged in the webbing between her fingers from trying out different concepts for her AP Art portfolio. Gael's fresh cut on his elbow, probably from his intentional wipeout. Malachi's smirk, directed at his phone in the exact way that means he's talking to a cute boy he shouldn't be. Yaya's eyes, looking at me, making me run so hot, I can feel my cheeks flushing. I turn, blinking away *that* detail before I can say something embarrassing, instead focusing back on Drew. Drew with her fuzzing edges. The hickey on her neck emerging from the blur of concealer.

The—

"You have a hickey on your neck?" I blurt out.

Malachi drops his phone and looks up, sharply. "*Andrea Harris*—" he starts, crawling over Leila's legs. "Who gave you that hickey?"

"We all know who gave her the hickey," Leila says with a wolfish smile. "*Avery . . .*"

"Can you *not*?" Drew asks, but now with the air of someone who wants to be asked everything about it.

"Did y'all fuck or no?" Gael asks. "You both disappeared after he did that weird demon-summoning shit."

Malachi's nose wrinkles. "You are so *vulgar*, Gael . . . but did you?"

Drew pulls her knees to her chest, leaning forward, looking each of us in the eye.

But then all she says is, "Avery gave me the hickey."

She says it casually like it doesn't cause a cosmic shift to my reality. Drew Harris doesn't know when a boy is into her. Drew Harris doesn't return the affection of random boys, because

53

they're distractions—her words, not mine—and Drew Harris is destined for greatness. But then I realize that means Avery isn't some random boy. Avery is *important* to Drew.

"Come on, Harris, that's all you're gonna give? Hope you didn't blue balls Avery as hard as you just blue balled *me*," Gael says.

Drew scoffs. "You are so disgusting. I can't believe I'm friends with you still." My skin ices over, but even as she says it, she's fighting to keep from grinning, thankfully.

"It's because he's like a fungus," Leila says matter-of-factly. "He just keeps growing until he's impossible to get rid of." Gael shoves Leila onto her back and she tumbles, letting out a howling laugh.

While the pair launch into the same cyclical argument they've been trapped in since childhood, I pluck the joint from Malachi's fingers and take another hit. I look over at Drew. "Excited for the zoo?" I ask her.

Drew shrugs. "I guess," she says, slightly uninterested. She tugs at the grass. "Can't we just stay here? Avery mentioned stopping by."

"No," I snap. "I changed my shift today so we could go. We all decided."

There's a beat of awkward silence, which even takes Leila and Gael out of their thing, for them to turn and stare. Malachi's eyes narrow, and he very carefully says, "Maybe you're not relaxed enough. Take a second hit and pass to Drew."

Drew's brow furrows but she doesn't snap back, just watches me. Turning onto my belly, I kick my heels up. I blow the brief moment of frustration away with my exhale of smoke. The party has made me think twofold on the concept of the Best Summer Ever. Once we started having fun, I was thrilled by the fact that Drew danced with us, pulled us around to introduce us to everyone, just wanted everyone to know *us*. But at the same time, then there was Avery. He's important to her. That makes him a threat to our plans. To *our* summer.

Not since *last* summer have I felt so calm, so wrapped in the embrace of my friends. Summers are always the best—no real responsibility, all of us together every day, just existing. At this moment I don't have to think about Drew deciding to graduate early without telling me. I don't have to think about how her leaving will turn into everyone leaving in just a year, and some of us might not be returning. I let the high tell me that it doesn't matter because it's not real. At least, not as real as *this* moment, when I can feel the heat radiating off Malachi's ankle, when I can drown in the lilt of Gael's and Leila's voices. I'm untouchable. *Infinite.* I feel—

Like someone's watching me. I scan and note someone across the street. It's too hot for what they're wearing. That's what catches my attention first, I think. A bulky oatmeal-colored sweater that disrupts their natural lines and a pair of thick dark-green cords. They must be blistering. I'm in cutoffs and my thighs are sticking together with sweat, the platinum eye shadow I use to define my eyebrows melting off despite my setting spray. I twist in the grass, squinting at them, and sure enough they're staring. Just standing there. Not moving, eyes on us.

For a moment the sounds of Brooklyn—the sharp honking of near-colliding cars, my friends' laughter, the shrieks of gleeful children—peel away. For a moment, even though I can't make out their features, I feel as if our eyes meet, and my heart comes to a screeching halt before it begins to thud in double time. Something is swelling in my lungs, thick and heavy, and then—

Yaya's laugh at something Malachi said bursts through the weighty silence, and I break the strange eye contact. The second I do, I can breathe again. My heart is still speeding, but for a different reason, as Yaya's hand settles on my ankle. I jump and she looks down at me, worried.

"You okay?" she mouths, not drawing the others' attention.

I blink hard. Once. Twice.

When I look back up, the person is still staring, but I decide they're probably just having heatstroke and I'm just being paranoid.

I roll back over to face my friends and grin. This is only a pit stop before our zoo trip, and I have about six fun facts about zoology that I want to tell Drew, in case she decides that she wants to spend college teaching apes sign language.

Someone watching us isn't a big deal.

After all, it's New York. Someone is always staring. Right?

CHAPTER FIVE

The day that I turned seventeen was the happiest of Mr. Ahmed's life, because it was the day that it became ethically okay to ask me to work night shifts. My shift at his bougie-ass bodega the next day starts at five and runs until midnight.

It's not a bad shift, really. It's never particularly busy. Mr. Ahmed checks in often, and half the time his son Rashid decides to work the shift with us, which gives me someone to talk to. We can even lock the doors at eleven, and spend the final hour restocking the store. It would actually be perfect . . .

If it weren't for Alexis.

Tonight she bounds in two hours late with the least apologetic smile possible gracing her face. She stomps through the aisle, elbowing a bag of chips off the shelf, only doubling back when I raise an eyebrow and point. When she gets up to the front, she leans in, instead of coming around the back, acting as if she's a customer instead of my extremely late coworker.

"You redid your eyebrows," she says. She doesn't compliment them or insult them, just flutters her pale lashes at me, rubbing her own eyebrow as if there's something in it.

"I did," I say, trying to keep it upbeat. Being nice to Alexis is on the *list* because if I get fired, I'll get grounded and that means *nothing* on the list can get done, and the list is law this summer.

But as usual Alexis makes it hard. She takes her sweet time getting ready, lingering in the aisles as she pins on her name tag, picks out her snacks, checks her phone, and generally is a nuisance to the customers by standing in their way. She doesn't bother to rush even when a bunch of middle schoolers run in all at once and beeline to the freezer section in search of cherry ice pops. I recognize one of them from my block, and I lean over to ask, "Ice-cream truck still skipping us?"

"Fuck Miss Kendra," the girl confirms with the kind of violently dismissive disgust that only preteens possess. Alexis looks scandalized but doesn't say anything, even as I grin.

"Language," Mr. Ahmed warns from the back as he juggles two boxes of the fancy yogurt bars that have been flying off the shelves since the new people started moving in. I wait for Alexis to go to help him, but it's like she doesn't even see him. Maybe she doesn't; her gaze stays focused intently on her long, professionally polished nails as she at last meanders to stand behind the counter next to me.

When she finally looks up, she raises her natural blonde eyebrow to question my staring.

"Why don't you check these kids out and I'll help Mr. Ahmed," I say, and then I swiftly sidestep her and grab the second box from his hands. He shakes his head before I can even open my mouth. He's already heard my many complaints about Alexis, and each time he's always quick to remind me that Alexis's mom is a kind woman, that she'd helped him and his family in a bad spot before and he owes her.

Once I put the box down, I help Mr. Ahmed stock. It's better than having to hear Alexis's endless chatter about things I don't care about. She's better at dealing with the smart-ass customers too. That's one thing about Alexis—she's so self-absorbed that she never notices when someone's being snarky with her.

Which is probably why Mr. Ahmed warns me to "Be nice" as he passes me the box of Ruffles and I stack six right behind the nearly expired ones.

"I'm always nice," I say.

Mr. Ahmed scoffs because that's not strictly true, and I just sigh, turning back to stocking the chips and other snacks, right beside the health bars that the yoga moms and young professionals moving in three blocks over prefer. Sure, Mr. Ahmed has had to trade out Honey Buns for gluten-free puff pastries, but at least he's still making money. He was even able to replace the decades-old linoleum floors last month, making everything that much shinier, but part of me still misses the old ones. My own personal bitterness combats regularly with watching Mr. Ahmed thrive. People with more cash to spend are good for business, but while the streets look the same, every day I recognize fewer of the faces walking them. Another reminder that everything is *changing*.

"Feeling better after yesterday morning?" Mr. Ahmed asks, with the audacity to still be a little judgy.

But I don't bother being embarrassed. Mr. Ahmed has been a staple of the neighborhood since before I was born. This is certainly not the most humiliating thing he's seen.

"Yeah, it was just Drew's graduation party. Did you know Drew graduated early?" I blurt out.

Mr. Ahmed nods. "Your father said something about it when he came to pick up his breakfast. Your sister has always been a very bright girl. She'll be off to do great things, I'm sure."

Someone is always off to do great things, I think glumly. That's what people like Drew do. Go to change the world and deign to come back for a visit just to *change.* My stomach churns, reminding me uncomfortably of the Thompson-Bryants.

I'm not built like that. Like them. Greatness scares me and changing terrifies me even more. I don't know what I want, but I know what would make me content—something close and warm that felt exciting for the next day and nostalgic enough to keep me grounded.

Looking for something to busy myself with, I resign myself to going back to the counter. But the minute I step behind it with Alexis, she swivels around on the stool she's sitting on and starts talking.

Maybe I don't need a distraction that badly.

"I like your braids. Super awesome. Your mom is, like, so good," Alexis says earnestly.

"Thanks," I say cautiously, waiting for the other shoe to drop.

"I wonder if she'd braid my hair too. Then I could tag her on Insta or maybe she'd post me," Alexis says, combing her fingers through her wavy flaxen hair. I try to hold back irritation behind my teeth, but Alexis doesn't give me the chance. She leans forward, pinching the curly end of one braid between her fingers. "The blonde almost suits you, Devon, really. Especially for someone with your undertone."

Hello, other shoe.

"What do you mean by that?" I ask flatly, though I know exactly what she means.

"You're so . . . cool toned. And this blonde is a little warmer. You should ask your mom to tone it again. To get it just right," Alexis says.

She is so full of unasked-for advice. Mr. Ahmed says she doesn't mean anything by it, and I almost believe he's right. Except no one could be *that* stupid for that long. Alexis is good at gaslighting everyone into thinking that she's not being malicious when she's being the most clueless person on the face of the fucking planet. She's a *victim* of *circumstance*. It's not her fault that she's late. It's the MTA, of course. It's not her fault if the ice pops sit out and melt in their packets. She doesn't have a great memory and, "Mr. Ahmed, you know that. You know it's bad, and you said it was okay." It's not her fault that everyone's so *sensitive*.

I'm fortunate in that she doesn't go to Midwood High with us, but Alexis has been pulling this shit around me since childhood. She started at the same day care as us, then the same after-school. Then we both attended Yaya's mom's dance studio and even quit the same year too. And now we work here together. So it stopped working on me a long time ago.

In fact, I'm convinced now Alexis makes such an art out of being as obnoxious and oblivious as possible, it has to be fun for her. A planned attack meant to put me in the worst mood ever and keep her in her "forever victim" status, provoking me to react so she can whine and fuss until someone asks her if she's okay. I know her. I *see* her. But it still doesn't make it easier not to blow up when she pulls this.

Still, I think of the list and let it hold me back as she continues to work my last nerve, busying her idle fingers with rearranging the candy I already carefully restocked when I arrived to our shift *on time*. She likes to put it in the order of the rainbow to be more "aesthetically pleasing," even though Mr. Ahmed prefers the stuff that's more popular to be right up front.

"Come on, Devon, you know Skittles look best next to the Starbursts," she says cheerfully, rummaging and pushing everything around.

Thankfully, customers come in just as I'm about to finally forget my pledge to "be nice." It's a pair of white men who look like they thrift all their clothes, even though they clearly make more than enough to buy full price, and love it when Mr. Ahmed calls them "boss." They go straight for the fridges. It's late, it's a Friday night, and I know what a desperate search for mixers looks like. Alexis sits up abruptly fast when they approach the register, elbowing me out of the way to serve them. Flirting with the gentrifiers is a well-celebrated pastime in Crown Heights, so that's not really my gripe. It's what comes next.

"Your name's Jacob?" she asks, looking at his credit card and sighing as she pops her stolen Hubba Bubba bubble gum. "My ex-boyfriend's name was Jacob. Wasn't as cute as you, though, and I bet you wouldn't cheat on me, huh? You seem like a good boy."

"Alexis . . . ," I say warningly, watching this so-called Jacob, who is probably way older than her ex, shift uncomfortably.

Alexis pouts. "*What?* I'm just making conversation."

That's what she always calls *oversharing*. "Making conversation." It's probably what she told Jacob the fifty-billionth time he found her flirting with someone that wasn't him. Not to say that he should've been cheating on her—I'm a girl's girl.

As she checks the two men out, she makes a whole show of scrawling her number on the back of Jacob's receipt, even when he tells her that he doesn't *want* a receipt. As the door swings closed, I turn to her and say, "You know you look seventeen, right?"

"What?" Alexis asks, nose wrinkling, still chomping on that gum.

"You look your age, and *they* are not your age. They're not gonna call you, and if they do, they should be in jail," I say flatly.

Alexis sighs indignantly. "I've been told I'm mature for my age."

"*Dude*, just stop oversharing with customers. You're gonna scare off the money," I mutter under my breath, turning to look down at my phone, hoping for at least *some* action in the group chat, but I see nothing. Listlessly, I look over at Mr. Ahmed again, but he's already prepping all the ingredients for tomorrow as he gets ready to shut down the grill and head home.

The next time the door swings open, my mood only drops more.

In contrast, Keith Thompson-Bryant seems delighted to see me behind the counter. "Hey, Dev."

"Don't call me that," I say, voice flat. "Keep it moving, Keith."

"I'm *hungry*, Devon. I need my bacon, egg, and cheese. I'm a growing boy," he sings to me with a wide-toothed smile. Nerd.

"Grill closes at eight," I say, tapping my phone on the counter.

"It's seven fifty-five," Alexis says unhelpfully. She leans behind me, smacking her gum, and shouts, too loud, "Mr. Ahmed, we got an order for a bacon, egg, and cheese! On a roll, Keith?" Keith nods. "On a roll!"

I sigh, exhausted by it all. I still have four hours of my shift left. They won't pass quick enough like this.

"Looks like I will be getting that sandwich," he says, with a laugh that to some might feel like I'm in on the joke, but to me just feels like mockery.

Keith turns away from me, looking over at Alexis. He has another book tucked under his arm that would make him look good and smart in a paparazzi photo. Kafka, because that's a normal thing to casually read. Not that he's remotely interesting enough for anyone to photograph.

Except to Alexis.

"How are you, Keith?" Alexis asks, voice a little breathier. She's sitting a little taller, Jacob already forgotten.

He favors her with a smile, giving her the full force of his attention.

"I'm good, Lexi. Spent the day reading and helping my mom out with the renovation. How are you?" he asks.

I could almost understand it. Keith is handsome, with a nice line-up and gleaming white teeth. He's always put together, with his tasteful fun-print button-downs and his cargo shorts, and a beanie in the summertime. I can't even accuse him of being ashy. Objectively, there is nothing *wrong* with Keith, at least on the outside. But *I* know better.

The others only find him annoying. *I* find him insufferable.

His mother is a menace. "Fuck Miss Kendra" isn't the only thing people in the neighborhood have to say about Kendra Thompson-Bryant. Besides being single-mindedly committed to destroying her father's historic brownstone in favor of creating six sizable apartment units and being generally an unpleasant person on the block, she's always complaining about the one-off yard sale, the permit-permitted hydrant parties, and *now* making the ice-cream truck go missing from our block. Forget hometown loyalty or class solidarity from Kendra Thompson-Bryant. She's not *that* kind of Black. And Keith has inherited her genes. Pretentious, condescending, and entitled. That's not exactly a crime. But to me his worst offense is his interest in—

The bell above the door rings.

Yaya.

I don't realize I've said her name aloud until she turns and smiles. "Devon." She's got on her sweats with the words BET-ON-IT STUDIOS going up the leg, and she's still in her leotard underneath.

"What are you doing here?" I ask. There's another corner store much closer to her mother's studio, with cheaper prices, too; they don't stock the snacks of the gentry at that one, but they do have the bag of Takis and classic Arizona iced tea that she's going to get.

"I remembered you were working today and I wanted to say hi," Yaya says. She doesn't even seem to notice Keith or Alexis, even though both are staring at her. She walks right up to the window.

Beyond her smile, I see that her edges are frizzing and she's breathing hard.

"How long have you been practicing without a break?" I ask sternly.

Yaya rubs the back of her neck and admits, "Ah . . . too long. Mami kicked me out and told me to go home." She pats her crossbody. "*But* I have the spare keys. I'll go back later."

"You really shouldn't. You're gonna hurt yourself," I chastise gently.

Yaya shakes her head. "I know my limits."

I laugh quietly to myself and lean forward. I shouldn't, but I reach out to poke her cheek playfully. "No, you don't." And Yaya's smile widens into a laugh. It sends a giddy rush of feeling through my veins, my heart thudding in time with Yaya's elevated pulse.

Unfortunately, Keith finds his voice. "Yaya," he blurts, tapering out on the second syllable. "Uh, how are you? I saw you on the way to your dance studio this morning and I wanted to say hi, but I was inside the parlor and you had your headphones on and I didn't want to startle you, so I just kinda stared but then I turned away, because I'm not a creep. I didn't want to creep you out."

How many times can someone say they're not a creep before it becomes clear that they are one? Stay tuned to find out.

"I wouldn't have been creeped out," Yaya says, because she is nice. The nicest. She tilts her head, looking him up and down with a long, considering look. From the corner of my eye, I can see Keith stand taller, proud and smirking. "You should just say 'hi.' I don't bite. I'm a person just like you."

Keith flushes and rubs at the back of his neck hard enough the skin should come off. "You're . . . right, yeah."

"And I'm fine. Just very tired," Yaya says.

"Yaya's going to be the prima ballerina of the world," Alexis says unnecessarily. "We've always known it."

"Well, I have to get into a school first before I'm a prima ballerina of anywhere," Yaya says modestly.

Yaya doesn't want to go straight into a company. It's Juilliard, UNCSA, or Tisch. Hard schools for anyone to get into, even someone as talented as Yaya, but those are the options. Her first audition tape isn't even due until the end of the summer, but you wouldn't know that from how hard Yaya works herself.

"I've seen videos," Alexis says. "You're gonna get in. Keith, have you seen the videos?" Before Keith can say what I'm sure is a "yes," she's already on her phone, jetting to YouTube to find that one video of Yaya in the *Swan Lake* production that her mother mounted just last winter. Yaya had been selected as the Swan out of a citywide audition, and she wasn't cast just because of her mom. There was a whole panel and everything, and *still* Yaya was picked.

I recognize the jaunty tune and without even seeing it, I can picture Yaya, in black and silver boning, tights a blinding white under the stage lights at BAM, performing thirty-two flawless fouettés in the Black Swan Coda last winter. She'd been magnificent.

Instead of trying to peer over Alexis's shoulder at the tiny screen, I look at Yaya now and see she's squinting down at a tiny version of herself, like she doesn't recognize the girl. I can practically see her correcting the infinitesimal mistakes that appear only to her. Her hands are moving slightly, like she's mimicking her own posture and relearning. Then she looks up at me, meeting my gaze, and shrugs with one shoulder like I've caught her. I smile in a way that says, *I know you,* and Yaya's grin back says, *I know you do.*

"Wow, you're really good," Keith says, pulling back to give Yaya an impressed look.

"'Really good'?" I say, unable to help my edge of mockery. "Yaya is *brilliant.* She's going to get into every ballet school under the sun."

Yaya flushes and shifts. "Maybe," she allows, lowering her gaze, and suddenly I'm jealous of the fan of eyelashes brushing her cheeks.

"You must be something else live," Keith breathes. "I'd . . . I'd love to watch you practice sometime—"

"No," Yaya blurts out, and it's so sudden and aggressive

that Keith takes a half step back. Yaya's blush burns hotter and she takes a deep breath and then corrects herself with "No one watches me practice except my mom or the other students in my class. Maybe I'll . . . maybe I'll show you more videos sometime. I don't know."

Keith brightens at the suggestion, and my already dismal mood *lowers*, if it's even possible. He looks about ten seconds from proposing when Mr. Ahmed slides a wrapped sandwich to me on the counter and taps the spatula against the flattop before he begins quickly scraping the grill clean a second time.

"Oh, look at that, your sandwich is ready and it's eight. Mr. Ahmed can walk you out, right?" I prompt. Mr. Ahmed rolls his eyes but salutes with a promise to send Rashid at eleven to lock up.

"If it's all right with Yaya, I'm gonna continue making conversation with her," Keith says firmly. He looks over at her, eyes softening. "That all right with you?"

"Can you at least pay for your sandwich?" I bark.

Keith pulls out a fistful of cash and passes it to me without looking. "You can keep the change," he says.

A better person would count it out for him and give him the change anyway. But a better person also wouldn't show off to me by handing over fifty dollars for a five-dollar sandwich. I open the cash register, break the fifty-dollar bill, and slide five dollars in. Alexis nudges me, narrow eyed, staring down at *my* emotional damage reward.

"Come on, Devon," she mutters.

To shut her up, I slide a twenty her way, while Yaya asks what he's reading now.

"Currently, I'm making my way through Dostoyevsky. You know Dostoyevsky, right?" Keith asks.

I frown, I thought he was "reading" Kafka. He's literally holding *The Metamorphosis*.

"Do you think I'm stupid, Keith?" she asks with a tiny smile, the kind that says she's joking though her words sound sincere.

"Oh my God, no. Not at all. Of course you know," Keith stutters, flustered beyond words.

Yaya's smile pulls wider into her shit-eating one. "I'm going back to the studio."

"Well, can I walk you?" Keith blurts out.

Yaya raises an eyebrow. "I don't exactly need an escort. . . ."

"What about company?" Keith pushes. "I could tell you more about Dostoyevsky while we walk. Or you can tell me about him, since we've established that you're not stupid."

For a moment Yaya looks puzzled by his insistence, but she just rolls her bottom lip between her teeth and says, "I mean, I . . . guess," without quite meeting his gaze.

"You don't have to say yes," I say flatly.

Yaya looks up and smiles. "Good thing I didn't. I said, 'I guess,'" she says as she leans in over the counter, pokes me in the cheek, and soft sings, "Bye, Dev."

"Bye, Yaya," I whisper as the pair leave. I can still feel the scorching fingertip-shaped mark of Yaya's touch on my cheek as Alexis groans, "Ugh, finally," and jumps up from the stool. She stands on her toes, reaching up to the button that controls the ancient camera sitting at the corner near the door. It spins a quarter of a rotation and then drones as it powers down. It's so old and spotty that Mr. Ahmed never questions when it "mysteriously" shuts off during our late-night shifts, especially since it's happened often enough during the day. He still hasn't replaced it as *no one's stolen from him yet.*

Alexis continues. "I've been dying for a snack. You want anything?"

"I'm good," I say.

"That was cute," Alexis says, whistling into the silence.

"What was?" I ask.

"The two of them," she says. She slides from behind the counter *again* and with way too much ease steals an Arizona from the case and a bag of fancy organic chips, the ones in the matte-black bag with truffle and salt. "Yaya and Keith. I can see it."

"I certainly can't," I say through clenched teeth. "And neither can she."

"No?" Alexis asks, and has the nerve to sound genuinely surprised. "He's super hot and older and interested. And she's . . . *Yaya*. Tall gorgeous boys always go for the tall gorgeous girls. They suit each other. She's just playing hard to get, I think. Guys love that. You saw his face." She shrugs, like it's all science, a foregone conclusion. "Don't grind your teeth, Devon. It's bad for you," she says, cracking open the iced tea and taking a long gulp. Her lip gloss is smudged when she pulls it away.

"I . . . no . . . Keith is a *sophomore* in college," I sputter. Alexis squints at me like, *So?* So I scoff, shaking my head. "I need to restock the Arizona."

"I only took one . . . ," Alexis starts.

"Watch the register," I spit, and then I throw myself from behind the counter and into the back freezer, refusing to let her see how flustered her words have made me feel.

As the heavy metal door closes behind me, I'm left alone with my own thoughts. My breath comes fast and harsh. I can see the shape of it in the air, as the coolness around me provides a welcome contrast to the sweaty heat that layers every other surface of the store. Staring down at my hands, I can hear Alexis's words echoing loudly.

"He's super hot and older and interested. Tall gorgeous boys always go for the tall gorgeous girls."

"The blonde almost suits you, Devon, really. Especially for someone with your undertone."

It "almost suits you."

"They suit each other."

I feel the annoyance in my teeth as they scrape together. Yaya has never expressed interest in *anyone* before—boy or girl. She is all about her work. Yaya was born to be on the stage. I've known that since we were kids.

But Alexis's words are like an infection, and it's all I can hear—that guys like Keith and girls like Yaya go together. That her disinterest might have been feigned all this time. Maybe that's true. I don't know how *heterosexuals* operate. Plus, Keith has money. And straight teeth. Is older and reads Kafka and Dostoyevsky.

And Keith is a fucking *boy*.

I feel like I'll die.

I peer through the tiny window that leads out to the rest of the store. Alexis is on her phone again. I can see her leaning over the counter, swinging one foot behind her. There's someone waiting to pay, and it takes her a good two minutes to even *look up*.

She's useless.

I scoff, pushing up my sleeves, preparing to throw out my

plans and tear her a new one. I reach out to grab the handle.

But a hand, big and dark, settles on the metal right next to the glass window first.

Breath doesn't come easy. It never does for me. I have no stamina.

But breath comes all too fast now. Panicked.

The hand is the strangest one I've ever seen. It is blacker than black, the kind of pitch darkness you can only dream about. The kind of darkness where your eyes never adjust. It's a never-ending thing that draws you deeper and deeper. The palm is too small for the six fingers that emerge, set wide and spindly, like the legs of a great spider. Each finger has the same number of knuckles as a person, but each segment, each bone seems twice as long. The hand pulls away from the door, suddenly ghosting over my throat as if to gently tell me, *Time to die*.

I am frozen.

Then I am screaming.

The hand slaps down on the door just as I wrench it open, slamming it shut again so hard that the echo is louder than my own thoughts. I can see Alexis jump, but the hand is coming back toward me again, so I drop to my knees and turn.

When I do, I see the hand is only the beginning.

The demon is tall, its skin a more purpling black than the fingers, like a bruise in the fuzzy blue light of the freezer. Its shoulders are wide and jutting, tapering into a rack of ribs that are pressed tight to thinly stretched muscle beneath its taut skin. Its legs are long and bowed, feet ending in long bare toes, each with an extra knuckle, tipped with dark claws. Most terrifying of all, though, are its big, big shiny black eyes and the perfectly normal teeth that appear when its mouth opens and it releases a sound like a soft rattle.

I look into the darkness of its mouth, trying to understand it.

My eyes do not adjust.

"Oh, absolutely *not*," I breathe.

It looms over me, slowly lifting its hands to look at them, like it's not sure of itself yet, and I take advantage of the hesitation. I reach up for the handle again and throw the freezer door open before crawling through. The second I yank my foot through, I kick the door shut behind me with another heavy bang.

"Stop slamming the—" Alexis starts.

"Shut the fuck up," I bark, breathing heavily, still crawling across the ground, up the short step to the cash register. Alexis makes an offended sound, but I just grab her arm and yank her hard until she falls down next to me.

My eyes shut so tight, I see red spots as I try to convince myself this is just a brief psychotic break. A moment of temporary, rage-induced insanity.

"You are *so* rude, Devon Harris. I can't even believe—"

The whine of the freezer door hinges cuts Alexis off, and she stills.

"What is that?" Alexis whispers as I peel my eyes open. "Mr. Ahmed—"

I press my hand over her mouth and shake my head slowly, squinting past the counter, at the freezer door to the left. It's open, but there's nothing there. I look to the right but there's only a tiny window, streaked from a poorly done wipe job, courtesy of Alexis, and covered with bars. The only way out is around the counter and then right out the front door. There's about twelve feet to get to it. But with how large and long that *thing* is, I don't feel confident.

Though the more seconds that pass, the more my confidence that I even saw anything leaks away too.

Where is it? Where did it *go*? Is it even real?

I look at Alexis again. There are about a thousand questions in her brown eyes, but I don't have time to answer a single one. I peek through a crack between the layers of old candy below the counter and . . . there. Holy shit, I'm not dreaming. I can't see into the face of the thing, but it's there, moving back and forth, sweeping the aisles. *Searching.*

I slowly lift my hand from her mouth and put a finger to my lips. Without breaking eye contact, I mouth a single word to her: *Run.*

Then I'm barreling from behind the counter, shoving the freestanding shelf right into the enormous thing on my way to the door. It doesn't make a single sound of pain on impact, but it stumbles, landing heavily underneath the shelf. For a moment I think I've managed to knock it out.

Until its claws snag around my ankle, shockingly cold, and pull me down too. I feel a shock run up my spine and burrow into the nape of my neck. I gasp as terror cracks through, rooting itself there in my spine, forcing me into action. I kick out and my foot connects despite how shadowy the creature appears, forcing it to release me. But it reaches out again immediately, its fingertips catching on my skin, digging in until blood drips onto the tattered tops of my socks and the white canvas of my sneakers.

It's a soft shock, the fact that this thing can draw *blood*.

That this thing wants to do *me* harm.

It's not a large leap to the ultimate conclusion: This thing wants to kill me.

I wrench my ankle away again, but I still feel its hand like a brand on my skin. I pull myself up and stagger toward the door, where Alexis grabs me by the shoulder, tugging me in front of her like a shield, as the *thing* gets to its feet again too.

"What the fuck do you think you're doing?" I bark.

"What the fuck is that thing?" Alexis demands instead.

"I don't *know*, but I'm not your shield. Get *off*," I say, shaking myself free as I press up against the door and then shove it open.

For a moment I linger. There's a mess of exploded chip bags on the ground and a crack in Mr. Ahmed's new linoleum. My good sense clashes with my responsibility. I'm supposed to be in *charge*. This is Mr. Ahmed's store, and there's something *infiltrating* it.

But Alexis has no good sense at all. "Wait, my phone is on the counter," she breathes. "I *have* to get my phone." She takes a step away from me. *Toward* the demon. Like an *idiot*.

I reach out, wide-eyed, nostrils flaring, and grab her roughly to yank her back. "Alexis, your phone doesn't matter—"

But the second I turn my head to berate her, the thing lunges. In the split second before it arrives, I throw myself and Alexis out the door, into the orange glow of the streetlights.

I stumble on my heels, wild-eyed as I look to the door I've slammed shut behind us.

From the outside, everything still looks okay. Everything looks *fine*.

"Is it . . . ? Is it gone?" Alexis whispers.

The words aren't even out of her mouth when the door flies

open, nearly off its hinges, and all the glass shatters. The thing emerges trembling from fury, from *existing*.

"No, no, *no*," Alexis whines, voice high, and I smell something sour. Like ammonia. Like—

I twist, looking at Alexis wide-eyed. "Did you just . . . ? Did you pee yourself?"

"No, no, *no*!" Alexis shrieks, voice growing louder and louder. More piercing. She stumbles back, nearly tripping. I grab on to her, trying to keep her with me, but she tears herself free from my grip.

"Alexis, *don't*!" I insist, her skin catching again underneath my fingernails. She doesn't even seem to notice. Her face stays contorted in a perma-mask of fear. She stumbles back, taking me along with her. "Alexis, come *on*. Run!"

But she's not running. Not really. She's still looking at the thing, eyes wild and darting as she makes aborted moves back and forth. Like she can't decide where to go. I try to decide for her, grabbing her hand, but she just shoves me.

Right toward the fucking thing.

I try to halt myself and stumble, banging my hip against the curb, my head falling back against the base of a streetlamp.

Alexis stands over me and demands, "Why did you make me do that? Why won't you *protect* me?"

I stare at her in disbelief.

In that moment the *thing* rushes toward us and my world is swallowed by darkness, interrupted only by the screech of tires and a thunderous thud that rocks my world.

Through spots in my vision, the world lights up again in orange, and when I can finally see clearly, I don't see the monster.

I see the hood of a black car, crushed in, like an accordion fold of paper, an Uber sign glowing above it. I see her—Alexis's—form, crumpled and twisted, blood dyeing her blonde hair pink. And I see the thing hunched over her, breathing heavily, shimmering like an oil slick. It claws its fingers through her blonde hair, tugging and tugging until a lock comes free. It doesn't even seem to notice me now as it tilts back its head and lowers that long strand of blonde right down its gullet.

I blink my eyes rapidly. This has to be a nightmare. A stress-induced delusion.

When I open my eyes, it's gone. But the world is still orange. The air is full of sirens.

And Alexis is not breathing.

INTERVIEW WITH DEVON HARRIS (and Guardian)
Sgt. Irvine
RECORDED INTERVIEW

SI: How are you, Miss Harris? You've had quite a scare this evening.

DH: You could call it that, yeah.

SI: Have you calmed down a bit? When we first arrived at the scene, you were in quite a bit of distress.

DH: Well, yeah, my coworker just got hit by an Uber. The Uber driver was in distress too.

SI: Of course. Understandable. All of it is very understandable.

DH: Is it?

SI: I think so.

DH: I don't.

SI: Don't what?

DH: Think it's understandable. I think it's very *not* understandable. I think it's ridiculous and terrifying.

SI: Well, that's the understandable part. You witnessed a horrifying thing.

DH: I feel like you probably have a different idea of what the *most* horrifying part was.

SI: Your friend—

DH: Coworker. Alexis and I were not friends.

SI: No?

DH: We were famously *not* friends, which I know is going to come up. I wanted Mr. Ahmed to *fire* her, but I didn't want her to die. That was . . . She was thrown in the street. But I think it was supposed to be me. Was it supposed to be *me*—

SI: Miss Harris . . . Devon, you know you're not in trouble, right?

DH: I didn't do anything so I shouldn't be, but I get that might be hard for your kind.

SI: My kind?

DEVON HARRIS LOOKS AROUND, DISTRACTED. DISORIENTED.

DH: I just hate you.

SI: Me, specifically?

DH: The concept. The execution. All of it. Just you.

DH's Guardian: Devon, be respectful.

SI: Miss Harris, we're trying to get to the root of this. I'm sure you are very tired and you'd like some rest. So, can we just finish solidifying a few of these facts before I let you and your father get home? Is that all right with you?

DEVON HARRIS TAKES A MOMENT BEFORE ANSWERING.

DH: Yeah, I guess that's okay.

SI: Miss Harris, do you remember what you were saying?

DH: I *(pause)* . . . No, I don't. I just . . . Alexis was . . .

SI: You called us, Miss Harris. *You* did. And do you remember what you said?

DH: No.

SI: You said that your coworker was thrown into the street by some-*thing*. Not someone. A thing. What thing?

DH: It was . . . I don't know . . . It doesn't make sense. It doesn't make sense, and all I can think of is Alexis screaming and running and I was trying to calm her down, but I couldn't because it didn't make sense, and then she *peed*—

DH's Guardian: It's okay, Devy. It's okay.

SI: Yes, calm down, Miss Harris. You're not in trouble.

DH: Sure.

SI: Is there a reason that you *should* be in trouble?

DH: Your type doesn't usually need a reason, do you?

DH's Guardian: Devon!

DH: Okay, okay, Dad. I'm sorry. Sorry. I'm just messed up about it. You wouldn't believe me if I told you, that's all.

SI: Oh? Try me.

DH: Is . . . Is Alexis really dead? Is this really happening?

SI: I'm afraid so, Miss Harris. Now, please, do your best to remember what happened. What you say could really clarify a few things. The lead-up to Alexis's episode is a bit murky. Now, to reiterate, when you called, you said that your coworker was thrown into the street. You've mentioned that she was screaming, urinated on herself, and then . . .

DH: Yeah. I was . . . We were in the store, and we were being *chased*.

SI: A thief? Gang activity?

DH: Dude . . . no. By the thing that pushed her. It chased us. I fell. It was . . . There was so much happening and I'm just so tired and confused, and you . . . You're not going to believe me. I barely believe me.

SI: Who saw this thing?

DH: Alexis and me. But the thing—

SI: Alexis saw the thing as well? What did it look like?

DH: It . . . It was tall. And hunched over. It had huge hands and dark, dark eyes. And purplish-red skin. But . . . it had human teeth. When you make me say it out loud, it sounds crazy, but it was real. We were chased by the thing, and then the Uber hit her. Well, first she tried to use me as a *shield*, which is so *fucked*, and then she shoved me and . . . the Uber hit her. But she wasn't running; she was pushed.

SI: Pushed?

DH: But not by me.

SI: Then, by who? Or . . . by what?

DH: The *thing*.

SI: Did Alexis share other distressing visions with you, Miss Harris?

DH: I'm not crazy, okay? I'm not—wait, what?

SI: I'm not calling you crazy, but what you've described—the thing Alexis saw—it doesn't sound like a human being. And sometimes suffering can mess with the mind, and Alexis seemed to be suffering greatly, didn't she?

DH: I think it was a pretty quick death. Very . . . immediate.

SI: I meant in life. Others we've interviewed have described her as beautiful but distraught. A cheerleader, but lacking in other areas of her life. According to a customer who came in earlier, she just lost a boyfriend, is that right? She'd been with him for some time, and I think he . . . cheated on her? Very distressing for a young girl. You must have brought her great comfort.

DH: I told you, we *weren't* friends. And what does this have to do with her death?

SI: What indeed. That's the question.

DH: Alexis was pushed in front of the car. That's what I saw. I heard her go crunch and I saw her neck snap and I saw the blood and . . . isn't there video of the thing? There are cameras all over the place in this city. You must have seen it. I know there's a speed camera up the block and there are other stores and . . . you don't need me. You really don't need me.

SI: I wanted to get your perspective. Since you knew her.

DH: Well, what's your perspective?

SI: Excuse me?

DH: What do you think happened? You keep talking about her suffering.

SI: Yes. We saw her emotional state on the video. Great distress. We saw video of her making impact with the car, both from dashcam POV and an overhead street camera.

DH: But you didn't see it? It was there! Chasing us. The Uber hit her, but it wasn't her fault and it wasn't my fault and it wasn't the Uber's fault either.

SI: Miss Harris, I think you're very tired.

DH: I am.

SI: Do you think Alexis was tired too?

DH: . . . what?

SI: Do you believe that she was tired of . . . the pressures of being a teenager in New York City?

DH: You can't be serious. She didn't commit suicide.

SI: Pressure can lead to psychotic breaks. . . .

DH: Oh, you *are* serious.

DH'S Guardian: Devon . . . well, Alexis had a lot going on at home.

SI: We'll be sure to make a note of that.

DH: Dad! Alexis did not kill herself. She was pushed.

SI: By society.

DH: I want to go home.

SI: Okay, Miss Harris. Thank you for your time. And you too, Mr. Harris.

CHAPTER SIX

*W*hen I wake up, I attribute last night to a very vivid nightmare. I used to be prone to those, in middle school, dreams full of the terrifying squeals of things that go bump in the night. Of toppling over onto the train tracks. Of being lost in the grid of the city.

It must be residual from the party. Finally, the creepy feeling must have snuck its way into my sleep.

But when I check my phone, it's nine in the morning, the exact time that my morning shift is supposed to start, and there are no calls from Mr. Ahmed. This spurs me into movement, which I immediately regret, gasping for air as my heart thunders in my chest.

When I sit up, my body *feels* the ache of exertion. My muscles twitch, overtired from adrenaline. I feel like I've clawed my way back from something. My ankle twinges with the sting of a half-healed wound, and when I look down, there's a bloodied super-sized Band-Aid already starting to peel off.

But I don't really accept it until I go to brush my teeth. It's there I notice the red-black blood crusted under my thumbnail. And hooked on a hangnail is a single straight blonde hair. Alexis's hair.

So. Not just a dream. A living nightmare.

Fuck. Fuckfuckfuckfuck.

When I get back to my room, the only thing that stops me from fully spiraling is that Drew is there. She's sitting cross-legged at the end of my bed, still in pajamas. Very untrue to form.

"How are you feeling?" she asks. "Did you sleep okay?"

I wrap my arms around my body like I'm holding myself together. "I am . . . okay."

"That's good. Yesterday was a mess. Mom and Dad were so worried," Drew says.

Dad and I had gotten in so late last night, but Mom and Drew had been wide awake. Mom had crowded me up against the door, kissing my forehead again and again, demanding to know if I was okay. I hadn't known *what* to say, and after I just stood there, quiet for minutes on end, Mom had sent me up the stairs to get to bed. Said we could talk about it in the morning after I got some sleep. I'd lingered on the step, though, waiting for Drew to say something. Anything.

But Drew just stood there until I gave up and ducked up the stairs for the night.

"Mom and Dad. Not you, though," I retort, letting the anger and frustration slip out. Drew startles at my aggression, and I backtrack like always, soften the tension with a smile. Drew tilts her head and gives me the same analytic stare she gives difficult math problems.

Then she's the one who surprises me when she says, "I'm always worried about you." I'd doubt her, but the way she says it is too honest, too real. It should feel good, reassuring even, but the room crackles with the awkwardness of it and everything we haven't said. Don't make us *talk* about it. The Best Summer Ever is supposed to be fun, not messy, not worried. Drew feels it too and changes the subject. "The cops weren't too bad, were they?"

"They were bastards, but what's new," I mutter. I crawl onto the bed, slinking past Drew, and settle against the plush mountain of pillows that I usually kick off in the night. "They didn't really believe me when I told them what happened."

Drew sits up, more alert than before. "Wait, so they think you killed her?"

The police at the scene had that thought, but only for a moment. After all, Alexis was . . . *Alexis*. Perfect victim Alexis. And it's no secret that I didn't like her. But . . .

"No. There's video evidence that shows I wasn't close enough to do anything or else they probably would have. They . . . think Alexis just kinda . . . snapped and killed herself. The 'pressures of society,'" I say, remembering the cops' dismissal of what I saw.

Drew's nose wrinkles, but she doesn't confront me. "Is that not what happened?" she asks.

"No, actually."

Drew and I don't have twin telepathy. We don't finish each other's sentences, and we don't accidentally wear the same outfits. We've never been the kind of sisters that tell each other everything. We're not the twins of sitcoms old.

It's why I don't say anything. Not yet. If I keep it close—what I saw and what happened—it means that nothing is quite ruined yet. I still have the Best Summer Ever with Drew, and nothing can touch us. Because if I tell her, she will not believe me because it's not logical. It's too fantastical, and Drew doesn't believe anything she can't touch. So instead of elaborating, I shake my head and trudge downstairs without changing.

Dad is actually home this morning, instead of at his tech job. His smile is straining at us from his seat at the kitchen table, and the scent of bacon fat and fried butter tells me he's made breakfast too. Along with it I can also smell hair—Mom's got someone in her chair in the living room, then.

"Morning, Devy-Doo," he says. He's the only one who has a nickname for me, and I smile at the sound of it, unable to help the Pavlovian response of it all, even if there's not much to smile about.

"Morning, Dad." I sit down in front of an empty plate. Drew ignores the third plate, sitting in the empty seat next to Dad, so she can look across the table at me. I try to ignore her, dragging the tines of my fork over the edge of the plate. But Drew doesn't deal well with being ignored.

"So, if she didn't kill herself, how did Alexis die?" Drew asks bluntly.

Dad rears back, appalled. *"Drew—"* he starts. *See, even when caught off guard he doesn't call Drew "Andrea."*

"Devon says that the police think Alexis killed herself, but she implied that's not what happened," Drew says matter-of-factly. Then she looks back at me, leaning forward. "So, what *did* happen?"

There is no real way to explain that a black slinking shadow turned solid and chased me out of the freezer, through the store, and into the street. There's no way to describe the mounting terror that had gripped me when it had me by the ankle. There's no way to explain that Alexis had been thrown into the path of the Uber by a thing that so conveniently knew to stick to the shadows so that it somehow wasn't captured on the cameras.

There's no way to explain my gut feeling that the thing was going after me but Alexis is the one who's dead.

"It doesn't matter how it happened right now," Dad says. "Devon went through something traumatic last night. It's fine if she doesn't want to answer your questions yet."

Drew's severe expression makes it very clear that it is *not* fine. And then I see her lean back, gripping the edges of the table, thinking hard, before she looks up and says, "I'll stop pushing." The "for now" lingers in the air and only makes me want to prolong breakfast for an eternity.

Dad makes an honest attempt to distract us from the elephant in the room by telling a story about something that happened at work. It's funny not in a funny-ha-ha way but a funny-dad-ha-ha way that I genuinely appreciate. But Drew's shrewd gaze almost never leaves my face.

I'm grateful when the doorbell rings and Mom shouts, "I'm midbraid; can someone get it?" I lurch out of the chair as the volunteer and thunder past the living room. My mom calls, "Oh, you're up, Devon?" but I ignore it in favor of opening the door.

Immediately, I'm caught up in Leila's arms. She hugs me so tight, I gasp, then allow myself to sag into the weight of her. Leila stumbles once before she locks her knees, anchoring us in each other's space.

"Fuck, Devon, can't keep yourself out of trouble, can you?" Leila asks breathlessly. Her laugh is a little watery as she leans back to look at me. She swipes her hands over her face, putting on a brave front, but I can see how shiny her eyes are, how puffy her face is. So different from Drew's undisturbed façade. I swallow the thought.

"Glad you care so much," I say, looking away, attempting to deflect.

Leila shoulders me away. "Fuck you, man. I thought you . . . That's scary. Alexis and then the *cops* and . . . I'm glad you're all right."

"I'm fine," I say, and it almost sounds true. A little bit. Kinda.

Except Leila doesn't look like she believes me either. She knows me as well as Drew does. Unlike Drew, she doesn't push, though.

"Did you eat breakfast?" Leila asks.

"Not finished yet. Join us?"

Leila nods and follows me to the kitchen. Dad relaxes when he sees her, as if he's been expecting her. And I realize he must have been since there's no other way she could have known what happened. My suspicions are solidified when Dad goes to make her a plate. "The pancakes and the eggs are good to go, but the turkey bacon isn't kosher. Sorry, Leila," he says.

"No problem. Thanks, Mr. H," Leila replies. She nudges me to my seat and then drops down into Drew's usual spot. She digs in with gusto, and it really seems almost normal, except Leila doesn't just come over for breakfast, unless it's after a sleepover.

"You're here for breakfast," I needle. "It's the summer. You don't usually wake up until lunchtime."

Leila nods. "I was up."

"Yeah?"

"Yeah, I was struck by some sunrise inspiration. Started a new portrait. I wanted to draw my avuela this time. It's going to be so good," Leila says. She's building out a portfolio, one that's going to be so spectacular, she's going to get into art school with it. Like Yaya, like Drew, like the rest, she knows exactly what she wants.

"Don't leave out your avuelo or he'll have something to say," I remind her.

Leila cracks a smile and nods. "I know, I know. Anyway, I was still in the sketching phase when your dad called," she says. She looks over at Drew and asks, "How are you this morning?"

"Fine, considering," Drew says through a crackling jaw. She hates having to hold her tongue, so used to wielding it like a sharp edge. And Leila's ill-disguised warning look just serves to piss her off even further.

We finish up breakfast in silence, but there's something about my dad being present and my mom coming in halfway through to steal a piece of bacon and a kiss from him that makes it less awkward. Mom drops a kiss to the top of my head too, but I know she feels a certain type of way only when her hands fall to my shoulders and she squeezes *hard*, like she'll never let go, until she does and goes back to her client.

"My turn to do dishes." I sigh, getting up to clear it all away. I don't miss the look Dad sends Drew's way.

"I got it," Drew sighs.

"Thanks." I grab Leila's hand and proceed to drag her upstairs. Drew will be sure to follow when she finishes up. I'm tempted to close the door, but I leave it open just a crack—an invitation I can't stop myself from offering despite her pursuit to know *more*.

I collapse onto the bed and Leila slides onto the duvet until she's lying on her side, facing me.

"You're not doing well, are you?" she asks quietly.

"No, I'm not," I admit, but I'm not sure if I'll ever want to speak about what I thought I saw last night.

No. What I *know* I saw.

It plays in my brain like a movie. I can see it crystal clear, in a way that no camera could really ever capture and apparently didn't. I see Alexis's fear and smell the sourness of piss. Most of all, I hear the thud of her body colliding with the hood of the Uber. The sight of those long wide hands, with long bony fingers, shoving Alexis flickers in my mind, even as I try to blink it away. It's only dulled when Leila rubs my shoulder, quietly giving me the comfort I've been craving.

It doesn't last. I can hear Drew coming up the stairs. I peek out from the pillow and see her shadow hesitate before she pushes the door open. Drew doesn't immediately join us, though. She doesn't immediately say anything at all. Instead, she wanders my room with no boundaries.

I can't even be mad at it. I feel the same proprietary feeling in her space too. Drew and I shared a bedroom for so long, it's still habit. We shared right up until Drew asked for her own, just before high school. She needed a place to focus and to study, to shut out the rest of the world and its distractions. But it sort of felt like now that she'd removed me from her school life, she wanted to shut me out of the rest of it too. I told myself I was glad to move into the guest bedroom, to be able to spread my interests wide without her judgment. Still, it's always felt weird to be separated by walls from the person you once shared a womb with.

Drew plays with my crocheted animals on my bookshelves. She carefully folds some of the crocheted tops I have thrown on the floor and sets them aside in neat piles. She's brimming with a frenetic energy I'm used to. Leila doesn't cope so well.

"Why don't you sit down with your sister and me?" she suggests in a tight voice.

Drew snorts, shaking her head like a filly. "I don't want to *sit*," she mutters. Strands of her hair peek out from underneath her silk scarf. The fact that she hasn't noticed yet proves just how distracted she really is. "I just . . . I don't get it, Devon. I don't."

"What is there to get?" I ask, face half hidden in one of my pillows.

"You *said* the police think Alexis killed herself. But then you say that she didn't, despite there being video evidence corroborating that she did. So, if she didn't kill herself and *you* didn't kill her . . ." Drew trails off, and she looks like it physically pains her to not ask her real question. No, more like it physically pains her to not *know*. Because that's what this is all about, after all.

She wants to know what happened more than she wants to know how I *feel*.

"Does it really matter *right* now?" Leila asks through clenched teeth.

Drew huffs out. "Of course it matters. Don't you see her? She's all fucked up over it."

"Of course she is!" Leila blurts out. "She saw her coworker die."

Drew shakes her head. "She didn't even like her. So whatever happened had to be really messed up, and I'm sorry, I'm not sure if Alexis throwing herself in front of a car would cut it."

"You think I'm that callous? That I'd dislike someone *that* much?" I ask quietly.

"No," Drew says almost immediately, almost too quick for me to believe. "But I still don't think that you would react like *this*. You're not talking about it. You don't want to talk about it. Every time you start, you stop. You clearly have a problem you won't let me help you solve, and that confuses me."

That's what does it. What transforms my listlessness into genuine frustration. I always understand Drew's motivations, but they never really annoy me until she says it out loud, without shame. It's the lack of shame that makes me shut down. She makes it sound like it's about me, but this isn't about me at all.

In one move, I roll away from Leila and plant my feet on the ground, leaning off the edge of the bed to make full eye contact with my sister. I imagine myself exploding at her, blowing past passive aggression into a fuller rage, the kind that sits deep, the kind that I don't want to think that I might be capable of feeling toward my sister.

It builds in my throat like word vomit—oh, no it's not. I rush to the bathroom and spew actual vomit into the toilet.

The acrid taste in my mouth grounds me. I flush and then brush the bile from my teeth, acting as if Drew and Leila aren't hovering in the doorway like a pair of panicking nannies. I stare at my own reflection and breathe heavily instead, focusing on the taste of chemical mint burning on the back of my tongue. With each exhale, the need to explode dissipates until I feel slightly less off kilter. Without the pressure of vomit or anger, I can think more rationally. Annoyed as I am at her motivations, this *is* an impossible problem, one I can't solve alone, and behind me is my sister, *notable* problem solver. When I'm finally ready to face them, I turn around.

"Devon . . . ," Leila says cautiously.

"I was upset last night. Alexis was pissing me off. More than usual," I say without preamble. "I went to the freezer to cool off. I was looking out the window at her ignoring customers and then, before I could confront her, there was this . . . hand by my head, pressed against the door. Someone . . . *something* was in there with me."

"Some*thing*?" Leila repeats.

"Yes. It wasn't human . . . but alive. All black. Shadowy but somehow solid. With long fingers that curved like claws and this terrifying *mouth*. I tried to shut it in the freezer, but it got out and chased me and Alexis out of the bodega. I was so scared, I thought I was going to die. My heart was pounding in my chest and Alexis was freaking out, but all I could think was that I had to get out. To get away. Because I could tell it wasn't chasing *us*. It was chasing *me*. It wanted to kill me," I whisper, and I can't quite make eye contact with either of them. Not when their disbelief is so palpable, I'm nearly choking on it. But now that I've started, I have to finish. "We managed to get outside, and I thought we were okay. But then it came out of the bodega, and she tried again to use me as a shield—"

"She *what*?" Leila croaks.

"She pushed me, and I fell just as the thing *lunged* and then my vision got spotty, but it must have gotten her, instead. Pushed her. I heard the Uber hitting Alexis and I knew just from the sound she was dead," I say, voice cracking on the finality of it all. Alexis Mendoza is *dead*.

There's a beat of silence.

"Dad was right. You had a time last night," Drew says with an uncharacteristic amount of compassion, her curiosity now fully sated and assured I'm just insane. "You should go back to sleep."

My eyes narrow. "I don't need to *sleep*, Drew. You wanted to know what happened and I just told you," I spit.

93

Drew nods. "You're telling me what you think happened. I understand—"

"I don't 'think' anything. I was there. I *know* what I saw!" I insist. "You sound just like those *cops*."

"And what did those cops say?" Leila asks gently.

"They . . . They said Alexis had a psychotic break. That she was depressed or going *crazy*. But she wasn't 'crazy.' She was *afraid*, and so was I! She didn't *throw* herself at the Uber! She was *pushed*," I insist.

Leila looks caught between pity and confusion. But it's Drew's expression that sets me on fire. She looks at me like I've committed the most egregious crime in her eyes—being *wrong*.

"Mr. Ahmed has cameras. What did the footage from the cameras inside look like?" Drew cross-examines me. It feels like I'm back in the interrogation room again. Like I'm being prodded and pushed and discounted.

I gear up to explain that everything's there. That they'll pull it up any day and I'll be proven right and then—

"Alexis . . . Alexis turned off the cameras so that Mr. Ahmed wouldn't know that she was stealing again during our shift," I admit, voice low. "And the thing that attacked us wasn't caught on the shitty street cameras anyway. You can't see that sidewalk, *just* the street and the *opposite* sidewalk, so it looks like Alexis just flung herself into the road."

Drew nods slowly, raising an eyebrow. I hate that eyebrow. "Riiight," she drawls.

"Hey, don't do that," Leila warns. Drew raises her hands, and Leila takes an unsteady step into the bathroom, holding one hand out to me. "Devon . . ."

It's too much. I storm out of the bathroom, shouldering past

Drew with more force than necessary, and I throw my bedroom door shut behind me. It doesn't stop Leila, who barges in, joining me by the window as I glower out at the street. Drew lingers in the reopened doorway, leaning on the frame, arms folded.

"I don't know what happened last night, Devon, but I think it's affecting you really deeply. And that makes sense. I know you didn't . . . *like* Alexis, but you watched her die. That's a whole lot," Leila says.

"*I* know what happened last night. I just told you. And you don't believe me," I say. I make it plain for them, no talking around it: "Some supernatural shit appeared in the freezer and tried to kill me, but then it killed my annoying-ass coworker instead."

It's so unbelievable, I know it makes sense that they're looking at me like I'm crazy, but Leila is always the first to give me the benefit of the doubt. I meet her eyes and can't help the way my face twists, pleading for her to *believe* me. Leila lowers her gaze to the ground, brow furrowing as she tries to make up her mind.

Drew. Well, Drew scoffs.

Her gaze hardens, and she leans in. "Are you making fun of Avery?"

"Avery?" I repeat.

Drew nods once. "Yes. Are you making fun of him because of the Ouija board thing at the party? Because I get that he's full of shit, but he was just having fun and he's my *friend*. I get that he's not part of the crew or whatever, that you're not interested in my life outside your narrative, but—"

The accusation knocks the wind out of me, and I feel over-whelmed with a sudden need to crush the argument before it can even start.

"I haven't thought about Avery once since we left his house, and definitely not since I saw someone *killed in front of me*, Andrea," I insist.

It's funny that what finally cows her into silence is her own name.

"You can both go," I say in the coldest voice I can muster.

Leila winces, rubbing her forehead, then nods. She leans forward to wrap her arms around my shoulders in a tight hug. Against my ear, she whispers, "I'll see you tonight, okay?"

I don't say anything else as she and Drew walk out. I slam the door behind them.

I'm supposed to go to Movies-in-the-Park with Leila, Yaya, and Drew—a girls' night, the next installment of Best Summer Ever. I can't believe how important it seemed just hours ago. I wouldn't have missed it for anything. They're playing some rom-com from the nineties that Yaya loves and Drew pretends to hate. I was on blanket duty, and Yaya was going to bring the snacks.

Even the promise of Yaya's presence, her smile, and her attention doesn't change the fact that I'd rather do literally anything in the world than sit next to my sister on a blanket and have to deal with her insufferable need to be *right* and *logical* when there's no logic in this. Not when my entire worldview has just shifted so absolutely and no one believes me about it.

So when Yaya texts to ask where I am, I mute the group chat swiftly, letting Leila and Drew fill her in. The least they can do is save me from having to say it again and seeing the same disbelief on Yaya's face.

Shockingly—or maybe not shockingly, with the current

THE BLONDE DIES FIRST

circumstances—my parents allow Drew to leave without me and don't verbalize a single question, though I can feel it in the weight of their eyes. In the face of last night's events, I'm allowed to sequester myself in my bedroom for the day to process, if not mourn. Mom comes upstairs only once, after her final client of the day, to ask if I want anything special for dinner. But I can't even imagine eating right now. Not when every time I blink, I see the shape of the supernatural thing on the back of my eyelids, its figure burned into my retinas. Its origin is elusive.

When had it gotten there? How long had it lingered, waiting for me? Did it come through the walls? The vents? Underneath? They all seem equally impossible, but so does its existence. Because all I know is that it wasn't a person and that was the most terrifying thing of all, how *inhuman* it had been. Six fingers and a void of purple-black shadow wrapped around muscles and stretched over oversized bones. I shiver and sink deeper under my duvet, attempting to ward off these obsessive questions, each one without a satisfying answer.

But as the sun approaches the horizon, the idea of staying home to hang out with my concerned parents and going over what happened again and again becomes less appealing. If I tell my parents I was attacked by a knockoff Slenderman, they'll commit me to a seventy-two-hour psychiatric hold. And I'm not ready to shuffle along in grippy socks through the halls of Mount Sinai.

Not yet anyway.

The answer comes in a stroke of genius—or perhaps in just remembering that it's nighttime in the summer and Malachi is a creature of habit.

I scramble out of bed to snatch my phone from the charger

97

near my bookshelf and thumb out a text, praying that the news of
Alexis's demise hasn't yet dissipated through the neighborhood, or
worse—my parents' group chat with my friends' parents.

DEVON
yo you have a date tonight?

Malachi has always been a fast texter. So fast that he tends to
get frustrated with anyone who isn't as quick as him, so I don't
even set my phone back down.

MALACHI
duh why

DEVON
you happen to need backup?

MALACHI
. . . gael's gma got him helping her move her furniture in the
living room so yeah I guess.
délivrance @ 8:45

My parents have never been the kind to demand to know where I am at all moments of the day. I tell them where I'm going and when I'll be back, and they follow me on Find My until they see I'm with one of my friends. But tonight when I tell them that I haven't changed my mind about not going to meet up with Leila, Yaya, and Drew under the Brooklyn Bridge, they're concerned.

Once I confess that I'll be heading to Bushwick to watch out for Malachi on a date, though, they nod. They love how we watch out for each other, love how we're close, and trust us because of it. It makes protecting one another a lot easier, and particularly protecting Malachi, because Malachi is the romantic kind, in the worst ways. The not-always-safe kind. The not-always-smart kind. For Malachi, romance is something to risk it all for, so the greater the risk, the better the reward, no matter how much we try to tell him those aren't the same thing. Live fast. Love hard. That's Malachi.

And so it's better for one of us to watch out for him, because he'll look out for everyone else but himself. At least that's how Yaya phrased it when we first decided that we needed to chaperone him.

I find myself at Délivrance a whole fifteen minutes early. It's in one of many warehouses scattered amongst stacked thrift stores and old-school bodegas off Flushing Avenue. It's a queer club that we found last summer, even though we were technically too young to get in. Our cousins are always shocked by how we know even these parts of New York like the skin over our bones, how we learned her every crack and bruise and scar. It's hard to explain the normalcy of that, though, unless you've grown up with it.

Shockingly, it was Yaya who discovered Délivrance. In our search for places to dance with good music, she found the answer in this spacious, repurposed sugar factory that's heavy on the eighties synth and light on the ID checks, *especially* on nights that are only eighteen-plus. We became such regulars those nights that the bouncer never even confuses Drew and me. So tonight he waves me in lazily, eyes glazed over in a familiar way.

Délivrance is already half full when I walk in. It must be a themed night, though, from the array of costumes. It's very space age, and at first I feel out of place. Usually, I love a chance to dress up and break out my glitter, but even if I'd known, it's not one of those nights. I'm not in a dressing-up kind of mood.

The costumes almost disguise how truly bland Délivrance is for a club. It's huge but feels unfinished, still bearing too much resemblance to the old factory that it is with its leftover gears and pipes along the walls that still hiss with heat, like a warning, and its standard cracked, black vinyl tiles. The bar is the only part that's new and shiny, with colorful bottles racked along the back wall, fairy lights hanging above them from overhead rafters. Tucked close to the bar are seven booths with cracked leather and sticky tabletops, and parallel, along the opposite wall, are an array of tall tables with mismatched stools. There's no VIP section, no fancy bottle service, or anything like that.

But there's something about having a queer space that lets us *be*.

Once my eyes adjust to the lighting, Malachi's easy to spot in tight silver vinyl pants and a lace-up vest with handsewn sequins—not his work but his grandma's for sure. He sits at one of the tall tables, drumming his fingers against the edge with one hand and scrolling on his phone with the other. I slip onto the barstool adjacent to his and settle my elbows heavily on the table, dragging his attention to me. I cradle my face in my palms and raise an eyebrow. "Really showing up and showing out tonight, huh?"

"You didn't even bother to get dressed?" Malachi complains. "You always dress up."

I shrug. "You didn't tell me that it was a themed night." I swing my feet and lean in, holding out my hand. "Lemme see him."

"I heard you had a rough night," Malachi says, ignoring my outstretched hand.

Damn the parent group chat. Straight to hell.

"Yeah."

"You want to talk about it before I see my date?" Malachi asks quietly.

I sigh. "No, and I had an equally rough day that I don't really wanna talk about either. Now, lemme see this old man," I demand.

Malachi glowers at me and protests, "He's not old," but he flips through his overfull photo folder anyway. He turns his phone to face me, not releasing the device into my hand.

The guy is handsome enough. Dark hair and thick eyebrows.

He's wearing khakis and a blue button-down shirt in this photo, slightly open over a chest that looks waxed. Racially ambiguous. Could be mixed. Could be Mediterranean. Too hard to tell off one photo. Straight teeth, the kind you pay for, which reminds me of Keith a little, but that could just be the leftover trauma from the night before. The Yaya trauma, not the demon trauma. But most of all . . .

"He looks twenty-five," I say flatly.

"And?" Malachi drawls.

"You're seventeen!" I retort.

Malachi purses his lips. "I turn eighteen in literally a month." It's not a lie, but still, seven years is a lot when you're in high school and he's probably out of college. He shakes off my judgment with habitual irritation. "Anyway, he's meeting me at nine."

"Okay. We sure that's what he looks like?" I ask.

Malachi nods and sucks his teeth when I raise an eyebrow. "Damn, yes, Devon, this is what he looks like. Here."

Another photo. This time, shirtless. "Ew."

"That is *not* 'ew,'" Malachi says, with eyes lit up and a sly smile crossing his face. He lets out a tiny laugh and stretches his arms over his head. I can hear his back cracking even over the synth. "We've FaceTimed, so I *know* that the photos aren't edited. We've been talking for a *while*, Devon. I, like, really like him. He works in the finance department of some creative firm. He's smart. Funny. Went to NYU. He's so sweet. So."

"Sure. Your little finance bro will have so much to talk about to his teenage boyfriend's teenage friends. You have *so* much in common," I say sarcastically, rubbing crust from my eyes. "Okay, let's go through the signals."

We created these universal signals after an unfortunate run-in that Drew had with someone who was too old and too pushy. Our first night out ended with Drew standing tall and the guy getting a deviated septum and a bruised esophagus courtesy of Malachi and myself. Now we go through the motions. A tug on the hair is an "all clear." A hand on the hip is a "please hold." A deliberate stretch of one hand over the head is a "get me away from this nigga."

And a finger over the teeth? That's a "make them bleed."

"I have a good feeling about this one, though," Malachi says after going through them, like he hasn't said the same thing a ton of times before. "Like a man named Marco can't be evil, you know?"

"He sounds like a villain on a reality TV show," I say, skeptical. "Also . . . finance bro?"

Malachi gives me the finger. "Hey, I know you're not at a hundred percent, but *you* volunteered to watch my back. I didn't ask for your opinion or your judgment," he says firmly.

I sigh and nod. Malachi rewards me with a smacking kiss on my cheek, nudges my chin, and then hops off the stool, all long legs, too much charisma, and wanting too much trouble for his own good.

"Come dance with me?" he asks.

I sigh again, shaking my head. "No, I'm good."

Malachi's eyes narrow, but he doesn't push.

He shimmies to the dance floor, greeted by a few of the regulars that I know by face, if not by name. They take him under their arms, giggling and laughing as he presumably shows them photos of so-called Marco. I check my own phone. Still

ten minutes until he's supposed to get here. As someone prone to
FOMO, Instagram is my least favorite way to pass the time, but
just to be a masochist, I immediately go to Yaya's Stories.

They're at the movie. Leila and Yaya are sitting on the blanket, mugging together. I can see the bottom of Drew's sneakers;
she's sitting in a lawn chair of some sort, legs folded. In the next
story, she's leaning down, cheek to cheek with Leila. So they're
starting to gel out. Our group is starting to fall into the comfortable patterns of friendship. Without me. In the next, Yaya is
filming their spread. And sure enough, there's the popcorn I like.
With me not there.

"Fuck," I whisper to myself. My guilt makes me actually look
at my messages.

The group chat that I've muted is going strong.

But then there's my individual chat with Yaya.

Today 11:37 AM
YAYA
Hey, I heard. Are you okay?
I mean, I know you're okay, because Drew said you're home.
But are you OKAY?

Today 1:42 PM
YAYA
Of course you're not okay. You can talk to me.

Today 8:29 PM
YAYA
Hey, I assume you're not coming.

Malachi says you're watching his back tonight. I'm glad.

We miss you.

I miss you.

Drew said you and her had a fight? And Leila said if we wanted to know what's going on, we had to ask you.

Gonna save your popcorn for the next time I see you.

And I will be seeing you, Harris. Tomorrow even.

I'm going to show up for lunch and make you take a walk with me and answer all my questions.

"Fuck, fuck, fuck *me*," I whisper to myself, irritation mounting. The self-loathing that unfolds isn't *unfamiliar*, but the addition of anger at *Drew* is. Because, really, I would've gone to the stupid movie if she wasn't such an asshole. If she hadn't pushed and questioned my sanity, and then made it all about her stupid boyfriend who had thrown her a stupid graduation party she wasn't even going to invite us to.

"That does *not* sound good," someone says. "All good there, pretty girl?"

I look up, irritation rearing its head. The girl standing next to me is someone I recognize from seeing here but have never actually met. She's not particularly tall, only an inch or so more than me, has a shaved head with hooded eyes and a generous mouth. She's dressed in all black, formless clothing that obscures any shape.

"Ah, yes," I say. But even I can tell I don't mean it. "Just, got a text."

"Good one or a bad one?" she asks, smirking at me.

"Kinda both. I can't do anything about it now," I admit with a sigh that makes my entire body rock on top of the stool. I hold out a hand. "I'm Devon."

"Trish," she introduces herself. "You're a friend of Malachi's." She doesn't say it as a question. "I recognize you. You always come in with your other friends. One of them's your sister, right? You look alike."

"Yeah, my twin, actually," I say tightly.

This seems to surprise her. "Oh, shit, word? You don't look *that* similar," she says.

"Actually, we're identical and everything. Must be . . . must be the hair," I say. *And everything else*, I don't.

"Maybe!" Trish says brightly. She licks her tongue over her teeth, a tiny pink slip over white enamel. Her lipstick is a little smudged on her upper lip, and a tiny bit of the purple bleeds onto her brown skin. "So, where do you go? I just finished freshman year at NYU, but I've never seen you, like, anywhere except here. Unless you're an upperclassman? Or wait. Here for an internship?"

"That's because I don't go there. To NYU, I mean," I say kindly.

"Oh. New School? *Columbia?*"

I bite my bottom lip. "I'm in high school. I'm seventeen," I admit. The confession lingers. I watch the knowledge wash over Trish, and it's like she has to recalibrate.

"Oh, shit. Whoa," Trish says slowly. She looks around, like she's looking for my mom, and I laugh.

"Dude, you're like, what? Eighteen?" I challenge.

Trish rubs the back of her neck. "Yeah, so?"

"Yeah, *so* much more mature than me," I joke, a slow smile tugging at my lips. "And definitely not supposed to be in here tonight either."

There's a stirring by the bar and I look over. It's always so strange, the way names and faces separate in my head. I recognize the shape of his jaw, but it's not until he smiles with those too-white teeth that it clicks back together. Marco is here, dressed as if he's only just come from work in a crisp white button-down and a Patagonia vest. He eases his way through the immediate rush of twinks who go to meet him with a wide smile, but he doesn't immediately go in search of Malachi. I purse my lips; there's still time for him to, before I consider him rude in addition to being a creep, but not much.

I point at the stool opposite me and nod at it. "Am I too young to even talk to now?"

"I mean, not if we're only gonna *talk*," Trish says as she slides into Malachi's abandoned seat. She pushes up her sleeves, revealing skinny arms rippling with gorgeous tattoos, flora and fauna wrapping along the planes of muscle, tucked into the crooks and twists of her joints. Trish grins when she catches me ogling. "Cool, right?"

"When did you start?" I ask. I have to stop myself from reaching forward to trace the lines.

"My junior year of high school," Trish says. She shakes her head. "So I guess I shouldn't, like, *judge* or be surprised that you're *here* as a junior."

"Rising senior," I correct. "Also, my presence here is not, like, surprising for a kid from New York, so I get the feeling you're not from here. Where are *you* from?"

"Michigan," she says, almost embarrassed.

"Very alt for someone from Michigan," I say.

"You think?" she asks, almost searching for approval, no

matter what she's proclaimed. She suddenly looks meeker. It's not a good look on Trish, who'd come in swinging.

I purse my lips. "Wouldn't know. I don't know anyone from Michigan." Tension leaks out of my shoulders. Trish makes me comfortable in the way a new friend does, where there's no expectations. Just kindness and an eagerness to talk about nothing in particular. I appreciate it.

This is just a night. This is any *other* night.

"So, what are you doing at Délivrance?" Trish asks.

I sigh, glancing at the bar again. Marco is still there, entertaining a pretty boy with a thicket of dark curls atop his head who looks very much my age but very much *not* like Malachi. Unpromising stuff.

"You know Malachi. Well, he's . . . very romantic," I say. "It makes him reckless. We usually take turns coming here to be backup in case one of his dates goes south."

"You keep saying 'we,' but I only see you," Trish says. "Where is the rest of the crew?"

Right. *Right.*

"My friends had other plans tonight," I say as diplomatically as possible. The glint in Trish's eyes tells me that she understands far more than I mean her to. "Do you know a Marco, by chance?"

"That whore?" Trish asks. She catches herself, letting out a tiny laugh colored thick with shame. "That wasn't very sex positive of me."

"Not at all." But I don't mind it. It just confirms a few uncharitable thoughts of my own. I look back at Trish, holding her gaze meaningfully.

"Oh, not *Marco*," Trish gasps. "I didn't think he was like that. He likes them pretty and young, but not, like, a minor."

"I wouldn't put it past Malachi to lie," I say.

I check in with him again, and for better or worse Marco seems to have made his way to the dance floor and found Malachi. They are pressed close together already, the sound of Tears for Fears bleeding into the more familiar thudding of the Eurythmics, and Malachi is beaming up at him. Marco hadn't seemed so tall at the bar, but he's a good head over Malachi, which is a feat when Malachi isn't particularly short. The lights are flickering brighter than ever, and Marco lifts a hand to Malachi's cheek, rubbing his knuckles against it, before he holds his hand out, as if to draw him deeper into the dance floor.

I narrow my gaze, willing Malachi to turn around. Like he senses it, he looks over his shoulder and tugs at one of his locs reassuringly. I watch them drift farther onto the dance floor, but not so far that I can't see them.

"You really keep a good eye on him. Who keeps an eye on you?" Trish asks.

I turn away from Malachi and scoff. "I don't need anyone to keep an eye on me."

"Sure about that?" Trish asks.

It takes me a moment to recognize that she's teasing. Flirting. Even though that's all she'll do. It's nice to be wanted, in some way. It's nice to know that someone looks at me and thinks, "Oh, she's beautiful," without any other qualifiers. No comments about the undertones of my skin and how they don't match my hair.

Malachi has his back to Marco's front now, their hips aligned. Marco's hands are huge on Malachi, too big and roaming. Proprietary in a way I don't like. I stand up, abruptly, stopping Trish midsentence.

I ignore her confusion, glowering as Malachi reaches for Marco's wrist and guides it back to his hip. Marco whispers something to him and he nods, but the bad feeling doesn't go away.

"You okay?" I hear Trish ask from the end of a long tunnel.

"Yeah, yeah, I'm fine," I mutter dismissively. I realize my tone and look back at her. "I'm sorry. Just watching."

"Oh, well, at least Marco seems distracted?" Trish says, looking over my shoulder.

"What?" I ask.

There is no one more focused on a singular person than Marco right now. He is wrapped around Malachi like a parasite attempting to burrow underneath his skin. Marco's wandering hand slides over Malachi's chest, settling against his Adam's apple this time.

But Trish says, "He's talking to that boy," and points in the direction of the bar.

I follow the tip of her acrylic-tipped finger and falter.

Impossibly, it's Marco. Back with that curly haired white boy with the cupid's-bow smile and the cherubic cheeks. Marco is curved around him, keeping him trapped against the edge of the bar, ignoring the irritated lesbian behind it. It's like he's forgotten Malachi altogether.

But when I look back to the dance floor.

Marco is still there.

With Malachi.

"Oh, shit," I whisper, jumping to my feet. The thud of the stool barely makes an impact over the synth-pop.

Malachi's eyes are narrowed to slits, but when he makes direct eye contact with me, a hazy smile crosses his face. Marco—who can't be Marco—drags his fingers over Malachi's chin, tilting it up and toward him, pointedly away from me.

But something in my face must make Malachi stare at me from the corner of his eye just a moment longer, even with the cocksure lift to his eyebrow.

I bare my teeth wide like an animal and drag my fingers over them deliberately, using our sign, before jerking my head toward the bar. Malachi looks annoyed at first but then follows my gesture.

And he sees it.

Marco.

Which makes the Marco behind him . . . not-Marco. Not-Marco's fingers drift higher, pressing strangely against Malachi's bottom lip, almost like he's attempting to hook the corner of his mouth.

I drag my finger over my teeth again.

Make them bleed.

This time Malachi bares his teeth and bites.

Not-Marco lets out a sound I remember down in my marrow— the wet gurgling kind of yell of something not human.

"Wait, that can't be *Marco,* can it?" I hear Trish ask just as Malachi yanks himself away from not-Marco, but the crowd surges as the beat drops, swallowing them from view.

"It can't," I say. Then I dart off through the fray, tossing elbows until suddenly the smell of sweat and blood fills my lungs, sitting heavy and wet in each heaving breath, a confirmation that the nightmare of last night isn't just real. It's back.

CHAPTER EIGHT

Everywhere I turn, there is another body, all of them pressed tight like sardines. Like thickets of brush, with nowhere to part them. I shove through anyway just to get shoved back with a snarled curse. I half-heartedly snap back as my panic mounts and my stomach lurches. The world is too hot, the music too loud, and my vision begins to tunnel, but then—

Between the shoulders of two Amazonian-tall queers, I see Malachi, hands pushing not-Marco's away.

Closer up, not-Marco doesn't look exactly like Marco, not really.

There is something fractured about him, like I'm staring at him from the end of a long kaleidoscope. It looks perfect until you twist just a little to the left, and then the fractals reflect something monstrous back. I recognize that something monstrous— the wet gurgling purr that oozes from his throat, the unnatural curve of his knuckles, fingers streaked with black, the same color lighting Malachi's teeth up like a gore fest.

For a moment I sway, frozen, just as not-Marco plants his feet and opens his mouth, revealing the dark cavern that had gaped at me last night. It's only hearing Malachi's yelp, sharp and terrible, as not-Marco's fingers dig into his shoulders, cutting through the silver vinyl of his vest like a knife to butter, that unfreezes me.

THE BLONDE DIES FIRST

Not *my* friend. Not after Alexis. Not again.

The chant of "not, not, not" echoes in my mind as I charge forward, swinging my fists and knocking not-Marco right in the Adam's apple.

He gags, lurching backward, his entire body contorting like he's spineless, boneless even, and yet I can still feel the crunch of cartilage against my knuckles, the slight give of it. I twist and look Malachi right in the eye. While the music is too loud to hear what he's saying, I can see his terror in the whites of his glassy eyes, and he's shaking. It isn't until he grabs my wrists that I realize—oh, I'm shaking too.

"You okay?" I ask, teeth chattering, and Malachi nods frantically.

"Yeah, I'm good, but we gotta . . . we gotta . . . ," Malachi stutters.

Then he inhales sharply, eyes trained over my head, and I turn back around, coming face-to-face with not-Marco as he— no, it, it has to be an *it*—recovers. One of my wrists is still locked in Malachi's hand as I press him back behind me, glowering at the thing as it lifts its terrifying hands again, the tanned skin flaking away and joining the pink confetti in the air as its claws come out.

Malachi whines in my ear, reduced to a childish kind of fear I haven't heard from him since day care. Not-Marco reaches out to swipe me aside, but at the tiniest contact, it hisses, like even attempting to touch me hurts it instead of me. There's something familiar about the movement, the way not-Marco's mouth curves with something that seems like petulance. But it's gone just as quickly, and then not-Marco is looking at Malachi again, sneering and snarling.

I kick out, hitting my target right between its legs. Not-Marco's gurgling yelp is loud enough to draw the attention of others *finally*, and one man yelps, tugging on a blue-haired girl's arm. She turns, and her expression goes slack as her pupils blow out. Not-Marco shrieks at her this time, and it's the distraction we need. Malachi is a half second quicker to move than I am, and he drags me out through the crowd.

I look behind me as we hustle, but I can't see not-Marco.

When we finally burst off the dance floor, Trish is gone and the air is a little less heavy, a little less wet. Malachi doesn't stop, though. He beelines straight for the side door, next to the bar, and drags me out into the slightly cool summer evening. We stumble into the narrow side alley, stuffed full of only garbage; we catch sight of only a few stragglers at the mouth of the alley, zipping by in the awkward time after dinner but before it's *truly* time to party.

"Oh fuck, oh fuck, oh *fuck*," I gasp, chest heaving.

"What the hell, Devon?" Malachi demands. "Like what the actual—"

"There you are! I was looking for you in there. Malachi, right?"

Malachi jumps violently, then throws me behind him.

Marco—the human, regular one, I can tell now from the light in his eyes—puts his hands up, surrendering.

But I don't think Malachi registers the difference, because he barks, "Get the *fuck* away from us," with more bass in his voice than I ever thought he could muster.

"Whoa, why are you being so aggressive?" Marco asks.

"Nigga, are you deaf?" Malachi demands.

THE BLONDE DIES FIRST

I wince and Marco takes a weak step back, holding up his hands. "I wasn't talking to John long, I promise. I really was look-ing for you," he says.

Unfortunately, Malachi knows nothing about that. "Who is John, and who the *hell* are—" The side door swings open, inter-rupting him. The hairs on the back of my neck stand straight up.

I expect not-Marco to move with the same aggression as before, but it slinks out instead, head crooked to the side. It opens its mouth and lets out a long, clicking croon, like the croak of a bullfrog, but I feel it in my bones. Marco's mouth falls open, eyes widening as he takes in this fun-house-mirror image of himself. My mouth runs dry as not-Marco swings its head back and forth like a pendulum, looking between the meal that it wants to make of Malachi and me and the man whose face it's stealing.

"Holy shit," Marco rasps. I can hear how heavy his tongue sits in his mouth. He doesn't look perfectly tanned now, just wan and small. But then I see him big himself up in the same breath, puffing out his chest.

"Don't," I warn, but my voice is lost in a frightened wheeze.

Marco takes another step, pushing up his sleeves past his elbows. "What kind of sick joke is this?" he demands. "Dude, do you know who I *am*?"

Oh, not him being one of *those*.

Not-Marco's crooning mouth unhinges wider than any human mouth should, revealing a circle of perfect, shiny white teeth that barely cling to its black-purple gums.

Marco jumps back, proving his courage was only for show, cringing away from the thing's soft rattle. He makes deliberate eye contact with us and then tries to turn on his heel, to abandon us to our fate. "Look, you're cute, kid, but not cute enough for this weird shit," he says nastily. "And, frankly, I've got a lot more to live for, I think. I'm about to get promoted at work—"

I see the moment not-Marco makes its decision. It catches up to Marco impossibly fast, latching on to the back of his neck, hooking a long arm around it. I expect it to be quick, like Alexis getting hit by the Uber, but it's not. Marco tries to tear himself away, using more strength than not-Marco is expecting, and the thing loses its grip for just a moment before resnagging the fleece shoulder of Marco's Patagonia.

Marco pulls himself out of his vest, stumbling away and crashing into the wall of the warehouse. He leans there, breathing heavily, perfectly coiffed hair falling into his eyes as he pales, recognizing the seriousness of it all. Then he lunges at us. I'm not sure if he means to grab us to use us as a shield—very Alexis-core—or just to get past us so that we're closer to not-Marco than he is, but we force ourselves back, clinging to each other. Before Marco's fingers can do more than graze Malachi's vest, the fleece of his Patagonia reappears, obscuring his handsome expression and pulling taut around his head.

"Marco!" Malachi gasps, compassion overriding the current need for some goddamn sense. I grab him and drag him even farther back as Marco fidgets and fights against the thing's strength, limbs wheeling around, fingers tugging at the fleece that's wrapping impossibly tighter, suffocating him.

It's so horrifying, it takes a while to realize not-Marco is looking up at us through all of it, mouth open into a Glasgow smile as it pulls. Marco claws at his chest, but his yells are quieting to the whistle of blocked airways, growing more and more sluggish.

I look around, begging for someone to *notice*, to *help*, but it's Bushwick, early-ish on a Saturday night; and by the train tracks, it's a little more deserted.

There's nothing either of us can do to help. I harden myself as the panic in Marco's body gives way to stillness and he slumps over, limbs drooping. Finally, not-Marco releases its hold and Marco's body drops to the ground in a lifeless heap. His eyes are glazed and wide, popped blood vessels contrasting the green of his irises. Not-Marco shudders, hunching over the body, and reaches for the man's pockets. With two fingers, it pulls out Marco's phone. An iPhone. It looks at it, baring its teeth oddly at the screen, like it's not sure the kind of expression one needs to make one seem human. Still, I hear the soft click of an iPhone unlocking, and the thing scrolls once and then croons.

Not-Marco flashes the screen at us. It looks like a dating app. And at the top are Marco's messages with Malachi.

It feels like déjà vu as not-Marco tilts its head back and opens its mouth abnormally wide just to drop the phone down its gullet like the most indulgent meal it's ever had the pleasure of consuming.

We don't stick around to see if it wants another course. Instead, we run, *fast*, faster than either of us ever has before, and we don't look back.

On the subway we don't get a second look. Who's paying attention to two gay Black kids, covered in body glitter, smelling like sweat? No one.

I sit in the corner seat, staring ahead for two stops. Neither of us says a word; we simply exist, until finally, Malachi whispers, "We just watched a finance bro get killed with his own Patagonia

117

vest. And then that *thing* ate his phone, and my messages with it. Devon . . . what the hell is going on?"

I turn immediately. "Last night I nearly got murdered by that thing. . . . I think it's a demon. It killed Alexis, when it was trying to kill me. And now it just tried to kill you."

I wait for Malachi to laugh it off. To do the same as Drew and doubt me. To do the same as Leila and pity me.

He stares ahead for a long minute, rubbing his shoulder and wincing. His fingers come away tacky with blood, and his nose wrinkles as he wipes them on his pants. He stares at them for a long minute, the five crimson streaks.

Then he looks me in the eye and says, "Girl, *fuck* you. Team meeting."

CHAPTER NINE

*T*eam Meeting" is not a phrase to be used lightly, especially not in our group chat. It's a phrase we've used only four times before— the first time being the false alarm that was Leila's parents potentially selling their brownstone and moving away in middle school. The second was the day that Malachi came out—which led to me coming out and then being accused of stealing his thunder. The third, the day of Mr. Thompson's funeral.

The fourth time wasn't long ago at all—the day I found out that Drew was graduating early. It was the first time one of us had been excluded from a team meeting, namely Drew. My breakdown had been one for the books. Before, Drew's eventual greatness was only that—an eventuality. Now, she was ready to graduate. Ready to *leave*.

My friends consoled me that we'd always have summers, at least parts of them. But to them, Drew *was* only summers. And the occasional weekend during the school year, but those had become fewer and farther between. Now I knew that was because she'd been studying extra hard, taking on extra coursework to graduate early.

Drew was going to go out and keep achieving, keep moving forward. What if she didn't come back for summers? I had to make this last one so memorable, she'd never want to miss another.

And now a supernatural demon was going to fuck it up.

Hence the need for this fifth team meeting.

Team meetings always take place at Leila's, like the first time, so I buzz the Benadys' alarm and speak into the intercom: "Uh, Dr. and Mrs. Benady, it's me and Malachi. We know Leila isn't back yet, but we wanted to go into the garden to wait for her. We won't be loud."

There's the muffled sound of movement over the intercom. I look over my shoulder and see Malachi is bouncing up and down on his toes, eyes flicking back and forth over the street like not-Marco will show up at any second. It could. It might. The threat of it makes the spit in my mouth dry up for a second.

Mrs. Benady's voice breaks through the terror as she says, "I heard from your mother this morning. Are you all right, Devon?"

Malachi hisses under his breath, "Mrs. Benady, just let us in."

I hush him violently and force a smile into my voice as I say, "Doing better. Think I just need to be around my friends." It's not exactly a lie.

Mrs. Benady tuts. "Of course. You know where the lockbox is. And if it gets too late, you kids sleep over on the garden level. The beds are made up."

Malachi falls into a squat immediately, fumbling for the lockbox in the dead flower bed that Dr. Benady always forgets to tend to. The code hasn't changed since it was set when we were twelve—1028, Leila's birthday—but we always ask anyway. When the lockbox clicks open, Malachi grabs the key and shoves it into the garden-level door.

The second we're inside, some of the tension leaks away. But even in the dark, I can see the black blood crusting in Malachi's teeth.

"Come on. Let's get you cleaned up," I say, voice going hoarse. Malachi clenches his jaw tight, keys tucked into a fist, but he nods. I grab his free hand, edging us past the too-nice navy velvet couches the Benadys keep in the basement. One of them is hiding what I'm pretty sure is a gnarly scorch mark on the precious wooden floors from Malachi and I fumbling a lighter. Once, hiding that mark was the biggest of our problems. It's nothing compared to our current situation, a murky thing that I still can't quite understand.

We crowd into the tight bathroom, all old tiles and pipework, and pull the chain to turn the light on. I hold my breath, expecting to see it in the bathroom with us, but no.

Just us, looking worse for wear.

Malachi's vinyl vest is ruined by three jagged tears in each shoulder. Through the rips, I can see welts and then a few places where the demon's claws had actually sunk into his satin brown skin. Malachi shrugs the vest off, throwing it immediately into the tiny waste bin, then soaks some paper towels with water and soap before pressing them tight to the wounds. He hisses.

"Do those hurt?" I ask stupidly.

"No, they don't," Malachi says in his sarcastic drawl. Then he frowns at his own reflection. "Yeah . . . yeah, they do. But it's fine. I'm fine."

I swallow. "It's . . . okay if you aren't. I'm not," I whisper. I wait for him to speak and can practically see the cogs turning in his head as he reckons with our new reality.

"I just wanted to go on a date with a cute boy," Malachi says helplessly. He's not looking at me directly, instead catching the line of my gaze in our shared reflections. He sounds *young* now.

We are both so *young*, and he seems to have finally realized it. "And he wasn't even interested in me. Then the guy that *was* interested in me wasn't so much interested as he wanted to . . ."

"Murder you," I finish.

"A demonic entity wanted me more than that guy," Malachi mutters. He runs a hand over his face and sighs. "This is hell to the self-esteem, isn't it?"

"Yeah," I say. He looks so vulnerable, and I swallow hard. "I . . . Do you wanna know why I was in the freezer when the thing came for me?"

Malachi raises an eyebrow. "Sure."

I take a deep breath. "Yaya came into the store. We were talking . . . almost flirting? I don't know. I'm sure she didn't see it that way. But then . . . Keith came in and was talking to her and they walked out together and the *first* thing Alexis said was how cute they were together. Like she is so . . . *was* so, oblivious, she literally didn't see how she was punching my heart into a pulp." The vulnerability of my confession flays me open and just brings me down lower into misery.

Malachi huffs and grips hard at the porcelain bowl. According to Leila and Malachi, my feelings for Yaya are visible from space; they think the only reason that Yaya can't see it is because it's hard to see the big picture when you're in the frame. It doesn't help that I've never been the most courageous person and I don't want to risk rocking the boat of our friendship any more than it already is from Drew's constant departing and returning.

Malachi mutters, "I never cared for that girl, you know. Her or her mama." And then he reaches an arm around my shoulders, pulling me tight against his side. I press closer, wrapping my arms around his waist and hiding my face in his neck, avoiding his wounds, as I tremble with the need to cry or not cry, I'm not sure which. Everything is tangled inside me, but Malachi is here. He bends down, pressing a kiss to the top of my head.

"It's all right. We're . . . alive," Malachi says, like he's not clear on that fact. Then, a little surer, he repeats himself. "We're alive."

We shuffle out from the bathroom to the backyard, refusing to untangle from each other until we get outside. The small span of green has always been an oasis for us in the middle of all the concrete. The green grass below the brick and wood deck is where I learned to do my first cartwheel, where Mrs. Benady had shown me how to hook yarn onto my crochet needle and make a slip stitch.

This is a safe place. If such a thing exists for us anymore.

We sit next to each other on one of the garden sofas to wait, ginger in our movements, overly careful with our limbs, and squint up into the dark, searching for stars but finding only the blinking lights of airplanes as they fly off in different directions, some to LaGuardia and others to JFK.

The rest of the group finally arrives together, the lightness of a night out clinging to them as they giggle their way in. I can hear Gael needling at Yaya and her slyly poking back. I'd usually laugh, to make sure she knew that *someone* heard her passive-aggressive jokes, the ones that are so dry, you might not be able to tell unless you were looking for them. But right now I don't feel much like laughing.

And when they come out onto the deck and take us in, their humor drains away.

"What . . . the *fuck*?" Leila breathes in horror as I lift a hand in greeting.

She drops her book bag on the brick patio with a thud. She and Yaya fling themselves into action, rushing down the deck stairs to meet us. But Drew stays up there, frozen in place. She's looking at me, but not. More like she's looking through me. Yaya steps into my line of sight before I can think any more about it, placing her hands on my shoulders, and then frantically dragging them up my neck until she's cupping my cheeks as she kneels in front of me.

If the context wasn't so traumatic, it'd be kinda romantic.

"Oh my God, Devon, are you okay?" Yaya rasps, brown eyes so big and wide and glowy. "I should've known you weren't when you didn't answer my texts, and I . . . I . . . I shouldn't have gone to the movie. I should've checked in with you." She wraps her arms around me tightly, drawing me into the warmth of her, and I sink in immediately, tucking my face into the curve of her neck. My need for tactile comfort trumps the no-touching-Yaya rule. That's all out the window now like every other law of the universe.

"What happened?" Drew finally croaks.

"What happened?" Malachi echoes from where Leila is checking him over. "What happened is that you should've listened to your sister when she told you that she was attacked by some weird-ass demon creature."

Leila stills. "Holy shit, what?"

"Yeah, holy shit, *what*? What did I just walk into?" Gael demands. He finally takes us in, frowning. "Dude . . . you look like you were literally mauled."

"Because I *was*, jackass," Malachi snaps. "I was mauled by a demon. Keep up."

"Okay, we need to run this all back." Gael leaps from the

deck, right past Drew, and falls into a squat in the middle of the bricks next to the firepit. He looks weirdly somber, and I know it's because of the text. Team Meetings are maybe the only thing Gael takes with the utmost seriousness besides horror movies. "First: Are you all right?"

I think about lying, but Malachi answers too quickly. "No," he blurts out. "No, I'm not all right at all. I was attacked by this thing that looked like my date but *wasn't. And* it was trying to kill me."

Gael nods slowly and then looks at me, waiting. Yaya's arm is still wrapped around my shoulders, keeping me close to the curve of her body. She looks down at me, nudging my temple with her forehead, and I dig my fingernails into the bare skin of my thighs, trying to grab hold of my bearings. *This isn't like the last time*, I remind myself. This time I'm not the only person alive who's seen it.

"No," I confess in a shivering whisper. "What Malachi said is true. The same thing attacked me and killed Alexis last night."

Drew lets out a ragged sound that makes me look up. She is still holding herself stiffly as she takes measured steps and then sits primly on the edge of one of the deck chairs. But then she looks me in the eye and says, "You said something about being attacked last night. By a thing. And I . . . discounted you. Tell us again. Everything. From the beginning. And we'll believe you." *I'll believe you*, she doesn't say.

She doesn't say, *I'm sorry*, either.

Even still, I force myself to recount the terrifying encounter from the night before again. It's not easier, per se, talking about it for a third time. The first time with the police, it was all too fresh, and I couldn't process it. The second time felt even more like an interrogation than the first. Repeating myself for a third time makes it feel more real, even though it all seems so distant in the face of our newest encounter. I go into detail this time, about the way it stalked us around the store, its gaze trapped on me. How it was shaped, how it moved.

"What did it do after Alexis got hit by the car?" Drew asks.

I frown, staring down as my fingers curl into my palms. "Just kinda kneeled over her. Looked at me, I think, but it had big black eyes with *no* pupils." Then I remember the weirdest part. "And it, like . . . ate some of her hair," I finish flatly.

Gael looks up, a little more alert now. "It ate some of her hair," he repeats. "And Malachi . . . how did you get away from the demon?"

Malachi folds his arms. His lip curls over his teeth, and there's still a bit of black staining them. Gael's eyebrows rise as he catches sight of it too.

"Well, first, it disguised itself as my date to try and *entrap* me. And then when we finally got away from it, my actual stupid date followed and then it suffocated him with his Patagonia fleece," Malachi says.

"It . . . *what*?" Yaya rasps.

"Patagonia fleece?" Leila adds, unhelpfully.

Malachi shakes his head. "It suffocated my finance bro date, Marco—hence the Patagonia—before I even got a chance to meet him. And then it ate his phone, like Alexis's hair."

"I don't think you ever would have," I blurt out. "Met him, I mean. That's what he was trying to make excuses for. I saw him come in and start . . . like, flirting with some white twink at the bar. Who also seemed . . . suspiciously young."

Gael shakes his head like a wet dog and then jumps to his

feet. It's a sudden movement that startles us into a disquieted silence again.

"Okay, wait, so it suffocated your date? And then . . . ate his phone. For real?" Gael asks. Malachi rolls his eyes, but Gael isn't playing. He grabs his shoulder and then frowns when Malachi winces. "Sorry, man, but this is, like, of the utmost importance. Did you see what was on the phone?"

Malachi leans back, giving Gael a wary stare. "Uh . . . yeah. The thing showed us because it was being a prick. It showed me our messages."

Gael blinks and then he claps his hands to his face, shoulders shaking. For a minute I think he's weeping from how crazy it all sounds, but then he throws his head back and lets out a deranged howling laugh.

"Yo, shut up. Do you want to wake my parents? Or worse, my *neighbors*?" Leila scolds.

Gael stuffs his fist into his mouth, bouncing up and down, shaking hard.

"He's lost it," Malachi whispers absently.

Gael spits his fist out. "No, I haven't. This is just . . . This is fucking *incredible*. This is absolutely beyond my wildest dreams."

"You dream about me and Devon being *attacked* by a wannabe Slenderman?" Malachi retorts.

"No, asshole, *us*, as a collective, being stalked by a demon." Gael spins around and pumps his fist in the air, far too giddy for someone who has seemingly just declared that Malachi and I aren't the only targets of a malevolent supernatural force.

"Oh, so we're not special?" Malachi asks sarcastically.

Gael shakes his head. "Sorry, my friend, but no. This is a

group project," he declares. He turns to all of us, tilting his head. "Do you really not get it?"

Yaya quietly says, "Gael, no. We're not . . . You're not . . . It doesn't make sense?" She says it so apologetically. It's the kindest way anyone has called someone an idiot. Like, ever.

"Explain it to us like we're four," Leila commands.

Gael throws himself stomach-first on the couch.

He looks at each of us before his gaze stops on me. "It went after Devon first. But it got Alexis. And it ate her hair. Her *blonde* hair. Malachi's date was a gay finance bro, and it ate his *dating messages on his phone*. It's *Read Your Rites*."

Drew's eyes fly open. "That stupid B movie you made us *pay* to see?" she demands.

"Yeah," Gael rasps. "The same one that your *little boyfriend's* mom consulted on. The one featuring that little athame and Ouija board you found so funny. I *told* you that we shouldn't mess with that shit, Drew."

"You've got to be joking," Drew says, voice flat. "You can't seriously believe—"

"I know that you're all logic, but the evidence—the facts—don't lie, Drew. Your sister and Malachi were attacked by something that cannot be explained by our normal reality. The closest explanation is the only visible connection. *Read Your Rites* is about a group of friends, a late night in a ski lodge, a Ouija board unleashing something. Said something follows them down the mountain, killing them one by one and collecting trophies to gain power and get back home to its hellscape." Gael sounds more excited than he has in *weeks*, like he's in the frenzied midst of storyboarding his latest short film.

"And you think that's happening to . . . us?" Yaya asks.

"Yeah, I do. Except with us, it was a party in Carroll Gardens and that *thing* followed us to Crown Heights. We've only done *one* thing out of the ordinary, and it involved a weird-ass knife, a Ouija board, and white kids who play too much," Gael says. "No offense, Leila."

"I'm Jewish," Leila says flatly.

"You're still white."

"So are *you*."

"I'm actually mestizo—"

"That is beside the point," Malachi bites out. His eyes are narrowed on Drew. "I warned you, *Andrea*."

Drew's mouth falls open. "Well, it's not my fault."

"Isn't it?" I don't realize the words are going to come out of my mouth until they already have. I shift underneath Yaya and meet my sister's eyes. "You said it was going to be fine. That it was no big deal."

"No, *you* did," Drew pushes back. "You said 'demons aren't real.'" It's always uncanny, when she mimics me, down to the rattling cadence of my sure-unsure voice. It's like looking in a fun-house mirror, hearing my own voice echo in my ears.

I don't know what to say to that because she's right. I'd dismissed the tightness in Malachi's shoulders, the way Yaya had clutched her rosary, and Gael's warnings. I'd ignored the way Leila was swaying, almost hiding behind the others, when she was not the type to hide. All because I wanted to be down. I wanted to show Drew and her friends that I was cool. That I could be cool. With all their weird shit.

And look where it's led us. Here.

With a demon haunting us and Drew still not on my side.

"Throwing blame won't solve anything," Yaya says, forever the sensible one. She sits up, and I immediately miss the weight of her arm around me.

"There were other people there, though. Why did it attack *us*?" I ask. "Why *me*?"

Gael shrugs. "Drew co-signed it, and Devon . . . you're the one who let it in."

The stark reminder of my own words makes me freeze up—"Come to me." So Alexis's death really is my fault. It's *all* my fault.

Gael continues, ignorant of my thundering train of thought, "Also . . . well, Devon . . . you're blonde."

I startle, stopping my spiral. "What?"

Gael's grin is positively wolfish. "Come on, Devon . . . the blonde dies first."

"Oh, *fuck* you," I spit out.

"No, thanks for the offer, though," Gael says, ignoring the absolute disgust that rolls off me. Then he points at me, even though he knows how irritating I find being pointed at. "The opening kill in *Read Your Rites* was blonde. She was played by that actress. Not Maika Monroe, she's too good for that movie, but sort of like her. Anyway, after that, the movie followed the standard kill order."

Malachi snorts. "And that was?"

"The Black guy who was queer coded. Sorry, man."

"I'm not *coded* anything," Malachi bites out.

Gael rolls his eyes. "Dude, I'm talking about *Read Your Rites*. You're just, like, the representative of the trope for the purposes of this exercise."

"I thought it was the Black guy who always dies first in these things?" Drew says.

Gael shakes his head. "Complicated question. Statistically, on the surface, it's untrue because you have to take into account how few Black men actually appear in horror films. But when you look at the proportion that die first when they *do* appear, it's easy to see where the misconception emerged from—"

"Okay, okay," Leila says, flapping her hand. "So, Malachi is the Black gay kid. Why does any of this even matter? Like, Gael, not to burst your bubble, but this isn't a movie. Why is a demon following a movie *kill order*—"

Gael groans, shaking his head with the drama of an award-winning actor. He sighs, then rolls into his squat again to look at each of us.

"Amateurs," he declares, like we're the stupid ones. "This demon is rooted in the real world. *Read Your Rites* was based on real lore. Something about the Middle Ages or whatever. Sure, it was exaggerated and messed up because that movie is shit, but you heard Avery: his mom was the consultant. The demon is following a movie kill order because real life *is* the basis of the horror movie." He lingers on it, holding his hands up and shaking them like jazz hands. Oh my God, we're supposed to be impressed.

"Holy shit," Leila rasps.

Gael nods, grinning. "It's so rad—"

"Now, hold on," Drew cuts in. Gael glowers, put out by the interruption. "If we're being hunted, then why aren't Devon and Malachi dead?"

"Do you want us to be?" Malachi asks coldly.

"Obviously not," Drew retorts. "But the question still stands."

"For being the genius, you're not very bright, Drew," Gael sighs. He ignores her pointed middle finger. "Oh, it's so nice being the expert for once. *Obviously*, they're still here because the demon collected stand-ins for our darling Devon and Malachi."

"A stand-in?" I repeat.

"Tell me, Devon, what color was Alexis's hair?" Gael asks. I still, thinking of the blonde strand under my fingernail this morning. Gael doesn't give me any time to answer, though. He turns to Malachi. "And your date? Gay, I presume?"

Malachi huffs. "We didn't get into specifics—"

"So, let's assume what the demon assumed. He was gay," Gael says. He rubs his hands together, looking around wildly. "And it collected trophies from each of them? The hair. And a phone."

"Yes," I confirm slowly. "You think it wants to go home? We told it to go home. Remember, at the party."

"Why would it listen to you?" Gael demands. "You already let it in. Now it needs to find its way home through the only way it knows how."

I resist the urge to say "we," even if I'm pretty sure it was a group effort. "And to do that . . . it needs to collect something from us. In that order?"

Gael grins. "Two down. Three more to go."

"Three?" Yaya says breathlessly. "But . . . there's four of us left."

Gael nods. "Exactly. Next is the asshole—yours truly. Then the nerd," Gael says, and he sends Drew a lofty look. She just gives him two middle fingers this time. "The independent kid. Leila." He walks right past her and kneels in front of Yaya and me, setting a hand on Yaya's knee, a little more serious now. "And then. There's you."

"Me?" Yaya whispers.

"Can't you see?" he asks with a tiny smile. "Come on, Yaya. It was always going to be. You're the Final Girl."

READ YOUR RITES
FROM WIKIPEDIA

Read Your Rites is a 2023 supernatural teen horror film written and directed by H. A. Nahr. It stars Victor Check, Michaela Torrance, Carrie Starling, Francis Dua, Chandra Kapoor, and Damien Armitage as a group of friends being pursued by a demon accidentally summoned during their brief vacation in a ski lodge. Despite their attempts at survival, a culling occurs as the demon collects its victims—and their totems—as keys to its entrance back to the dimension from whence it came.

Self-proclaimed as a well-researched and historical portrayal of a demonic haunting, *Read Your Rites* was jointly written and promoted by Nahr and Dr. Diane Spring, a senior curator at the Museum of Metropolitan Art. Spring's focus on the iconography of the Middle Ages lent itself to Nahr's thematic interests, and Nahr hoped that this would be the beginning of a long association building a franchise. In reality, Spring's work was heavily critiqued by contemporaries and critics alike as losing sight of historical accuracy and contextualization in favor of bolstering more cliché elements of the genre.

The film premiered at SplatterFest 2022 before being picked up for distribution by Boogieman Productions. It received generally negative reviews for the writing and special effects, though praise was directed toward the cast's performances. It was ultimately a financial failure, grossing $10 million against a $12 million budget.

CHAPTER TEN

F inal Girl?" Yaya whispers to herself. She seems more frightened of the title than the potential demon that might be pursuing us. "What makes you think that's *me*? And not, like, Leila or Drew or Devon?"

Gael shakes his head. "Well, it clearly can't be Devon; she was already attacked. Drew absolutely fits the bill on the nerd trope. Genius that she is." He somehow makes the title "genius" sound derogatory, and I hate the thrill I feel about it. "And let me tell you, Leila is no Final Girl."

Leila scoffs. "And why *can't* it be me?"

"Final Girls are three things—smart, sober, and above *all* . . . virginal. Which you aren't," Gael says, waggling his eyebrows.

Leila barks out a laugh and nods. "Touché."

"I smoke weed," Yaya says bluntly.

Gael waves it off. "The definition gets wider with modern Final Girls. Yaya, well . . ." He trails off and we all get it. She fits.

"But . . . someone else died instead of Devon. And then that guy died instead of Malachi," Yaya says, voice trembling with a quiet desperation. "So, it's not a one-to-one fit. It could be someone else."

"We can't have a stand-in for the Final Girl. She's the only one who can finish it off. The last one standing. The girl that gets the killer. Or in this case, demon. If you're gone, that means game over, the demon's won. But as long as you're standing? There's a chance for us," Gael says emphatically. He's all lit up and frantic with his excitement, but Yaya's face drains of color, clearly not sharing his enthusiasm. She stands suddenly, wrapping her arms around herself, shaking her head.

I reach up to grab her wrist, but she's already tottering forward, mumbling, "It can't be me. I'm not . . . I *can't*."

Before Gael can insist again, she stalks away, stumbling through the back garden door and then shutting it behind her.

"Was it something I said?" Gael asks.

Malachi scoffs. "'Was it something I said,' he asks." He pushes himself up off the couch and sighs. "Should I go talk to her?"

"I think she needs a gentler touch," Leila says, shaking her head. "Devon?"

I startle.

"What are *y'all* gonna do?" I ask.

Drew sits up. "Plan. Gael, get over here," she commands, pulling out her phone, ready to activate her note-taking superpower. It's so easy for her to put aside her panic in favor of doing something productive. She believes so strongly that she can outsmart anything, I doubt she's worried at all.

Leila sidles closer, which gives me an opportunity to ask, "Are you trying . . . ? Are you trying to wingman me? Right now, Leila?" I say it under my breath to keep from attracting everyone else's attention.

"Dude, no," Leila says. Then she squints. "Kinda."

"*Leila.*"

"Only kinda! I also think that you are the best person to talk to Yaya right now," she insists.

I set my jaw and nod once, looking into the living room. There's no reason for this to seem more daunting than punching a demon in the throat, but it is. I leave Gael and Drew to their planning, trying my best to ignore the unshakable weight of Leila's eyes.

Yaya is curled up tightly in the corner of the L-shaped couch, strategically positioned so that she's not visible from where the chairs are on the deck. She's not crying, at least. But she's mindlessly scrolling through her phone, not even bothering to look at the screen.

I slide open the door and slip inside, my stomach twisting violently. It almost makes me feel normal again, the intensity of my feelings. She looks up at me, and her expression is *lost*. I've never seen her so unsure.

I don't know what to say immediately and neither does she. So I shut the door behind me and take an uneasy step as she finds the words.

"Two days in a row you've almost died. Can you at least *try* to stay out of trouble, Devon?" she asks with a weak smile. Her attempt to make a joke out of our circumstances falls miserably flat, but I laugh. For her.

"I could, but I won't," I say, sitting down on the edge of the couch, leaving at least a cushion and a half of space between us. "Plus, I think Malachi was really the one in danger this time around."

"Right," Yaya whispers. "Gael has to be wrong, right? About all of this? Especially about me?" She ignores my self-imposed attempt at space, edging closer, her eyes so big and round and *wanting. Me?* God, I wish it was me. But what she actually wants is an answer. Yaya has never needed the feel of a reassuring shoulder or hand to steady her—her balance is too good—but this has finally knocked her off her axis.

I frown. "How could he be wrong about you?"

Out of everything that Gael has said tonight, Yaya being the Final Girl—the heroine of our story—is the only thing that *has* made sense to me.

"I mean . . . God help us if I'm the hero . . . protagonist or whatever. I'm not. . . . I'm not anything. I'm not a genius like Drew. Not headstrong like Leila. Not *brave* like you." Yaya laughs to herself. She doesn't even seem to notice when I mouth the word "brave" to myself—it's not something I'd ever describe myself as.

She's so close now, her knees pressed against my thigh. "I'm just a neurotic perfectionist with dreams that are too big and too high. You can't vanquish a demon with a pirouette. I'm not *built* for this."

"Who *is* built to be stalked by a demon?" I retort.

Yaya seems surprised by the question. "What?"

"I'm being serious. Tell me exactly who would be the perfect type of person to kill a demon?" I push back, and Yaya's mouth opens and closes several times. "You can't. Because this is not something that *happens* to people. It's something that happens in Gael's shitty movies, and we just happen to be living in one. You can't prepare for that."

Yaya crumples like wet paper and I want to let her dry, smooth her out, make her feel whole even if she's a little tattered. But she does it herself. "Here I am freaking out about something that's a *theory* when you're the one who was *actually* attacked by a demon. If there's anyone with the grounds to freak out, it's you," Yaya says.

"I don't think there's a competition in who deserves to be more freaked out by a demonic stalker," I say patiently.

Yaya frowns. "I think there can be when you've *actually* been attacked. You and Malachi."

"Look . . . Yaya, I know this is scary. Like, I *know*," I emphasize. "But you're gonna get through this. Because the Final Girl *never* dies."

Yaya flinches, and then suddenly she's closer, too close, and I can make out the fractals of browns and greens in her hazel eyes. "But what about you? And Malachi. And Leila and Gael and Drew. What happens to all of you?" she asks.

And here lies the root of the problem. I should've known that Yaya's preoccupation rests in our safety. Because if Yaya is the Final Girl, it means she's the only one left, alone. And if she's alone, it means that we're . . . that we'd be . . . no.

I don't know what to do with my hands so I grab hers in mine. She startles but doesn't pull away. I turn one of her hands over and look at the lines of her palms, tracing them as I try to refocus my thoughts into something that would help her.

"Nothing. That's the great part—this may be following a movie, but it isn't one. We're . . . We're all going to make it through," I say, mustering up as much confidence as I can. Yaya looks at me, hope beginning to overpower all the doubt. "You are . . . a bit neurotic. And you push yourself too hard. And you *really* don't spend enough time celebrating your wins. Always on to the next thing with you. But you also take care of us. You always remember what snack I like. And you're the one who started the whole accompanying Malachi to his dates thing, which probably saved his life tonight. You did that. The Final Girl is the glue that keeps us together. And we won't let you fall apart either."

Yaya's hands tighten around mine, so much that I start to lose feeling in them, and then she tips forward to hug me, pulling me tight. "Thanks, Devon," she murmurs against the shell of my ear.

I hug her back immediately with a quiet "Always, Yaya."

When she pulls back, I force myself to jump up off the couch, taking three steps back toward the door. With each abrupt step back, I find it easier to breathe, to not try to lean in and kiss her like an asshole. As if that would be the answer to her distress. "Now, let's go make a plan with the others."

Yaya stares up at me for a beat, expression more opaque than ever. Then a wry smile finally twists her mouth. "Okay, let's make a plan."

CHAPTER ELEVEN

*W*e actually do spend the night together. None of us wants to split apart, not even Drew, so we pass on the guest beds and pile together like puppies, stealing each other's warmth, all hidden behind the couch. Like that would be enough to throw a demon off the scent.

Even still, it's a full night's sleep. Fear doesn't quite touch me when I'm surrounded by the people who make me feel strongest.

In the morning Dr. and Mrs. Benady don't even notice that we're jittery or quiet. That makes sense; Leila's always been the most latchkey of us all, super self-reliant. They don't pry too much with her, so they don't with us, either.

It's Yaya's mother who senses that something is off, and only because Yaya takes the morning off from practice. When we swing by so Yaya can explain in person, it takes an extra twenty minutes for Yaya to convince Ms. Betancourt that everything is good, and even then she still squints at us, suspicious, from the window of their third-floor walk-up as we head to our first stop on the journey to destroy a demon.

"Listen up, kiddos. Keep vigilant," Gael says. Despite being the next one up, he's the only one thriving in the face of our new reality, mouth curled into a shit-eating smile, sunglasses tangled in his loose curls. He walks backward, leading us like we're lost ducks.

I feel a bit like one.

"It's broad daylight," Malachi says stiffly. He's wearing a sweatshirt with shorts today, even though it's scorching, to hide the welts and scratches littering his shoulders. He seems to be handling himself better than I did, already at least close to baseline.

"Yeah, but the movies are different now, man. You *can* die in daylight," Gael says.

Leila sneers. "Who gives a *fuck* about movies?"

Gael lowers his sunglasses very deliberately to glare at her. Then he looks over at me and Drew, and with surprising tact, asks, "How are you doing? You're awfully quiet."

"Fine," Drew says simply. She sounds so confident, armed with the first phase of our developing plan—information gathering.

In contrast, a plan has never kept me from being high strung, so I don't bother lying. "Gotta admit, I'm still kinda messed up over this." I gnaw on my bottom lip, keeping my eyes on the gum-ridden pavement. It's not like I'm even the target anymore. As the should-be blonde opening kill, I set the tone, but I don't matter much to the narrative. I should be more grateful that I've survived unscathed, but still, my fear for the others overpowers anything else. I'm both surprised and not surprised when Yaya links her arm with mine, leaving my skin tingling where it touches her.

"Don't be. I've got you," Yaya says. "We've got you."

Gael nods. "You hear that? The Final Girl's got us." If he notices Yaya's sudden tension at her newly appointed title, he doesn't say so. He turns his back, leading us to the subway. "Anyway, it's not like you're going to get attacked again. It's the ass-hole's turn." He flashes a cocksure grin over his shoulder.

"Is it bad if I want to see it happen?" Drew mutters under her breath.

"What is wrong with you?" I snap.

Drew looks up, shocked at my sudden aggression. "I wasn't being serious."

"Well, you *should* take this seriously," I warn. I *impress*. Because she didn't take me seriously before, and I still worry that Drew thinks it's something she can just find an explanation for or *solve* with her genius.

The idea of something being unsolvable doesn't fit into Drew's understanding of the world. She has always been teeming with factoids and corrections to the point of callousness. She was never one for make-believe games, not unless they drew from her "Learn About . . ." books. Now, here she is with something that she can't correct, with facts that do not fit, and she's reduced to deflection and *jokes*—Drew doesn't make jokes—to deal with the fact that this might be bigger than something she can tackle with her mind.

"We are all taking this seriously," Drew says slowly. Her face screws up like she's sucked on something sour, which means she wants to say something but can't quite figure out how to say it without being *Drew* about it. Ultimately, she decides not to say anything, instead moving past me and Yaya to walk side by side with Gael. "This better bear fruit, Gael. I can't believe we're going to *Midtown*."

The name itself sends a shiver up my spine. *Midtown*. Christ.

"It's Kips Bay," Gael deadpans.

"Also known as part of *Midtown*," Drew says, spitting it like a vile curse.

"Ooh, Keith isn't outside on the stoop for once. Move fast," Leila says.

Yaya's nose wrinkles delicately as Gael howls.

Malachi elbows him and says, "Stop. If he hears *you*, he's gonna sense us."

"He's not that bad," Yaya says weakly. She looks down at me for help, but I turn to stare straight ahead, mouth pressed into a firm line. Golden rule and all that. "Come on. Keith is *nice*, if like . . . overeager."

Yaya *would* describe him as nice. It's because he's never been anything but nice where she can see him.

"He is not *nice*. That goofy boy is an annoying, pretentious loser," Leila declares. "Thinks because he reads Faulkner and Proust and is an English major that it's not weird that he's always trying to find a reason to talk to you."

Yaya rolls her eyes, but at least she doesn't try to defend him further.

It's not even the worst part about him. The worst part is how he basically tracks Yaya like a *dog*.

"Also, remember how Mom *really* doesn't like his mother? They're a pair, Keith and his mom," Drew reminds her. It's enough that Yaya tilts her head in reconsideration. My mother likes just about anyone, so if she doesn't like someone, it's something serious.

As always, Gael hops the turnstile and then taps his foot while us law-abiding citizens pay to get through to the platform.

We crowd together, and I remember coming home just last

night on the opposite platform, huddled together with Malachi. I remember how no one gave us a second look despite us being ragged. Two Black kids who looked like we had gone through hell and no one had said a word.

I sigh to myself as we wait for the train. Today would've been a perfect day to ride the carousel at Brooklyn Bridge Park. And instead, we're going to find out how to kill a demon.

So much for the Best Summer Ever.

Freaks & Leeks isn't the kind of place I was expecting.

For one, it's cleaner than I imagined for a cult video store, which might make sense, since it doubles as a farm-to-table café, but really, food standards don't matter in a city like this. It's brighter, too, with big wide windows only partially obscured by the mannequins dressed as the serial killers of horror cinema's past. The most suspicious thing I see is that the blood on Michael Myers's navy-blue suit looks the rusted dark brown of real blood.

Still, it's weird that the goth anarchists dripping with safety pins and the clean-cut patrons of Kips Bay are all brunching here like they belong. Brunch is very un-Gael.

"Did you take us somewhere for *brunch*?" Malachi asks, voicing my confusion. "I thought said it was a video store."

Drew groans. "We're being haunted by a demon and Gael wants *brunch*."

Gael puffs his chest up. "No, I'm taking you to see the expert in all things horror."

"Thought that was *you*," Leila taunts.

Surprisingly, Gael doesn't take the bait. "All students have a teacher," he says, "and you guys say that I don't get down to basics enough."

"You get bogged down in the details. We don't need to know the originating movie for the first jump scare," Malachi says rather generously as Gael marches us right past the hostess, who salutes like she's seen him around a thousand times before. We shuffle past the tightly packed tables into the retail space, full of rows and rows of DVDs and, inexplicably, VHS tapes.

"So, it's a horror Blockbuster?" Drew asks.

"Physical media, Drew. It's the future," Gael says, his repeated mantra suddenly making more and more sense. "One day streaming is going to disappear, and boom, where will that leave us? Do you know what the world would be like if we lost *Killer Klowns from Outer Space*?"

Drew purses her lips. "A better one?"

Gael shakes his head. "You are so lost." He doesn't allow her to retort; instead, he scoots through the long, uniform rows until we reach the back of the shop, where a short counter separates us from the man behind it and a gallery wall of alternate horror movie posters. "Now, all of you, show some respect. This man's a legend."

"This man being?" Malachi prompts.

The man is not *old* like the title of "expert in the genre" or "legend" might suggest. He's maybe early thirties, actually pretty nondescript, with the only distinguishing characteristic about him being his crooked nose. My eyes would glaze over him in the street.

"What's up, Gael?" he says, leaning forward, elbows propped up on the table. He sounds even younger. "We don't have the tabletop space to accommodate six of you today, man. Unless you wanna wait the forty-five minutes?"

"Nah, we'll do to-go," Gael says.

Politely, Yaya whispers, "I thought we weren't here for brunch."

I'm not as polite when I add, "Can you be even a *little* serious, Gael?"

"Ugh, fine, we'll figure that out after," Gael groans. "Team, this is Jack Strode. He owns Freaks & Leeks, and he's also, incidentally, the one who helped me source my VHS of *Halloween*. Jack Strode, this is Team."

"What can I do for you, Team?" Jack Strode says.

"They've got a couple of questions about horror cinema," Gael says easily.

Jack Strode raises an eyebrow. "What would *I* know that you wouldn't?"

"It's more like they don't trust *me*." Gael purses his lips, casting us all judgmental looks.

For a moment we all look at one another, no idea where to start. I already know what happens when you tell people that you're being stalked by a demon with no evidence of that stalking to show—they don't believe you.

"We kinda want to know . . . the rules," Yaya says. "*I'm* not particularly well versed and I think Gael's knowledge might be a little advanced for me."

Leila pushes forward, cutting through Yaya's diplomacy. "Gael says a lot of bullshit. We want to hear it from the source."

If Jack Strode thinks we're a bunch of weirdos, he refrains from saying so.

"This your girlfriend?" Jack Strode asks. "Only a girlfriend would neg you that hard."

Gael and Leila's faces screw up in disgust.

"Ew," Gael says with a cringe.

"He *wishes*," Leila retorts. "Now, like I said, we want to know from the *expert*."

"You want to know the rules of horror?" Jack Strode asks with a light laugh. "What is this? *Scream*?"

"Suppose it is," Drew says, slightly too sharp. She forces herself to gentle her tone when she adds, "Suppose it's *Scream*, but it's 2024 and it's a bunch of kids from Brooklyn, and instead of Ghostface hunting them down, it's a demonic entity. What would the rules be?"

"Then first I'd say you're not in *Scream*. That's a slasher. You're in a supernatural horror," Jack Strode says, his tone suddenly authoritative.

"Are the rules different?" Malachi asks, leaning against the counter.

"Somewhat." Jack Strode steps back away from the register and points to the closest poster. I recognize it from the hazy memory of a sleepover: *Paranormal Activity*. "What kind of demon is it?"

"I didn't know there were types," I say flatly.

Jack Strode looks over at Gael like he can't believe the words that have left my mouth. As if with his eyes alone he can say, *This is what you bring into my store?* Gael simply shrugs like we're lost causes to the world.

"Yeah, there are types. Are we talking the typical Christian-based demon?" Jack Strode asks. He's got none of the frenetic energy that thrums through Gael at any given moment, but he does have that same *holier-than-thou-I-know-more* vibe that borders on insufferable. "Think *The Omen, The Exorcist, The Conjuring*."

"No, definitely not Christian demon. Think general hellscape demon. Not religiously affiliated," Gael jumps in. "But something that could, mayhaps, be summoned by way of, say, I don't know . . . a Ouija board?"

Jack Strode barks out a laugh. "Man, are you talking about garbage like *Read Your Rites*?"

"And if we were?" Drew questions sharply.

Jack Strode's laugh tapers off, and he holds up his hands in surrender. "No need to get upset. I'm just kinda shocked. That movie blows. Gael and I have talked about it," he explains. He sighs to himself, rubbing at his clean-shaven jaw. "Okay, so I get your *Scream* vibe a little now. *Read Your Rights* does function like a slasher, as in the fuckers die in a particular order, but it's foremost a supernatural. I have a beef with that, you know. Sure, they bragged about all the research going into the writing of the demon, but not everything has to be a subversion, especially if you're not going to *subvert* anything."

"I totally agree, man. It's like, horror is *in* nowadays, but nobody has any care for what came before. Art isn't created in a *vacuum*, and you're not original just because you haven't seen the classics. You know these fuckers have never seen *Possession*? The '81 one with Isabelle Adjani—" Gael rants. He just keeps going, not noticing the way Leila, Malachi, and Drew are all collectively losing their patience.

Before a blowup can occur, Yaya, gently but firmly, says, "Gael, please," before she turns to Jack Strode and asks, "Can we stay focused?"

He nods, taking it in stride. "So, for a shitty supernatural movie like *Read Your Rites*, rule one—"

"Don't have sex," Gael blurts out. "You have sex? You die."

Jack Strode raises an eyebrow. "Okay, yes, but again, this isn't a slasher, so that's like rule five. Rule one: You're dealing with a demon? Figure out how it got here and where it came from. You can probably kill it with something related to how it came to you. Like in *Read Your Rites*, the Final Girl managed to kill it with the athame because that's how it got tethered to their world. Demons are tied to their identity as much as you are to yours. Where you come from matters as much as where you're going."

It's hard not to let Jack Strode's words affect me. "Where you come from matters as much as where you're going." When I look over at Drew, she's already looking back at me, but for a different reason. Knowledge is her greatest weapon, and she knows where to arm up now. Drew's boyfriend is related to the resident expert in the demon that's haunting us.

"Okay, rule two?" I prompt.

"Your characters shouldn't go into creepy places. Liminal spaces. The demon wants to isolate, and it'll do what it can to divide and then get its victim somewhere alone," Jack Strode says.

Just like the demon posing as Malachi's date. If I hadn't been there to look out for him, eventually Malachi would have found himself alone and then strangled just like *real*-Marco.

"That sounds like common sense to me," Leila says.

Jack Strode nods. "It is, but fear . . . fear makes us all go a little stupid. A little *mad*." Leila doesn't know what to say to that, so he presses forward with: "Rules three and four: Don't go toward the loud sound and *don't* split up."

"That's a warning for you two," Malachi says, gesturing vaguely at Gael and Leila.

"Wait, why *us*?" Gael demands.

Yaya's mouth twitches. "The rest of us are Black."

"Fair," Gael sighs.

Jack Strode looks amused by our antics. Almost vaguely charmed. "Rule five: *Now* we're at the 'don't have sex' rule."

"That's so old-school horror," Drew says. We all look to her, wide-eyed. Drew has always been the one to *least* enjoy the movies that Gael makes us watch with him. "What? I did a lot of research last night."

"Yeah, it's old-school in *slashers*. This is a genre-bender supernatural horror meets slasher," Jack Strode pushes back. "So, it's not just no sex. Don't do drugs. Don't get drunk. Abstain from vice until the problem is over. Abstain from sin or you're marked."

I swallow hard. Aren't we already marked by no sins of our own except maybe being dummies?

"We said non-Christian!" Gael protests. He's holding on to his fanny pack for dear life, like Jack Strode is about to stop and frisk him.

But he shrugs. "It's America. Christofascism is all over the fabric of our society."

"Fine," Gael bites out.

"Don't worry. Weed isn't a drug," I say, patting his shoulder.

"Weed is absolutely a drug. No more smoking," Drew warns, pointing at the two of us.

Jack Strode snorts. "I meant in the movie."

We still. "Surrrrrre," Drew drags out the word like it's being pulled from the back of her throat.

"Anyway, the sex piece of things matters most for the Final Girl. I mean . . . someone always has sex. And then they die. It just can't be the Final Girl."

"Why not?" Yaya yelps.

Jack Strode shrugs. "You need her not *completely* mindfucked when her love interest dies in the third-act twist. Imagine: she's just being intimate for the first time with someone, and then *boom*, they're dead and it's probably her fault."

"What if there's no love interest?" Gael pushes back. "For anyone?"

Jack Strode sounds bored with the idea of a sexless horror movie and moves on.

"Okay. Final rule: Have faith," Jack Strode says.

"'Have faith'?" Yaya repeats. With her free hand, she's holding her newly repaired rosary like it's a lifeline.

Jack Strode nods. "Yeah. Have faith. I know, super simple, but, like . . . supernatural horror is at its heart about the lack of that. Faith. Christian or not. The thing is . . . demons are terrifying, impossible beings. Their rules don't work the same as our rules in this real world. So for it to work, you need the characters *and* the audience to have faith that the impossible—beating a demon—is *possible*. You need them to believe in the unbelievable power of the Final Girl. She's impossible. And if she is, you'll win in the end. And your audience . . . they will too."

Yaya is swaying into me, her weight resting on mine as she processes his descriptor of the Final Girl. It's like she doesn't think it fits her at all, when I can't picture anyone else when I hear it. None of us has the type of impossible strength that Yaya has. Her flaws—someone who pushes past endurance, someone who won't stop when sense says she should, someone who dances and goes for it until her toes bleed—only make it more clear, and I know that, even if she doesn't.

"Okay, but what if the 'Final Girl' isn't technically . . . final?" Leila asks.

Jack Strode frowns. "What do you mean?" he asks.

"What if it starts with the opening kills narrowly surviving or someone being sacrificed in their place? Does that change things?" Leila asks.

Jack Strode acquiesces: "Potentially. But if it does, sounds like it would be a *very* lame movie. More likely it'll come back around to anyone who makes it through at first, just to subvert expectations. Otherwise, where's the horror? Where's the suspense? The tension? How else will the Final Girl reach her full potential and actually take out the monster at the end?

"Unless there's already a green-lit sequel where their deaths will have more shock value?"

Malachi hisses through his teeth. "I'm sorry, sequel?" he blurts out.

"Everything's got a sequel or a reboot nowadays," Jack Strode says. "Nothing's ever really over. Hollywood's run out of ideas so they just remake their own IP over and over again, and the general populace eats that shit up. It's embarrassing." He sounds like all the nerds on Twitter that Gael circle jerks with through DMs and then regales us with their opinions like we care about the "state of cinema" or whatever.

"Respectfully, we're not interested in a sequel," Yaya says tightly.

Jack Strode nods sagely. "Tired of the corporate machine discarding art for dollars too?" he asks.

"Totally, man," Malachi drawls.

"Look, if the whole cast lives, then the perpetrator and all its associates—in this case, the demon and its affiliates, which may or may not include who summoned it—*need* to die or you're going to have a problem," Jack Strode says severely. "And even that might not stop a producer from pushing back. Look at *Paranormal Activity*."

Gael shakes his head. "That won't be a problem. This is a self-funded production." And then he looks at each of us as he declares firmly, "No sequels, no requels, and definitely no remakes. One and *done*."

CHAPTER TWELVE

"Well, that was bleak," Malachi says into the tense semisilence between us as we wait on the platform for our train back to Brooklyn. He takes a sip from his to-go coffee, courtesy of Freaks & Leeks.

"You think so?" Drew asks.

Malachi handles it better than I would. "Uh, yeah. He basically told us we were going to die and then sent us on our way with coffee and pastries."

"To be fair, they're, like, really good," Leila says. She's munching on an almond croissant, her mouth covered in powdered sugary goodness. Yaya passes her a napkin, which Leila does *not* use, instead choosing to wipe the back of her hand across her mouth and *then* smear it on the napkin. "Is this all baked in-house?"

"Yeah, Jack finally hired a pastry chef. I think mostly because she was an extra in the newest *Evil Dead*, though," Gael says.

I'm about to interrupt when something prickles in me. It takes a minute to place it as the same feeling from the night before in Délivrance. The same weird feeling on the back of my neck when I was in the freezer. I look up sharply, but across the platform there's only a harried woman with a writhing toddler strapped into a stroller and a tourist family who look lost.

"Let's focus up a bit," Drew says, calling everyone's attention back to her. "Jack Strode confirmed a lot of what I was thinking. I checked out a few books from Libby last night and spent all night reading about supernatural horror cinema and the genre. Most of the rules were basic common sense, and we have that in abundance. But the first rule about information being power? That resonated. In other circumstances, I would suggest that we watch the movie again and pore over it, but we can do one better. We can go to the source: Avery."

Her breakfast dangles from her other hand as she waves her phone screen. I focus on it and see it's open to her text thread with Avery, full of long sweeping paragraph exchanges. Avery's verbose texts don't surprise me, but *Drew's* do. I can't quite make out what they're talking about, but it's clear that she responds to each of his texts thoughtfully. The past few days are more threadbare, full of double and triple texts from him, with hours between where Drew doesn't respond. Finally, the last text is from her: **Can we talk?**

"I guess he *is* the one who summoned the demon. Accidentally or not," Yaya says.

"I think we should jump him," Malachi sneers.

"Him or the demon?" Leila asks.

"You can't jump a demon," I interject meaningfully.

"No one is jumping anyone," Drew says firmly. "I say we go to Carroll Gardens and ask him about everything. The athame, the Ouija board, the . . . demon."

"To Carroll Gardens, then," Yaya declares.

I hear the telltale rattle of a train. The prickling feeling grows and grows until it's less of a tickle and more of a *sting*. It actually feels painful, and every second I try to focus on my friends, it hurts more and my hindbrain howls that something isn't right. I fall out of the conversation and take a deep breath.

On the exhale is when I see it.

Directly across from us, on the opposite platform, is a figure, long and shadowy. The inky blackness of it is spreading, and my tunneling vision grows and grows. It opens its yawning mouth at me, human Chiclets teeth inked with pink.

My scream, torn and ragged, is lost in the screeching brakes of the train and the demon's scream.

Shockingly, Drew's belief in the existence of the demon isn't shaken after not seeing for herself *why* I'd been screaming bloody murder on the platform while they shuffled me onto the train car, out of the burning sight line of the demon.

I try to catch my breath, but my heart is thundering in my chest like I just ran a ten-mile race. "Does anyone have water?" Drew asks. She squeezes onto the seat next to me, ignoring the glare of the person she's basically just booted out of it.

"*Excuse* me," the man huffs.

"Fuck off. Can't you see we're having an issue?" Malachi hisses, gesturing at me violently.

I must look just as bad as I feel, because the man relents, but not without storming down to the opposite end of the car. Drew squeezes my wrist, drawing my attention back to her, while Yaya presses her water bottle to my lips and I take a long gulp that burns on its way down.

"Okay, five things you can see?" Leila asks.

"What?" I gasp, shuddering.

"It's how you calm down people having panic attacks, I think.

157

I don't know. I saw it on TV," Leila sputters, and I shiver so bad, I bite my lip hard, the taste of copper beading on the bruised flesh.

Yaya presses her hand to my mouth and says, "Don't do that." The heat of her hand against my lips makes me want to lean in and flinch all at the same time.

Things I can see. I look around, categorizing each of their reactions. Drew is careful about her expression, refusing to reveal a single emotion she doesn't mean to. Leila lets her worry show, her eyebrows drawn tight together. Gael has finally realized it's not a game; his grin is gone. Malachi is spooked, and I wonder if he felt it, even if he didn't see it. If he's marked like *I'm* marked. Then Yaya pulls my attention back. *Yaya.*

Against her skin, I mumble, "I—I see you five."

"Okay, good. Four things you can touch?" Leila prompts.

I look around. "The seat under me. The air-conditioning. Drew's shoulder. Yaya's hand," I say, finally drawing back from her touch, slumping against the chair. Each recounting does help me feel more grounded. Reminds me that I'm solid and that I'm *real*.

"Three things you can hear?" Leila asks.

My breathing is coming slower now, and the train is finally rattling along faster than the pounding of the muscle in my chest. That's good. That's *normal*. "Um . . . the train. My own voice. *Your* voice." Leila smiles at me.

"Two things you can smell?" Gael prompts.

I smirk and say, "Your breath. Also, someone has *awful* BO on this train."

"Fuck," Gael says, huffing into his hand and sniffing his own breath. "Hey, screw you. I smell extremely minty fresh."

"Anyone have gum she can taste?" Malachi asks.

Drew shakes her head and leans closer, blocking everyone else out. "One . . . more thing you see?" she asks.

I focus on her hard. "You. I see you."

"Maybe that should be two. We're identical," Drew says, mouth twitching.

"Okay," I agree, even if we aren't really. Not anymore.

Drew pats my knee and sinks back into the seat next to me, staring up at the ceiling of the train car. Someone's managed to scrawl across it in black permanent marker, the letters too bubbly to make out any of the words. "So, you saw it across the platform."

"Didn't you?" I demand.

Drew shakes her head solemnly. I look at the others, and all of them shake their head. Even *Malachi*, despite my hopes.

"Yes, but I felt it first. I think I've been feeling it. I thought . . . I thought I saw something in the park, when we were getting high before it had even come after me. I mean, I'm *sure* that was it, because it's this same feeling I got last night and the night before. Like something is *just* about to touch me, and then I get sick to my stomach, and then, I'm just . . . I'm so *afraid*," I admit, because it doesn't feel weak to say anymore. It's important that I say it out loud, give a name to the feeling that's rushing through my veins, more powerful than my hate for Keith, or my irritation with Drew, or even my crush on Yaya.

Fear.

"Why you, though? What is it about you that makes you the only one who can sense its presence?" Leila asks. She looks at Gael when she asks, "Wouldn't it make more sense for it to be Yaya?"

"Why *me*?" Yaya blurts out.

"Because you're the Final Girl," I remind her, hoping that saying it over and over again will help her believe it. "I'm nobody. I'm supposed to be dead. The opening kill."

"Maybe that *is* why you can sense it," Gael speculates, rubbing at the nonexistent hair on his chin. "You're, like, the exact opposite of Yaya. You were part of its emergence and you were supposed to die. But you didn't. Maybe that connects you."

I should probably be offended about how much he kinda sounds like he wishes I *had* died.

"Then how come she's the only one who can sense it?" Drew demands. "Malachi should too, by that logic."

Gael shrugs. "Look, I haven't even had the pleasure of meeting our demon friend. I can only make so many conjectures."

"Fine. We *have* to figure out the demon's backstory," Drew allows. She looks at the overhead map and says, "We can transfer to the F at Bleecker."

"Did he respond?" I ask.

"Not yet." Drew looks surprised by this, and I almost roll my eyes.

"You had sex with him, and then you basically stopped responding to his text messages. Then, out of the blue, you say that you need to talk to him."

"So?" Drew asks.

Malachi purses his lips. "So if I were him, I would've already blocked your number."

"Avery is my best school friend. He'll understand," Drew insists. She looks away and shrugs a single shoulder. "Besides, no matter how he responds, we need information, and he has it.

We're going, unless someone would rather put Avery's personal feelings over destroying the demon that is after all of us? Anyone?"

"You know *I* don't care about the fucker," Gael says. "But we can't just say, 'Oh, look, there's a demon haunting us and you're the reason why.'"

"Why not?" Drew demands.

"Because if he's anything like you, either he's going to call us crazy or, even if he really believes in all of this, he won't trust we're serious after how we reacted to it. Especially not after you broke his heart and he realizes you're just there to try to needle him for info," Gael says pointedly, and Drew looks up at the subway-car ceiling as if that'll help her. "I've got this, don't worry, Drew. Let's disrupt his peace."

Avery doesn't exactly shut the door in our faces when he sees us, but I can see that he thinks about it, long and hard. He takes us all in, faces that he'd only met in a drunken blur, before his gaze falls on Drew and hardens. He purses his lips, leaning into the doorframe, but doesn't say anything just yet.

He'll be waiting a long time if he expects an apology from Drew. She looks away quickly, lashes fanning her cheeks in momentary defeat, but sure enough, she doesn't say anything.

"Why are you here?" Avery asks finally. He's still looking at Drew.

Drew opens her mouth, and I can already see her need to be upfront being our downfall. Gael elbows her hard, masking it as a stumble, to remind her of our planned excuse, while Leila takes over. "We forgot some weed we stashed at your house. We were bored and we thought it would be funny. A joke."

161

"Well, I'm sure it's still around somewhere. No one's doing drug busts *here*," Avery retorts.

Okay. Asshole.

"No one's doing drug busts where we're from either," Drew says sharply, finally speaking up. Avery winces, like he regrets his words, but doesn't apologize. "Look, we forgot our weed and we want it back. Can we not stand on your doorstep? Can you let us in?"

"Why should I?" Avery asks childishly, but he steps aside anyway and lets us through. His eyes follow Drew as she stomps into his home, the rest of us following on her tail like kindergartners.

Avery shuts the door behind us. He leads us into his kitchen, and everything looks bigger without the bodies of teenagers packed in like sardines. There's no lingering smell of alcohol or body odor or sick, just the clean smell of Pine-Sol, and maybe a load of laundry that has been freshly washed. I recognize the detergent smell from the Laundromat we used to frequent as a family. It's surprising how familiar the scent is in a space that is so unfamiliar. I look at Drew from the corner of my eye, wondering if she recognizes the scent too.

I sit up at the breakfast bar and Yaya sits next to me. Malachi makes himself comfortable leaning against it, as Gael and Leila stand in the corridor, like bouncers. It almost feels like we're trapping Avery, and the thought prickles. Not like it does when the demon is watching, but it still itches all the same. *We're not doing anything nefarious,* I remind myself.

Except preying on his complicated feelings for my twin sister to get access to information . . .

"Where'd you leave the weed?" Avery asks.

"Can't remember," Leila admits. "I went upstairs with someone for a bit, and then, I was so crossed. You know . . ."

"Well, our cleaning lady, Magda—you know Magda, right, Andrea—she's really thorough. She might've thrown it out?" Avery suggests. "How much was it?"

You know Magda, right, Andrea. Christ.

"An ounce," Gael says, pacing like a caged lion now. He looks over at Avery. "You mind if Leila and Malachi look for it?"

Malachi usually hates being volunteered for things, but he gives in easily now, standing at attention like a soldier called to battle. This is part of the plan too. The weed is a ruse and the primary reason we'll need to roam the house without restriction, to search for the very thing that brought the demon to us in the first place.

Avery nods. "That's fine." Malachi and Leila don't wait a minute; the two of them clamber up the stairs. Avery makes a move to the couch where Drew sits, before aborting the idea, instead standing taller and murmuring, "Can we talk?"

As if he doesn't hear the painfully obvious vulnerability in Avery's voice, Gael says loudly, "Yo, I was thinking about the Ouija board thing from the party. Wanted to apologize, man. I was such a dick to you about it all."

"Yeah, you were," Avery says wryly, "but I've been informed that's your default setting, so . . ."

"Touché," Gael says with an unbothered grin. He saunters over, and when his shoulder glances against Avery, one *could* call it an accident. But I *know* Gael. It's deliberate, and it's just enough to knock Avery off-balance enough that he lands on the couch next to Drew. "The Ouija board you used . . . any significance?"

"Nope. Ordered it from Amazon," Avery says. He probably thinks he's subtle, cutting a side-eye look over at Drew, but she's already staring right at him, catching him. I give him points for not sagging under the weight of her gaze.

"What about the athame?" I speak up. Avery looks surprised to hear from me.

"Oh, yeah. They made a prop athame for the movie, but my mom found the real one that inspired it in, like . . . the archives of the museum she works at," Avery says. Then he stills. "Andrea never told me you were into horror. Is it more the spiritualist aspect you're into?" He gets excited at that, leaning forward.

"Sorry, I'm not," I say, and then fumble to cover with, "I'm interested in curating actually. Your mom's a curator at the Met, right?"

"I see that for you," he says, even though we've never had a real conversation in our entire lives. "Yeah, she is. Anyway, unlike the one in the movie, that athame is the real artifact. Circa, like, 1350."

"That's right around the Black Death, right?" Drew says, sitting up taller.

Avery turns to look at her fully. "Yeah, that's right. That's part of its origin. To dispose of bodies during the Black Death, they burned them, but, uh, there were some physicians who were intrigued. They thought there was something in the body that could reveal the disease's genesis. So, at first, that specific athame wasn't used for spiritual stuff at all. It was for autopsies."

"A knife with purpose," Drew recites.

"That wasn't in *Read Your Rites*," Gael says.

Avery shrugs. Sourly, he says, "Dude, that movie got so many of the actual facts wrong. Even the demon was *wrong*. Hellscape? Give me a break."

"Maybe if the facts had been in there, the movie would've been better," Gael says generously. Avery takes the offering of peace with a tight smile. "So, how did the director turn your mom's research about autopsies during the Black Death into a demon?"

"That's kinda part of her research too. The physicians were curious, but they weren't careful. They were callous. When they cut up the bodies and couldn't find answers, they didn't burn them or bury them. They just . . . threw them in the River Thames like they were trash. Everyone in London knew, so they made up stories," Avery explains, and he sounds the same as he had that first night, when he'd accidentally—or maybe not so accidentally—summoned the demon in the first place. *Serious.* But, also, a showman.

"What kind of stories?" Yaya asks.

"That their bodies were desecrated and their souls were lost. All that malignant energy improperly disposed of meant a demon was born," Avery explains, as if this is common knowledge.

"What else did the legends say about the demon?" Gael demands, intrigued. If he could be taking notes, he probably would be. "How did it choose its victims? How did they get rid of it?"

"You've seen the movie. The demon follows the friends. People thought it was just tropey, no real reason to the order. But if you actually pay attention . . . it moved like an infection. A plague," Avery says. He waits for us to nod our understanding, but I don't think any of us gets it.

Before Avery can answer, though, Drew proves me wrong and speaks up in typical know-it-all fashion. "The demon infects the lives of the heroes, and it burns its way through them all. Like the plague spreading during the height of the Black Death. Isn't that correct? Starting with the person who invited it in and moving to the next person they were in contact with."

For a beat, Avery looks at her with the same awe he regarded her with the first night that I met him. Then his anger hits him all over again, and his hands ball into fists in his lap.

"Right as always, Andrea," he says, sounding resigned. Then he sighs and pushes himself up from the couch, looking around.

"Wait," Gael calls, when it looks like Avery might go looking for Leila and Malachi. "In the movie, the demon collected trophies. Why?"

"That's part of the stories too. That the demon would take things from its victims and get stronger. Those tokens, full of sad, malignant energy, just fed it. But my mom says that's the part that's probably not true. More likely that the physicians and healing women just stole from the dying," Avery says with a distracted shrug. Now that he's been reminded of Drew's presence, he keeps cutting a look at her and then away again.

"And the knife?" Yaya asks. "How does the athame factor into destroying the demon?"

Avery clears his throat. "Remember what I said? An athame is a knife with purpose. To cleave. To bring together. To split apart. The athame splits the souls apart. Puts them to rest, so the cycle is finished. The infection has been diagnosed and treated," Avery says. He folds his arms over his chest, biting his bottom lip. "Haven't they found the weed yet?"

"I'll text them," I say quickly. I shoot a look over at Yaya, one that's intended to say, *Keep him busy*. It's clear that I've sent the look to the wrong person by the way she looks back at me, absolutely bewildered by the unspoken directive.

DEVON
he's asking if you've found the weed.

LEILA
we're not done. we're in his mom's office.
looking for the athame.

My heart starts beating in my chest and I set my phone back in my lap. Gael looks down and I know he's read it too when he sucks his teeth, then looks up sharply and smiles over at Avery with a toothy grin.

"Leila says she thinks she split it up into quarters. Drunk Leila is an absolute idiot," Gael says easily, probably because insulting Leila does come easily to him.

"That's actually kinda hilarious," Avery says. I don't know him well enough to be able to gauge his sincerity. "Andrea, can we talk?"

I jump up, startling them both into looking over at me, and Gael frowns, raising an eyebrow.

"I think I just remembered where Leila hid the weed," I blurt out. "You two . . . talk. I'll go tell Leila."

Drew will agree, I'm sure, and that's for the best. She's more than capable of drawing out a conversation, so I don't worry about her. It's Leila and Malachi I worry about; they're taking too long.

Before Drew even has a chance to verbally agree, I rush up to the second floor and peer through open doors into empty rooms, searching for Leila. There's a bathroom, a guest bedroom, another guest bedroom, another—how many guest bedrooms does a family of three need?

When I stop at the fourth door and look around, it takes only a second to tell me it's Avery's room, though it isn't as extravagant as I thought it would be. If I didn't know better, I'd think he'd gotten his furniture from Ikea, for how little character it all has. His textbooks are what clue me in—I recognize them as the same ones Drew has, though his don't even have cracked spines. Avery doesn't seem dumb—my sister is not friends with "dumb" people—but he's clearly not as studious as Drew.

The room has the smell of a teen boy, despite how impeccably clean it's kept. There are a few photos of Avery as a child, but a more recent one catches my attention. It's a photo of him and Drew, in a group setting. She's tucked on one side of Avery, his arm thrown over her shoulder, Christophe's thirsty ass on the other side. Next to him is a brunette with a tiny button nose, bright green eyes, and dark hair, who looks like an actress from a bad teen drama on Netflix. Lydia, maybe? I didn't see her at the party, so she has to be the group's exile. Drew is absolutely beaming at the camera.

I don't have time for this. I stumble back, forcing myself up the next flight of stairs before Avery and Drew can come up behind me. I jump when I see Leila standing wordlessly on the next landing, one hand on a cocked hip.

"You're so nosy." Leila grins anyway.

"Did you guys plant the weed?" I demand.

"Of course we did. You came to 'help' Malachi find it?" she asks. "Or are you here to help me with our other mission?"

I nod. "The second one. Let's get the damn athame. Drew's gonna talk to Avery," I whisper. I can hear Drew's murmur getting closer and I dart up the next landing to meet Leila, grabbing her wrist, leading her up to the next floor.

"Good. About time she talks to her boyfriend," Leila mutters.

I glare at her. "He's not her boyfriend."

Leila tilts her head. "That's probably part of his problem, isn't it?"

I hear Drew's voice floating up the stairs.

"We can go talk in your room," she says. I should feel bad for eavesdropping, but it's not my fault, really. A flight of stairs in a brownstone is not *nearly* enough space.

"You *ghosted* me, Andrea," Avery says, and he sounds absolutely gutted, like Drew has personally taken the knife we're looking for and driven it through the soft flesh of his side. He lets the words linger in the air, like he's waiting for Drew to speak up, but she doesn't. Not right away. I know she's thinking about how to respond, but he continues. "I told you how I felt and you told me you felt the same, we had sex, and then you *ghosted* me for three days!"

I look over at Leila. She's wide-eyed as she mouths, *Brutal*, at me, before gesturing violently for me to creep up with her.

Avery might live in a brownstone like me and my family, but they couldn't be more different. There's something about Avery's home that *smells* new. The floors don't creak with age here, and the stairs aren't so close together like they are in Crown Heights. The dark wood has all been replaced with light wood, with modern details everywhere. One of my mom's most prized possessions in our entire home is the antique medallion and chandelier that hangs in the parlor, but I'm about 1,000 percent sure Avery's family hasn't kept a single original detail, even if his mom *is* a curator of historical artifacts.

Leila nods toward a half-open door, and I slide in with her. My shoulders are up to my ears as I push the door closed, waiting for the whine of hinges, but it never comes. There's only the softest click of the latch.

"Okay, where have you already searched?" I ask, looking around the room.

More light wood. Norwegian-looking bookcases filled with heavy, dark tomes. The massive work desk that occupies half the room is right in front of a wide window that overlooks the back garden, complete with a window seat of powder-blue crushed velvet. There's a single photo on the desk, in a frame the same sandy wood as every other surface. It's Avery and presumably his mom— they have the same freckles—and likely his dad in a ski lodge. His dad is still wearing obnoxious yellow reflective goggles atop his head, while his mom is in après-ski wear that looks fashionable but far less functional. Smart woman, staying off the slopes. Skiing is a one-stop shop for bumps, bruises, and breaks. At least, that's what I assume. I've never been, but the single time Drew had, she'd returned with a broken elbow.

"We think it's probably locked up in here," Leila says, tapping at something underneath the desk. She's squatting so I can see only the top of her head. I round the too-big desk and collapse to my knees next to her, squinting into the dimness.

It's a small, gray metal lockbox, the kind that might hold important documents like birth certificates and passports. It has one of those rolling locks, so not something finding a key could easily solve.

"What makes you think it's in here?" I ask, grabbing hold of it and shaking lightly. It doesn't make the soft whispery sounds of paper. No, it rattles, answering my question. Then Leila turns it upside down and I see on a tiny little peel-away sticker that's been haphazardly stuck to the bottom—PROPERTY OF THE METROPOLI-TAN MUSEUM OF ART—along with another sticker declaring BOOGIE-MAN PRODUCTIONS.

"That," Leila says smugly. "Now you see what was taking Malachi and me so long. We were trying to figure out the passcode. We went through all his mom's agendas and notes, but she doesn't take many physical ones, and there's *no* way we're getting access to her desktop."

"Where is he now?" I ask.

"He's wandering around the house, opening a ton of drawers and making noise to draw attention away from *us*," Leila says.

I bite my bottom lip and when resting in a squat starts to hurt, I fall back on my butt, crossing my legs. I pull the lockbox into my lap, racking my brain for an answer. The lock combination should be made of six numbers, which means practically an infinite number of possible answers. And I've never had the brain for math, except for counting stitches in a crochet project that I'm working on.

"Anniversaries, birthdays, and death dates," I rattle off. "Those are the most used combinations."

Leila huffs. "Well, I know *that*, genius, but I don't know the lady. For fuck's sake, I don't even know Avery's last name," she bites out.

"I do. It's Spring," I say. Leila looks at me for a long time, and I feel the need to blurt out, "She's cited on the Wikipedia page for *Read Your Rites*. When is Avery's birthday?"

"No idea," Leila sighs. She's looking down at her phone, thumbs moving fast across the screen. She looks up like she can sense my exasperation. "I'm Googling wedding records, dude. That's public record."

I nod. "Okay, but go on Insta after. Look through Drew's page, what she's tagged in. Maybe someone's posted something about one of Avery's birthdays?"

"Oh my God, so true," Leila rasps. "It'll probably be a few days off, but I'll find something."

As she works on her phone, I lie down flat on the ground, pressing my ear to the wood, hoping that I might be able to catch even a whisper of the conversation happening in the bedroom below. If I close my eyes hard enough, I can picture it—Drew and Avery sitting side by side on the bed. It's probably the bed they had sex in, which . . . gross, but Avery is probably pouring his heart out to her, telling Drew about all the things that he finds so great about her.

Wait, not Drew. The things he finds great about *Andrea*. It makes me even more curious about what he's saying. Because I don't know Andrea, not like I know Drew. I'm not even sure how similar they would be. Would *Drew* ghost Avery the way she did? Or is that more of an Andrea thing? Will she ghost us, too? As soon as the demon's gone, will she be spending her Best Summer Ever with him?

"Don't call me Andrea," she had said so emphatically to Gael. He didn't have permission. None of us did.

Not to call her "Andrea" or to know all of her either.

"Hello?" Leila sings, snapping at me. I sit back up, nearly

cracking my head on the underside of the desk. "We don't have time for you to have an existential crisis."

"I'm *not*," I whine, even though I am. "Did you find something?"

"Try April seventeenth," Leila says.

I put in the date and then linger over the year. He's a rising senior too; I set him at our age. The box doesn't budge.

"Up or down?" I ask.

"Up first, we'll go five days in both directions," Leila decides.

It's tedious work, going through the combinations, and with each wrong one, it grows more frustrating. There's a franticness to my movements when we have to start going down, counting back toward April 12, when Leila's phone starts buzzing rapidly. She frowns.

"What? What is it?" I ask.

"It's Malachi," Leila says. She answers, putting it on speaker immediately, "Yo? Still upstairs?"

"No, I'm downstairs. I was gonna go into the basement next, maybe get him down there, but, girl, there is a bitchy brunette that looks like a doll slamming on the door, demanding to talk to Avery? Now what kind of *mess* did we—oh, shit, he's coming down with Drew," Malachi hisses. His voice changes immediately, presumably no longer addressing us, as he says: "Heyyy, we found three-quarters of the weed. We're looking for the last quarter, but um . . . yeah, that."

There's a slightly distant: "Oh, shit," presumably from Avery.

I rack my brain as Malachi's description itches at my ear. I pause. "Wait . . . dark hair? Green eyes?"

"I don't know the color of her eyes. . . . Oh, shit, can't talk—"

"What the *fuck*, Andrea? You hooked up with my boyfriend?" a voice bellows.

Leila gasps.

"Oh, is this Lydia?" she asks in delight. She pulls the phone closer and says, "Keep the phone on, I need to hear this."

And much as I want the tea too, I snap my fingers in her face. *"Focus,"* I bark as I land on April 12. *Wrong.* "You go look for more combinations. Just . . . set the phone there." Leila reluctantly abandons her phone to me and goes to search the room again.

I lean in, listening hard, too preoccupied with the unfolding drama.

"He's your *ex*-boyfriend," I hear Drew say.

Lydia lets out a disbelieving laugh. "Oh, give me a break. I thought we were *friends*, Andrea," she bites out, her voice drawing closer, louder, and then quieting again, like she's pacing through the space. "I always knew this would happen. You don't think I knew, Avery?"

"There was nothing to know," Avery says.

"Yes, there was. You two were always *like* this. So *close*, and you knew it made me uncomfortable. I told you that, Avery—" Lydia rattles off.

"And I told you that there was no reason to worry!" Avery shouts. "*I* should've been more concerned. You tried to fuck Christophe, of all people. He's *gay*, Lydia."

"At the time he said he was bisexual!"

"Yeah, but you were dating *me*!"

Leila *tsks* under her breath, shaking her head. "Don't shit where you eat, kids," she mumbles under her breath.

See? Friend groups that date each other are messy. It's why the thought of even confessing my feelings to Yaya sets my stomach churning.

"Maybe I did it because you have *always* looked at her like . . . like that. Like the sun rose and set with her. Do you know what it's like? Competing with that?" Lydia hisses, voice growing lower and more distant. I can picture her stalking up to Drew, and I can picture Drew not flinching, not even blinking as she stares Lydia down. "Do you know what it's like competing with you?"

"You need to leave. Actually, you all need to leave," Avery says. "Andrea, we can figure this out later. . . . I'll look for the weed myself—"

Leila looks over at me, alarmed. Our time has run out. I hiss and look back down at the lockbox, swallowing hard, brain rattling for the answer.

Then I stop.

Of course.

I open my phone again, going into my Safari app, and breathe a heavy sigh of relief when I see that the Wikipedia page for *Read Your Rites* is still open.

"What is it?" Leila asks.

"Produced by *Boogieman Productions*, dude. It's the day *Read Your Rites* came out," I say, then flip in the premiere date. I gasp in delight when the lock clicks open.

I flip the metal box open.

Common sense tells me that it's rare and fragile, that a single touch could shatter it, but nothing about being haunted by a demon has felt like common sense so far, and once again my expectations are subverted when I pull it out. The hilt is a solid wood, not even rotting a little bit. The blade is black, jagged, and shiny like new. That first night I thought it looked like glass, but now I can't tell the material, and I suddenly wish for one of those museum cards explaining the origins. I wonder if Avery's mom is the one who writes them up.

"Come on, Devon." Leila hisses. "We gotta *go*."

I push back up on my haunches and slam the lockbox closed, feeling it click back into place as I hear the sound of thundering feet. I shove it back where it came from like nothing happened. We'll figure out a way to return the athame once we use it to get rid of the demon—though I have no idea how that works—and no one will be the wiser. I scramble out from underneath the desk, holding the knife tight in my hand, as Leila goes about making the room look undisturbed again. Finally, I tug her out of it, before Avery can come up here.

In the hall I shove the knife into the waistband of my jeans, by the small of my back. Leila adjusts the hem of my cardigan to hang just the right way, and then we rush down to the second floor, where we're met with Avery arriving, Drew and Lydia on his heels.

Lydia doesn't look nearly as camera ready in real life as she does in the photo. Now she looks painfully human, and I wonder if Leila regrets her snide comments when faced with the dark sleepless bruises that hang beneath Lydia's eyes, the blotchy flush across her cheeks, and the burst blood vessels in her eyes. I don't have to guess if Drew regrets anything—she's as pristine and emotionless as ever.

"We found it," Leila blurts out. "In your mom's yoga studio."

"It's my dad's," Avery says flatly. "And good. Because you need to go." Then he looks back at Drew and Lydia, his face creasing with his confusion. "I need to *think* about this."

"What is there to think about?" Drew asks.

Avery stares at her in disbelief. "Well, first off, whether or not I still want to be friends with you, Andrea."

Finally, to my surprise, Drew's expression cracks open, and when it does, it's so vulnerable, it hurts to look at. "What?" she asks, voice small.

Avery flinches, like the ability to make *Andrea*, of all people, feel small, weighs heavily on him. And instead of feeling annoyed he made my sister feel bad, like I usually would, right now I just feel *envious* of his superpower to break through to her.

"You fucked me up," Avery says, and I'm not sure whether he's talking to Lydia or Drew at the moment, but they both seem to hear it, to feel the weight of his words. "You fucked me up, and *I* have to figure out what to do with that. So, like, give me a minute. And when I call? Pick up your phone."

CHAPTER THIRTEEN

With the athame in our grasp, we're riding a high that not even Drew's unfamiliar emotional state can dampen. She doesn't speak the entire train ride home, so I overcompensate, throwing myself into conversation with anyone who'll listen. It's a bit of a debate, who'll keep ahold of the athame, but one that's settled by giving it to Gael for now. His mom won't find it weird if she sees a goofy-looking knife in his room, especially if it's in one of the bags from Freaks & Leeks. She'll assume it's a prop toy.

"But it's gotta go to you eventually, Yaya. Jack Strode said that's how we'd kill it, and you're the Final Girl, so it's gotta go to you," Gael warns.

Yaya looks green at the idea but doesn't say no. Not anymore.

"So . . . the demon is a sickness," Leila declares into the brewing silence, repeating what I've just relayed from Avery's explanation. "And it'll infect us one by one."

I latch on to the conversation, unable to deal with sitting in the ambient noise of the train car.

"It's almost like an STI without any of the sex," I say jokingly. Gael elbows me and I raise an eyebrow at him. "What?"

"I promise you won't die a virgin," he says solemnly.

"Oh, fuck you," I bark sharply, and he does his obnoxious

little jackal laugh that draws all the stink eye from the other passengers on the train. I stink eye right back at them. It's one in the afternoon on a Sunday, they should be wide awake.

"No one is going to die at all," Malachi says decisively. "None of y'all are allowed."

"Hey, why don't you tell the demon that," Leila jokes.

Malachi smirks. "You don't think I will?" Then he stills. "Maybe we can have Yaya say it. Give it a proper scare. What do you say?" It's a kind way to check in on Yaya, but she still starts at her own name and looks over at both of us.

"I don't think I'm up to saying anything to it," she says quietly.

"Secretly, the villain is always afraid of the Final Girl," Gael says firmly.

"Don't say that," Yaya mutters. "We should get inside someone's house before it shows up." She shakes herself as if that'll make the nerves slide off her. "I need to . . . I'm not *ready*."

"Not yet," Malachi agrees. "But you will be. You've got it."

There's something isolating about it, I realize. The way we keep insisting that she's different, even if we mean to inspire confidence. It's not so different from when we gas up any of the others when they're about to do something great. Something amazing. Like Gael with his films or Leila with her art or Malachi when he puts his heart on the line again. Except the stakes are higher. They mean more, and that means the confidence we're channeling is *unshakable*. And for the briefest of moments and for the first time ever, I'm jealous of Yaya.

I only wish they would have that kind of confidence in me. That I had that confidence in me.

· · ·

Despite my itchy neck, nothing happens that night as we unwind at Leila's. Eventually we all have to go to our own homes before our parents start really getting suspicious.

For three days after, we're on high alert, waiting for a sign. We make it our business to be home by dark and make it a point to follow rule #4 to a T and never go anywhere alone. Which isn't that hard since I no longer have to go to work until Mr. Ahmed and the insurance company fix the mess caused by what he and the cops assume to be Alexis's psychotic break. The one time I do visit him, though, I'm packed tightly between Leila's and Malachi's bodies, both of them on high alert. Yaya and Drew take to the library daily, searching for more about the athame. They come up with little, but Drew always comes back with a book anyway, apparently taking to horror cinema scholarship more than I ever thought she would.

Gael is the most closely protected as the next in line. He's escorted around and he takes to it far too well, as if he's a little prince, demanding that we fetch him chips or a slice whenever he feels like it or he'll roam by himself.

But there is no demon. There isn't even a sign of it. No creeping fear or twitching shadows.

There's nothing. And when there's nothing . . . doubt comes in.

My father always says that true insanity is repeating the same thing over and over again, expecting different results. The longer we wait, the crazier it feels that I expect the demon to appear. With each passing day, the sharpness of the memory, the details of its shape disappear. Dread lingers, but the gutting terror dissipates slowly and the doubt swells. It feeds on everything around me and grows into resentment over the Best Summer Ever, which is rapidly slipping through our fingers.

As I watch Drew fiddling with the books on my bookshelf, I wonder, though, if she even *cares* that it's her last summer with me before she has to go off and be better and smarter and everything in the world, while I still wait to grow.

"I'm tired of . . . of just *waiting* for it. What if we . . . like, went after it?" Yaya suggests before I can say anything. She's sitting on the center of my bed with me, legs folded in such a way that both of her feet are on top of her bony knees. Her toenails are cracked and ragged, and when she sees me looking at them, she reaches forward, grabbing them and covering them self-consciously.

"We don't know where its lair is," Gael says, shaking his head.

"It has a lair?" Drew challenges with a raised eyebrow.

"They always do. It takes damage, doesn't it? It's gotta go heal *somewhere*," Gael says.

"Yeah, Devon punched it in the throat," Malachi confirms.

"Right on," Leila mumbles, squirming her way onto my full-sized bed, officially making it a little too crowded. She doesn't seem to care, lying across both Yaya's lap and mine as she rubs at her chin, thinking hard. "It's just weird, isn't it? We finally have the means to kill it and it suddenly disappears?"

"Maybe that's why it disappeared," I suggest. "Maybe it knows."

"How would it know?" Gael asks.

"I'm not the demonologist of the group. I'm throwing out suggestions. Feel free to contribute," I say sharply. Gael just shrugs.

"Maybe . . . we're going a little crazy," Drew drawls slowly.

She looks over at me and almost manages to seem a little apologetic. "I think you saw something. Of course I do. On the train and at the bodega and at the bar. But I'm just . . . Maybe there's another explanation, Devon. And I . . ."

"You don't trust in things you haven't seen," I finish, doubling down again.

"I know *I'm* not crazy," Malachi bites out. "I saw what I saw. I *felt* what I felt."

"Were you drinking?" Drew asks. "Maybe you were drugged?"

"No, I was sober," Malachi retorts. "So tell me, if I wasn't drugged and it apparently wasn't a demon, *how* was my date in two different places? And *don't* say twins, Drew."

Drew makes a half shrug, like it's not a bad option, but she doesn't say it. "It's not *logical*," she says, like she's finally been defeated by a question.

"But you believe that we're made of, like . . . cells, right?" Yaya interrupts. "You believe that the earth is round, and you believe that we're all breathing oxygen and a ton of other little bonded atoms of terribleness?"

Drew frowns. "Of course."

"Okay. You can't see that. At least, not without the right tools," Yaya says firmly. She reaches out and grabs my elbow, and I should find it gross because she just was holding on to her terrible-looking toes, but I feel anchored. Yaya smiles at Drew in that disarming way that makes everyone want to believe her. "Just because we can't see it right now doesn't mean it's not real. It's real, Drew."

Drew purses her lips, and I can see another argument rising on her tongue.

"The thing about you, Drew, is that you're convinced that

you are *always* right," Leila says, slowly sitting up, her eyes narrowing as she zeroes in on my twin. I can see the way frustration has a hold on her, stiffening her shoulders. Leila brings her chin to her hand, refusing to release Drew from her line of sight. "You should *probably* evaluate why that is. Why you feel the need to know all. Why you need to have the *last word*."

Drew opens her mouth and then closes it again, but whether she gets the last word or not, she loses and she knows it. I grab Leila's wrist, anxiously, and she looks at me with a light frown, shaking her head once. She won't tolerate me being doubted. Not about this. Not again. She's still trying to make up for the first time.

"Yikes," Gael mutters, shattering the tension. "*Anyway*, there is a logical explanation for the pause here. I'm next up and it probably hasn't shown up because I'm not doing anything to tempt it." He hops off my desk and starts dragging his fingers over my bookshelves, playing with some of the crocheted dolls that I've made from boredom since I can't possibly think of drafting patterns right now. Usually at this point in the summer, I'd have already dreamed up patterns for my back-to-school wardrobe—crochet dusters in intricate patterns, granny square skirts, and meshlike vests. Not this year. No, my attention is preoccupied with bigger things. "Besides, even if I did, I don't think it's abnormal that it hasn't shown up yet."

"No?" Leila asks, raising an eyebrow.

"Well, we've just discovered that it's a demon, and we're at the third kill," Gael says, like that's supposed to mean something.

Whether to steal his thunder or to save the non–horror nerds in the room from a three-hour lecture, Malachi explains. "I think he means that it's the part in the movie where the villain tries to lull us into a false sense of security, you know?"

"Is it smart enough for that?" Drew asks, lips pursed.

"It's smart enough to hunt us in the order of the movie, and when it doesn't get us, it's *very* quick to find a substitute. I think odds are that it's a very intelligent kind of beast that we're dealing with," Malachi argues.

Drew flinches at the dismissal, pulling her knees to her chest and looking away. Without glancing at her, Leila puts a hand on Drew's knee, squeezing, as if reassuring her.

"Okay, so when do we reach the end of that lull?" Leila asks.

Before Gael can say whatever he seems jittery to say, my mom's shout echoes like she's in the room with us: "Kids! Come down here and help move this shit!"

"Move what shit?" Malachi asks us.

Gael groans. "I have to do physical labor?"

"Dude, she's gonna feed you," Leila says, and she rolls off me, laughing when I grunt at her elbow landing in my solar plexus. "Plus, it's probably for the block party."

"Oh, that's happening soon. I nearly forgot," Drew says absent-mindedly.

I lurch, turning to stare at her in shock. I don't understand how it's possible to forget the block party that our mother plans extensively every year before I realize . . . in the midst of every-thing, I nearly forgot too.

We make a silly parade, clomping and shoving our way down the stairs to see what my mom is talking about. We pack our way into the living room to find that Mom has shoved all her hair stuff into the back room. All the blinds are pulled wide, filling the room with the bright light of summer. Everything is spotless, gleaming and polished, which is a feat for a house as old as ours. There are already about six women sitting in the room, all picking at the feast of hors d'oeuvres my mother has set out and sipping at what I recognize as her summer pink punch, a fruity delight packed with vodka and tequila that she makes in an enormous cooler and keeps in gallon jugs in the downstairs fridge. It's *always* finished by the start of the school year.

"Mami?" Gael blurts out.

Mrs. Aguilar smirks at Gael. They share the same curls and wicked smile. "*Mijo*, go help Mrs. Harris take the junk from my trunk and put it downstairs, yes?" she says, tossing him the car keys. Gael fumbles as he lunges to catch them and nearly tumbles to the ground.

"You're helping plan the block party?" Gael asks, still bewildered by his mother's presence.

When we were young, Gael's mom worked a lot. During the school year she was an admin for the NYC Department of Education, and in the summers she'd do temp work at one of the consulting firms off Wall Street. But she was promoted to school administrator just last year, which has meant *much* more free time at the exact moment Gael never wants to be in the house.

"Yeah, thought I'd get a little more involved in the community," she drawls. "Now, go."

"Listen to your mother," Mom says, as she comes out and sets a fresh glass of pink punch in front of one of the moms who lives three blocks over. "Drew, you know where the key is."

We all know where the key is: at the very bottom of the key bowl. Drew rifles through it for a moment, and then we file out of the house without much complaint, especially after spotting some of the snacks we're sure to steal from the planning committee when we're done.

"Shit, she packed it really tight." Gael sighs as he opens the back door to find bags stuffed on the floor and crates piled on the backseats. The front seat even holds two cardboard boxes. "If this is in the back, I can just imagine what's in the trunk."

"What even *is* all of this?" Malachi asks, peeking in one of the boxes. "Plastic cutlery?"

"Probably her overdoing it because this is her first year on the committee. Mami wants to impress," Gael says, pursing his lips. He grumbles the whole time as he pulls out a box, but I can see the way the corners of his lips turn up.

"Let's have a system," Yaya declares. "Leila and me on the backseat, the boys at the trunk, Devon and Drew with the front seat. Sounds good?"

"There's only two boxes in the front," Malachi complains.

"So I'll help wherever I need to help after that," I suggest quickly, before Yaya's plan gets derailed. I'll just move . . . *very* slowly with the little I have to do.

With the roles divvied up and Drew having finally unlocked the door to the garden level, we begin the painstaking work of unloading the car. It really wouldn't be an issue if the boxes weren't filled to the brim and the sun wasn't so high in the sky on this clear day. More than once, one of us wonders out loud how Gael's mom got the boxes into the car in the first place. She's a small woman.

It's daytime, but Gael's warning rings clear. The demons come out in the sunlight now, and every few moments I look over my shoulder to check if there's someone across the street watching us.

I should've been looking down the block.

We're just about wrapping up when I hear someone clear her throat and say, "Excuse me. Hello."

Kendra Thompson-Bryant has a voice you could never forget, even if you wanted to. Prim and high pitched, and edged with animosity. I wince as I turn to look at her; the last time I'd seen her, I'd basically pelted flyers at her door.

"Andrea . . . no, Devon," Kendra says awkwardly. She tilts her head and folds her arms and then thinks better of it, putting her hands on her hips, like she doesn't know how to speak to someone under the legal voting age.

"Uh, yes?" I ask, lingering on the bottom step, fingers straining around the stack of tablecloths I've got clutched to my chest.

Kendra is tall and fit, the kind of fit that tells me she works out at Equinox four times a week. Her hair is blown out, big and soft like a nineties Black sitcom villain. I want to know whether it's a perm or if she just has a roller set, just to see if my mom could affect the same on me when it's fall. She's dressed like an HGTV host when they're trying to pretend they're actually the one doing the renovation work—expensive jeans and a plain white T-shirt that probably cost $400.

"Can you get your mother for me? I'd like to speak with her," she says firmly, regaining her insufferable sense of authority.

"Sure," I say slowly. I scurry up the steps, shoulder my way back into the house, and turn into the living room.

"Okay, the balloon vendors are confirmed. I don't mind if Mr. Martinez is on the grill, but we need two others, too. For halal food and for kosher food," Mom says, her voice not allowing for argument, as if it's something she's had to deal with before. "It's not hard to be considerate, yeah?"

"Mom?" I interrupt.

She looks up from her iPad and raises an eyebrow. "You get lost, baby?" she teases.

"No, Mom, it's just . . . um, Miss Kendra is here," I explain. "She wants to talk to you."

The moms all exchange varying looks of distaste. Gael's mom snorts and shakes her head, tapping her foot on the ground as she mumbles, "What does that self-righteous woman want now?"

Mom holds up her hands. "All right, all right, I'm sure this isn't a huge thing," she says, even as she pastes one of her fake customer-service smiles on her face. That tells me exactly how little she wants to deal with Kendra.

Sure enough, Mom takes the tablecloths from me and marches to the front door like she's marching into battle. When we emerge, we find Kendra has migrated halfway up our steps. The others are still by the back of Gael's mom's car, huddled together like they're preparing to watch the showdown of a lifetime.

"Hello, Kendra," Mom says pleasantly, leaning against the banister. She doesn't take a single step away from the door. I slide around Kendra and rejoin the others.

"*Hi*, Carole," Kendra says, practically cooing. "I just wanted to check in about this?" She pulls out a folded flyer from her back pocket. I recognize the pale-blue copy paper. "This . . . block party."

"Mhmm?" Mom nods. "We've been doing it since the girls were just kids. I think it's our . . . tenth year?"

She *knows* it's the tenth year. That's why this one's going to be bigger than ever.

"That's so . . . *nice*," Kendra says with the air of a woman who doesn't think it's nice at all. She tilts her head, squinting up at the sky. "I don't remember my father mentioning it."

"Oh, Mr. Thompson *loved* it. He made a mean fried catfish. That was always your favorite, right, Devon? The catfish and the macaroni and cheese," Mom says.

I nod quickly. "Yeah, and the yams," I throw in.

"Yes, the candied yams were real good," Mom agrees, still wearing her tight smile. She takes another step, and Kendra stands even taller, like there's a metal rod slipping through her spine. Mom is shorter than her, but she's always had the energy of someone you don't want smoke with. "Have you come to offer to help, Kendra?"

"I'm sorry?" Kendra asks.

"We always love to have more organizers. It's a big thing around here. Ever since the neighborhood's . . . shifted, we've made a conscious effort to continue to create events that center the community. To encourage a coming together of sorts," Mom says. It's such a nice way to say, *We're doing this so that the gentrifiers will feel invested instead of trying to shut our shit down.* "We'd love to have you."

Kendra squirms, false discomfort twisting her expression. "Oh, no, I just . . . I wanted to share my concern, is all. The noise—"

"Ah, the *noise*," Mom murmurs in mock concern. "Like the noise of the ice-cream truck?"

I lean forward, intrigued to hear the way *this* will go . . . until I feel the *prickling*.

Immediately, my heart begins to race. My mouth dries and fear chases goose pimples down my spine.

I whip around, preparing myself to be confronted with a gaping maw.

Instead, Keith leans against the gate, three books tucked under his arm as he talks softly to Yaya.

I'd rather have been faced with the demon.

Yaya brushes her hair behind her ear, looking at him with an indiscernible expression. I take a step toward them before I mean to, my focus shifting entirely. Kendra doesn't matter anymore. The block party doesn't matter.

Only this and my mounting irritation.

"—thought you'd be at practice?" Keith says. His voice sounds creaky, like there's a frog in his throat or he's getting over a summer cold.

"Why would you think that?" Yaya asks.

Keith laughs awkwardly, then says, "Come on, Yaya, you're always practicing." He rocks forward and then back on his heels. "And, like, yeah, I *may* have swung by to see if you were there, but only because the library is, like, two blocks over."

"There's a library closer to here," Leila says flatly, leaning back against the side of the car. She darts a quick look over at me, checking in, but I try to ignore it, like it doesn't mean anything.

"Yeah, but the one over there is renovated and has a better selection," Keith says with a light shrug. As if it was all reasonable and coincidental and not *planned* like the creep he is.

"That one is really nice," Yaya agrees. She leans against the iron fence and toes at the box of decorations on the ground, between her legs, like she's searching for something else to say. "I'm taking today off. I've been told that I might be overworking myself."

"I'm sure you know your own limits," Keith insists, like he knows it's me he's contradicting. He clears his throat, opens his mouth, and then closes it again as he notices that he has an audience. He looks over at Drew and Leila, who are both raising an eyebrow at him. "How are you all?"

"Fine," Leila says flatly.

"The summer is going well so far," Drew lies, as if we've been having the exact summer I planned.

"Oh, congratulations, Drew. On graduating. My granddad always said you were the smartest girl in the neighborhood," Keith says. He doesn't sound sad recalling his grandfather, and I wonder how close they were, exactly. "He said you reminded him of my mom when she was younger."

"How kind," Drew says. Keith does a double take like he can't tell if she means it or not, which I can't blame him for. Drew rarely speaks with inflection to begin with. He turns back to Yaya and Yaya shrugs, reaching for the box of decorations. She gestures with it, like it's a Get Out of Jail Free card, and I bite my bottom lip to keep from grinning.

"Wait, uh . . . Yaya, I wanted to ask you before at the bodega, but it just seemed like a weird time," Keith begins. He doesn't have to look at me to make it clear that *I* was the one making it weird. I don't miss how he hasn't looked at me once since he arrived. He's content with pretending I don't exist, and I squirm, wanting nothing more than to make my presence to him *known* and unforgettable. Keith continues: "And I know you're busy and your friends . . . take up a lot of your time—"

"Don't make it sound like a chore," Malachi mutters under his breath.

Keith winces but presses on: "If you had some time, though . . . actually, what about the block party, would you want to . . . I don't know, go together?"

Yaya nearly drops the box of decorations in her hands with an "Oh." I have to stop myself from shouting the refrain of *no no no* that's running through my head, but she says nothing at all.

Gael squints at Keith, and then, like Keith didn't just awkwardly ask Yaya out, he asks, "Hey, you seen any weird shit lately, man?"

"Pardon?" Keith asks. He looks befuddled, as he always does when he's confronted with Gael's particular brand of brashness.

Gael shrugs. "Just wondering if you've seen anything . . . strange."

"Strange, how?" Keith asks, quirking an eyebrow.

"Demonic," Gael says flatly.

"Gael? What kind of question is that?" Yaya squeaks. She looks over at Keith and shakes her head, sighing. "Sorry about him. We think he was dropped on his head as a baby. More than once." It's the most outwardly mean thing she's ever said.

"Ooooh, burn," Gael snarks, unbothered as always.

Yaya shakes her head and then says, "I've been going to the block party with these heads since I was, like . . . seven. I gotta go with them." She turns away easily, marching off with the decorations. Class dismissed. Triumph feels so *good*.

"Shouldn't you go off and read your books, Grandpa?" Malachi drawls.

Keith snorts, letting the insult roll off his back. "I'm not that old. And aren't you the one who likes older guys?" he says, cheeks burning.

"I'm over that," Malachi says flatly.

Keith huffs. "Sure." Then he cranes his neck to look past me at the garden-level door. He startles when I step in front of his gaze and our eyes meet. I can't help but glare at him, my body tensed by my annoyance, but this time he stares back, unruffled. Then he says to me, "Tell Yaya I say bye."

It's a pointed dig and I can't help it—I give him the finger.

But Keith is already going back up the street, abandoning his mother to her current issue with *my* mother.

When he's halfway down the block, Drew turns a glare on Gael. "What was that about? Interrogating him about something demonic. Were you trying to make us sound crazy?" she accuses.

Gael shakes his head. "Of course not. I just . . . Well, what if he's the *guy*," he suggests with an apologetic look over at me.

"What guy?" I demand.

"Remember what Jack Strode said?" Gael asks. "The third-act twist—the love interest dies and mindfucks the Final Girl."

My brain short-circuits.

"He's *not* the love interest," I yelp. "She doesn't even like him!"

It's loud enough that whatever conversation Kendra and Mom are having breaks, drawing their attention to me. My face burns and I look down at the pavement, squirming with discomfort. I train my eyes on Leila's beat-up Converses until she bumps my chin.

"Hey, hey, it's just a thought," Leila says quietly. She rubs at my shoulder. "We're flying into this blind besides a Wikipedia page, Jack Strode's rules, Avery's secondhand info from his mom, and Gael's considerable horror cinema knowledge."

I ignore Gael's preening at this rare compliment and try to shake off the sympathetic looks they're casting my way.

"Okay," I mumble. "Okay, I'm fine, I'm fine."

Despite my obvious frustrations, I'm smart enough to privately admit that Gael could be right. It would be best to keep an eye on Keith, in case he really *is* the love interest. I won't let anything get in the way of protecting us or our Final Girl. Especially my Final Girl.

CHAPTER FOURTEEN

Kendra does *not* want to help with the block party. Drew and I hear that loud and clear over family dinner as Mom recounts the rest of her afternoon confrontation with mounting ire. She's shoveling rice and beans into her mouth in between ranting, destroying the quiet harmony of our Mexican takeout, using her free hand with gusto.

"You should've *heard* her in that uppity voice. Speaking to me like I was a bill collector," Mom sneers. "She thinks she's better than us because she's got an *education*. Well, honey, you're not the only one who went to school."

She says it like Kendra is right there to hear her.

"I'm sure she didn't mean it that way," Dad says, attempting to placate, and then winces at the look my mother sends him. He takes a careful bite of his skirt-steak taco and then tilts his head. "You're right. . . . She probably did. But I don't remember Mr. Thompson being so . . . you know."

"He wasn't," Drew speaks up.

"Except he was," I mutter.

Mom frowns. "What?"

I sigh, looking up from my plate. "He *was*. It was just different. Like . . . a respectability politics thing. Old-school way of thinking," I say. "He was nice to *you*, Drew, because you bootstrapped your way out of what he thought of as beneath the respectable kind of Black people. Mind you . . . we live in Crown Heights . . . which is not what literally *anyone* would consider the hood."

Drew frowns at me. "Well, I don't think that way. I don't think I'm better than anyone," she says.

I turn my attention back to my plate.

"You know she got our *permit* restricted? We can't have the block party on *our* block because it'll disrupt the construction on her building, but we can have it a few blocks down. As if it makes that much of a difference. She's just mad because I shut that shit down when she had those big ugly dumpsters on the street past the time we *agreed* on," Mom rants. "That woman is a piece of work."

"I don't like her, and I don't like her son, either," I declare.

"Well, we all know why *that* is," Drew says.

Dad raises an eyebrow. "He said something fresh to you?" he asks, an edge of hardness in his voice.

"No," I say at the same time as Drew, unhelpfully, volunteers my exact issue: "He's got a thing for Yaya."

"Oh my *God*, Drew, shut up," I hiss, leaning forward.

She stares back at me, waiting for me to say or do something to her. When I settle back in my chair, she seems almost *disappointed* by it all. Disappointed in me.

"Ah," Dad says awkwardly, looking over at Mom for help.

She's staring at Drew, mouth tight. I know all Mom's tells; she's frustrated with Drew but doesn't want to rock the boat further. Finally, she asks, "Well, does Yaya like him back?"

"No," I say sharply, but Drew doesn't bother to step in this time.

Mom nods. "Does she know *you* like her?"

"Mo-om," I groan, letting my head fall to the table next to my plate. My phone buzzes next to my forehead, but I know not to grab it. My parents have *rules* at the dinner table, and "No phones" is at the near top of the list, right under "Family dinner is required unless a formal request is made three days in advance."

"Sorry, sorry," Mom chatters.

My phone buzzes again, and I hear a soft echo from Drew's side of the table. The group chat then. I stare at my phone worriedly and then flicker a look up at my parents. Mom looks ready to tell us to put our phones out of the room, but then they buzz *again*.

"Mom, please?" Drew asks.

Mom sighs. "Fine. Once. And then you're done."

I'm quick to flip my phone over, taking a glance at the preview.

GAEL
ETA to the Harris house is 15 min. Going to Leila . . .

"Everyone's coming to pick us up in fifteen. Can we go?" I ask quickly.

Mom and Dad exchange looks. "Where are you going?" Dad asks.

"Leila's. We might sleep over, I don't know," Drew says with a shrug.

Mom nods. "All right. You kids be safe. Make good choices." It's what she always says when we go out. Never a "No." Never a "Don't drink." Never a "Don't do drugs." Just a "Make good choices." It's a strong guilt inducer, right up there with "I'm so disappointed in you."

I start shoveling food into my mouth, only showing enough decorum not to drip guacamole all over the table. Once I scrape the plate clean of crumbs and rice, I drain my glass and stand up, moving to clear up as many of the empty plates as I can so that I'm not accused of not helping out. But Drew is still pacing herself, looking deep in thought, and my impatience starts to mount as I look over at the clock above the archway to the kitchen. Three minutes until arrival—when the group sets an ETA, they're usually within the expected time, especially now that it's getting dark.

We want to be on the move as fast as possible.

"Don't rush me," Drew says as she finishes eating her last taco.

"I didn't say anything," I protest.

Drew raises an eyebrow. "Then why do I feel rushed?"

Before it can become a real disagreement, Dad says, "Hey, just finish your food. I'll do dishes tonight." Then he looks at me severely. "But you do them tomorrow night, you hear me?"

"Yes, Dad, fine," I groan, rocking back and forth. I look over at Drew and sigh. "I'm going to put my shoes on." I don't wait to be acknowledged and pound down the hallway into the foyer, where a pile of our shoes awaits. I sit on the bottom stair and shove my feet into my Converses just as my phone buzzes again.

I don't need to look to know what it says. "They're outside!" I shout, probably too loudly.

"I'm coming," Drew says, voice closer than I'd expected. She looks down at me with a raised eyebrow, slipping into her already-tied sneakers before she rushes to open the door.

"Hey-o, kiddos," Gael says, saluting at us with his free hand from the sidewalk, his skateboard in the other. He's got Yaya's dance bag hoisted over one shoulder.

Yaya's swaying from side to side, and she lifts a tired hand that immediately flies to her mouth to stifle a well-earned yawn. Leila stands at her side, and my eyes light up on the massive tote bag that she carries. She grins, shaking it at me.

"I picked up extra paint and yarn while Gael and I were on our way to meet up with Yaya. We can have a craft night while we plot," Leila says.

Drew locks the door, then bounds down the steps, and I'm quick to follow, slotting myself next to Leila and Yaya.

"Death to the demon," Malachi says grimly.

Leila loops her free arm through mine. "We're gonna take care of this," she says boldly. "We have all the information. We just have to piece it all together into something that makes sense before this pause is over."

She sounds far more confident than we all felt just hours before.

"I think we lost any semblance of sense a long time ago," Drew says, expression dour and brooding. She glances down at her phone again. I wonder if she's texted Avery again. Or if she wants to.

It's a quiet night for Crown Heights in the summertime. That's not exactly *not* normal. People always have the same idea about New York—bright and loud and something always happening. But there are so many pockets all over the city where there's *nothing* happening. Not quiet, exactly, but a chill ambient noise that settles just right in the soul. Still, with everything going on, it doesn't feel as comforting.

Gael chatters about the number of horror films he's rewatched in the past few days to inspire our takedown. He even managed to squeeze in a third rewatch of *Read Your Rites* while he ate dinner with his mom.

Gael has a captive audience in Leila, Malachi, and Drew for once, so I don't feel bad for slowing down to check in with Yaya.

"How are you doing?" I ask in a soft undertone.

Yaya shrugs. "I think . . . I don't know how I'm doing," she says. "It's a lot. I've been trying not to focus on it because I'm still working on my audition pieces, but it's . . . I think about it all the time. Like . . . the Final Girl. It should've been *you*."

"I don't know about that. I was the opening kill," I say, self-deprecatingly.

In a horror movie, the first to die is always the easiest pickings. She practically deserves it, half the time, for her grating stupidity. She doesn't pay attention; she baits the killer, the demon, the avenger—the whatever. She's always last in the rolling credits, and by the end, everyone always forgets her name. There is nothing "great" about the blonde except if she has a particularly memorable end.

"But you *didn't* die," Yaya says quietly. "You outmaneuvered a demon, not once but twice. You *saved* Malachi the second time. You're basically a hero."

I giggle until I realize that she's being serious. "A hero? Yaya, come on . . . ," I say, rubbing the back of my neck.

Yaya stares at me solemnly and says, "You know, Devon, you have a lot of doubt."

"What?"

"You're just . . . You always *doubt* yourself," Yaya says. "It's the most frustrating thing about you." She says it so plainly, like it's something she's tread over and over again in her own mind, only biding her time until she told me.

"I don't doubt myself," I insist.

"You do. You're so quick to cheer everyone else on. You do it all the time. With Drew, with the others . . . with *me*. But you don't cheer yourself on. You feel very comfortable being the cheerleader instead of taking action," Yaya says, and it feels like she's saying something else, too, but I can't figure out what, for once.

I flinch at the cutting assessment. "Well, *maybe* I'm not all that driven," I bite out.

"How do you know?" Yaya pushes. "You don't put yourself *out* there. I don't know if it's because you're afraid, but you don't have to be, you know." She takes a deep breath and then looks down at me with a tiny smile as I try to push away the wounded twist to my expression. "I'm just saying, if I can be the Final Girl, then you *can* admit you're a hero. That you could do this just as well as anyone else."

I sigh, shaking my head, and suddenly, I feel *nervous*. I don't usually feel nervous talking to Yaya, not anymore. I'm so used to the overwhelming love I feel that it sits normally inside me, a constant growing thing that lives somewhere inobtrusive alongside my liver. But now it's making itself known, and I feel my breath catching in my throat as I meet her eyes and then have to look down again.

"I . . . I guess," I whisper. Then Yaya beams, and I turn away, nauseous with it all. "So . . . you and me. The Heroic Opening Kill and the Final Girl. A pairing for the ages."

"You and me," Yaya confirms, and she nudges me with her shoulder, her smile gentling into something secret. I want to know every single thought in her head, to pick them out of her brain matter and cherish each one.

I want to tell her, I realize, right there at the corner of Saint Marks and New York Avenue.

For the first time, I want to put myself out there. I want to tell her that seeing her makes my day. I want to tell her that every time *she* doubts *her*self, I get angry. I want to tell her that I brag to everyone I know about her like she's already mine. I want to tell her that I've loved her for years and I don't think I'll ever stop, even when we're dust. I want—

"Hey, Yaya," I say, barely above a breath. But she hears me anyway.

"Yeah, Devon?" she asks, looking down at me with a smile.

"I—"

Terror has become an old friend, at this point. I feel the prickle at the back of my neck, calling me to cut a glance behind. I don't have to search; it's like my nerves are locked in, and I know exactly where *it* is.

The shadow beneath one of the flickering orange streetlights greets me from half a block away. I can practically hear a gravelly voice coming from it, a scraping "Hello." I stare into what should be its eyes, but it's in its true form, like at the bodega, long and liquid blackness, crooked and cracked.

"Devon?" Yaya whispers. She slowly tries to turn, and I stop her, squeezing her elbow.

I narrow my eyes, turning my back on it, and then I say, "You guys . . . *run*."

I thread my fingers through Yaya's, and then I take off, feet pounding against the pavement. Just as we pass under the next streetlight, a sound echoes behind us. I recognize it, the terrible screech that sounds like steel scraping against steel. But it's the first time the others encounter that unholy sound, and I can see it worm deep into their brains, branding itself on their amygdalae. A terror that will persist, a forever sort of thing. Drew looks over her shoulder, and what she sees makes her screech to a halt. Her mouth hangs open, her limbs refusing to work.

It makes me glance over my shoulder and I see that it's coming.

Not just coming.

It's *running*.

I grab Drew with my free hand and I push harder, sprinting down the block, skirting around an oncoming car, ignoring the honk of a horn. Leila, Gael, and Malachi bound across the street ahead of us, another car swerving out of their way.

"We're not making it to Leila's," I gasp out.

"No. Mine," Gael says, and then he grabs Malachi by the hand and Leila by the elbow and takes off even faster, his fanny pack thudding against his body in time with my racing heart.

I keep my eyes locked on the nape of his neck as we run, taking the corner sharp. I nearly fall off the curb, but Yaya corrects my momentum, swinging both Drew and myself ahead of her. We're three blocks from Gael's apartment building, a perfect halfway point between my and Drew's house and Leila's. But it's like the demon senses where we're going—it doesn't hesitate after each turn we take, doesn't stop when a car's coming, only twists and bounds over it like the shadow it is. There's nothing that will stop it. *Nothing*—

We crash into the small atrium of Gael's building, and he immediately goes rifling through his fanny pack, muttering, "Keys, keys, keys." I take a step back from the front door, crowding up against Gael.

"Come *on*, Gael, now is *not* the time to be losing your damn key!" Leila cries out helplessly.

"I'm *trying*—got it!" Gael cheers. But immediately he fumbles it, fingers shaking as he goes to open the door. "Trying, trying, trying—"

"Try harder!" Malachi and Drew shout in unison, finally frightened out of their general coolness. Just as Gael gets the key in the lock and turns, the glass in the front door behind us shatters.

We tumble through the second door into the lobby proper, slamming the heavy metal door shut just as the demon reaches for us. For a moment we linger in the dinginess of the lobby, staring right at the demon through the window. In the yellowing light, the demon looks even more terrifying than it had in the dark. The strange eyes set in a long face, dark jaw swinging unhinged to reveal a mouth full of human teeth. The long, long fingers tipped with long, low claws. The way its back curls over in the shape of a sickle.

"Oh my God," Leila whispers. "Oh my God, oh my *God*."

"That's the demon. It's *real*," Drew murmurs, processing slowly. Malachi swallows. "It can't . . . enter. Can it?"

Gael forgets some of his fear, returning to himself. "It's not a *vampire*, Malachi. Of course it can." And as if to prove him right, the demon lifts its knee and slams it right into the lock. The door rattles hard in the metal frame but doesn't give. Impatiently, the demon does it again, and this time the metal door flies open with a slam so hard, it cracks the brick wall behind it.

"No more waiting," I gasp, grabbing Drew by the wrist again and tearing off to the elevator. I press the buttons, hoping that one might be on the ground floor. We have no such luck.

"Up here!" Gael shouts, and there, right next to the elevators, are the wondrous but daunting *stairs*. All ten flights of them.

There's no time to even consider how impossible the task of sprinting up all those stairs feels. All that's understood is that there needs to be as much space between us and the demon as possible. Gael takes them up two at a time, long legs stretching over each step, Leila and Malachi quick on his heels. Yaya is the most in shape out of all of us, and it shows, the power that she moves with. Drew and I pull up at the rear, keeping up as best we can, keeping close.

Stumbling up the stairs, we hear the echoes of spitting and gagging and shrieks below.

"My mom," Gael gasps, as adrenaline starts to lose the battle with his limits. "I can't lead it to my mom. I'm the target, I'll draw it away. Yaya, get the athame." He throws his keys at her and she catches them, wide-eyed, before she settles into a determined stance and sets off again, blazing past us up the stairs. Gael stumbles away toward the door that leads onto the third floor, seven whole floors away from his own.

"No, you *don't*!" Malachi snarls. "Get back here, Gael! Yaya! The rules! We are *not* splitting up—"

But that's exactly what we're doing. Breaking the rule.

"Well, if we're doing this, we better give Yaya enough of a head start." He switches tacks.

"Wait, don't!" I cry out just as he latches on to Leila and hauls her off up the stairs.

I hear the fourth-floor door slam open and then swing closed.

Now it's only Drew and me in the stairwell.

The shrieking behind us has stopped. There's only us, taking deep gasping breaths as our heart rates slow.

It takes me a moment to realize there's a third breath.

I look up at Drew, three steps above me, and hold a finger to my lips. Drew is shaking, eyes so wide, I can see the whites of them. Slowly, I take another step up, keeping my gaze on the corner.

For a minute I wonder if it'll also leave, following after Gael, in pursuit of its prey. I wait to hear the creak of the door below, but it never comes. I can sense its hesitation, like it doesn't know what it'll meet.

And then, with a long breath, it gets over it. Its long fingers curl around the corner, and it pulls itself around slowly. We're caught in the headlights of those big, glossy eyes, and its mouth curves open. No, not quite open. That's when I realize—it's smiling. It looks at me, spitting and chittering, but when it looks at Drew, just behind me, it makes another sound.

A death rattle.

It's not Gael, I realize. It wants—

"Drew . . . go," I say between clenched teeth. I grab Drew's wrist, dragging her up behind me.

As we scramble up the steps, I can feel it lunge, fingers reaching out. Drew cries out, and I look over my shoulder just enough to see long nails digging into the soft meat of Drew's calf. Drew tears herself out of its grip and grabs on to the railing, hoisting herself up to meet me.

The demon's death rattles echo in the infinity of the stairwell. It isn't moving as fast now, instead stalking us slowly up the steps, enjoying the way it causes panic. Like it knows the higher we go, the less likely it is we'll get away.

"This floor," Drew pants, slamming out onto the sixth floor when it's clear we can't make it any farther.

I follow her, chest burning, as we stumble out into the hallway. Drew limps back and forth, shaking and cursing under her breath. Gripping the wall, I slap my hand against the elevator buttons, but then push off, grabbing Drew away from the window just as the door next to it slams open and inky black spills out of the dank stairwell.

"Help!" I force out from my throbbing vocal cords, looking over my shoulder as we run down the hallway. *"HELP US!"*

Drew pounds her fists against the doors that we run past. Behind each heavy, solid door, we can hear sounds of life—heavy conversation, the drone of *Wheel of Fortune*, the ding of a kitchen timer. We smell the scents of people cooking—a fry-up, curry, and old Chinese food all mixing. But no one comes to our aid. No one hears us over their own lives, and that'll be what makes ours end.

I'd never thought the bystander effect would ever happen to me, and then I remember—this is New York City. Everyone's a goddamn bystander.

When we reach the end of the hall, we both look left, then right. Each takes a turn somewhere unseen—one to another staircase and the other to a dead end. Drew is shaking as she presses her back up against the wall, holding on to it like it's the last thing keeping her up. I stand in front of her, my should-already-be-dead body a shield, and I feel her breath hot against the back of my neck. Her fingers dig shakily into my sides before she stills.

"Devon, don't, I'll—" Drew says. I can already hear it—*I'll face the demon.*

Like she has to take care of me. Like she has to do everything. Like she's going to *sacrifice* herself—

"Shut up, Drew," I mutter.

The demon skids to a stop right before me, hunched beneath the low ceilings. It swallows a last death rattle until it's silent again except for the three of us breathing.

"I won't let you kill her. You can't . . . You can't kill her because you'll have to kill me first," I stutter. "And I won't let you."

The demon immediately proves me wrong. It reaches out with a single clawed finger and presses it against my bare shoulder, where my hoodie has slipped in the chase. It digs in, carving a mark into my skin. A warning.

Then, point made, the demon opens its wide hand, clamping it around my throat like a well-fitted collar, and shoves me back so hard that Drew cries out in pain behind me. She slips out from around me, driving her knuckles into the demon's wrist around my throat, and the demon actually yelps. It's a disturbingly human sound, which makes it all the more scary.

"Get *off* my sister," Drew hisses, shaking with her rage or her terror, I'm not sure which.

For a moment the demon seems to consider it, turning its gaze from me onto Drew. It leans forward, almost over my head, baring its teeth. Drew's the target. Drew is what it wants.

No.

I rocket my foot forward, feeling it connect with its knee, and the demon's stare snaps back to me. The demon's hold tightens, and air hisses from my deflating lungs like an old balloon losing its helium. I feel light-headed, and this time Drew's voice sounds far away. "GET OFF HER—"

But just before I lose consciousness, there's a feral scream that comes from neither me nor Drew.

The demon twists, releasing me, and the sudden rush of air is just as painful as being cut off from it.

Vision spotting, I look past the demon, and see Yaya's hand stretched out and touching its slick, leathery skin, trying to jerk it back. It curdles from her attempted touch, flexing and squirming away, revealing something warm and brown underneath, like the top layer can't touch her. Even bright with tears, Yaya's eyes are furious as she lifts a black and jagged object in her other hand.

"Get *away* from them," Yaya says, swinging the athame down.

With surprising dexterity, the demon jerks away from her reaching hands and presses against the brick wall just like Drew had. But then, like a spider, it scuttles up against the ceiling until it's backed into the corner above us, letting out a terrifying spitting shriek as it glowers down at Yaya.

And Yaya—beautiful, ferocious Yaya—screams right *back*. She doesn't stop screaming as she holds up the athame like someone who knows how to use it, warding the demon off. It scuttles to the cracked window, still hanging on to the ceiling, head twisted completely around, staring at Yaya straight-on.

When her breath runs out, the screaming ceases, and the distant sound of police sirens on the streets below replaces it. For a minute I wonder if someone has called for a noise complaint. At least it's something.

The lights on the ceiling flicker just a little, and I expect the demon to move in the blinking moment when the building is washed in darkness, but it just slowly turns its stare to Drew. The way it stares is so *familiar*.

But before I can take another look, the demon falls to the ground on its feet and in one move crawls right out the window, like the vermin that it is.

For a long moment none of us speaks, and then Drew whispers, "So, *I'm* the asshole. Huh."

On the phone of Leila Benady:

Quiz Corner

PERSONALITY QUIZ
would you be haunted by a demon?
Quiz introduction
what lurks in the shadow of your fear?

START QUIZ >>
By theevilliving

Question 1 of 8
pick a song
○ all along the watchtower—jimi hendrix
● teenagers—my chemical romance
○ sweet dreams (are made of this)—eurythmics
○ something in the way—nirvana
○ every breath you take—the police
○ red right hand—nick cave and the bad seeds

Question 2 of 8
pick a verb
○ to run
○ to hide
○ to seek
○ to lie
○ to weep
● to sigh

Question 3 of 8

pick a scent

○ sulfur

● incense

○ tom ford electric cherry

○ red wine

○ smoky wood

Question 4 of 8

what is your favorite time of day?

○ witching hour

● dawn

○ noon

○ sundown

○ midnight

Question 5 of 8

it's getting dark outside. what's the plan?

○ going out to party with friends

○ curling up with a good book and hot cocoa (no matter the season)

○ start prepping dinner. it's getting late

○ never too late for a nap

● turn off all the lights. let the darkness in

Question 6 of 8

pick a location

○ farmhouse

○ townhouse

● park
○ lake

Question 7 of 8
there is a woman lingering on your doorstep.
she tells you, "i have nowhere to go. my mother
has sent me away and my father does not know
my face." the road is deserted. the streetlamps have
yet to light up. you cannot see her face beneath the
brim of her hat. you hear her plea for shelter. what
do you do?
○ let her in
○ tell her to go
○ promise her honey and meat as a tribute, then banish
her before it's too late
● get thee to a nunnery

Question 8 of 8
pick poetry
○ "my name is Ozymandias, king of kings: / look on my
works, ye Mighty, and despair!" —percy bysshe shelley
○ "the mind is its own place, and in itself can make a
heaven of hell, a hell of heaven. . . ." —john milton
○ "deep into that darkness peering, long I stood there,
wondering, fearing, doubting, dreaming dreams no
mortal ever dared to dream before." —edgar allan poe
● "before i got my eye put out— / i liked as well to see
/ as other creatures, that have eyes— / and know no
other way—" —emily dickinson

YOU ARE:

run, run, fast as you can.

"it's coming, it's coming, it's here. close your mouth, shut your eyes, hold your nose. don't let it in, and all is not lost."

CHAPTER FIFTEEN

*N*owhere is safe now, not even Gael's apartment. But it's somewhere to catch our breath. Even still, Yaya keeps the athame tucked between her thighs. Just in case.

"Did you hear all that screaming just now?" Gael's mom asks, sucking her teeth. "You know, when you were growing up, *mijo*, it wasn't like this, not at all. Now it's full of nonsense here." We don't have the heart to tell her we're the nonsense, so she continues her well-meaning rant, finishing with how glad she is that we turned out to be "good kids." Gael nods, humoring her, as he rubs at his face, trying to make sense of what's just happened.

I feel like a veteran now. The fear and its face are almost old hat. I smile encouragingly at everyone when they look at me with that same question in their eyes—*This is what you've been up against all this time?* Everyone but Drew. Drew, who won't look at me at all, like if she does, it will upend her worldview again.

She lingers in the doorway, eyes focusing on nothing, as she reckons with her own fear. I know that feeling well.

I rise to my feet and creep my way over Malachi and Yaya to her. She jumps when she realizes that I've moved, and I tilt my head toward the door. Drew turns on her heel and walks out of Gael's apartment without another word. I let the door shut lightly behind us.

"Hey," I say awkwardly.

Drew's eyes narrow at me, already back to her usual annoy-ance. "He-*llo*," she says, dragging the word out. "Do you need something?"

"Oh, I just wanted to check in with you," I say. "You seemed . . . not yourself." Not confident. Not fearless. Not calculated. She seemed wholly human back there, and it's not something I'm used to. It's not something I hate to see, though.

"That will happen when you're presented with the unfathom-able existence of the supernatural," Drew says sharply. She shifts back and forth, lifting her chin as she meets my gaze, like she's trying to look down her nose at me—hard to achieve since we're identical twins and thus the same height. "I'm fine."

"It's okay if you're not," I say.

"But I *am*, so." Drew says it in such a way that I know she means for the conversation to be over. Ended. On her terms. Like always.

And she transforms her face so she looks . . . fine.

But I wish she didn't. I wish she'd *show* that she feels the same biting terror that I did. I wish her heart still raced and her breath still caught and she let herself feel the world come to a shattering end, because that had happened to me. I want her not to just know, like she does now, but to *understand*, because they aren't the same thing, and it's a common thing, for us to get confused by the two.

Drew shoulders past me hard enough to make me stumble and shoves the door open.

Before I can manage my anger, I rasp, "Makes sense that you're the asshole, Drew. You really are a jerk."

Drew's the asshole. *The* asshole. She's the jock who gets with a friend's ex and thinks it's nothing. She's the bully who belittles the nerd. She's the overachiever who makes everyone feel bad about themselves. She's the *fucking* asshole, and now that I see it, now that I've said it, I can't stop thinking it.

Drew holds the door open for me only so that she doesn't prove me right. I slip in under her arm and march past her into the living room. Gael's mom seems to have gone to her bedroom, so it's just the six of us now. I take a knee next to Leila and lean into her side.

She bends her head close to my ear. "All good?" she murmurs against the curve of my lobe.

I snort. "No. Whatever."

Leila sighs, sitting taller, and I slump farther across her lap, looking up at Malachi and Yaya.

"Thanks for that, badass," I say.

Yaya looks up at me, startled. "Huh?"

"You saved our lives." I explain, "Final Girl shit if I ever saw it."

Yaya at least tries to smile. "I guess. . . . I do what I can."

I laugh. "Yeah, you do," I agree. I twist to look over at Gael, raising an eyebrow. "What now, genius?"

"Huh?" Gael says.

"Is there an echo in here or what?" I joke.

"How are you . . . so calm?" Leila asks, looking down at me with big eyes. I turn to lie on my back, head tilted up in her lap as I meet her gaze.

"Because she's faced it *three* times and lived," Malachi says. "She's still afraid but . . ."

"It's manageable," I finish. "And now that *you've* all seen it, we can *officially* stop calling me crazy." I can't help the jab at Drew, and it feels *good*, no longer holding back.

"You said it didn't try to isolate Drew. It followed both of you. *Again.* You're always there," Leila mutters. "Do you think that's why we've avoided being killed? You?"

I shake my head. "No. I'm just the opening kill. The forgettable one." Yaya makes a noise of disgust at the notion, but I push on. "I think it just means it's escalating, more sure of itself. It's not going to go away, so we need to stop waiting and get rid of it. *Fast.*" I'm not saying anything they don't know, but I emphasize the last word, to show exactly how serious I am. It's what they need right now—someone else who can be in control. Tomorrow, maybe it'll hit me again and someone else will pick up the slack, but I know the role I serve tonight. "So, ideas, thoughts, observations?"

"We should jump it," Gael says grimly, apparently fresh out of horror-trope ideas.

I frown. "I'm not sure we can jump a demon, but . . . sure, we'll write that down. Drew, you love a list. Why don't you take notes?" I suggest acidly. She follows my direction without even glancing at me. "Anything else?"

"It can't touch Yaya. Or Yaya can't touch it," Drew volunteers.

"What do you mean?" Leila asks. "Like it . . . avoided her?"

"No, it *screamed*," Yaya admits. "When I reached out to touch it, and its skin, like, parted to *avoid* being touched by me. But it only ran when I showed it the knife. So I don't know if it's the athame or me that it was really afraid of. Rules of the Final Girl or demonology."

Drew leans forward, eyes brightening. "So . . . we should test it, then."

Malachi frowns. "What do you mean?"

Drew's not *slow* to come to conclusions, but she likes to think through every scenario before she presents a hypothesis, because she can't let herself be wrong. So she pauses until finally her face sheds the mask of uncertainty for a slow, settled smugness. She smiles at all of us.

"When scientists do experiments, they are often motivated by what they know rather than what they don't. We should focus on what we know. We know the demon can't touch Yaya. We know that it's stalking us. And we know it follows *rules*. Let's force it to follow them and catch it while it tries," Drew suggests.

"You want to lure it out," I say slowly. "And use yourself as bait?"

And after all that hard work I'd done to keep her alive.

"Well, it wouldn't be me, but I don't want to volunteer anyone," Drew demurs.

"How couldn't it be you? You're next," I press, a harder edge to my voice now.

Drew challenges, "The demon operates on rules, correct? We've established that we all fill typical archetypes. You, Devon, the opening kill. Blonde. Malachi, Black and queer. And me, apparently, as the asshole." Apparently. Hilarious. Leila tries to catch my eyes with a smirk, but I don't quite meet hers. "The demon attacks us in this order. But it has yet to *get* one of us. In fact, when it doesn't, it moves on."

Gael sits up taller, staring at Drew in wonder. He finally looks like himself, excitement coloring his cheeks again as he grabs on to the idea. That unnatural stillness that had seized his limbs drains away, and he vibrates with overstimulation.

"It can only move forward. Not come back. That's why it didn't kill Devon to get to you," Gael says.

"I mean, it certainly tried," I interject.

Gael shakes his head. "Nah, if it really was trying, it would've gotten you, right?" he asks. I try to interject again, but a giddy chuckle slips from his mouth. "*I'm* next. For real this time."

"Exactly. It won't come after me, because its focus is on its next victim. You," Drew says decisively. "I think we should use its penchant for rules to try to kill it." She looks proud of her proposal.

"Why should we tempt fate *on a guess*?" I ask. "We should take a minute. Think this through."

"You're the one who just said we shouldn't waste time. The demon has rules. Let's force it to follow those rules. We'll have plans in place, and then Yaya will strike. We can do this together and put this mess behind us."

Except it doesn't curl all the way over. Not for me, at least. Because Gael might be latching on to this, but I remember what he said the first night after Délivrance. While Malachi and I were safe, the people we were with *weren't*. Alexis had died a grisly death, her body smashing into the front of an Uber. Malachi's date, Marco, had been strangled by not-Marco. People had taken our place and paid for the sin of being just a little bit similar to us, and the demon had taken a token from them. No one has faced "consequences" for Drew's actions or provided anything to satisfy its need.

Drew sees my skepticism and answers it before I can even

voice it. "We know the demon's history. Jack Strode said that was key. It's an infection, right? An infection spreads. It passes to the next carrier whether or not it kills its victim. We have to diagnose it—at least confirm the rules it follows if we can't kill it—if we want to have any hope of speeding up its . . . prognosis—death, rather." I look over at Malachi and Yaya.

Malachi looks like he's considering it. Yaya's expression is harder to discern. I turn to Leila for help, but I can see she's swayed by Drew, forever the genius. Forever the smart one. The one with a *plan*.

"How could we even lure it out to test it?" I challenge.

"The demon works on rules. So do we," Malachi says slowly.

"What do you mean?" Yaya asks.

"All the demon's rules are about what it must do and in what order—its next person to kill must be Gael, et cetera. Ours are about what we *can't*. So if we broke a rule—a big one—wouldn't that summon the demon?" Malachi says.

"And which rule is that?" Leila asks with a raised eyebrow.

I remember it well: "Don't have sex."

CHAPTER SIXTEEN

The plan has a hierarchy of goals, and at the top is "kill the demon." There are two prongs to Drew's plan, one depending on if it follows its own rules and one if it cares more about us breaking ours. I want to doubt that its reasoning powers are so great that it would follow Drew's predicted path, but I know that the demon is smarter than it looks. One would think that a demon doesn't need to have a reason to harass poor, unsuspecting teens, but there's something about it all—its deliberateness, the way it tracks like a horror film's nasty arc, the way it seems like there's something hiding inside the nebulous shape of it. So if there's even a chance Drew's right and we can slaughter it before it manages to kill one of us? We're going to take it. Failing that, we'll at least know more about how it operates for a future attempt.

Peering out from the window, I look both ways, checking the street. Empty. For now.

"We don't have to actually kiss, right?" Gael asks, nose wrinkled as he regards Leila with a haunted look in his eyes. He curls up against the frilly pillows that she has piled up at the head of her bed, her hyena Squishmallow being squeezed into a pulp between his knees.

Leila scoffs. "You *wish* I'd kiss you."

"I really, really don't," Gael insists. He turns back to Drew, the de facto leader of this plan. "So . . . do we?"

Drew looks over at Malachi. He leans against the doorway, rubbing at his chin, but there's a glint of something wicked in his eyes.

"Well, the demon has to think it's real," Malachi says slowly. Gael fakes a gag and Malachi snorts. "Boy, it's really not serious. You two have kissed before, right?" He's referencing what-must-never-be-mentioned, an unfortunate game of Spin the Bottle, which had resulted in our hastily called Team Meeting back-to-back coming out after we refused to touch lips.

My mind goes back to the night of the party, when Leila and Gael had appeared out of thin air to witness the Ouija board debacle. Leila had looked . . . rumpled. And Gael had looked quite pleased with himself. I cringe from the line of my thoughts.

"I don't know, have we?" Leila deadpans, not giving him the satisfaction. She slides off the side of her bed and approaches me. She lowers her chin, lips drawing closer to my ear. "We really gotta do this, Devon? You think . . . you think anything's gonna come of it?"

"Yes," Drew answers for me, drumming her fingers against the windowsill. "Gael is next. We're not going to beat around that bush. But we can see what rules are most important to it. Will it attack Leila and Gael for rule breaking, or will it just go after Gael because he's next? Either way, we can get the jump on it and Yaya can outright kill it."

Yaya shifts anxiously, the athame clasped between her fingers. She's holding it so tightly that her knuckles go white, and she only looks up when she feels the weight of all our eyes on her. Yaya's mouth curls into a half smile that doesn't really reach her eyes, and I fight the yearning to go to her side, to talk her up. Malachi easily fills that role instead. He whispers something to her that I can't hear and taps her on the nose with a tiny smile.

"Okay, so we know our positions?" I ask. Everyone nods, ready to be done with all of this. "Leila, how long are your parents out?"

"You know my parents are always out. We've got a while," she says. But she's less confident than usual, squirming in her own skin. I take her by her wrists and draw her out of the room, as Malachi does us the courtesy of stepping into Leila's bedroom and shutting the door.

"Are you good?" I ask her seriously. "Because I need you to be good."

Leila jerks. "Uh, yeah. I'm good. I'm just . . . freaked out."

"About hooking up with Gael while we film you or about the possibility of a demon showing up?" I ask sharply.

The filming aspect was Drew's idea. She'd referenced experiments done in labs with live subjects, like mice. The mice were constantly under surveillance so that the scientists could run back the tape and see specific reactions to stimuli. So in this case, Gael, Leila, and the demon are our three little mice. Unless we kill it and then hopefully we never even need this footage.

"All of it. All of it freaks me out," Leila rasps. "Like . . . this shit is *real*. It's actually not a game."

"Did you still think it was?" I ask, brow furrowing. The realization dawns over me slowly, and I can't find it in myself to even be angry. I smile bitterly. "You really didn't believe me."

Leila drops her head onto my shoulder and she sighs. "Look,

I . . ." She sounds so lost. I stare at her door for a long moment, waiting for her to compose herself against my shoulder. She stands up straight again. "I believed you, Devon. You have to believe me, I *did*. But seeing it is something else. Being chased by it and hunted is something else. And now, Gael is next, and after Gael is *me*, and that's . . . That's some shit."

There's a beat of silence where we just look at each other.

"It really is some shit, isn't it?" I say shakily.

Leila squints harder at me. When I don't feel the prickle of the demon's presence, I frown. "What?"

Leila giggles. "We've got to bleach your eyebrows again. They're getting dark at the roots."

It's meant to crack the tension between us, but I hold myself stiller than ever. I swallow hard. I know what my eyebrows look like. Dark hairs coming through the blonde. A normal color. One that doesn't make *me* a target. But that also doesn't feel like me. Will I ever feel like me again?

I bite my bottom lip hard to ground myself, and I lean into her, sagging as fear leaks from my bones, just for a moment.

"Okay, okay. We'll do that after this. Demon or no," I decide.

"We really do need to," she says, nodding with the utmost seriousness, and then, with this other goal to focus on, she marches back into her room with more bravado than necessary. She zeroes in on Gael, lounging on her bed, and says, "Okay, honey, just lie back and think of England."

Gael snorts back, "Oh, fuck you," but as Leila's tension has noticeably given way, Gael relaxes too. Leila slides onto the bed next to him, balancing her body on her elbow, facing him.

"We never speak of this afterward, agreed?" Leila asks.

Gael nods. "Agreed. We can spit and shake on it if you want?"

"Don't be gross," Leila retorts.

"You're both so *dramatic*. You're just making out," Drew sighs. She turns around and claps once. "Okay, everyone, places. Malachi, guard the front door. If you hear something going down, slowly come up. We want to box it in so it's got nowhere to go. I'll cover the back door. Yaya, Devon, in the closet."

"Yikes," I say jokingly.

Drew rolls her eyes. "You know what I mean."

I smirk, then reach out, making grabby hands at Gael. "Hey, time to let 'er go."

The "'er" in question is Gael's most precious possession—his used Canon EOS Rebel T7 camera. The very same camera he made his award-winning short film on. Gael presses a kiss to the body, stroking it lovingly.

"Take good care of my baby," Gael says sharply. "I'll kill you if you break it."

"Relax," I insist, taking the camera from him, cradling it like the precious thing that it is. I back up toward Leila's closet, half emptied to make room for Yaya and me. I press myself to the back wall, and Yaya approaches slowly.

She steps in close, not even looking away as Drew shuts the closet door entirely. Drew squats to look at me through where the doorknob had been before we removed it.

"Good?" she asks.

I'm not sure if she's checking in on me because she feels bad about earlier or what, but she must not feel too bad if that's the case because she makes an impatient noise in the back of her throat and says, "The camera, can you shoot from this hole?"

"Yeah, it's fine," I say, annoyed. "Go to *your* position."

Drew draws away, leaving just Yaya and me. I set myself up, holding the camera carefully as I aim the lens at the hole. It's harder than it should be since Yaya's chest is pressed up against my shoulder.

"You okay?" I whisper, looking back at her. There's so little light, I can just make out the shininess of her eyes.

Instead of Yaya answering, Gael shouts, "Yeah, we're good."

"Um . . . maybe play some music," I suggest. "So this can be as *painless* as possible."

"What do you mean?" Leila then.

Yaya's lips tug into a slight smile again. "We mean we don't want to actually hear you two going at it."

"Uh, gross, Yaya," Leila says, but I hear her fumbling with her phone anyway, followed up with the crooning sounds of Kehlani. Real hookup music, through and through.

Yaya leans over my shoulder, and her breath whispers across my ear as she says, "Can't believe she pulled that up on her Spotify that quickly."

I smother my giggles as best I can without the use of either of my hands and end up hiccuping. But that just pushes Yaya to giggle, soft huffs against my skin that send goose pimples running over me. It's cramped in here, with very little space between us, and I have to crane my neck to get a look at the viewfinder, to make sure that it's aimed correctly. I gasp when I feel my back pressed up against Yaya's chest this time.

"Sorry," I whisper in a rush.

"No need to apologize," Yaya says quietly. She shifts even closer and I feel something cold and metal press against my lower back, where the hem of my tank top has risen up and exposed the skin over the waistband of my shorts.

"Is that a knife? Or are you just happy to see me?" I whisper. I turn to look over my shoulder and meet her eyes, ready to dissolve into laughter again, but I find myself stricken by the solemnity that she stares back at me with.

"Yeah, sorry. Sorry," she rasps back.

"Were you scared?" I ask quietly. "In the hallway?"

"It's complicated," Yaya says. "It's kinda like . . . when I do a show, right? I'm just nervous until I get out there. Until I have to perform. Like . . . I . . . I'm terrified right now. But I wasn't scared when I had to protect you and Drew. I'd never been less scared," Yaya admits. She lets her chin fall against my shoulder, and I move quickly, like I'm uncomfortable. But her spine curves, hands tightening on my hips to properly draw me to rest my weight against her. "Better?"

"Hmm," I sigh, giving in and sagging into her.

"Can you see the viewfinder better?" she asks.

"Oh," I try to stop myself from sounding flustered. "Uh, yeah. Totally." I squint down at it, getting a proper look to confirm, and I pause. "Oh, they are . . . not shy, are they? They're really selling it."

Yaya leans even closer, and I can *feel* her surprise rather than see it. "Oh."

Gael is on his back, half buried in the pile of frilly pillows, while Leila looms over him, kissing him like she's trying to suck his soul out of his body. Her fingers are buried in his hair while his hands are roaming her back, one of them sliding lower and lower and then—oh, there Leila goes, redirecting his hand back up firmly without ever breaking away to breathe. Doesn't she need to *breathe*?

Maybe Gael doesn't need to either because now he's up on his elbows, burying one hand in Leila's mass of hair, tugging her even closer by her hips. Which just makes me think of Yaya's hands on my hips.

I make the mistake of looking up over my left shoulder, and Yaya isn't watching the viewfinder. She's watching me, an uncertain look on her face.

"What?" I mouth, even though I'm afraid of shattering the tension in the closet.

The feeling of something crawling up the back of my neck comes back with different implications.

Yaya's free hand comes up to ghost over my right shoulder, pressing lightly to the bare skin over my collarbone. Her lips part, and her gaze flickers down, over the shadow of me, over the camera, over—

"Devon," she whispers, but it's tinged with fear, not desire.

I look down at the viewfinder again.

No, same implications as always. Damn. At the slightly cracked window next to Leila's bed, there is something dark slithering through. Leathery fingers reach in, and the crack slowly begins to widen. The prickle on the back of my neck intensifies.

Neither Gael nor Leila seems to notice; so shockingly entwined with one another, they've forgotten that they hate each other, too busy sucking face to remember our goals. But they'll soon be reminded.

I freeze as the demon stands up. Here it is.

Yaya's hand tightens on my shoulder, and then she whispers,

"On my count, move." I nod, but the demon isn't moving, only looming, slowly tilting its head back and forth as it watches them.

Look up. Breathe, for God's sake, I think viciously.

Gael leans back, lips finally parting, and whispers, "Jesus *Christ.*"

But it's not because of the demon. I want to scream at the two of them, but we can't.

Yaya is slowly pushing me to the side, getting into the tiny gap between the door and my body. She's shaking, but her voice is steady as she breathes, "Three . . . two . . ."

"Not my ministry," Leila says with a smarmy grin, still oblivious too.

"One."

We don't get a chance to act, though. The unholy scream the demon lets out is finally enough. Leila and Gael are forced violently from their own private world, and Leila gasps, rolling off Gael into a crouch on the ground. But Gael is frozen on the bed. I wait for it to make its choice, to go after Gael or corral both of them, but Yaya doesn't.

She knees the door open, and it hits Leila's wall with a slam. She throws herself against the foot of the bed, holding up the knife like it's a gun. I slowly emerge after her, clutching Gael's camera on my chest, pointing it right at the demon. Leila armycrawls toward me and I crouch, then pull her up with me with my free hand.

The demon turns immediately to face off against Yaya.

"Yeah, you . . . back the fuck off," Yaya barks. It's not something Yaya would ever say, but it comes out near natural. Like lines that she's rehearsed in the mirror again and again. Or a dance that she's committed to her bones in the practice room.

The demon draws itself up again, and it's *tall*. But being up close is not the same as seeing it at a distance, and I can make a more clinical assessment from behind the camera. It's not the same unnatural height that I'd thought it was, more like six foot seven. A basketball player's height. I could meet someone this tall in real life, theoretically. That's somehow more unsettling than even its leathery skin, its webbed fingers or dark claws.

Gael scrambles off the bed, backing away toward the door. The demon looks up, its pupilless eyes tracking him, but it takes a slight step back toward the window as Yaya advances.

"Stop moving," she insists, and the demon *listens*. It's just standing there, looking, and as it does, it feels like there's something *mounting*. It flickers its gaze over our faces, and then back to Yaya, and it smiles that wide human tooth smile. Yaya flinches, unsettled by the Chiclets grin. "I'm going to . . . I'm going *to* . . ."

Yaya falters in her advances. Her hand—with the athame—droops just slightly.

"Wait, Yaya, *don't*—" I warn.

The second the knife tip points a hair downward, the demon lets out another howl and bounds over Leila's bed in one long stretch of its legs.

"EVERYTHING OKAY?" I hear Drew shout, followed by the thudding of her feet coming up the stairs, while Yaya turns with the sound, tightening her grip on the knife again.

The demon stills, jerking up at the sound of Drew's voice.

I know immediately and instinctively that Drew and Gael are wrong. Gael's not next.

It's still *Drew*.

"Drew! Don't come in here—" I start, just as the bedroom door slams open.

Drew hovers in the doorway for a moment, looking down at the demon crouched before her. "Oh, *fuck*," she blurts out, and then she throws herself to the right just as the demon begins to *crawl* toward her like scuttling vermin. Drew hops over an outstretched arm and lands uneasily on one of the steps leading down to the parlor floor. "Malachi, second plan! Front door!"

Gael pushes himself to his feet, shuddering, unaware the demon has turned its sights on a different sort of prey. It tilts its head as its eyes follow her, smiling widely. The asshole is *back* on the menu.

"Drew is *not* for consumption!" I shout, but the demon scurries out of the room and lets out a spitting screech, kicking the door shut behind it in an attempt to slow me down. In my panic, my fingers slip over the doorknob twice before I wrench the door open.

"Wait! Devon, wait!" Yaya shouts. "Let me go first—"

The death rattle is loud. I hear Drew's gasp from the first floor but can't see her, and it only makes me move faster.

"Get away from her!" I shout as I run down the hall, run down the steps toward the parlor floor, before colliding with something. Someone.

I gasp, seeing my own face looking back at me. Drew grabs on to me, tugging me toward the door. "Come on," she insists. I fumble with the camera, attempting to loop an arm through the free-hanging strap and secure it to my shoulder.

But if the demon isn't here, it's—

I turn around, seeing the demon lingering at the top of the stairs, only just jerking out of the way of Yaya's wild slashing.

"Get down here! Forget it!" I scream, just as the demon lunges for Yaya. She just avoids it, only for Gael to jerk in and crack his skateboard down on the demon's head in response.

The demon *roars*, throwing its head back in pain. Yaya runs past it, ducking under a flailing arm, ashen, but her grip on the athame never loosens. Not again. Leila and Gael run past it too, pounding down the first few stairs. But it recovers and follows hot on their heels. It's close behind Gael, reaching out.

"Come on, Devon!" Drew shouts as I try to reach back. I can see just past her, to the street, where Malachi lingers, anxious.

Then I hear Leila shout, "Gael!" I turn around just in time to see Leila's shoulder collide with the demon's rib cage as it looms over Gael, fingers wrapped around his shoulder. There's the clear sound of a snap, like a tree branch breaking off its trunk. Then Leila's floating in midair.

Reality crashes, just like gravity, which brings Leila down hard, with the demon. It's a forever sort of tumble, the sound of Leila's body thudding down each step, the demon rolling with her, while Gael stares frozen in horror near the top of the stairs. The demon hits the wall next to the landing first with a thud and Leila stops just a step ahead. The demon's next sound is a weak hiss, and then it looks directly past me, at Drew, before it pushes up, hands fluttering over Leila's prone body, like it can't decide how to kill her. Leila, who is not supposed to be next.

Sure enough, it tilts his head, as if beckoning Drew toward it. Offering her the chance to sacrifice herself for our friend's life.

I can't make myself move at all as I stare at Leila, wondering if this is like Alexis, like Marco, all over again. But Leila isn't an asshole. She *isn't*.

And then Yaya throws herself forward and swipes down directly on the demon's long leg, catching it in its thigh, plunging the athame deep into what on a human would be tender muscle. The demon roars, tugging back, and a flush of black oozes from the purple-gray wound, revealing soft tissue beneath. It practically shoves Yaya away, and she stumbles back, slamming into the wall hard enough to give me pause. Its eyes are locked on Yaya, but Yaya doesn't falter, just pushing off the wall, primed to leap.

"Come if you wanna," she threatens.

The demon lingers for just a second more. It makes an aborted move forward and then it hisses, awkwardly favoring its noninjured leg, and scuttles back up the stairs. I hear a door slam and then . . . nothing.

"Leila," Gael croaks, and then he slides down the stairs to her, quicker than even me, who's only feet away but can't move. He grabs her, dragging her between his legs, propping her up against him like she's nothing more than a doll.

And then she makes a soft groan. "Holy shit, *ow*." Leila blinks bleary-eyed back into consciousness.

"Oh my God, you're okay," I gasp, shoving my way past Yaya to Leila, grabbing her free hand. "You're *okay*."

Leila blinks again, slowly, shaking herself from the grip of grogginess. "I . . . I am. I . . . *ow*," she groans, and it's more than just the pain of a fall. She grabs tighter at my hand, her grip bone white as she looks down, panting. "Ow, ow, ow, my ankle . . . fuck, *my ankle*."

Yaya kneels, poking at the swollen flesh, causing Leila to curse loudly. She looks up severely and says, "We have to get you to a hospital."

"Oh my God, I'm going to be in so much *trouble*," Leila says.

Drew frowns and says, "I'll call an Uber XL. Come on, get her up."

And then everything gets worse.

"That won't be necessary," a familiar voice says, in a cadence eerily similar to Leila's usual meaningful nonchalance.

The Benadys have come home early.

CHAPTER SEVENTEEN

The hospital waiting room isn't empty, like it is in TV shows and movies.

The overhead lights do wash the room out in a stark white like you'd expect, making the linoleum floors look dingy in comparison, but the old chairs are packed with the sick and waiting. No one's coughing or sneezing, thankfully, but there's a heaviness to knowing they're all there for ailments, visible or not. There's one small child, about seven or eight, sniffling as their mother cradles them, rocking them back and forth. For a short moment I feel bitter with my jealousy, yearning for my own mother.

Looking around our small circle, I can see my own thoughts reflected in the others' expressions. Malachi looks drained of life, hunched over his phone in the threadbare waiting chair, the stuffing coming out at the seams under him. Gael is curled up into a ball next to him, face buried in his knees. His shoulders are shaking with suppressed sobs, and I make an awkward move to comfort him, then stop, unsure of how I can. Malachi doesn't even look up as he wraps one arm around Gael's shoulders and tips him so Gael presses his face into his shoulder.

Yaya's arm is a hot brand against my own, and her shoulders are so low and hunched with the weight of her guilt.

"It's not your fault," I whisper to her gently as I fiddle with Gael's camera in my lap. Yaya doesn't tear her eyes away from where they're concentrating on the space between her sneakers, where there's a suspicious stain on the ground. "It's not your fault, Yaya, please—"

Drew's voice cuts through, fine edged like the sharpest knife. "She didn't follow through. If it's not her fault, then whose is it?"

Malachi jerks, looking up swiftly. "Don't go there, Drew," he warns through clenched teeth.

Drew leans against the bump-out in the wall, no chairs available to her. She's tightly wound, both emotionally and physically, arms folded against her chest, mouth twisted into a knot. She lets her head fall back against the wall and then she leans forward just as quickly.

"I'm just *frustrated*. We had a plan and it just . . ." Drew groans into her hands.

"It didn't work. That's it," I bite out. "Drew . . . if you're not going to say anything helpful or encouraging, it might be best not to speak at all."

Drew sneers at me, leaning in. "I'm just saying—"

"Stop *just saying*!" I bark.

"You guys . . . ," Malachi says, as the tensions crackle and rise. He jerks his chin across the waiting room. "It's Mrs. Benady."

Leila has always looked a lot like her mom. It's never been more evident than now as Mrs. Benady approaches us. She keeps a neutral expression on her face, no hint of rage or relief, and that's somehow scarier. I hold my breath until she's just in front of our chairs, towering over us, despite not even clearing five feet.

"It's a broken ankle," Mrs. Benady says. "A clean break. No surgery will be required."

"Oh." Yaya exhales in a rush, looking up with watery eyes. "That's good."

Mrs. Benady looks away from her, refusing to soften at Yaya's earnestness.

"She's awake. Her father is with her, but she is asking for you," Mrs. Benady continues, and this is what makes Gael finally look up. He jumps to his feet, still wan and wrung out, and it's usually funny, how much taller he is than Mrs. Benady. But nothing is funny about how she looks up, neck craning, when she asks him: "What happened?"

Gael swallows hard, Adam's apple bobbing. He doesn't say anything, just makes a soft wheeze, but Mrs. Benady doesn't look away.

"We got rowdy," Malachi says, slowly standing up and discreetly grabbing on to Gael's elbow, like he means to anchor him. "We were just playing around, and then Leila fell down the stairs. It was an accident." It's not technically a lie. Not all of it, at least.

Still, Mrs. Benady only gives Malachi a cursory look before she redirects the full weight of her searching gaze back on Gael. Gael only just stops himself from shuddering. The truth bobs in his throat, and he swallows it back only when Malachi's nails dig into the skin of his arm.

"Were you getting high?" Mrs. Benady asks.

There's a beat of raw silence. Gael's reputation precedes him in the worst ways sometimes. It's not even true, but to Mrs. Benady, the possibility is obvious. It's like the time he got me in trouble with our homeroom teacher, but so much worse because someone actually got *hurt* this time. *Her* girl got hurt. Gael rocks back and forth from the balls of his feet to his heels, and when he nods, it's a horrible thing. Just a sharp bob of the head, and then he tears his eyes away, because telling the truth—that we were trying to kill a demon—would be so much worse, would seem like the bigger lie.

Mrs. Benady lets out a low whistle. "Okay," she murmurs. She doesn't even sound angry. "Okay. I should let the doctor know, right?" I stiffen; if she tells the doctor and they test, we might get caught in the lie.

"She . . . she wasn't high," Drew blurts out, having come to the same conclusion as me. "Just . . . Gael. And me." Drew ignores the sharp look that Gael sends her.

"And me," I add in solidarity.

"Right," Mrs. Benady says. Her brows are drawn so tight, there's no skin visible between them. Leila has her eyebrows—thick and heavy and enviable. "But whose weed was it?"

"Mine," Gael croaks, because it's *always* his weed, and Mrs. Benady knows it.

"Leila's father and I give you *all* so much leeway. You think we don't smell it? Or hear you? But we want you to have a safe space to do these things. That's what we agreed to with all your parents when you entered high school," Mrs. Benady says.

My stomach drops out from under me—the idea that my parents have *any* idea of what I might be up to at any given time is shocking, even if it shouldn't be.

Mrs. Benady continues: "But I am so disappointed in you. Leila got *hurt*. Any one of you could've been hurt, and I have the feeling that you weren't going to call one of us. You're all going to enter college soon—Drew, you're practically leaving already—and if you'd had even a *modicum* of sense . . ." She trails off. Her voice never rises, but the intensity doesn't let up either, and my eyes prickle with the ghost of hot tears, threatening to spill.

"I'm so sorry, Mrs. Benady, I am. This is me. This is all on me. *I* messed up," Gael blurts out, taking the entirety of the blame and hoisting it on his shoulders. It's clear to us that he means to take the fall for all of it. After all, Leila had been trying to protect *him*.

"No, I should've done something," Yaya insists, speaking up for the first time. Gael looks at her, wild and blurry eyed, shaking his head.

"Yaya, no—" Gael starts.

Mrs. Benady holds up her hand, interrupting the blame game to hand down a verdict. "I blame all of you. Now, Leila would like to see you. While you visit with her, Leila's father and I will be making *quite* a few calls, won't we?"

My stomach twists up tight. My parents are going to be so pissed.

The only reason all five of us are allowed to enter Leila's room is because Dr. Benady is a well-liked cardiologist at the hospital. We pile into a hospital room that is far nicer than the waiting room. Leila is sitting up against a pile of pillows, in a hospital gown.

"I know, I look like I'm dying," Leila says, pursing her lips. She pinches the ill-fitting fabric of the gown. "They made me change, and now I'm sitting here with my ass out." She jokes as if she doesn't have her splinted ankle hoisted up on a pillow.

"No cast?" I ask.

Drew answers for Leila: "They have to wait twenty-four hours for some of the swelling to go down."

Leila nods in confirmation. She looks over at her parents, who linger in the doorway apprehensively. Finally, Dr. Benady nods and simply closes the door behind him, presumably so they can go call all our parents. She leans forward, raising an eyebrow. "Well, that was something, wasn't it?"

There's a beat where we all stare at her in collective disbelief.

And then Gael bursts into ugly, messy sobs. He unravels quickly, sinking onto the edge of the bed and grabbing Leila by the shoulders, dragging her in close to crush her in a hug.

"Oh my God, Gael?" Leila wraps one arm around his neck, looking over at me in confusion. She flinches as Gael accidentally jostles her ankle. "Ow, *fuck*."

"I'm sorry," Gael gasps, tearing himself away, wiping at his eyes frantically. "I'm so sorry, Leila. If you hadn't tried to save *me*, if I had just gotten out of the way myself—"

Leila hushes him sharply. "Hey, no. It was going after you. Well, to get to Drew. We thought we could manipulate the demon and we were wrong. Kinda wrong, because I mean, we *did* get it there. But at least no one died," Leila insists.

Gael scoffs. "You nearly did!"

"I fell down the stairs," Leila protests. "You know how many times I slip down those stairs a day? They're really steep."

"Yeah, but it could've been worse. Man, you're my best friend," Gael rasps. "I don't even know what I would've . . . I don't . . ."

Leila's gaze softens. "Oh, you idiot," she sighs, pulling him in again, patting his shoulder. "I know, Gael. I know."

It should be a painfully awkward thing, watching one friend cry and the other comfort him, but it's almost like I feel like I *am* Gael. Like she's comforting me, too. Watching Leila sigh and snipe like she always does makes everything feel, maybe not normal, but next to it. Gael calms down slowly, matching his breath

241

to the steady beep of Leila's heart monitor. When he pulls back, face flushed from emotion, he doesn't even look embarrassed. He just sits next to Leila in the bed, and I slowly creep forward, sitting on the other side of her when she extends a hand.

"I'm sorry too, Leila," Yaya says painfully.

Leila narrows a look at her. "Don't you start too. It was a messed-up situation all around," Leila insists. "Look . . . no more apologies. We had a plan. It didn't work out the way we wanted it to. But it was worth it."

"Worth it?" Malachi demands. "You are in a hospital bed. Your ankle is *broken*."

Leila scoffs. "And it'll heal."

"It shouldn't have happened at *all*," Yaya insists, and this time she refuses Leila's attempts at consoling and absolving her. "I had a job—Final Girl—and I didn't do it. I know that. That's on me."

It sounds like her doubts, but the words—that's a Drew job. Drew, who has yet to say anything at all, standing closest to the door, like she's ready to leave. Like *always*. I honestly wish she just would. But she meets my glare and takes a hesitant step forward.

Hands clasped behind her back, she offers a limp-dicked acquiescence of *maybe* being wrong. "The demon is smarter than we gave it credit for. And its rules are more complicated than we foresaw."

"Exactly. So, let's see the data," Leila says, playing into the experiment metaphor of it all.

"The . . . the video?" I ask. I look over at Gael helplessly. He holds his backpack straps even tighter, like he can't move. "Are you sure, Leila? It's late, and you're tired and in pain and—"

"And this can't wait," Leila says severely. She nods down at her ankle, and I force myself to look, to take her pain in. "If this isn't going to be in vain, I'm going to need to see the footage. *We* need to see it." Her gaze softens just a tad when she looks at Gael, and she nudges him with her elbow.

It sets him into motion, and he nods, beckoning me forward. I crowd closer, holding up the camera, and I know enough to be able to fetch the footage I shot. Yaya, Malachi, and Drew crowd around the bed, so all of us are squinting down at the viewfinder while we play it back.

It starts as awkwardly as I'd expected it to—Gael and Leila going for it in her bed. Neither of them is a coward about it, though, both watching the screen with a lack of embarrassment I admire.

Even when Malachi whistles between his teeth and says, "I thought we were doing a fake-out-make-out, but my *God*, you're eating him alive," Leila simply shrugs.

I shift closer to her, holding the camera out more as it refocuses on the demon cracking the window wider. From the closet it had looked like it floated in, but from this angle, it looks like it's shimmying, attempting to fit through a gap just slightly too small for it. When it pulls itself upright, it lingers and stares at Leila and Gael, taking them in. It's grossly voyeuristic in a way that feels . . . *different* from our filming.

Gael points. "Pause it," he says sharply.

I press the pause button quickly. "What?"

"Don't you see it?" Gael says, tapping the tiny screen.

I do, but it's hard to put into words. A shadow layered upon a smaller shadow. A shape of something familiar—

"It's shaped like a person. There's a *person* inside of it," Drew says, her cool composure cracking with her surprise.

And there . . . is. It's a demon as it's always been; I can still see its leathery skin and long tipped claws and yawning mouth. But in the low glow of Leila's bedroom lighting, the camera makes it seem like it's backlit, and inside its demonic shape, there *is* the shape of a person. With slim shoulders and long arms and everything familiar.

Malachi huffs gently, looking at Drew in worry.

Gael's expression rages between mournful and excitement. "Demonic possession?" he begins to suggest just as the door slides open again.

The Benadys aren't the interrupters. Instead, it's a doctor I don't recognize. He's the kind of doctor you *would* see on TV, in the kind of shiny waiting room you expect. Smarmy, with a full head of dark, slicked-back hair, big blue eyes, and full lips. He's in dark scrubs, and his white lab coat says LAURIE underneath the pocket.

"Hello, Dr. Laurie," Leila says with a pointed lack of enthusiasm. "He's the assistant director of Ortho. My dad asked him to check on me himself, even though it's not really necessary."

Dr. Laurie purses his lips. "Well, you aren't the doctor, are you, Miss Benady?" he retorts. Before she can answer, he looks at all of us with distaste. I can just imagine what we look like— exhausted and bruised and run ragged by the thing that haunts us—and I can see him forming judgment as he looks at each of us. "Visiting hours are over. I do believe you should all see your way home." He doesn't leave it up for debate, just holds the door open.

None of us moves right away.

"Dr. Benady said we could visit her," Malachi says slowly.

"Dr. Benady is not her doctor. *I* am her doctor. I am in fact doing Dr. Benady a favor by *being* her doctor. Get out," Dr. Laurie says sharply. When we still hesitate, he *snaps* at us like we're dogs, and that shocks us into moving.

From her seat in the bed, Leila gags, making an apologetic expression that Dr. Laurie wrinkles his nose at. He stands next to her bedside, reading over her charts, and says too loudly, "There are better ways to rebel against your parents than befriending people like *that*, Leila."

The door shuts behind us and Gael glares back at it. "Elitist prick," he says, loud enough that I know his voice carries inside, because Leila's bark of laughter is loud enough to reach us.

That's the sound that finally starts to assuage some of my guilt. Leila is *laughing*. Leila is *alive*, and that makes all the difference.

But leaving doesn't feel right. Not yet. We shift back and forth, looking up and down the hallway for any sign of the Benadys. Instinctively, we huddle closer together, trying to make ourselves as small as possible, pressed out of the way of everyone else in the busy hall. Gael rocks back and forth, swallowing hard and rubbing at his arms.

"I'm glad she's okay," he says quietly. "I don't know what I would've done if she weren't okay."

"Me neither," Malachi says, letting out a breath so heavy that it feels like he's been holding it for hours. He rubs at his eyes, trying to brush sleep away. "I'm so . . . I feel like I've lived a thousand lives."

It's a sentiment I feel too. The Best Summer Ever should only be *just* starting. But Drew's graduation party feels like it happened months ago, even though it's only been a week. I can feel myself aging.

"Well, we only have one. Let's try not to lose any of them," Drew says coolly.

Malachi shoots her a narrow-eyed look. "Do you have something to say?"

"No," Drew says with the energy of someone who *definitely* has something to say.

She's only said the one word, but it's enough. This never-ending week has been more than enough. Every itch of frustration and anger that I've swallowed back for years rises and rises like bile, and there's no swallowing it back now. There's only the sour venom of it, forcing me to grab Drew by the bicep and drag her away from our friends and around the corner. I move too quickly for Drew to even fight back until we've fully turned into another, quieter hallway.

"What is wrong with you?" she demands, finally tearing herself away.

Everything, I want to laugh in her face.

"You need to get off your high fucking horse, Drew," I snap, my voice echoing nastily in the empty corridor. I pause for a moment, listening for footsteps, but the distant sound of a wet cough is all that I receive back. "You blame Yaya. You blame Gael. When, really, we *should* be blaming you. *You're* the reason that Leila broke her ankle."

"Me?" Drew gapes.

"Yes. It's your not-boyfriend's demon that's after us. And you're the one who wanted to use *us* as bait, to kill it so you could get back to your fancy life and *Avery*. You made Gael and Leila shields just like Alexis and Marco did to me and Malachi, because if you'd listened for one second you'd have known, that demon was after *you*. Asshole," I accuse.

"We thought . . . I thought it skipped me. I thought it had already attacked me and chose not to . . . ," Drew insists, shifting uncomfortably.

"When are you going to realize you can't reason your way out of this?" I say severely. "You're always trying so hard to be *right*, and you just constantly fuck us over in the pursuit. You've always been like that. You've always been a know-it-all, but it's been . . . it's been . . ."

"It's been what?" Drew asks, voice dripping with mockery.

"You have been *insufferable* since the day you said you were going to graduate early," I say.

For a beat, Drew just stares at me like I'm an alien, and then she has the audacity to roll her eyes. "I knew it was going to be about this," Drew says, shaking her head. "It's always about *this*."

"About *what*?" I ask, incredulous.

"Your fucking inferiority complex," Drew says, like it's something that she's brought up time and time again when she's never said anything of the sort. "Don't project your own insecurities onto me, Devon. Don't do that."

"You think . . . you think I feel *inferior*?" I ask in hushed wonder. And then I giggle quietly; it's so gentle that it throws Drew off kilter. "Inferior to *you*? Drew . . . Drew, be serious."

"Excuse me?" Drew asks, voice hard.

I take a step toward her, squinting at her as I look her over. "I don't want to be *you*. I've *never* wanted to be you. You're smarter than me. That's true. You're a whole genius. Graduated early. Gonna do great things. Probably solve world hunger or create world peace or whatever . . . whatever you wanna do. I know that. I've always known that. But, Drew . . . at least I'm fucking *real*," I blurt out.

She is shaking as she looks at me. "What does that even mean?" she demands.

It means so much that my hands are trembling as I try to put the disdain, the hurt, the anger, and the price into words. It means everything, because I know right now, this will change things between us, and that change terrifies me. It's what I've been fighting against all this time.

I can't fight anymore.

"I make mistakes," I say slowly. "And when I do . . . I say sorry. You don't. Did you know that? You don't say sorry, because you don't think that you *make* mistakes. You don't think you're capable of it, because everyone's always told you you're better than the rest of us. But you're not *better* than us, *Andrea*." I can't help but use the construct that she's created out of the name that our parents gave her. I don't need to explain that; she knows.

"I *never* proclaimed myself to be better than anyone," Drew forces out between clenched teeth.

Drew is so close, her forehead is pressed against mine, and I know her. I know her like I know my own reflection. Up close, it's terrifying, the fun-house-mirror reflection of our rage. She grabs at my shoulder, rooting herself in the ground, pressing hard.

"I'm *not* going to solve world hunger. Or create world peace. Or cure cancer," Drew barks. "I don't want to do any of that shit."

I pause and step back. "Huh?"

"*You* want me to do that shit, Devon," Drew grinds out between clenched teeth. "You and Mom and Dad and literally everyone we know, since the day I read you *Brown Bear, Brown Bear*. Do you even know what I'm *doing* next year? Have you thought to ask?" She doesn't let me answer. She's always loved her rhetorical questions. "I'm not doing anything. I didn't *apply* for college because I don't *know* what I'm *doing*. I'm not *going* anywhere."

She doesn't give me a chance to step back, to be windswept by her confession. Instead, she just gets closer again, and I feel like I'm being boxed in.

"You're . . . not going to college?" I ask.

And then I think. I think to that moment when she told me. I think about how she always talked about graduation but nothing else. Nothing more. Nothing *after*.

"You didn't know because you didn't want to *know*. You stopped asking. All you cared about was how you thought it would affect you."

She'd said the same thing to me before, after I tried to tell her about the demon the first time. That I wasn't *interested* in her life outside of my own narrative. She *said* that. And I—

"You don't know anything about me or what I want to do or my friends or my life because you stopped listening to me. I don't think I'm better than you. *You* think I'm better than you, and you . . . you fucked me up, Devon. *You* and everyone else. With your expectations and your dreams and everything that you've cooked up for me, without my *fucking* permission. And then you resented me for it!"

"How . . . ? How is any of this my fault?" I blurt out, floundering. "Mom and Dad are the ones who put you in private school because you're a genius or whatever."

"*You* put me on a pedestal that I'm constantly trying to escape," Drew says.

"Well, stop trying to escape!" I shout.

Drew is shaking. "What?"

"Stop trying to run *away* from me," I beg, feeling myself cracking. "You've been running away from me our entire lives. You're *abandoning* me."

And there it is—out in the open.

I've always known that was the word to describe how I'd felt the day that Drew announced that she was up for early graduation. While my parents had cheered and congratulated her and asked her again and again if she was sure, I hadn't asked at all. I'd known that Drew was sure, because she wouldn't have said anything if she weren't. Drew was absolutely sure about her plan to abandon me one last time. To go off and be an actual adult and start to finally live her life without me like she'd been preparing to do for years, leaving me behind to go places that I couldn't chase her to, *again*.

But to say it out loud makes it real. To say it out loud is to acknowledge that lists and a can-do attitude won't ensure that Drew comes back or fix anything between us. Nothing will, because Drew is sure about this and sure about *me*. Even with the bombshell reality shift that she's not actually leaving, not yet at least, the gap separating us doesn't close, not even an inch.

And then Drew says, each word deliberate, "I didn't leave you behind. You stopped walking next to me."

It's like a punch to the gut, and the distance between us is a cavern that I can't even fathom how to cross.

But then the death rattle sounds, and Drew goes pale.

CHAPTER EIGHTEEN

For a split second I think about doing what Drew is doing to me. What Drew *has* been doing to me for years now. Abandoning her to her fate. I don't imagine she'd make it very far. Drew may be the asshole, but she's no track star. She'd make it down the hallway, sure, but sooner or later, her limbs would lock up from the fear. Or she'd trip. Or she'd—

The possibility of her suffering the same fate as Alexis overpowers my anger, and in a way that just makes me even *more* angry. She probably won't even thank me, will say she was just fine on her own, but I'll do everything I can to save her anyway.

"Fuck *you*," I growl, grabbing the end of a gurney and preparing to shove it at the demon with all my might. Until I look at it. Properly.

It's a woman in light-blue nurse scrubs, a surgery cap covered with clown fish dangling from a crooked pinkie. She scrunches her nose at us and doesn't say anything, just presses her finger to her lips as if to say hush. But she doesn't speak.

"I'm sorry. We were loud," Drew says immediately. She rocks forward, hands held up as if to explain herself, but I grab her by the wrist and jerk her back. Violently, she turns toward me, wrenching herself from my grip. "What's your problem?"

"Hold on," I say, with enough edge in my voice that it cuts

through her anger, right to her logic-brain. I look at the nurse again. The nurse who still hasn't spoken. "We're visiting Leila Benady. Sorry we were loud but we're allowed to be here."

The nurse shifts uncertainly. Still doesn't speak. I lean forward, squinting to look at her name tag, but where her name should be, there's a smudge.

I look down the hallway. There's still nothing but the nurse. Except I'd heard the death rattle and I *know* Drew did too.

"The demon . . . Malachi said the demon pretended to be his date, right?" Drew asks. Sometimes it really does help to have a genius sister—even if she pisses me off. It means I don't have to spell out the connections to her.

Instead, I say, "Run." And then I push the gurney with all my might. It slams right into the center of the nurse, who folds over like her hips are on a hinge, head bowing forward as she grips the gurney and lets out a terrible scream.

The demon's scream.

Yup. Thought so.

I turn on my heel and run down the hallway in the opposite direction from the others. Drew doesn't even hesitate to fall in line for once, just keeps pace as we take the turn. Not-Nurse doesn't make noise in its pursuit, and so every few feet I have to whip my head around to see how far it is behind us. The shape it has chosen is smaller than its usual form, so it takes smaller strides. A clear disadvantage. But there's something else. Each time I glance back and see it coming closer, I catalog a *change*.

Not-Nurse moves more labored than before, like each stride hurts, and its breaths come out wheezing now, instead of the panting of a predator waiting for its prey to make a single mistake.

It occurs to me as we take the corner, skimming against the wall, that Leila isn't the only one that fell down the stairs. The demon did too, tumbling after her, making solid contact with stair upon stair before it rolled its elastic body into a standing position. The demon hadn't been warded off in Leila's house; it had been hurt and had *run*. Just like a person would.

A demon, I had no hopes of stopping. A *person*?

I might be able to escape.

"This way!" I cry out, turning right again, going in a circle, moving close enough to the wall that not-Nurse collides with it in its pursuit, forcing one of the corkboards to rattle. I push harder, putting as much distance as possible between us, before it pushes off the wall and runs after us again.

We skid down the next hallway, and I hesitate for a split second at the end. We're back to where we started—way too close to Leila, who can't escape, plus Gael and the others. Drew must sense the same thing because she goes left, pointing.

"Staircase!" she cries out, shouldering into the next doorway. I fully expect to tumble into the stairs in a replay of what happened in Gael's apartment building. But a heavy thud repels Drew back.

Drew gasps, grabbing at her shoulder. "Locked."

"Come on," I insist, too focused on staying alive to acknowledge when she cries out at the sudden jostling of her sore shoulder as I pass. We go back down the hallway we'd first turned down, restarting the circle like dummies.

This time I reach out with my free hand, shoving and rattling each door we pass. Only one gives and it's a supply closet, full of scrubs and surgical gloves and dead ends. Finally, we reach the last door before we have to turn the corner, and it gives, but there's no staircase in sight.

Instead, it's an empty patient room, the bed stripped bare, only a few monitors and machines around it. It's so dark outside, the windows function more like mirrors than a portal to the rest of the world.

The second we shut the door behind us, I know we've made a mistake, set ourselves up for failure. We've entered a room with no way out. I back up farther into it, clutching at my braids, shaking my head as I search the room for something that proves me wrong. Anything. A miracle.

"No, no, no," I mumble to myself, rushing toward the window again, cupping around my eyes to see how far up seven floors really is.

Far enough we'd die if we jumped.

Drew wrenches open the only other door across the room, but I already know what's behind it.

"It's the bathroom," she gasps. She looks properly afraid now, and when she reaches for me, I can't find the wherewithal to deny her. She's shaking as she drags me closer and whispers, "What do we do? Devon, what do we *do*?"

"I don't . . . I'm going to call Yaya," I blurt out. "Barricade the door." I fumble for my phone, punching in my code as fast as I can.

A terrible sob tears out of Drew's throat, and she seems surprised by the fact that she can make a sound like that, one so utterly human and *weak*. Drew doesn't cry, but the fat droplets that gather at her chin and stain the collar of her shirt prove otherwise. Her fingers dig into my forearms painfully for one more second, and then she releases me, rushing to shove two of the visitors' chairs up against the door, angling one to lock up under the knob. I look down and dial Yaya immediately while Drew moves on to heaving the nightstand halfway across the room to add to her barricade.

Over Drew's sniffling and the ringing, I can hear slow, measured steps.

Something—no, *someone*, I remind myself—is coming.

"I don't want to die," Drew confesses in a panicked whisper.

I want to say, *You won't*, but it catches in my throat, because I don't *know*. There's nowhere to go.

Finally, the phone clicks. "Hello?" I hear Yaya say. "Devon, are you there?"

The door starts to rattle.

"Get down," I rasp, tugging Drew down to her knees, and we crawl beneath the hospital bed. In any other situation, I'd complain about how tightly we're packed, but this time I just press even tighter around her, like a cocoon.

The demon will have to go through *me*. Again.

The door creaks open but stops when it meets the chair. There's a pause. Then a harder shove, and the first chair falls with a clatter that makes me flinch. The door opens a bit wider.

Then I hear: "What the hell is going on?"

One more shove and the nightstand and chair both skid across the scuffed-up linoleum, far enough for the door to open properly.

But instead of heavy-duty, nonslip nurse shoes, I see a pair of HOKA sneakers and the hem of dark-blue scrubs.

"I know you're in here," the voice says.

Dr. Laurie. Drew sags with relief against me, but I just hold tighter.

Dr. Laurie's *voice*, I remind myself. For all I know, this could be another nonperson, like not-Marco.

Dr. Laurie—or maybe not–Dr. Laurie—says loudly, "I thought I told you all that you needed to go *home*." He rattles around the room, walking into the bathroom, like we'll be revealed somewhere amongst the green tile and the old toilet. I watch his feet as he exits and paces the room. "This is not Dr. Benady's hospital, I hope you know. Right now, it's *my* hospital. And you are not *authorized* to be here."

For a moment he stands with his back to the door, and I can picture him—probably with his hands on his hips, his lip curled into what I think might be a permanent sneer. Then he turns and bends over to glare at us, where we're hidden beneath the bed.

"Get over here. Right now," he shouts.

Drew lets out a soft sob, clinging to me, and I stare at him, squinting, trying to find something that reminds me of not-Nurse. But there's no emptiness to his eyes. His skin fits well on his body. Everything seems . . . remarkably normal. And he's *talking*.

"Do I have to repeat myself?"

"No," I choke out. I slowly stand, attempting to pull Drew out of her prone state. She resists, grabbing hard to my shirt, trying to pull me back down. I look back, frowning. "What?"

"Are you sure he's . . . ?" Drew trails off.

"Yes, I'm sure," I say firmly, standing to my full height. I offer my hand to her. "He's regular. A normal. I promise." She takes it, and I slowly guide her from under the bed, meeting Dr. Laurie in the middle of the now-messy hospital room.

Dr. Laurie looks unimpressed. "Is she on drugs?"

It's that question again that makes me snap, "And if she were, would you do anything for her?"

"What?" Dr. Laurie asks.

"If she were on drugs, belittling her wouldn't be helping her or treating her. Do no harm, you dick," I say fiercely, something besides fear rising in me. Something a little more familiar now that seems to grow each time I experience the same horror: rage.

"What is there to harm her here? You're the ones causing havoc in my hospital," Dr. Laurie says coldly. "You can do that in your 'hood' or whatever, but not *here*."

I hear Drew's sharp intake of breath, and Dr. Laurie seems to think it's about what he's said. He looks at the pair of us, triumphant at finally silencing us, and says, "The Benadys really do need to keep better company." He waits for us to react to that, too, but neither of us is looking at *him*.

Not really.

We're more preoccupied with his shadow.

Drew falls onto her ass, back pressed up against the bed, and lets out another gasping sob. I stand before her, planting my feet, looking just over Dr. Laurie's head.

"Hello?" Dr. Laurie asks, snapping at us again. "*Hello*. What are you looking at?"

Grimly I whisper, "Look behind you."

He glances quickly over his shoulder and then stills when he's half turned back to us, like he's only just registering what he saw. He frowns.

"Nurse Katie?" he asks, looking over at her with a raised eyebrow.

So that's the name of the woman who the demon is pretending to be. Not–Nurse Katie neatly steps into the room and closes the door behind it. It leans back and stares for a long moment.

"Were you two *harassing* Nurse Katie?" Dr. Laurie demands.

"That's not Nurse Katie," Drew chokes out.

Dr. Laurie rolls his eyes and looks back at not-Nurse. Then double takes. Its eyes are a glossy ink black now, and its teeth—while human—don't fit its mouth right. The death rattle that emerges is too inhuman. Dr. Laurie gasps, taking a half step back, colliding with me and making me trip over Drew.

"Nurse Katie . . . Nurse Katie, I think something's wrong—" he yelps, grasping around him for anything to put between him and not–Nurse Katie. Unfortunately, the first thing he grabs is Drew, and he practically thrusts her by her shirt at not-Nurse. I shove him hard in the back like a reflex, then whiplash Drew around behind me.

The doctor pitches forward with the unexpected force, right into the loving embrace of not-Nurse.

The asshole doctor.

Not-Nurse's long fingers chase up Dr. Laurie's scrubs, settling right over his name tag, as if it wants to commit the name to memory. And then it drifts to the stethoscope hanging around his neck. I know what's to come before it even happens.

Not-Nurse grabs the aural tube in one hand and the diaphragm in the other and pulls tight across Dr. Laurie's throat, crushing the man's Adam's apple and stopping his screams before they ascend any louder than a yelp.

This is so much worse than with Marco, because this time we can see his face. This time Dr. Laurie really fights back. He claws at not-Nurse's hands, stumbling, and the skin doesn't give, not like it would for a human. Drew and I have to scurry out of their way as they tussle. Dr. Laurie is a solid man, the kind whose muscles aren't for vanity. He shakes and fights until he tumbles back onto the hospital bed, but not-Nurse leaps up, landing in a squat over him, hands never leaving the stethoscope.

For a moment I think Dr. Laurie might sit up and shove it off, but then not-Nurse *twists*—and crack. Dr. Laurie collapses onto the hospital bed and doesn't move. Not-Nurse's chest heaves with each breath, and then it lets out a harsh shriek in Dr. Laurie's face before it leaps off and drags Dr. Laurie's body by the stethoscope. The body lands in a heap on the floor, and the demon draws itself up to full height again.

For a moment we just look at one another. And then not-Nurse tips its head back, opens its jaw, and slowly drops the stethoscope down its gullet, consuming another token, grunting as it swallows hard, working the metal and rubber down not-Nurse's throat to its belly. When it's finished, it lets out a strange belch.

Not-Nurse shudders with delight, all of those twitchy broken moments from before long gone. Now it moves like it's *too* full, having had too indulgent of a meal after a long period of starvation. Drew was wrong. It always needed to get to the asshole next.

It takes a step back. Not-Nurse has no use for Drew or me anymore. It's well sated on asshole now. But there's a film-nerd boy somewhere else in this hospital that could be dessert. And if not-Nurse was *really* a glutton, an independent girl that now can't defend herself because of the mistakes that we *all* made.

The very idea of Gael and Leila being next is what forces me to speak up.

"Hey!" I bark, even as Drew gags and heaves, bent over the crumpled body of the asshole doctor. "Hey, you piece of shit, I'm talking to you."

Not-Nurse—no, the *demon*—stares at me, locked there, and makes a shuddering throaty sound, as if to ask, *What?*

"We're going to kill you," I warn, pointing up at it. "You don't hurt my friends . . . my sister . . . *me* without being dealt with. The next time you come back—the next time I see you—that'll be the last time. I promise."

I let the challenge linger in the air between us.

And then the demon licks its teeth and leans in until I can smell the sharp tang of metal on its whisper of a breath. It only stops when we're an inch apart and it makes a chittering sound.

Again, I don't need a translation.

Challenge accepted.

CHAPTER NINETEEN

We don't make it back to Crown Heights until the early hours of the morning, and in the first hint of daylight, everything seems a little softer. The demon doesn't show its face, but I don't expect it to. The only thing I'm sure of is that the reprieve won't be for long. According to Gael, we're entering act three.

The Benadys offer us an Uber, but at this point we need the soothing rattle of the subway car and the extra time to think. Even after the ride, no one is up to talking, so we walk in silence, moving like a single organism that might die if we're split. Drew hasn't let go of my hand since we left the hospital, after staging Dr. Laurie's body to be found by someone else. I've no idea what anyone might say once they come across it, but Leila promised he would not be a missed man. Gael's innovation and horror knowledge had been a star in this particular production, helping us arrange the appearance of an accident involving a fumble with some misplaced hospital sheets and a stolen stethoscope. And despite the circumstances of covering up a crime we didn't actually commit, I was glad to see him push past his guilt. I don't ask Drew how she feels about it, that someone had to die for her. I just hold her hand tighter and pretend that the harsh confessions that we spilled just before aren't out there in the open and raw to the touch.

When we finally reach our block, so close to at least an attempt at sleep, it's just our luck that we're met with an annoyingly familiar face. It's too early for it, and yet, he's here. As always.

Keith jumps up from his stoop, not even pretending to have been reading this time, and bounds down the steps two at a time. He looks worse for wear, haggard with exhaustion, dark circles under his brown eyes, as he hangs over his gate—clearly, he could've done with a few more hours of sleep. He still should've been *asleep*. Only Yaya slows down when he says her name.

"Hey," she says, rubbing at her eyes.

Keith is looking her up and down, frantic. "I heard one of you was in the hospital. It's not you," he says, before even asking. His voice scrapes with a roughness that I've never heard from him and I frown, folding my arms over my chest as he sags under the weight of his relief and smiles sheepishly at her. "I'm so *glad* it's not you."

Yaya recoils. "Excuse me?"

Keith doesn't seem to notice that he's said something wrong. Something that Yaya doesn't like. "I said I'm so glad you're not hurt."

"*I* didn't get hurt," Yaya agrees. "But . . . my friend did. Leila got hurt. She broke her ankle."

Keith nods and he swallows hard. "Yeah, that's . . . that's bad. Leila's . . . nice, I guess. And I'll sign her cast. But I just . . . You're a dancer, Yaya. A *dancer*. You need your ankles. You need those to do what you love."

It should be a sweet sentiment, and it probably would be from literally anyone else. But Yaya just stares at Keith like she doesn't understand him. It's funny, because the problem is that *he* doesn't understand *her*. At all. Yaya's love for dance is consuming, but it comes second to her love for us every time. I see her retreat inside her head, marking Keith finally as someone not to be humored. Not anymore. In any other circumstance, I'd take it for the victory that it is, but Leila isn't here to share it and there's nothing celebratory about tonight.

"Thanks, Keith. I have to go," Yaya says stiffly, and she pulls away from the gate. Malachi joins her, lip curling as he looks Keith up and down, giving him all the disdain.

"Wait, Yaya, I didn't mean it like that—" Keith says, reaching out, fingers quick to latch on to her wrist.

"Ow," Yaya says, and I realize his grip is so tight, it's practically bruising.

"Get off her!" I shout, shouldering past Malachi to plant both hands in the center of Keith's chest. He stumbles back and releases her, and then he winces and clutches his chest, like I shoved him with way more force than I actually did.

"I didn't—" Keith starts to say again.

"You absolutely did," Malachi retorts, burning with anger.

Keith looks up in disbelief, but before he can react, the front door swings open, and there's Kendra in her standard HGTV uniform, looking far too awake and determined for this to mean anything good. She marches down the steps, arms folded over her chest.

"You're all being *awfully* loud for this early hour," she says coolly.

"We're just making our way home," Drew says roughly, not making eye contact with her this time.

There's something about Kendra's stare that weighs heavily

as it drifts over each of us, cataloging us as *something*, though I'm not sure what. She takes a step closer, smoothing one hand over Keith's head. He ducks out from under her quickly, looking at her as if she's just betrayed him by acting like his mother in front of the girl he likes.

"Is that what you're doing?" Kendra challenges. "I thought you were yelling at my son."

"I was," I say flatly.

Kendra doesn't look shocked by my words, more pleasantly surprised at how easily I admit it. "Oh? And why is that?"

"He grabbed Yaya. Maybe you should teach your son how to keep his hands to himself if you don't want him getting yelled at," Malachi bites out, and he looks over at Yaya, lacing his fingers with hers. "You okay?"

Yaya nods, but Kendra is already dismissively saying, "I'm sure it didn't quite happen that way. My son is a respectful young man. He sits on the stoop and reads and is *perfectly* polite, while you and your little group. Well, you've not a kind word, have you? Insulting him and then disturbing the whole block, running around unsupervised, making noise. You would do well to learn something from *him*." She's looking at me and Drew this time, like she's waiting for us to agree that *we're* the problem.

"I don't think your son could teach us anything," Drew says stiffly.

"I'm afraid he could," Kendra says, stepping around her son, ignoring his quiet attempts to rein her in, and she pushes her gate open. She steps off her property onto the sidewalk, and she's not tall, but there's a quiet intimidation that comes with age that she possesses in spades. "The lot of you run wild, causing disruptions with the builders, harassing my son, *hindering* my apartment showings, and you think that no one else would have a problem with it? That no one would notice—"

"What are you accusing my kids of doing?"

I've never been more relieved to hear the sound of Mom's voice. She's still in the sweats that she sleeps in, her bonnet on her head, but she wraps one arm around my shoulders protectively, cleaving me to her side. "My kids have never run *wild.*"

"I hear them at all hours of the night. Just last night they were carrying on out here after dinnertime," Kendra bites out.

We weren't carrying on. We were walking to *Leila's.* Talking at a normal volume isn't carrying on.

"It's New York City. Everyone was carrying on except you," Mom says sharply. She's rubbing my shoulder hard. For a long beat there's tense silence, and then my mother blurts out, "Out of respect for your father, I've held my tongue, but enough is enough, Kendra."

"And what is that supposed to mean?" the other woman demands.

"You find a problem with everything on this block. Everything is beneath you down to the damn ice-cream truck. You want to change everything about the place where you grew up, because you're too good for it? But this place is *our* home, not yours, and we shouldn't have to change because you outgrew it. Have you considered that might mean *you're* the problem?" Mom asks.

Kendra *feels* the slap in her words and rears back.

"How could your kids *not* be the problem when they were the ones harassing *my* son?" Kendra demands.

265

Mom sniffs. "Because your son won't stop harassing this little girl."

Kendra's fingers ball into fists. "Well, you'll have to find a way to deal with us soon. My husband is wrapping up business in California, and he'll be moving here quite shortly. I intend to stay here as a live-in super on the penthouse floor, and I already have renters that plan to sign the other unit leases on concept pictures alone. You should get your kids in order. Who *knows* what kind of neighbors these will be? Maybe more *law-abiding* than I am," Kendra says, lofty and smug. "Law-abiding." I know what that means. The threat of the cops hangs over our necks like a guillotine, sobering us swiftly.

Keith gapes at his mother's words. So clearly it's the first he's heard of this too. "Now, Keith, come inside and help with breakfast."

Intent on having the last word, she turns on her heel and marches right up the stairs.

"Wait, Mom, we're not going back to California?" Keith asks as he dogs her steps. He tosses one look back at Yaya, but she averts her eyes, turning to stare at the ground. Brow furrowed, Keith looks back at his mother, and the last I hear as he follows her inside is, "Are you serious? Were you just not gonna tell—" before the door swings shut behind them, leaving us on the sidewalk.

I turn to look up at Mom, and she's still staring at Kendra's door, her jaw tight like her fingers on my shoulder. "Mom," I start, squirming in her grip.

"Oh," she says, releasing me swiftly. She doesn't apologize like she normally would. Instead, she looks at us and the tension doesn't dissipate. She turns to Gael and Malachi. "You two. Walk Yaya back to her apartment and then straight home. Both of you."

She knows.

I'd known she would. But there's something even more foreboding than I was expecting about the way Mom is acting. She's not exploding with rage or worry, which means she's gotten that out of the way. Instead, she's calm, which is scarier, because it means she's already decided on the punishment that Drew and I have earned in our secret escapades to murder a demon.

"Mrs. Harris, it was my fault," Gael says softly, repeating what he's been saying all night. "I made a mistake."

The look Mom levels at him is the same as Mrs. Benady's—one aching with disappointment—and I can't stand it.

"Actually, we—" I start.

But before I can finish, Drew interrupts and says smoothly, "We all messed up. We all made a mistake." She's making a point not to look at me. I bite my bottom lip, looking down at the toe of my shoes.

"That's unlike you, Drew," Mom admonishes. "Well. You three, *go*. Before I call your parents to pick you up." It's an infinitely worse threat.

Malachi murmurs his goodbyes, and I nudge Gael into a hug, holding him tightly as I whisper, "It's not your fault," into his ear. My goodbye with Yaya is infinitely more awkward, a fumbling of clasped hands.

"Thanks for defending me," she says quietly, and then she releases me and shifts to walk between Malachi and Gael, off to their respective fates.

For a moment it's just the three of us in front of the Bryant-Thompson brownstone. I look back up at the window and Keith doesn't even try to pretend that he's not glaring down at me. I don't turn away until Mom speaks.

"Come on," she says. "We need to chat."

Our parents don't grill us on what happened. The parent group chat has clearly been alive and kicking since the Benadys called last night. It's not the first time that they think we've gotten high and been dumb, according to the Benadys, but it's the first time someone's gotten hurt, and that makes all the difference.

"You know, we let you both do a lot of things. Drew, we let you go to the Hamptons with your friends. Go on family trips with your friends. No curfew. All because you are supposed to be *smarter* than this," Mom says snippily as she paces the living room. She stops in front of Drew, where she's sitting on the couch next to me, and says, "Drew, I am *so* disappointed in you."

Drew looks frustrated, hands balled into fists. I can see her fighting to hold back her words, but she loses the battle, muttering, "And what about Devon? Or is she not smarter than this too?"

I rear back, eyes widening, and she glares back at me.

"I was getting to her, too. Don't get smart with me," Mom snaps. She glares at me. "We've been too lenient with you kids. We trust you to have each other's backs. To keep each other safe and not to be *stupid*."

"*I* said that you should be done for the summer. No more going anywhere for a while, until you've proven responsibility," Dad says sharply.

"How do we prove responsibility when you won't let us out?" I complain, though I know I have no place to, not when it comes to this, not with Leila hurt. It sounds wrong even to me.

After all, this might be better. The demon hasn't attacked me at home. And Drew's off the chopping block now too. My sister is safe, so I feel *safer*.

"And what about the block party?" Drew asks suddenly. "It's the tenth anniversary of it. It's important, and we shouldn't have to miss it because of one mistake."

It takes everything in me not to turn my head around and gape at Drew. Drew's barely had anything at all to say about the block party for the past week, and suddenly, she's all about it?

"Don't talk back," Dad warns. "That's what I said *should* be done."

Mom plants her hands on her hips and says, "You're allowed to go to the block party, but that's *it*. For a month. And then after that, no going out late and no going out without telling us where and when you'll be back. That's over. Now *go* upstairs, and I want you both to write the Benadys handwritten apology notes." As if it's the nineteen hundreds and not something that we've already done in person.

But neither of us argues further. We take our licks with grace and rise from the couch, not speaking a single word as we walk in sync up the steps, swaying into each other's sides like magnets. For the first time we feel like *those* kinds of twins—the kind that can finish each other's sentences and live in each other's pockets.

At the second floor we stop and the feeling of sameness intensifies.

"Thanks for saving me again," Drew finally says, surprising me.

"Anytime," I say, because it's not a lie, no matter how angry I am at her. The hesitation only ever lasts a moment. I look at her and don't know what to say, which isn't an abnormal thing. I never know what to say to her, but it's especially strange now, with truth finally living in the thin plane between us. "We have a lot to talk about."

"We do," Drew allows with solemnity. But then she looks away, like it pains her to meet my eyes, as she says, "We have more important things to do first, though."

In another scenario I'd disagree. I'd fight her on that. Ask when I'm finally going to be important enough to her to come first.

But this time she's not wrong.

"We don't have much of a window now to draw it out and end this," I say softly. "We only have the block party."

The dread starts to set in. We're safe in here for now, with us both off the demon's menu. But how can we protect the others or figure out what to do when Leila can't walk, and we're not allowed out? We still have our phones, so we're able to coordinate with the rest of the crew, but it isn't enough. My stomach clenches, twisting up tight, and I can taste the sourness of bile rising. I swallow hard, squeezing my thumb to steady myself.

"Then we'll kill it at the block party," Drew says, as if it's as simple as that. She's still so sure of herself even after her spectacularly failed first plan.

"We didn't kill it this time. What makes you so sure that we'll be able to get it at the block party?" I ask.

Drew's eyes narrow. "Because we'll try, try, try again until we do."

This isn't her usual cockiness. She's more like me now, I realize. Her fear has become second nature, and now she's angry.

Anger is something I can work with. Something we can weaponize.

"The block party, then," I agree. I rock back and forth on my heels, waffling, before I settle on my decision. I go into my bedroom and leave the door open behind me, a clear invitation for her to slip in with me, so we can get to work planning.

She doesn't take it. Instead, she marches past me to her own room. It's only inches away, but just like that, the canyon's never felt wider again.

The Best Summer Ever™—<u>REVISED</u>

1. ~~Go to one of Drew's friends' parties. Bring the crew.~~
~~Remind Gael to not be a piece of shit. Remind friends to~~
be ~~friendly.~~

2. ~~Go to the Prospect Park Zoo (We've never been,~~
~~it'd be funny.) Drew likes animals—maybe interested in~~
~~zoology? [NOTE: What DOES Drew want to do in college?~~
~~Ask, maybe?] [ADDENDUM: Drew isn't going to college??]~~

3. ~~Ride the carousel at Brooklyn Bridge Park like we used to.~~

4. ~~Make nice with Alexis so that Mr. Ahmed doesn't have~~
~~to tell me off for making her cry again → parents won't~~
~~be mad at me for Alexis's snitching to her mom → shows~~
~~Drew I can just ignore Alexis like she's always telling me~~
~~to.~~ [ADDENDUM: Alexis is dead. Send flowers to her mom.]

5. ~~Girls' night at Movies-in-the-Park biweekly. (Checked~~
~~the schedule and there's a summer series of rom-coms. W!)~~

6. ~~Vet each and every one of Malachi's dates—no repeats~~
~~of what happened last summer. Be on Malachi-shift with~~
~~Drew?~~ [ADDENDUM: No more dates for Malachi for
the rest of the summer. ADDENDUM ON ADDENDUM:
Malachi can only date boys his age from now on.]

7. Make the Block Party the best Block Party ever. ~~It's~~
~~Drew's last one (maybe).~~ [ADDENDUM: Apparently, it's
not. My fault, I guess.]

8. ~~Don't. Fight. With. Drew.~~ [ADDENDUM: Failed this so . . .]

9. Kill the demon.

    9A. Gael and Malachi escort Leila to our house. Gael carries the athame.

    9B. Group walks to dance studio to meet Yaya. We wait for the demon.

    9C. Surround it. Leave it no way of escape.

    9D. Yaya executes the demon.

10. Survive.

CHAPTER TWENTY

*L*eila's discharge comes the next day, and it's the last time we're allowed to see her until the block party next week—which is the last time any of us will be allowed outside before it's a lockdown for the month. Just as we'd colluded on our demon-hunting plans, so did our parents on doling out punishments that would at least feel equally shitty. We were allowed to meet today only because Leila nailed the guilt-trip thing with her painkiller-hazy eyes, gesturing pathetically at her ankle as if to say, *But behold, I'm already miserable and sad, won't you please allow me visitors a final time before my jail sentence?*

Crowded back in Leila's room, it's hard not to remember what only just happened here. It's all been put right, everything that was upended from our escape of the demon's pursuit. Her mom's even managed to change the sheets. It really does look nearly perfect. Except, if I look at her closet door, I still see the tiniest little peephole to remind me it did happen.

"We don't have much time, so let's do this," Drew declares.

I look over at her, dreading hearing her plans, but she's, surprisingly, not saying anything. Instead, Drew is looking at Malachi, who's perched on Leila's opposite side. I curl in closer to Leila, letting my head drop on her shoulder.

"What are you looking at me for?" Malachi asks. "Do I look like leadership material?"

"You have a commanding presence," Drew says. It's a surprisingly tactful way to say "loud." "And . . . *my* plan clearly didn't work, so . . . any other ideas?"

Yaya speaks up: "I should make the final decisions. I'm the one who's supposed to be delivering the final blow. So I want to . . . be comfortable while I do it."

"I'm not sure that you'll ever be comfortable fighting a demon, Yaya, but you have a point," Malachi says, seconding the motion.

So we discuss do-or-die day, which is set for the block party. Gael makes it clear that he doesn't think the demon will go for Drew again, not after Dr. Laurie's unwilling sacrifice in her stead.

"It'll move on to an easier target then," Leila says. Her lips curl into a smile and she waggles her eyebrows. "So . . . me."

I glare at her. "That's so not funny."

Leila rolls her eyes, far more relaxed than the situation calls for, and I can't tell if she's affecting a blasé attitude to deal with what happened or if the painkillers are just doing her an immense favor.

"Don't say that, Leila," Gael says, still more solemn than he ever is with her.

This seems to be what makes Leila a little more serious too. She shakes her head with a quiet sigh. "Gael . . . it makes the most sense."

"No, it doesn't," Gael says stubbornly. "The movie kill order still stands. Clearly. I'm next. I'm the film nerd."

"What about the third-act twist?" Leila challenges.

Gael stills, jaw unhinging just a bit. He leans in, squinting at Leila. "What do *you* know about the third-act twist?" he demands.

Leila sits back smugly and shifts, hissing slightly when she jostles her elevated foot. Drew leans forward to readjust the pile of pillows, and Leila nods, grateful but stiff.

"You know I listen. To Jack Strode *and* you. There'll be a third-act twist. What if the third-act twist is that *I'm* next?" Leila challenges.

"I'd prefer if there weren't any twists at all, thanks," I add unhelpfully.

"As few twists as possible would be great, but they can't possibly be avoided," Drew says. "What we *can* control is the space where we confront it. Somewhere far from anyone else. No one else . . . No one else should get hurt because of us." I'm taken aback that it sounds more like, *Because of me.*

"Well, how do we know it won't attack *before* the block party? A week is a long time," Malachi says quietly. "And if it does, we . . . won't be able to help Gael *or* Leila. Not when we can't leave the house."

"It'll wait," Gael says, suddenly sure. "In the third act, everything takes place in a final set piece where the Final Girl confronts the villain and ends it, and the block party has all the makings of it."

"The dance studio," Yaya blurts out.

I raise an eyebrow at her. "You want to kill a demon in your mom's dance studio?"

"I want to kill a demon where I think I *can* kill a demon," Yaya amends. "Where I feel comfortable. And powerful. Besides, no one else will be there during the block party."

"The dance studio then," Gael declares with a new sense of dread that doesn't suit him.

The others lose themselves in the planning of it all, and I try to pay attention, to keep everything straight. But it's hard not to get lost in my own head as I watch Drew, for all her new micro-expressions. Every time she looks like she might offer something up, she holds her tongue. She doubts herself. Because she was wrong about the demon. And I hope that she's wrong about me, but somehow after a few days to process . . . I think she isn't. I hear her words echoing in my head over and over again. "I didn't leave you behind," her voice shouts. "You stopped walking next to me." Is that what I did?

"I can see you."

I jump, looking over at Leila. The animation in her expression from before has drained away, and she looks tired and wan. She lets her head drop against the headboard and turns to look at me, her smile weak.

"See me what?" I whisper.

"Thinking," Leila says gently. "You okay?"

It's a hard question to find an answer to. Slowly, I say, "I . . . don't know. I just feel like this is my fault. Somehow. All of it."

Leila rolls her eyes. "I don't think us being hunted by a demon is your fault."

"Isn't it?" I insist. "At the party I was so *blinded* by Drew and what I thought she wanted and in my own head about it, and this all started because of the stupid Best Summer Ever list. *I* invited it in."

Leila shakes her head, frowning. "I think you and your sister's thing started a long time ago, Devon. A *long* time, and I don't think it's necessarily just your fault. You and Drew have a lot to talk about. And Drew has a lot of shit to make up for."

Privately, I think I might too, but that means . . . *acknowledging* Drew's words, and the maybe-truth in them, something I still don't feel ready to do. Leila does it for me.

"You do too. Don't worry, you'll figure it out when the time's right. I *did* warn you about forcing it. About not listening," Leila mutters.

I look over at Drew again, and she's looking at us now, probably having heard us whispering her name. She quirks an eyebrow.

"What?" she asks. "Aren't you both going to pay attention too?"

"Yeah, yeah, but I got distracted by Devon's horrendous eyebrows," Leila says.

My hand flies up to my brows and I recoil, insulted, "Hey! They aren't that bad yet."

"They really aren't," Yaya says soothingly.

Leila pouts her lips. "'Yet' being the primary word here. You think we can Instacart bleach?"

"Why?" Gael says suspiciously.

Leila grins. "We're gonna bleach Devon's eyebrows."

The day of the demon slaying really does feel just like any other block party morning. Excitement and terror don't feel all that different. They both leave a jittery chatter in my teeth, a twitchiness that results in me fumbling with each and every item in my room that I happen to touch. Dad even brings up my sudden clumsiness at breakfast, after hearing me nearly trip down the stairs over literally nothing.

Mom is already gone, project managing her army of Crown Heights mothers and fathers. So Dad lays out the spiel that I know she's impressed upon him, with his own flourishes: "If I had my way, you two would *not* be going out today. And I want to remind you that after this you two still are being punished for an entire *month*. But your mother doesn't want you to miss out on something this important to our family and the community. Especially not with the . . . Kendra of it all. She won't want her to have the satisfaction."

"We know we made a mistake," I say in earnest.

Dad tuts. "But you're not the one who paid for it, are you?" he asks, and that's enough to ensure a silent breakfast until we're finished and I take my turn to do the dishes.

Alone in the kitchen, I let his words wash over me again. Leila did pay, and here she is, willing to pay even more. It isn't fair.

But neither is being hunted by a demon. It's the least fair thing of all, and all because I couldn't deal with change. With growing *up*.

I try to stop myself from thinking about it, since there's nothing to be done until all of this is over anyway. But it's hard when there's nothing to do but wait, not even my eyebrows. It had been odd to do them with everyone around, when it's normally just Leila and me. But even with more eyes, they're as perfect as they can possibly be, an icy blonde against my brown skin. It doesn't escape me that I was the maker of my own almost-demise the first time. Now I've done it again because if I die, I'll want to die looking like me, even if it does make me the blonde.

I grab my favorite makeup products—bright neon-pink liner and electric-green eye shadow and my freckle marker. I'm

279

definitely going to look like me. Crayon makeup and all.

As I begin to assemble a face, Drew's voice penetrates my focus.

"—come up. I'm sure it will," Drew is saying carefully. "When was the last time you saw it?" She's silent for a long time, and I can picture her pacing in her room, can hear it too with the way the floorboards creak. "And you locked it up after the Ouija board session?"

It doesn't take a genius to know she's talking about the athame.

"Okay, then, it must be in the house."

I gently open my bedroom door and stare down the hall, right into Drew's room.

"Your mom what?" Drew asks, voice going softer. I can see everything soften, even the sharp juts of her shoulders. She huddles against the phone at her ear, whispering like Avery's right there in front of her. "Okay, okay. No, I can't help you look. Avery, I got in trouble because of . . . some shit that I did at Leila's. My fault. I fucked up. And my mom's block party is today—" And then Drew looks up suddenly, as if she senses me.

"What does he want?" I whisper.

She holds up a finger, shaking her head. I know it's only meant to mean *Give me a moment,* but it feels more like a dismissal. I scoff, stalking away.

I go back to my vanity and break out my trusty eye-shadow brushes, going back to creating the garish green shade of my dreams around my eyes. I'm preparing to dot freckles on my cheeks when Drew appears in my doorway, arms folded and phone discarded. I don't even get to ask before she speaks up with a damning "He knows we took the athame. We have to give it back."

"Sure," I agree easily. "Tomorrow."

"I know, but . . . his mom knows now. That he took it out. He blames me," Drew pushes back. She sounds *lost*. "And he wants it back."

I search the planes of her face for a joke, but Drew is notoriously unfunny, and there's certainly nothing to laugh at or about with this.

"Oh, you've lost your fucking mind, that's it," I say flatly. "You want to give up our only weapon against the demon because your boyfriend is in trouble for pulling it out in the first place and siccing said demon on us?"

Drew's brow furrows. "He's not my boyfriend. And he didn't do it on purpose. And I didn't say we're going to—"

"Oh, I'm sorry, he didn't do it on purpose. That makes it *so* much better that we both almost died and three other people did," I say sarcastically. I turn to strip out of my pajamas and decide on my clothes for the day. It's got to be a demon-killing outfit. It's got to be a block party outfit. It's got to be a combination demon-killing block-party outfit.

Sturdy shorts. A crochet top, so I don't get sweaty. Sneakers. Excellent.

Drew still doesn't leave.

"Something . . . happened. Someone found it was missing from the archives, and his mother went to take it back to the museum and it wasn't there. She's freaking out. On him. On everyone. We *need* to make sure we get it back to him," Drew insists.

"It's really not our fault that she didn't return it when she was supposed to," I drawl.

It's so absurdly easy for once to block Drew out as I decide between two pairs of denim shorts that look the same. The one with the deeper pockets would be best. Then my crochet top. There's something about wearing something of my own making that makes me feel powerful, and I need that today. There, that's good. Dressed. Makeup done. *Blonde.* Here we go.

"You're not *listening*. I'm just telling you what he said. I . . . I didn't say that we had to give the athame—" Drew says, following me out of the room as I shoulder past her again, thundering down the steps. "Devon, don't *leave*."

I stop suddenly, and she nearly crashes into my back.

"Why not? *You* do it all the time," I bite out viciously.

Drew inhales sharply. "Oh . . . so we're doing this again? Now?"

My fingers ball into fists, and I continue down the steps. I sit heavily on the bottom step, feeling it creak with age. "No, not now. Later. After this is done. If we make it."

"Where are you going?" she demands as I finish tying my shoes. "The plan is for us to all gather here. We have to *wait*."

I stand up so that I'm properly toe to toe with her. "Drew, I don't . . . I don't really feel like being around you right now," I admit. It feels weirdly freeing. "I guess I finally know how you feel."

There's something delicious about having the last word with Drew.

Probably because it doesn't happen often enough.

CHAPTER TWENTY-ONE

*T*he ballet studio is unlocked. That's not surprising. It's early in the afternoon, the sun still high in the sky. But the wall of sound that hits me the moment I step into the old familiar space sends me off-balance, forcing me to reorient myself. I didn't expect it to be so *loud*.

The general common room is narrow, lined with padded chairs up against the gleaming wide glass windows and walls. I know that part of Yaya's punishment was cleaning the room from top to bottom, and I can see the fruits of her labor in the vacuumed and power-washed carpet that looks a brighter green than normal. The secretary desk against the left wall has been wiped, and the scent of bleach lingers in the air. I bet if I look in the file cabinet, each folder would look pristine too, not an attendance sheet out of place.

On the first floor of Bet-On-It, there are two dance studios. It's where Ms. Betancourt, Yaya, and two of the other teachers instruct the younger students. Those rooms are where I learned each of the five positions, how to hold my arms aloft, how to pretend that I had a modicum of grace. But I know that's not where Yaya trains. The music swells from the second level, full of dramatic strings and brassy horns. I ascend the iron spiral staircase tucked up against the right wall that leads up to the much more massive ballet studio.

It's a wide-open space, and each step brings me deeper into the cradle of music that surrounds Yaya. She is halfway through her combination, all grace and power, arms held in careful control, legs locked as she inches herself across the floor *en pointe*.

I am always in awe of Yaya's dancing; she's extraordinary. But never so much as I am now. Even when she notices me and falls out of a pirouette, she does it with more grace than I could ever have. For a moment there's just us, staring at each other, and then her face splits into a smile and she walks with purpose to the sound system, pausing it until the only thing that echoes is the silence.

"Hi," I say, wincing because it comes out far too loud and enthusiastic for the quiet, betraying too much about . . . everything really.

"Hi, Devon," Yaya says at a more appropriate volume. Then she raises an eyebrow and says, "I'll let you keep your shoes on just this once."

"Oh, shit, sorry," I say, scrambling to peel off my sneakers. I know the rules here.

"I'm joking," Yaya says with a shrug. "I have to mop anyway."

"More punishment?" I ask.

Yaya sighs. "No, the custodian just has the week off." She sits down on the floor and pats the space in front of her. She makes quick work, pulling off her pointe shoes, flexing her ugly toes. The big toenail is cracked, covered by a ragged Band-Aid. She moves like she doesn't feel it at all.

I join her, gingerly settling down on my knees, wincing at how hard the ground feels beneath my knobby bones.

"It's not time yet, is it?" Yaya asks, her smile faltering just the tiniest bit.

I want to ask her, "Time for what?" before I remember *exactly* what she means. "Oh, no, not yet. Drew was driving me crazy and I just wanted to get out of the house and be . . . be with you." It's surprisingly easy to be so honest, even though I haven't tried to say anything about how I feel since the night the demon chased us to Gael's.

Yaya looks surprised, but she doesn't question it.

"I've been practicing. Trying to get into the right headspace to do . . . this," she says, and she gestures vaguely at the space around her. I know that she's not talking about choreographing for her filmed audition—today's the day Yaya Powell kills a demon. "What was driving you crazy?"

I huff, shaking my head. "Just Drew. It's not a big deal."

"Clearly it is if you came all the way over here, neglecting the *plan*," Yaya teases, already reaching back for her dance bag, rifling through it for her socks. She pulls them on, and then grabs her Vans, holding them in her lap, as if she needs something to do with her hands.

"Drew is freaking out because Avery finally realized the athame was missing. I swear, instead of apologizing for being an asshole to him, she wants to return it and hope that it's enough for him to forgive her," I say uncharitably. It's all wrong, full of conjecture, and biased by my own personal beef, and Yaya seems to see right through it.

"I think she really likes him," Yaya says with a strange amount of certainty.

"I didn't get that impression," I retort.

Yaya laughs to herself, and she looks up at me, raising an eyebrow. "You know, Devon, your sister is . . . a lot. She can be an asshole, but you can ease up on her a little, you know?"

"Are you serious?" I blurt out. "Are you on her side?"

Yaya rolls her eyes, leaning back on her hands to take me in fully. "In case you didn't notice, you are *both* my friends. I'm not on anyone's *side*. I don't think there are sides to this." She shifts her balance, taking her time to think through her words like Drew might, except when she does it, it's not annoying. "I think that you're really hard on her sometimes. She's not perfect, you know."

"Oh, I *know*," I drawl.

Yaya laughs again. "Do you?" She teases. "You *love* to talk about how much of a genius she is."

"Well, she is," I say pointedly. Her IQ is genius level; it's just a fact.

"And that she's going to cure cancer or something," Yaya sings.

"Well, she . . . actually, she doesn't want to do that. Apparently," I say, nose wrinkling. "That seems like such a waste, though."

Yaya tilts her head as she looks at me. Then she says, "You have such high hopes for her. All the time. And then you get upset when she disappoints. You should ask her what she does want, from time to time. You did this with the Best Summer Ever list, too."

"What do you mean?" I ask.

Yaya shrugs. "I know it would've been nice . . . surprising Drew with all these cool things, but she's not really one for surprises, is she? She probably would've appreciated having some input. That's all."

I wince. Another reminder that I'm not great at that. Asking.

It's everything that Drew was telling me in the hospital, except in a way that makes sense. Communicated with kindness, something Drew has never quite mastered. But in the same breath, I realize, neither have I. I can hear Drew's bluntness and hear myself responding to her tone, not to what she's saying. I think back to the conversation we just had, and this time I hear what's underneath, too. *Don't just hear me. Listen to me, please.* I haven't been doing much of the latter lately.

"I . . . I've known something was wrong," I say half-heartedly. I glare down at the glossy wood, slightly smudged by footprints. "So I've been trying really hard to make this summer perfect. For her. For us."

"Why?" Yaya asks.

"Because I thought it was our last summer," I blurt out, and the words hang there between us. I force myself to continue and explain myself in ways that hurt. "When Drew decided to graduate early and didn't tell me, I was sure she was going to go be an adult and do things and be places where I'm *not* again and not tell me about them, either. Sure we won't be together."

Yaya knows that when I say "we," I'm not talking about our friend group. I'm talking about Drew and me. My *twin.*

"At least when she just went to a different school, she had to come home every day," I whisper, closing my eyes tightly to fight back the ache of tears welling at my lash line. "She told me I had it wrong, that she's not leaving yet, but she will. And when she does, I'll *never* know what she likes to do. Who her friends are. What she wants to be."

"Oh, Devon," Yaya says gently.

"I know we're getting older and everything. But I have always felt like I've been staring at the back of her head. She never turns around to look me in the eye. So it's easy to put her up where I can't touch her at all. It's easier because if she's not human, if she *can't* come down, then she's not abandoning me on purpose," I confess, and I pull my knees tight to my chest, forcing the air from my lungs. Without air, I can't sob.

"Have you ever told her how you feel?" Yaya asks.

"Yeah, and then she *yelled* at me. 'I didn't leave you behind. You stopped walking next to me.' Like, what does that even mean?" I snap. Even though I know what it means. I do. I just need someone else to say it out loud to make it real.

Maybe I'm more like Drew than I thought.

Yaya hesitates, then says, "The day we all found out Drew was graduating was . . . so bad, Devon. You completely freaked out. You ran out. Then you called a Team Meeting and *didn't* invite her. And I was thinking about why Drew didn't push back on that and just show up, but I think it reminded her of all the other times you didn't want to talk about her school stuff. You didn't want to hear it, so she stopped."

"Well, why did she stop trying?" I demand. "Why did she not care enough to keep fighting? I *cared*."

"No . . . you didn't, though. You both got comfortable. In existing together instead of *living* together. I'm not saying Drew's faultless," Yaya says delicately. "She can be so cold and dismissive, and she's . . . a very sometime-y friend. I mean, I love the girl, but that party? Come on. I'm just also saying that you ask her for the impossible. You want her to not change even while she's living this entirely different life . . . and yet you ask for greatness too. That's *heavy*."

Hearing it all, I bury my face in my hands, groaning to myself. It's always been easy to frame Drew in my head as the best and worst of us. But I can hear and see my part in it too. I really *hadn't* ever wanted to know, to have to acknowledge there were parts of her life I couldn't reach when nothing was out of reach for her in my life. I'd make jokes about her going away with her friends or about her richy rich classmates, all while having such lofty goals for her because of them, and the place she was in, and never asked how she *felt* about any of it.

All so I didn't have to deal with the fact that I *didn't* have that. I didn't have direction and I still don't. I'm not like Gael, the future filmmaker, or Leila, the artist, or Malachi, the romantic, or Yaya, the ballerina.

I'm not like Drew, the genius. Except . . . in all the ways I am. Because she doesn't know what she wants either.

All the roles I've cast for them seem arbitrary now. Even the demon's typecasting of us feels so arbitrary, because if Drew and Gael are both the nerd *and* the asshole . . . more than one thing . . . why can't I be too? More than just the blonde. More than just the friend, forever suffering in silence.

When I open my eyes again, Yaya is still smiling at me, and the warmth of her eyes sends a contrasting chill down my spine.

"You . . . told me that I always cheer other people on," I say quietly. "That I just live in all this self-doubt. You're right."

"I know," Yaya says cheerfully.

I'd roll my eyes, but that would spoil what I want to say next. Finally. Because I don't want to live in that self-doubt anymore.

"I love you."

The words come so naturally that they feel like nothing. It's not like when we were walking to Leila's, when it felt so hard, like I might tell her only in a gut reaction to her accusations. Now it comes freely and honestly and bravely, too.

"I love you too," Yaya says with a smile.

I swallow hard. *Be brave again,* I tell myself.

"No," I insist. "I *love* you, Yaya. Like I'm *in* love with you, and I have been, I think, since we were six years old. I love your kindness and your determination. I love how thoughtful you are and how sometimes I can't tell whether or not you're joking because you're being kinda petty and passive-aggressive. I love how you call me out on my bullshit. I love how you don't really know when to chill out and give yourself a break—and don't worry, I'll remind you because it can also be really annoying. But I love your grace and your dedication. I love how brave you are. I love how good of a friend you are. I *love* you, and that's . . . something I *don't* doubt."

Yaya's smile slowly crumbles, and yet my heart doesn't. It just thuds even louder as she regards me with a long look and doesn't say anything.

"And it's okay if you don't love me back that way," I find myself saying and meaning. "It's okay because I always want to be your friend. Being your friend matters the most to me, and it's why I've never told you this before. So. Yeah. I love you. I hope we're still friends. It's okay if we're just friends, of course. Yeah. But also, I'm a catch, so. Yeah."

Yaya takes a deep breath and releases it like a whistle between her teeth. She shuffles forward until her knees are touching mine, and she says very quietly, "Devon Harris, I've never wanted to be *just* friends with you."

And then she kisses me.

It's a chaste kiss at first, that tastes of the salt of her upper lip, but then her hands frame my jaw, tilting my head just slightly until our lips latch perfectly, fitting together like long-lost puzzle pieces.

I've kissed girls before. I've felt hands on my waist and softness underneath my own fingertips. Girls who've tasted like cherry candy and smelled like good soap or shampoo. But Yaya doesn't smell like anyone I've ever smelled before. She doesn't taste like anyone I've ever kissed before.

Because this kiss doesn't feel new. As I sink in, pushing closer to her, it feels familiar, like a warm hug or the well-worn plushness of my childhood bed. A kiss I'll never get tired of.

When we pull apart, a goofy smile pulls Yaya's lips wide. "Wow, that's better than I thought it would be," she says.

"You didn't think kissing me would be good?" I tease. Then I blink. "Wait, you thought about kissing me before?"

"All the time," Yaya says in a quiet, awed voice, like she can't imagine that she's finally saying it out loud.

"I didn't even know you liked me," I whisper.

"I more than like you, Devon. But . . . I'm afraid of being brave sometimes too. Especially when the prettiest girl ever likes *me*. It's intimidating." Yaya sighs. She leans in to press another kiss to my lips, quick and stolen, before she leans back and squints at me. "Did you . . . ? Did you think that you were hiding it?"

I feel my cheeks get hot and I look down, squirming under the sound of Yaya's laugh, the kind that swells up from her belly. She tries to swallow it back, but it burbles out from between her teeth until she throws her head back and it chimes through her throat into a snort. It's a terribly ugly sound, and it makes me like her even more.

"Do you wanna be my girlfriend?" Yaya asks.

"Uh, what?" I ask.

"I mean, I can take you on a date first if that's what's required. Or a FaceTime date since we're . . . grounded," Yaya says, and this time she's the one blushing.

"Of course I want to be your girlfriend," I whisper.

"Cool," Yaya says, as she pushes my hair back from my cheek.

This time I kiss her first, slotting my lips against hers, running my tongue over her bottom lip, and holding her close. I sigh into it, and again, it's nothing like what I expected but everything like I hoped. No fireworks. Just the steady warmth of a firepit. I smile into the kiss, and I can feel her responding until we're not kissing at all, just smiling into each other's mouths. Yaya pulls back first and we're still being hunted by a demon, but I feel like I've already won something somehow.

"Thanks for asking me to be your girlfriend," I say awkwardly, and Yaya laughs again.

"Thanks for finally being brave enough to tell me how you feel," Yaya says firmly, holding my hands in hers, lacing our fingers together. "Oh, and you *are* a catch. You're one of my best friends, and I'm glad that you know that."

There's something about the reassurance that our friendship is here to stay, no matter what happens between us, that steadies me. It makes me feel more sure. About this, our relationship, but also about the plan. Because we've all been friends for years. We know one another, probably better than ourselves, for sure better than this demon.

Maybe Jack Strode is right. Maybe we just have to have faith in that.

"I need to call Drew," I say, slipping my hands out of Yaya's, mourning their warmth immediately. "Put on your shoes."

Yaya frowns as she easily slides into her Vans. "Call Drew?"

It's strange. I always thought I'd call Leila first if this moment ever came. But there's no one I'd rather tell first than my sister. I want her to tell me when she makes up with Avery. I want her to tell me the things I don't want to hear. Even if it's messy, I want us to just . . . talk.

I fumble around for my phone, shaking with the need to hear my sister's voice. I see a text from her in the group chat, a brief: Plan is a go. Devon with Yaya. Meet on stoop in 20 min and we'll walk over to them. I punch in the passcode, then tap over to Drew's contact info.

Before I can press call, though, I hear the last thing I want to.

The death rattle.

It's a shaking thing that rises and rises from below, and I nearly drop my phone as I process it. Yaya sits up, alert, and she puts a finger to her lips as she slides back across the floor on her bum, until she's next to her half-open bag.

This isn't how this is supposed to go. It's not how it's supposed to happen. We're supposed to all be here, where it's safe, because there's power in numbers. We're supposed to bait it in with Gael accompanying Leila as she hobbles in on her crutches, appearing soft and vulnerable. We're supposed to seal the doors. We're *supposed* to slay the demon, because this is the third act and we have the Final Girl and the athame and we're the *good guys*.

We're supposed to win.

The death rattle grows louder and louder, like it's creeping closer, before it stops entirely. Yaya looks like she's holding her breath as she pulls the zipper of her bag ever so slowly.

It sounds louder than an avalanche.

The death rattle roars again in response, and I can see the top of the demon's head peek over the floor's horizon. First the slick black skull, then its sunken eyes and concave cheeks. It looks more hollowed out than before, nothing more than bones and a few solid strips of muscle under squirming black skin. I can count its ribs clearer now, more than a human would have, but there are parts of it where it bulges uncomfortably. Even so, it looks gaunt.

Hungry.

That's not the confusing part, though. What's confusing is why it's *here* instead of pursuing Gael or Leila. We haven't broken any rules. And it's not the Final Girl's turn.

But when the demon pulls itself off the steps, it barely catalogs Yaya's presence. Instead, it slinks across the floor, eyes drawn to me and me alone.

We've guessed the third-act twist wrong.

"Text the others," I whisper.

Yaya pulls her phone from her bag, eyes flickering between the screen and the demon's face again and again.

But before she can press the send button, the demon opens its mouth wide.

I expect the rattle. Instead, I hear a singular word:

"Don't."

CHAPTER TWENTY-TWO

The voice comes out of the demon's mouth with the quality of an old tape—grainy and chipped. But I recognize it and so does Yaya.

Keith.

There's something that doesn't compute about his voice coming out of that inhuman body. The Keith I know is annoying, but I would still hesitate to call him demonic, especially now that I've encountered a demon. The Keith I know is an obnoxious creep, but he isn't a *murderer*.

Except, if this is him, in there, then he's *all* of those things.

"Why are you . . . ? You're possessing him. Why? What did he do to deserve being made into your puppet?" Yaya demands. She takes another uneasy step forward, her gaze unwavering as she keeps the demon—no, *Keith*—in sight. "Keith! Keith, if you're in there . . . it's . . . You have to be stronger than it. You have to—"

The demon death rattles again.

It occurs to me only then that it's not a signal of its pursuit. It's not a warning. It never has been.

It's a *laugh*.

The same one Keith mocks me with constantly.

"He's not being controlled," I say sharply. Yaya looks back at me alarmed, but I don't meet her gaze. To take my eyes off Keith would be a mistake, and I'm not willing to make *any more* of those. "He's *in* control."

Yaya's hand tightens in mine, and her breath catches before she slowly turns to look at Keith again. Her voice is tiny this time when she whispers, "Keith?"

The rattle-laugh echoes louder and louder, the demon's shoulders shaking and twisting before it—no, *he*, it's Keith, I remind myself, *Keith*—gets control of his demonic giggles. Now that I've heard him in there, I can see it too. It's there in the way his stare is so absolutely unwavering.

"But how did you do it?" I demand. "How did . . . ? How did you know about the Ouija board and the . . . ? It doesn't make sense."

It doesn't. None of it does.

But Keith doesn't explain. Instead, his long tongue unfurls from his mouth, gnashing his teeth.

"I'm hungry," he moans in that trembling, raspy voice. "Since the day construction started, I've been so, so hungry."

Construction. It's been *weeks* since construction started. Before the party. Before Drew's graduation even. Suddenly, the methodical nature of the demon makes sense. It's been watching.

Keith's been *planning*.

"But what about the Ouija board?" I ask again. How did he even know we'd go to Avery's? "What about *Read Your Rites*?"

"This isn't a *fucking* game, Devon. There is no Ouija board, and *Read Your Rites* is just a terrible horror film with great production design. Drew really is the smart one; I would've thought you'd have done a little more research," Keith groans. "It's time for my meal, Devon. Sure, you've fed me a bit. Alexis. That man that Malachi

THE BLONDE DIES FIRST

was into. Then the doctor. But it was, like . . . McDonald's, when I should have caviar. *It* gets hungry and impatient so *I* get hungry and impatient, and we have to make do. The two of us. The demon and I. Me and the demon. But it doesn't matter now because . . . you're finally serving up the good stuff, Devon."

He still has eyes for Yaya, even as he speaks to me. He looks at her like he always looks at her. Like he wants her. Like he wants to eat her up and never let her go.

"I am?" I ask carefully, slowly shifting in front of her.

Keith death-rattle laughs again and returns his attention to me. "We didn't . . . The research never said anything about hunger. But I get it now. I *get* it. A virus . . . an illness . . . It infiltrates and eats up everything in sight. All the healthy cells are destroyed. But it's always looking for more to *live*. And it can't wait anymore, so now I get to skip to the main event. My filet mignon," he says. "A Michelin-starred tasting menu."

It's funny how we're nothing but sustenance to him. Something to keep him going.

The blonde. The queer kid. The asshole. The nerd. The independent one. We were all small plates. Tapas.

Until the Final Girl, that is. The one who's supposed to finish it all.

But something about the way Keith is looking at me now tells me I've got it wrong still. It takes a second for me to realize there's one other I've left off.

"Oh, it's me again," I conclude softly.

I don't just fulfill one role anymore. I'm not just the blonde who dies first. I'm something *else* now.

Yaya's grip is so tight, I'm starting to lose the feeling in my fingers, but I refuse to let go. Not yet anyway. Her hand in mine makes me braver.

"There's always an appetizer before the main course. The Final Girl's love interest." His voice is a quiet purr, pleased I've figured it out. But then he sounds . . . surprisingly regretful, a wrinkle of irritation and disgust tainting his lilting words. "I did try to avoid this."

His roving eyes lock back on Yaya, and for a split second I can see a small bit of hesitation in those big glossy eyes, even more strikingly human now that I know they are. Yaya's mouth parts, and for some reason, she takes her eyes off the demon to look at *me*.

"What, Yaya?" I hiss, stare flicking back from Keith to Yaya again and again.

Yaya's hand pulses in mine. "It's you. It's always been you," she whispers. "*You're* the Final Girl."

There's a brief split second that feels almost outside of time when I process her words. I'm not the blonde that dies, frozen forever in the tableau of an opening kill. Or I'm not *just* the blonde. The Final Girl is someone who adapts. Who leans into the change. And I'm too afraid to stand still anymore. The split second ends.

"I can't say I'm not still going to enjoy this, but I do wish we could've gone out at least once, Yaya," Keith says, and then he *lunges*, clumsy but still dangerous.

I react more with adrenaline than sense, swinging Yaya out of the way as he swipes at the air where Yaya just stood. The force of my swing causes our fingers to unravel, and I stumble back, nearly slamming into the ground, before I right myself. Disoriented, I spin around, and there's Keith rearing back again, fingers curled, opening his maw as he approaches Yaya.

Suddenly, I'm in the hospital again. I'm at Leila's house. I'm running through Gael's apartment building. Fighting at Délivrance.

At the bodega. In the freezer. Alone. *Terrified.*

And it was *Keith*.

Keith in demon form, sure. But it's *still* Keith.

And I fucking *hate* Keith.

"Get away from her!" I shout, and I throw my entire body into him.

He stumbles back, and it's a reminder that it's different this time. It's easier to throw myself into fighting him physically when I know that beneath the impossible monster is just that boy who won't mind his business. Keith staggers sideways and I slide past him, elbowing him in the gut as I go, forcing another screeching yelp from him. Beneath the unholy sound this time, I hear the shout of just a regular dude.

I reach under his outstretched arm and grab Yaya's wrist, tugging her toward the stairs as he doubles over. It's easier with her than with Drew or Leila. She doesn't question me, simply runs down the stairs, her phone clutched tight to her chest in her other hand. I can hear Keith snarl behind us, clawing his way across the ballet studio floor, probably leaving gouges and grooves in the smooth wood, ruining Yaya's happy place.

We storm down the steps, and Yaya stumbles, then pauses.

"Come on!" I shout, racing toward the door.

"I need to lock him in—" she insists.

"You really don't. You lock him in and he'll just shatter the glass and what then?" I say, trying again to pull her away. Stopping any longer than two point five seconds will only invite Keith to murder us. "Besides, I'm the Final Girl, so I make the decisions. Apparently."

"Oh, you acclimated to that revelation quickly, huh?" Yaya teases.

Well, no. Not quite.

"I'm not on the menu, Yaya. *You* are, and I'd like you to be my girlfriend for longer than fifteen minutes!"

Yaya laughs, and it's a lovely sound, so unfitting of the moment, but it fills me with hope. Faith. We dart out of the dance studio, our burbling laughter clashing with the spitting screams behind us. I back out onto the sidewalk, keeping my eyes on the storefront, as demon-Keith comes down, lingering in the studio. He looks smaller in the daytime.

I don't feel the strange prickling at the back of my neck. Not anymore.

The fear leaks out of me at that, until I'm hollowed out. And all that's left is rage.

"Is he . . . not going to follow us?" Yaya asks.

But she speaks too soon.

Keith raises his claws to his face and then begins to peel back the black skin, the purple muscle, until his own curly hair peeks out. I watch him until the person beneath reveals himself, slimy with gore. The demonic body falls to the ground in a dark leathery pile that Keith scoops up in his hands, and for a moment it's just a suit, just a *thing*, until it sinks, viscous, beneath his skin, like his pores are absorbing it.

Even through the slightly shaded windows, I can see what he means about being hungry.

He looks the same as when we'd seen him right after we got back from the hospital. There's a gauntness to his face. Eyes sunken in. Without his long-sleeved flannel, I can see the bruises and marks that track up his arms. *We* did that when we reminded him that we weren't just *food*. We fight back. He moves with a steady limp toward the door, much slower than when he's in the demon's skin.

But Yaya suddenly stops breathing.

"What?" I whisper.

"The athame is with Gael still," she realizes, voice crackling.

I look into Keith's eyes. They aren't brown again.

They're still an inky black, glossy like the eyes of a fish.

"We have to go get it, then," I whisper.

"Don't," he repeats through gritted teeth, swinging the door open with unnecessary force.

And then we run.

Ten streets away, the block party is in full swing.

That's where I should be. Where we should all be. Dancing and running back and forth to different fruit and food stands, laughing and playing children's games, stealing the prizes from the younger kids. Yet here I am, running away from the demonic motherfucker who wants to kill my girlfriend.

It's a straight shot from the dance studio to my house, and as we run, I can already see my block coming up. My stamina hasn't improved. My chest stings and my legs burn, and I feel like any moment now my strings will be cut and I'll collapse. But then I feel the back of Yaya's hand brushing against mine, and I push myself with a new burst of energy, my entire body swinging with action.

I look behind my shoulder. Keith is more than a half block away. He definitely isn't moving as fast as he would in the demon suit, with its weird supernatural power. In the proper daylight, I see the bruises blooming around his eyes. He's favoring one leg over the other, the one Yaya *didn't* slash during our confrontation at Leila's house.

"They'll be there, right? It's almost time?" Yaya asks, not sounding out of breath, as opposed to my wheezing and huffing.

"I don't know," I whisper, shaking, even though I want to agree, to reassure her.

Because I don't. I don't know what time it is. I don't know where they are, how far they are. All I know is that going back to my house, I could be leading Keith to my dad. To my *sister*.

I look back again. And—

Keith is gone.

"He's not behind us," I whisper.

Yaya winces. "Fuck, fuck, fuck—who's that?" she asks, nodding toward the figures in front of my brownstone. Despite her worry, some of the tension leaks away as we get closer, bringing them into sharp relief.

Leila is sitting heavily on the stoop, leg propped up next to her, crutches leaning on the railing near her head. Malachi stares at us, alarmed, and I can't imagine what we look like. Gael turns slowly, thrown by Malachi's expression.

"What the—" Gael starts.

"Where's Drew?" I demand in the same breath that Yaya blurts out, "It's Keith."

Leila shifts, disgruntled. "One at a time, *please*. I'm still coming down from my last painkiller."

Malachi demands, "What did you say? *What's* Keith?"

"The demon. It's not . . . It's not from the Ouija board. It's not just about *Read Your Rites*. Avery had it right all along—it's what the movie didn't keep in. And fucking *Keith* is controlling it," I explain, trembling from the adrenaline of it all. I back up, eyes darting around, searching for the man in question. "Now why are you standing out here? Where's Drew?"

"Holy shit. The third-act twist," Gael blurts out, not answering my question but sounding more like himself than he has in a while.

"Enough with the movie bullshit," Malachi snaps, before he turns back to look at the pair of us. "Wait, so it's *Keith*? Like he's been possessed?"

"It's not possession. Like I said, he's *in* control of it somehow, I can tell. He's doing this for . . . some reason. I don't know why," I spit.

"Probably to get with Yaya," Gael sniffs.

"No, because he's trying to *kill* me," Yaya growls, sounding angrier than she ever has.

"What do you mean he's trying to kill you?" Leila demands. "How did he even find you?"

"He came at us at the ballet studio," I try to explain, words tangling on my tongue. "But it wasn't because of the plan. I don't think he knows our plan. He came because . . . because . . ."

Yaya's burst of anger melts away into something else. Something like wonder. "Because I'm next," she says.

"No, you're not. There's still me. There's still Leila. The nerd. The independent kid. It's not time for the Final Girl," Gael pushes back. He stands on his toes, looking down at the street, like he'll find Keith himself, but he's not there.

He's still not there, and I can't understand why. I can't parse his motives. There's something more to this puzzle, a piece that's missing, that's just out of my grasp.

"He said he was skipping to the main event. But there's someone else before the Final Girl," Yaya says. "The Final Girl's love interest. *That's* what I am." She beams over at me.

If Leila wasn't still on painkillers, she would've caught it first.

But it's Malachi who proves to be the most insightful. He looks between us and says, "Oh, so you finally got brave."

Leila finally gasps, clapping her hands together and then hissing when she jostles her foot. "Oh, *finally*. Devon, your suffering in silence was getting so old."

I redirect my gaze to the ground and then back at Yaya's face, shyly, and she smiles, reaching out to loop my arm through hers and press her cheek to the crown of my head.

Eventually, Gael gapes. "Oh, shit. Oh, *shit*. You . . . you and Yaya. Devon and Yaya. Yaya and . . ."

"Devon." My name comes out distorted, Gael's words swallowed up by someone else's.

In an instant I jerk around, and there Keith is, across the street, slinking out of the shadow of someone's car. He's put the demon suit back on, the great hulking twisted thing that's been haunting me apparently since before the very first day of my supposed Best Summer Ever.

"Fuck off, Keith," Gael shouts, braver now that he knows what/who we're dealing with.

Keith takes a staggering step, rocks back on his heels, and then he launches himself forward, across the street, right at Yaya. I try to shove her out of the way, but we're packed too closely and all lunging in different directions, all except Gael, who stays firm, right in front of Leila as she fumbles and tries to stand, grabbing her crutches. I trip over someone's ankle, and Malachi gives a cry, but then I'm scrambling up the block with Yaya, Keith skittering on our heels, snapping like a rabid dog.

There's nothing to dodge behind, no trees or trash cans. And no witnesses, with everyone at the block party.

"Get away from them!" Malachi shouts, and I look behind me to see Malachi and Gael chasing after the three of us.

It's in my distraction that Keith finally catches me with a hand to the side, swatting me into the iron fence, knocking me clean on my ass, breaking my grip on Yaya.

I gasp, winded, and I look up and back. There's a certain irony to this, landing right in front of his house, so close to the subway, a potential escape. I try to get up, but Keith looms over me, *screeching*, a deafening sound that forces me to fall back against the fence. He clutches his hand to his chest, and I see it blistering, ever so slightly. From touching *me*.

"I'll enjoy this," he says in that distorted voice. "Always getting in my way. I was just trying to be *nice*. Well. I know I'm going out of order. I've always been taught to follow the rules, but they really do feel more like guidelines to me. Besides, after this I think they'll forgive me. I'll finish my leftovers after. *Promise*." He nips his teeth at me, death-rattle laughing, and then he looks up sharply. "Don't get any closer. Or I'll tear her in two. I can do portion control."

I try to look past the vastness of him to see which of my friends he's talking to, but he's so close, curled over me, that there's nowhere to look *but* at him. I tilt my head just as the steady creak of a door opening behind us sounds.

Kendra doesn't step out right away, but I know it can't be

anyone but her. She's the only one not at the block party.

"Mrs. Thompson-Bryant!" I shriek, reaching out for her as I press back against the iron gate leading onto her property, gripping at the bars. "Please!"

I have to look nearly upside down to get her in my line of sight. But she doesn't move. Not right away. Instead, she peers, tilting her head back and forth, probably trying to make sense of the nonreality before her, as she lingers at garden level.

And then, "Keith," Kendra says, terrifyingly nonchalant, "it's best not to make a mess in public. If you mean to rip her limb from limb, bring it inside."

CHAPTER TWENTY-THREE

I can't even find it in myself to feel betrayed. Or surprised.

Fucking *Kendra*.

I try to shove myself up, to dart between Keith's overlong legs, but he pushes me down with one heavy hand to my chest, claws pressing in with just enough pressure to threaten the integrity of my tank top. I turn my head, shuddering, refusing to look my end in the eye, focusing instead on the blue, blue sky.

Not a cloud in sight.

And then the blue sky is interrupted as Keith scoops me right off the ground and makes three bounding leaps toward the garden-level door. My stomach churns as I flop around, attempting to deaden my weight. Keith drops me, and I roll on the stone stoop, scraping my hands but salvaging the rest of my life. Kendra looks at me with the gaze of someone who would *hate* to get her hands dirty but certainly wouldn't mind the end result—a true sign of a burgeoning HGTV star.

"Please, don't—" I beg, as Keith takes a step forward.

Then there's a crutch flying down, cracking Keith right across the back of the head, unbalancing him and forcing him to topple backward into his mother, right into the house. I can breathe now, without the pair looming over me, and I'm dazed by the freedom of it all. Then the view's interrupted again by

Drew's face, her eyes so wide I can see the whites all around.

"Get up," Drew gasps.

For a moment I stare up at her and she stares at me, and I'm looking into the fun-house mirror again. Everything about her is like me. Her voice has always sounded like mine, except we're never saying the same things. Now, though, I hear an echo of the same urgency I'd felt at the hospital when I'd defended her. She is *defending me.*

Drew grabs me by the forearm and yanks me to my feet. I stumble into her, head knocking into her shoulder, and she squeezes me hard. Then she turns her glower back to the house. "They want to take this inside?" Drew asks. "Then let's take it inside."

She isn't even the first to enter. It's Leila who hobbles forward with one crutch, utterly fearless, holding the other up as a weapon as she declares, "That first one was for making me fall down the stairs, you dickhead." She swings her crutch again, clipping Keith in the forehead, just missing Kendra, who dodges. Keith crumples under the hit as Leila nearly tips over. Her only saving grace is Malachi lunging forward to catch her. But Leila doesn't even seem to notice as she adds, "And that's for being a creep."

Yaya casts a look at me over her shoulder, relaxing only when she sees Drew by my side.

"You okay?" she demands.

Dazed I whisper, "Yeah, I'm . . . I'm . . . okay." I'm not fine, but I'm okay. For now.

Malachi follows Leila in, Gael guarding her other side, uncharacteristically serious. For a moment I consider *not* entering with them. But then Drew is going in and I know—I can't stop walking beside her. Not again.

When we enter the garden level, Keith and Kendra have retreated farther in. It's still unfinished, a beautiful brownstone stripped for parts and left bare except for the wash of millennial gray and cheap gentrification brick lining the walls. This might be a kitchen—it's full of cabinetry—but there are no appliances. Just open wiring and tarp. They should probably get *fined* for how dangerous everything looks.

It's not the dance studio, but here, they're truly cornered. Keith crouches like a dog, his gaze swinging between us and his mother. Awaiting her command.

"It's you," I accuse.

Kendra plants her hands on her hips and confirms it. "It's me."

"She's on her Mrs. Voorhees bullshit," Gael says.

The name sounds familiar. "Mrs. Voorhees?"

"*Friday the 13th.* Jason's mom was the original villain, not Jason. We gotta take them both out or we're gonna be trapped in a franchise of sequels that don't need to happen, except maybe *Keith Takes Manhattan*, which might be extremely innovative," Gael says, voice grating harder and getting faster. "But how did you . . . ? How did you *know about the demon*? About all of it?"

Kendra looks at Gael, unimpressed. "Aren't you supposed to be the horror expert? Do tell me, boy, who was credited for production design on *Read Your Rites*."

Gael frowns. "Well . . . I don't know because the production design wasn't very good."

I wince. "I think the question was rhetorical," I whisper.

I remember Mom telling me that Kendra was a production designer. I'd had no idea what her credits might be, and it wasn't supposed to be important. Except suddenly it is. It's *all* important.

"You're the one who reported the athame missing," Drew accuses. "You knew about the athame because you worked on the movie. You knew the *lore* because you worked on the movie. You knew how to summon the demon because you worked on the—"

Kendra rolls her eyes. "Yes, yes, I worked on the movie. But really, summoning the demon wasn't all that hard. There's misery everywhere. All you have to do is *invite it in*. Promise to help it fulfill its purpose . . . if it'll help you fulfill yours."

"You got your son to invite it in and then sicced him on *us*?" Malachi asks, voice dripping with the kind of disdain we only have for adults who don't make sense. "Why?"

"Because . . . ," Kendra says listlessly, reaching for the right words for her motive, and then she settles on them. "You're all annoying."

"Oh, you're so unserious," Malachi rasps.

"You're trying to kill us because we *annoy* you?" Leila sneers.

"You are loud," Kendra says carefully, taking a step forward. "You are rowdy." Another step. "You bring down the property value." Another step. "You complain about my attempts to better this neighborhood." Another step. "And so does your mother." Finally, she's past her son, assuming a position of true *threat*. "Your mother won't have much to complain about when you're not around. None of your mothers will."

"You're a nasty piece of work, you know that? You and your creepy son," Gael growls in disgust. "We didn't do shit to you. You're the one who comes here to try and act like the way our neighborhood operates is an *inconvenience* to you."

Kendra scoffs. "Do you hear that? That tone?" she demands. "You're all the same. All of you. So unwelcoming to newcomers. To my son. How do you think my tenants will feel when they move in? I'll get calls and I do not have time to deal with that. It's best to clean out the vermin before they arrive."

Kendra barks, "Keith—"

Yaya interrupts with a soft, "And you, Keith? You agree?"

He hasn't moved since Leila's attack. He instead watches, inky eyes glazing over each of us, cataloging each twitch and movement. He really is just like an animal now, and we're his prey. Make one move too hasty or threatening, and he'd turn us into corpses.

"Keith, I've always known you to be an okay guy; you can't . . . ," Yaya says weakly.

Keith lets out a disbelieving laugh, shaking his head. "An 'okay guy.' I'm a *really* nice guy. All my exes' moms say so."

I raise an eyebrow.

Keith continues on like he hasn't said something questionable: "And you ignored me. Let your stupid friends laugh at me behind my back. They're not going anywhere, Yaya. They're dead ends. They go to *public* school."

There's a beat of silence where we just let the elitist-ness of it all sink in.

And then quietly, Yaya says, "So do I."

"I wanted to avoid this, you know," Keith insists, growing more and more hysterical. "You weren't supposed to be Final Girl's love interest. *She* was." He points at me viciously, like a child throwing a tantrum, growing more and more unhinged in his disconnect. "She was supposed to die first, and I could've . . . We could've . . ."

"You could've *what*?" Kendra bites out sharply, enough to make Keith falter.

"*Yeah*, whatever you thought? Not going to happen," I say with a smug smile.

But it's a mistake. Keith's attention turns to me again.

"It doesn't matter now," he says, slowly pulling himself up to his full demonic height. "None of it matters now. Because I'm going to kill you. All of you."

This is the moment that Yaya should step up, like she has the entire time. Yaya's moment to shine. Except, she doesn't. Not exactly. Instead, she looks at me. For a moment I squint at her, confused, and then . . .

Right. Because she's not the Final Girl.

I am. Right, right, *right*.

"Um . . . no, you won't," I say uncertainly, fingers flexing into fists. I take a step forward, slower than I should.

"What are you doing?" Drew hisses, grabbing hard on to my shoulder. "Don't . . ."

"I'm the blonde who should've died first," I say, swallowing hard around the knotted truth of that to clear the way for another truth. "And I'm the Final Girl."

Drew's fingers loosen. I hear her soft gasp against the shell of my ear.

"And what do you think that means?" Keith asks. "That you could hurt me, airhead? All you've done, Devon, is *run* from me."

"Keith, be careful," Kendra warns. "Don't be reckless. They have the—"

He doesn't wait for me to run again. He throws himself right at me. This time *Yaya* moves. She lets out a scream and shoves at him with her entire shoulder, throwing him and herself both off-balance. They topple over, narrowly avoiding a toolbox, screaming in each other's faces, and he looms over her, fingers curling around her throat.

I snap into action, jumping onto Keith's back, fingers digging into his shoulders.

"Get *off*," I insist, wrenching back so hard, I hear a crack.

Keith's head snaps back and he gargles on air, black spittle flying out and flecking Yaya's face. Keith shakes me like a wet dog, and I slide down his spine to grab Yaya as he stumbles away, his hands crossing to grab at the scorched parts of his skin. She jumps up, shaken, but still determined.

"Yaya, no. We have to . . . We have to run," I insist. I look past Keith at Gael and Malachi, both of whom are backing up, shielding Leila with their entire bodies.

"Keith, enough of this. Yaya first. Then Devon. You need to eat. *Eat*," Kendra encourages with the soft coo of a mother coddling her toddler into taking a bite. "Before they gain some sense."

I flinch as Keith lashes his tongue out.

"No running," Yaya says.

"We can't . . . We can't get past him," I explain breathlessly. "And I don't want to die."

"You won't. I won't let you," Drew says, stepping forward to my other side, glaring past Keith, right at Kendra.

Kendra lets out a tired sigh, fanning herself from the beating heat. "You really could have been something great, Andrea. There was a bright future ahead of you. My father saw that in you. I saw that in you. Almost reminded me of . . . a young *me*."

"I'm not like you. I'm an asshole, but I'm not a class traitor," Drew sniffs. Keith slowly turns to look at her, and Drew narrows her eyes. She points at Gael. "Gael, *the athame*."

Kendra blanches. "No—"

Gael gasps, grabbing for his fanny pack. "Devon, *catch*."

And then he pulls his hand from his fanny pack and *lobs* the athame in a perfect arc over Keith's head. I watch it spin, spin, spin, and Keith lets out a whistling cry, as if just being in proximity to it is enough to cause pain. I spring forward just as Keith regroups to scramble toward me.

For a moment all I can see are those glossy black eyes.

And then my fingers wrap around the sturdily made hilt, and the weight feels *right this time*. I swing it up, blindly, and it makes contact right beneath the last row of Keith's ribs. It doesn't quite sink in easily, like I imagined. It's not like butter. It's gristly and hard. Even still, Keith gasps and he reaches for me, grabbing my shoulder to steady himself. He doesn't cringe from the burning this time, only clings harder.

And then his eyes are no longer glossy black. They're brown again. A human brown.

The demon suit around him loosens, an ill-fitting thing now.

It starts to writhe, flapping in a nonexistent wind, parting over his skin and slithering, shaking clean of him. A shed skin of a snake with some life to it still. Keith staggers back as the demon fully slips off him, landing in a crumpled heap on the floor. Keith looks worse for wear, clutching at his belly, and I can see the light blue of his T-shirt staining purple, then red. He looks surprised.

"You . . . stabbed me. You, like, *really* stabbed me," he says, wounded, as if I've hurt his feelings with my act of self-defense.

"Is . . . it over?" Yaya asks uncertainly.

But it isn't. Keith is over. The demon's just getting started.

It's still hungry.

"Keith?" Kendra asks, her voice soft for once. She leans over him, reaching a trembling hand. She's close enough to touch him, yet she doesn't. "Keith, honey, do I need to take you to the hospital?"

But Keith never answers.

He never has a chance to. Because Keith, stupid, *nerdy* Keith, starts screaming instead.

The demon suit writhes toward him, its empty puppet mouth opening wide, snapping around his ankles, at his legs, claws tearing the denim and into his skin. Keith tries to run, but the demon is fast, even without him to pretend to control it.

The demon leaps forward, and its flopping arms reach out, wrapping around Keith's neck like leathery ropes, collecting the meal it is due. Kendra screams again while Keith's shrieks are choked off.

And then Keith is gone.

"Keith . . . ," Kendra moans out.

For a brief moment there's nothing, and then the limp arm slides down Keith's chest and flimsily picks at his cargo pants pockets. A slim book slides out from the bulky pocket—*The Great Gatsby*. High-school-level-ass book. Still, it's disturbing to watch it disappear into the demon's dark maw, turn into nothingness. Another totem gone.

Kendra registers it, and it stuns her grief from her as she takes an uneasy step back.

The demon shifts, twisting its nothing eyes to gaze at Leila.

Leila doesn't shrink away. If anything, she stands taller, leaning into Gael's side to steady herself, as if daring the demon to come at her.

So Kendra's yelp as the limp hand of the demon locks around her wrist comes as a surprise. It turns back to her.

The demon has a menu to finish, and Kendra is alone, I realize. Kendra's always been so *independent*, wanting nothing to do with the community that raised her.

She shakes her wrist, as if that's enough to jostle it off. She looks up at me and then down to the athame I hold close to my chest. "What are you . . . ? Are you just going to *stand* there and let it take me? Stab it again! Kill it!"

I swallow hard, looking over at my friends. Drew shakes her head once, chin stiff. "She tried to kill us. All of us."

"Screw her and her son," Malachi hisses.

Leila leans heavily into Malachi's side. "You're lucky my parents have great health insurance or my ankle would've been *expensive*."

Yaya doesn't even look at me. She stays staring at Kendra as the demon's tight, winding grip moves up her arm, up her shoulders, and her screams become muffled by a big leathery hand.

"Yaya?" I whisper, searching for an answer.

Yaya just squeezes her hand in mine. "Do what you think is right, Devon."

"Screw right," Gael shouts, and meets my eyes. "No sequels, no requels, and no *fucking* remakes."

"You're a 'boy mom' and a landlord and you're just . . . annoying," I say, finally.

And like I've given it permission, the demon opens its mouth over Kendra's face. She doesn't bother screaming anymore. Kendra goes to death with dignity, and when she's gone, the demon takes great delight in swallowing the shiny brass keys she keeps on her hip.

But it's not over. Not yet.

I adjust the athame in my hand and take a shaky step forward, keeping my eyes on the leather back of the demon as it crunches through the keys, more sluggish now. It's eaten so much, so quickly, I wouldn't be surprised if it was ready to take a nap. I'm as quiet as a church mouse as I step over Keith's tangled legs and meet Kendra's glassy orb eyes over the demon's shoulders. There's nothing left there.

When I bring the knife down between where its shoulder blades would be if it had a skeleton, I hear a soft wheeze of breath. I'm not sure if it's Kendra's final breath or the demon's release, but when the demon collapses, I finally know.

Now it's all over.

CHAPTER TWENTY-FOUR

*W*hen it's finally done, the demon pile doesn't resemble anything but an old coat, draped over Kendra's and Keith's bodies.

"Holy shit," Yaya says, letting out a sigh of relief. She turns to me, grabbing me by the shoulders, and draws me in, planting a firm kiss on my lips.

My entire world zeroes in on it, the feeling of Yaya's mouth moving against mine. The whoops and cheers of our friends are just the background soundtrack to the best kiss of my life. There are fireworks this time. Like the real fireworks going off illegally from five blocks away at the party, lighting up the summer sky, which still isn't yet dark but getting closer to it. She pulls back with a wet pop and smiles down at me, then sneaks in one more peck, before Malachi grabs her wrist.

"Okay, enough of that. Come here, Final Girl," Malachi says, gathering me into a tight hug.

Yaya's hand is still on mine and so I drag her into it as Gael wraps an arm around my neck, leaving a smacking kiss on the top of my head. Leila gloms on to Malachi's back, hooking her chin over his shoulder, smiling at me toothily.

"Your eyebrows still look good for someone who just fought a demon," she says.

"Thanks, it's a new setting spray I'm trying," I say, beaming back. I giggle, leaning forward, feeling lighter than I have in weeks. Feeling invincible.

And still, when she enters the group hug, Drew's arm feels like a hot brand against mine. I turn to look at her.

She's watching me like she hasn't since before. Before the demon. Before her graduation. Before she ever went to that school.

"Let's get out of here. Before we get arrested for trespassing," Drew says.

"Who would report us for trespassing?" Gael asks.

Drew considers the question and then shrugs. "Fair. Before they arrest us for murder. Then." That's enough to get us out of the Thompson-Bryants' wannabe-never-will-be apartment complex, creeping up the three steps and carefully sliding past the gate. When Gael closes the door behind us, he's sure not to touch a single thing with his own fingers, using his T-shirt as a barrier. Standing on the street for a moment, we look at one another, not sure of what to do now that the looming presence of the demon has fizzled away into relief.

Drew nudges me with her shoulder, and I nudge her with mine. It doesn't feel like old times when she loops an arm through mine, because it's something we've never done. But it does feel *new*, and new might not be such a bad thing, I think.

When we separate from the group, no one says anything. They all know that we need this moment for just the two of us. We don't go far, just back toward our house. I hesitate in front of the fence for a moment, like maybe we should go sit on the steps.

But Drew sits right down on the curb and dusts off the spot next to her.

"You didn't even hesitate," I blurt out as I join her. "You just believed I was the Final Girl. The minute I said it."

She nods, drumming her fingers against her knee to a beat only she knows.

"Yeah, I did," she says.

"Why?" I ask. It's a heavy "why." Drew is a student of logic. Drew believes only what she can see. And Drew questions *everything*. But not this.

"Because I . . . I was thinking after you left. And I was so mad that you weren't *listening* to me *again*. I wasn't going to give the athame to Avery today, you know. I just . . . freaked out because I didn't know what to do, and it didn't come out right, and for a split second I wanted to go 'Fuck it, she can do this without me,'" Drew whispers. "But I came to the conclusion that I was being a hypocrite. Again. I believed that you were the Final Girl because . . . it's about time I start believing in things I can't touch. Or at least trying to. This whole time I doubted you, even from the start of it all with Alexis. And I regretted that, not believing you when you said something. I didn't try harder. This is me trying."

I let out a soft whistle of air. "I feel like I don't get you at all."

Drew laughs. "You think I get you?"

"I'm really not that complicated," I say coolly.

"You underestimate yourself," Drew informs me. "You are so opaque to me. I know all about your Best Summer Ever list, you know."

It's so sudden, I choke on my spit. "You, *what*?"

"You're not subtle. Sneaking your little notebook around to show our friends. Also, Malachi has a big mouth," she says.

Despite Malachi not looking our way, I throw up an angry middle finger at his back. Drew laughs under her breath.

"I wasn't upset about it. I was actually really excited. A little skeptical? Yeah, of course. But suddenly you cared so much about exactly what I was into. What I cared about. After years of . . . not caring. And then . . . shit, I, like, wasn't even on that list. I don't like the zoo. Zoos suck. And the last time we went to the carousel, I got sick. And . . . I really didn't want you to go to the party because, outside of Avery, my school friends are kinda shallow. I didn't think you'd ever enjoy them because they don't really talk about much."

"Then why are you friends with them?" I demand.

Drew smiles down at her knees. "Because it was better than being lonely at school all day."

Well, that would've been nice to know.

"I always cared," I blurt out. It's true. "I . . . I cared too much. It hurt. When our parents switched you to your new school and you didn't fight to stay with me, the only way I could get past that was not listening and just pretending like you didn't have this whole life without me. In my head, it made sense that you had to leave me to go and be great, but my heart didn't want to let you."

Drew reaches over, grabbing my hand out of my lap and taking it in hers. She turns her entire body to look at me. "It was never like that, Devon. When we were younger, being at our school wasn't *easy* for me even though I had you. The schoolwork was, but . . . the social and everything else wasn't. I got distracted. I couldn't focus. I finished everything early and I'd do my own things and the teachers would get *mad*. . . . It wasn't easy. Leaving was logical. But I never thought you'd take it personally."

I nod slowly. All these things I didn't see. I didn't know.

"You're right that I didn't want to hear you," I whisper. I press my hand back to the curb and observe a tiny ant crawling its way back home. "But I'm right too. I feel like even if it didn't start that way, you're running away from me now. I made mistakes when we were growing up, but you never looked back. Ever."

"I know I stopped trying. I gave up. I haven't been the greatest friend. Or the greatest sister. And I know I can be a know-it-all and condescending. I made the mistake of thinking those things made me . . . ambitious or smart like everyone expected me to be, when I guess they just made me an asshole," Drew admits, staring down at our joined hands. Then she shakes her head. "But, look, in the end, I still don't know what I want out of life. I'm only seventeen. I'm not ready for college and I don't know it all, and I've been just trying to figure that out. All I do know is I outgrew that school like I outgrew the first one. I'm going to keep growing and changing. But I'm never going to outgrow you. It's impossible." And then she looks up at me with a small smile.

It's not an apology. Neither from me or her.

But it's a start.

And that's what everything feels like right now. A new start.

I take her hand in mine and squeeze hard, looking back at the street for a long moment, just feeling my sister next to me for the first time in a long time. I take a deep shuddering breath, my eyes suddenly burning with a need to sob in relief.

I try to swallow it back, and then I hear a hitched breath.

I look over at Drew. She's staring determinedly at the street, tears rolling down her cheeks, as she squeezes my hand hard. There's nothing to say. I just lay my head on her shoulder and we sit together and cry, sitting in this moment, until our hitched sobs dissipate.

When they do, Drew shakes herself once, and then she looks up the street, where our friends are pretending not to pay attention to our talk. "You guys can come sit with us!" she shouts.

"Right on," Gael calls, and then he stoops over to pull Leila onto his back.

Leila whoops, dropping her crutches to cling to her piggyback ride. Malachi sucks his teeth as he gathers them and chases Gael and Leila down the block. Only Yaya moves like a dignified being, at a soothing pace, the only thing out of place, the athame tucked almost comically into her waistband. She slides in to sit next to me, nudging her pinkie against mine. A reassurance that she's here.

"Let's catch our breath before we head to the block party," I say calmly, as if Drew and I haven't just had one of our first honest conversations ever. "What are we going to do about the bodies in there?"

"Oh, shit," Malachi mutters. "I almost forgot."

"How did you almost forget the two dead bodies inside?" Yaya demands, raising an eyebrow.

Malachi shrugs. "Out of sight, out of mind."

"The demon ate Kendra's keys. You think Keith has keys?" Drew asks suddenly.

"Yeah, probably. Why?" Leila asks.

Drew squints up at the brownstone. "You think they turned off the gas?"

"Arson, *Andrea*? In addition to being demon murderers, you want us to be *arsonists*?" Gael demands, probably too loudly. "Drew, we're not white people. Sorry, Leila."

Leila guffaws. "I'm Jewish."

"Leila, you're still *white*," Gael groans.

I sigh, shaking my head, looking over at Drew. I can practically see the gears turning in her head. "What are you thinking?"

"I'm *thinking* that we stage them as a murder-suicide with an addition of a carbon monoxide poisoning. *Not* as arson," Drew says. She leans back on her hands. "But in a bit. You two boys have to help me when we do."

Gael is quick to complain, "Why just *us*?"

"Final Girl privilege," I bite out.

Leila smirks. "Fucked-up ankle privilege."

Yaya purses her lips and sighs out, "I'll help, I guess."

I sigh, looking up at the sky. "Our Best Summer Ever is pretty much over when the block party ends."

It was over from the moment it started really, but somehow I still got what I wanted. My sister back.

"Our parents might relent," Leila says hopefully.

"Doubt it. My mom *railed* at me." Gael groans as he drops onto the curb, arm thrown over his eyes. "She's making me get *employment*."

"Poor Gael," Leila deadpans.

Gael shoots her a look but doesn't say anything.

"My parents aren't relenting on anything. As my mom said, 'My ass is grass.'" Malachi sighs, leaning against the gate next to Drew.

"Well. There's still tonight," I say. I start to push off the curb but stop when I hear it.

There's still the soca music. The rap. The jittery pop. But floating over them, there's this one jingle. The familiar, comforting melody that brings to mind every summer of my life. A constant balm against the muggy heat that overtakes the streets of Brooklyn every night.

The big white and blue truck creeps steadily along the road, the inside lit up in a washed-out white. The man in the driver's seat squints at Kendra's house, suspiciously, prepared to keep going, but then he notices us on the curb. After a moment's hesitation, he slows to a stop right in front of us.

The ice-cream truck is back.

ACKNOWLEDGMENTS

Writing this is just as hard as the first go-around. I want to thank my agent, Quressa Robinson, for, as always, being my champion, as well as everyone else at Folio Literary Agency. Thank you, Jenny Meyer, for championing my book globally.

Thank you to my incredible editor, Alexa Pastor, at Simon and Schuster BFYR, for holding my hand through this process. Writing a second book is so hard, and you made it possible. Thank you to all my friends at S&S, including, but not limited to: Alma Gomez Martinez, Dorothy Gribbin, Sara Berko, Laura Eckes, Justin Chanda, Kendra Levin, Lynn Kavanaugh, Karen Sherman, and Cienna Smith. Thank you from the bottom of my heart.

Thank you to my team in the UK! As always, you are wonderful. Thank you to Amina Youssef, my editor over there. Thank you to Lindsay Sethia and Chloe Parkinson and everyone at Penguin UK.

Thank you to family. I appreciate your constant support.

Friendship is important. Thank you to Shelly Romero, Molly X Chang, Racquel Marie, and Jake Maia Arlow for keeping me grounded. Thank you to Christina Li and Camryn Garrett for allowing me to blow up your phones at any time of the day, with errant thoughts like the Sims or a really weird dream that I'll forget in the next thirty seconds, and for telling me every idea is worth exploring. Thank you to Susie, Sarah C., Connor, Amber, and Penta for reminding me to touch grass. I wouldn't if you didn't tell me that I work too much.

To my favorite potato gang—Circe Moskowitz, Ashia Monet,

and Joel Rochester—I appreciate y'all so much. Thank you for cheering me on.

Once more, Sarah DeSouza, Alexandra Young, and Selina Mao, I love you to the stars and back. Thank you, thank you, thank you.

To Mom and Dad, thank you. There are not words big enough. You have given me everything. To Alyssa, thank you. You inspire me.

Thank you to me—this book was really hard to write, and I'm really proud of myself!

Finally, thank you to Wes Craven, my hero.

INT. BRYANT-THOMPSON BROWNSTONE—NIGHT
Credits have rolled. *A POST-CREDITS SCENE? GROW UP.*

The sound of soca music still fills the air, at a
distance. The block party is nearing its natural
end. The sound of laughter as a group of children
runs past.

In the middle of a half-finished kitchen, broken
tiles, and open paint cans are two bodies, feet
apart, collapsed in heaps. The oven door is open.
The sharp beep of a carbon monoxide alarm sounds.
Beep. Beep.

KEITH is face down. KENDRA is on her back, hand
still stretched out toward him. They could be
sleeping.

Between them is what looks to be a leather jacket.
It twitches. *UM . . . OKAY NO*

Carbon monoxide alarm. Beep. *Beep.*

                    DEVON (V.O.)
          We thought it was over. It wasn't. *IT ABSOLUTELY*
                                              IS OVER.
The carbon monoxide alarm gets faster. It sounds
less like an alarm. More like a heart monitor.
Beepbeepbeep—flatline.

The leather pile unfurls. It isn't a jacket. It's
a suit. A demon suit. It lifts its hands. An empty
mouth opens.
                    NO, IT IS NOT! WHAT DID I SAY?
                    NO SEQUELS, NO REQUELS, NO REMAKES!
The demon is hungry. *GOD, IT'S OVER. WE WON!*
                    GO HOME.